FORGED FOR ROYALTY

By Andrew Knighton

FORGED FOR DESTINY

Forged for Destiny
Forged for Prophecy
Forged for Royalty

FORGED FOR ROYALTY

FORGED FOR DESTINY:
BOOK 3

ANDREW KNIGHTON

orbitbooks.net
orbitworks.net

This book is a work of fiction. Names, characters, places, and incidents are the product of the author's imagination or are used fictitiously. Any resemblance to actual events, locales, or persons, living or dead, is coincidental.

Copyright © 2026 by Andrew Knighton

Cover design by Alexia E. Pereira
Cover images by Shutterstock
Cover copyright © 2026 by Hachette Book Group, Inc.
Author photograph by Richard Wilson

Hachette Book Group supports the right to free expression and the value of copyright. The purpose of copyright is to encourage writers and artists to produce the creative works that enrich our culture.

The scanning, uploading, and distribution of this book without permission is a theft of the author's intellectual property. If you would like permission to use material from the book (other than for review purposes), please contact permissions@hbgusa.com. Thank you for your support of the author's rights.

Orbit
Hachette Book Group
1290 Avenue of the Americas
New York, NY 10104
orbitbooks.net
orbitworks.net

First Edition: March 2026

Orbit is an imprint of Hachette Book Group.
The Orbit name and logo are registered trademarks of Little, Brown Book Group Limited.

The publisher is not responsible for websites (or their content) that are not owned by the publisher.

The Hachette Speakers Bureau provides a wide range of authors for speaking events. To find out more, go to hachettespeakersbureau.com or email HachetteSpeakers@hbgusa.com.

Orbit books may be purchased in bulk for business, educational, or promotional use. For information, please contact your local bookseller or the Hachette Book Group Special Markets Department at special.markets@hbgusa.com.

Library of Congress Cataloging-in-Publication Data
Names: Knighton, Andrew author
Title: Forged for royalty / Andrew Knighton.
Description: First edition. | New York, NY : Orbit, 2026. | Series: Forged for destiny ; book 3
Identifiers: LCCN 2025036110 | ISBN 9780316588300 trade paperback | ISBN 9780316581776 ebook
Subjects: LCGFT: Fantasy fiction | Novels | Fiction
Classification: LCC PR6111.N63 F69 2026
LC record available at https://lccn.loc.gov/2025036110

ISBNs: 9780316581776 (ebook), 9780316588300 (print on demand)

Printed in Canada

To my mum, Margaret Knighton, who taught me the vital and unglamorous work of striving for a better world one small step at a time. I promise, the parenting seen in this book isn't based on you either.

Chapter One
Chosen One

Raul stood in the fighting line, shield in one hand and sword in the other, facing the Dunholmi charge. Hooves thundered across a meadow crisp and white with spring frost, the horses' breath billowing like smoke. Spear tips gleamed starkly in the early morning light.

Even after a year of war, Raul wasn't used to these moments, when the choices had been made and all he could do was wait for their brutal consequences. He shifted the sword in his hand, forcing himself to unclench. But as soon as he loosened the tension in his muscles, it came back, shoulders tightening beneath his arming jacket and the chainmail over that. He felt the weight of the helmet on his head, of the shield on his arm, of the whole army's expectations bearing down on him.

Halfway across the field, a Dunholmi horn sounded. The spears lowered, pointing straight at Raul.

His da had been right. The enemy were smart enough not to fight inside the town, where they would lose all the advantages of cavalry, but to come out and face the attackers. He had to hope that Valens had been right about the rest too, and that they weren't smart enough to see what the rebels had planned.

He turned his head and opened his chest so his voice would carry down the line, just like Yasmi had taught him, then raised his sword so that the ruby in the hilt caught the light, gleaming red as fire.

"For Estis and for freedom!" he yelled. "A new moon rises!"

"A new moon rises!" the warriors roared, and the battle cry ran down the line, a thousand voices becoming a single cheer.

On the edges, the combat had started already, skirmishers from both sides shooting arrows back and forth. But it was in the thick of it that the hardest fighting would be done, and that was why Raul was here, despite the protests of his closest friends and advisors. How could he ask anyone else to face this if he wouldn't do it himself?

The Dunholmi were nearly on them. All along the line, the Estian infantry raised their shields to form an overlapping wall. Raul slid his foot forward, resting the back of the shield against his knee, and raised his sword to defend his head.

The sound of the charge was deafening, the Dunholmi so close he could see the hatred in their eyes.

"Brace!" he yelled, and they leaned into their shields.

The charge hit.

A spear slammed into his shield, the force of the impact jolting through his arm, his knee, and the leg he'd stuck back to keep him from being knocked over. The very tip of the spear punched through the wood of his shield, splinters flying inches from his eyes, but behind it the shaft snapped. Raul and his shield held. The horse in front of him reared, hooves thrashing, threatening to smash Raul's head open. But polearms reached over his shoulder from the ranks behind and those were enough to fend the animal off, to stop it trampling through. Its rider cursed in frustration, drew his sabre, and tried to turn his steed to take a swing at Raul.

No time to check the rest of the line. If it had broken, then they were all dead anyway. Raul tried to ignore the shouts and screams, the crash of weapons and thud of blows, the smell of blood already on the air, to focus on what was in front of him in the place where he could make a difference.

He slashed at the horse, his stomach churning with guilt as blood ran down its neck. The horse hadn't chosen service to the armies of Dunholm any more than Estis had. It twisted sharply away from the attack and its rider tugged at its reins even as he swung at Raul. It was an easy blow to parry, wild but not strong, the whole movement flung off by the jolting of the horse. Raul batted the sabre aside, then lunged. He felt the moment of resistance before his strength drove the tip of his sword through the warrior's chainmail, through the padding beneath, and into his belly.

The rider screamed and jerked harder on the reins, trying to draw back as blood streamed from his side. Down the line, a Dunholmi captain was shouting for a retreat, but her order drew another shout from further back, this one alarmed.

Raul grinned, despite the hammering of his heart and the shaking of his blood-slicked hand. Valens must have appeared at the cavalry's rear, using local rebels' knowledge of the terrain. Deprived of space to pull back, the Dunholmi couldn't regroup for a fresh charge, but they were still an intimidating force, hooves and spears and blades battering at the Estian line.

Fortunately, Raul still had one more trick. Relying on the others to protect him, he sheathed his sword and drew a whistle from where it hung around his neck next to a protective charm. He pressed it to his lips and blew. The shrill blast ran down the line and was picked up by captains on their own whistles. In their hiding places at the edge of the field, Quintae and his engineers waited, ready to respond.

There was a rustling sound, like snakes through the grass, then a series of thuds. Amid the Dunholmi cavalry, wooden stakes sprang from the ground, sharpened tips slashing at the bellies of horses. Panicked steeds snorted and whinnied, tangling themselves in the ropes and jerking to break free. Warriors were flung away with thuds and curses and the crack of breaking bones.

"Forward!" Raul bellowed, flourishing his sword.

"For Prince Raul Warborn!" one of his captains shouted.

Others echoed the cry. "Warborn!"

That cry plucked a guilty string in Raul's heart for the lie that drove these brave people on, but he couldn't help feeling proud too. After all, he was the one they believed in.

The infantry advanced with slow, steady strides like Valens had taught them, shields in line, overlapping where they could, the points of polearms waving past their heads. Some of the Dunholmi tried to stand steady, sheltering behind their own shields and lashing out at the Estian line. But horses weren't suited to holding ground and those who'd been flung from the saddle weren't trained for infantry fighting, if they were even in a position to stand. The Estians advanced across a litter of broken and groaning bodies, parting only to pass around the stakes or the horses that lay thrashing in pain and panic between them.

At last, the Dunholmi couldn't retreat any further. A circle of rebel banners with their red moon and blade closed around them. Pressed by infantry from ahead and behind, held back at the edges by archers and stakes, the Dunholmi were packed in too tightly to move, never mind to fight. Killing those who remained would be the easy part.

"Yield!" Raul demanded, catching the eye of a mounted Dunholmi warrior in an officer's white sash, her visor raised to survey the desperate fighting. He had to yell himself hoarse to be heard over the crash of combat, but she looked like she'd heard. "They're not worth dying for, not your king and not your count."

Her gaze went from Raul to the warriors around him, then back across her own blue-clad troops. There was a moment of hesitation, her expression twitching as loyalty to her leaders battled with loyalty to her followers, and Raul feared that this might end worse than he wanted, one more bitter moment fuelling generations of hate. But her shoulders sank and she sheathed her sword before laying her hands on her saddle.

"It's over," she shouted. "Lay down your arms."

One by one, the Dunholmi warriors obeyed, some swiftly and with looks of relief, others with reluctance. Some had already given up and were being herded through the Estian lines. The clang of sword against sword faded and the battle cries died, leaving the shuffle of hooves, the snort of nervous horses, and the groans of the injured.

"Are you in charge?" Raul stepped into the gap where blades had swung a moment before, taking off his helmet as he went, showing them his face and making himself vulnerable, trusting that this surrender was real.

The Dunholmi officer looked around.

"That depends on who else is alive," she said. "But I'm as good as you'll get right now."

Warriors shuffled aside, making space for her and Raul to approach. He reached out and stroked her horse, doing his best to soothe the anxious beast.

"You're him, aren't you?" she asked, unbuckling her sword belt. "The rebel king."

"Just a prince." Raul accepted her sword, wrapped in its finely decorated scabbard and white leather belt. Alongside it was a silver-handled dagger with a charm for sharpness stamped into its hilt, her badge of authority. "Can't have a coronation until we've got our country back."

That drew a round of cheering from his side, including those too far down the line to hear. It was hard not to feel like cheering when you'd fought and won.

"At least we lost to someone who matters."

The officer climbed down from her horse and Raul realised that she was holding one arm tight against her side, trying to keep a wound from bleeding. Her face was pale, but she faced him with dignity.

"Your Highness, I beseech mercy for my troops. Many

warriors here will fetch a fine ransom, and there is no honour in harming the rest."

"There won't be any ransoms," Raul said. "Not while the war's still raging. But don't worry, we won't be harming anyone either. In fact..." He stepped forward and caught her as she stumbled, sliding his arm under her shoulder to keep her on her feet. "Our physicians are waiting to see to your wounds."

The crowd cheered again as the lines parted, his title rising from a thousand throats, swords beating against shields in celebration. He held his head high and smiled brightly, catching the eyes of everyone he passed, and the cheers grew louder, a wave of jubilation that washed over him.

"Warborn!"

He was the freedom fighter.

"Warborn!"

He was the heir to Estis.

"Warborn!"

He was the hope for an end to a generation of tyranny.

"Warborn!"

He was a fraud playing his part, and if his people found out, then everything was doomed.

---•---

The remnants of a fire burned in the hearth of the small timber house, a pot hanging over the flames. The inhabitants had probably been cooking breakfast when word came that war had arrived, and they had wisely fled. Raul wrapped his bloodstained shirt around his hand and took the pot off the heat. The porridge inside was burned, but he wouldn't want the pot to be wrecked. He should ask someone to stock the log pile and the larder, to make up for the fear they'd caused these people.

"Here." Yasmi handed him a fresh shirt. Raul's calloused fingers lingered on the fabric as he pulled it on. He had never known silk before this year and it felt strange against his skin. "No time to wash, but we can do our best to make you look the part."

She pulled a doublet from her basket, deep black with red embroidery.

"We just fought a battle," Raul pointed out. "Looking the part would mean bloodstains and sweat."

Even as he protested he held his arms out. He knew he wouldn't win this argument and he couldn't afford to waste vital time. By now, word was likely racing to Pavuno that the rebels had taken another town. They needed to regroup and build defences before the counterattack.

"In battle, you needed to look gritty and fearsome." Yasmi stepped around him, sliding the doublet up his arms and settling it in place. "Now you need to play the part of the prince, regal and refined."

Raul started on the lacing but Yasmi stepped quickly around him, the masks on her belt clicking against each other, and batted his hands away.

"I'm quicker at this than you," she said. "And neater."

"You're better at most things than me."

"Flatterer." She smiled and treated him to a quick kiss. "But we both know that I'd be a terrible battlefield commander. By the time I finished my first speech, the war would already be lost."

Raul fidgeted with his cuffs while the laces hissed through their holes. His heraldry was embroidered on one sleeve, a moon-pierced blade to match the so-called birthmark underneath, the brand with which his parents had marked him for destiny. Another piece of theatre, his clothes a reminder that he was the chosen one, the embodiment of years of prophecy.

Even his clothes were lies, another thought that made him squirm.

"You'd be better at the politics," he said. "You're used to pretending."

Yasmi took a step back and placed her hands on her hips as she looked him up and down. Midmorning sunlight through the open shutters brought out the bright colours of her loose trousers and tunic, gleaming off a silver bangle he'd given her and lighting up her long strawberry blond hair.

"I'd enjoy the dressing up," she admitted. "But it all seems far too serious. 'Let lesser mortal fight for the fates of nations, I am bound by a brighter beat.'"

"Is that from *Princess Pitura*?"

"You remember that one?"

"I liked the part where you played a monkey stealing from the duke's treasure chest."

Yasmi laughed. "Tenebrial doesn't write a lot of slapstick, but it's fun when he does."

"Come closer," Raul said with a smile. "You haven't finished lacing me up."

"That's deliberate." She placed a finger on the small triangle of skin she'd left exposed beneath his neck. "You have a good body. We should remind people of that."

"Flatterer."

He pulled her close, luxuriating in her scent and the warmth of her body against his. As they kissed, all his worries went away.

Then he forced himself to let go, to raise his chin and puff out his chest, to take on the pose of the prince. He buckled on his sword belt, ruby pommel gleaming at his hip, and headed out into the street.

Hewed was a dark town, its buildings smeared black by the smoke from its foundries. The workshops of smelters and blacksmiths were built of stone to withstand the heat of their work and survive if fire broke out. Around them was a patch of dark mud before the timber houses in which the people lived, scattered between vegetable plots. Three well-worn dirt roads ran past its edges: two coming in from the hills where coal and iron were mined, the third from the lowlands and the markets where Hewed ironwork had been sold for generations, until the Dunholmi claimed it all for their armouries. For nearly twenty years, that road had run only to the governor in the palace of Pavuno, but today that changed. From now on, Hewed would arm the rebels instead.

No, not rebels. True rulers. Raul had to think that way, in hopes that he would talk like it too.

As he stepped out the door, half a dozen people bowed to him. It was unsettling to see his friends and companions bow, especially when he'd known some of them before any of this began, so he turned his attention to the one who forgot etiquette and stared at the frames of the buildings instead.

"Good work on the stake traps, Quintae. You saved us a lot of hard fighting today."

"Good, yes, good." The scrawny engineer patted the side of his own scarred head. "Easy work. Ropes and hinges, hidden in the grass. Not like the great machines. Oh, you should see them, yes..."

He flailed a hand in the direction of the road, back along the route they'd marched. His eyes gleamed excitedly and he clapped his hands together.

Behind Raul, Yasmi cleared her throat. Quintae's eyes went wide.

"You should see them, *Highness*." He flopped into an awkward bow, fingers trailing in the sooty dirt. Raul wanted to tell him that there was no need, but they were all actors in his play and he needed them to play their parts, whether they knew what they were doing or not.

Still, he laid a hand on Quintae's shoulder and eased him upright before turning to face the others. Valens, his da, a towering mass of muscle dressed in the armour and red-on-black livery of their new Imperial Legion. Ferra, grey hair shaved down one side and with a bow across her back, the closest the Withered Hills warbands had to a leader. Silvano Ironhead, who had worked the docks in Pavuno and now led a company of refugees from the city's work gangs. Biallo Lavelle, lead actor turned infantry captain, living the war stories he had once performed. Others who Raul knew less well, but who he trusted with his life and more importantly with the lives of those who followed him. Every day, their ranks seemed to grow, though there were losses too, people he couldn't protect no matter how hard he tried, all the way back to Appia lying dead on the palace flagstones. It had been over a year since they'd returned from the Withered Hills, nearly two years since the failed rebellion in Pavuno, and the wins were adding up, but so were the losses. More people than ever wore black mourning rings.

He set that aside and focused on what they needed in this moment, on who he had to be.

"The town is secure?" he asked.

"Yes, Your Highness," Biallo said. "We've checked all the buildings and secured the local Dunholmi lord's entourage."

"The roads in and out?"

"We've folk fixing to watch them now, Highness." Ferra nodded. "Clear a day's good ride out at least."

"And the wagons for the arms and armour?"

"Coming up now, yes." Quintae nodded eagerly. "Many wagons. Many horses. Yes, Highness."

"Good. I'll tour the positions shortly and make sure we've got sentries set, then the rest of the troops can relax. Council will meet this evening to discuss our next target. Until then, back to business, though I'd like a word with General Valens before he goes."

"Highness," they chorused, and all bobbed their heads before hurrying away, leaving Raul with Yasmi and Valens.

"I still can't get used to that." Valens shook his head. "The general bit, I mean."

"If it helps, I can't get used to it either," Raul said. "Feels weird to call you anything other than Da."

"Get used to it," Yasmi said. "Our people know how you're related, but they need you to keep up the atmosphere, to make them feel like they're part of a real nation and a real court."

Raul sighed. They'd been through this conversation many times, and he knew in his head that she was right. Still, his heart ached for a different way of doing things, and he couldn't keep from pushing at the edges of what was allowed.

"Come on." Yasmi nudged him. "It's good for our warriors to see you after a victory. It links you to a good mood in their minds, reminds them that they won thanks to you."

"Thanks to all of us," Raul said.

"Of course, but one matters more than the rest. So straighten up and get ready to perform, because they need their chosen one."

It wasn't like he didn't enjoy these moments. It was fun meeting people, learning about who they were and what had brought them here, watching their faces light up as they told their war stories to royalty. It was like being back at the inn, listening to the locals and travellers talk about their days, except that he didn't have to serve the drinks anymore.

Smiling and striding proudly, he headed into the liberated town.

Chapter Two
Sparks in the Darkness

Bonfires blazed to either side of the stage and the wagons it rested on, warming the audience of weary warriors and illuminating the actors of the Company Dellest. Sparks burst free as logs cracked in the heat, blazing orange motes spiralling on the currents of hot air toward the stars. But none of it—not the fires, not the sparks, not even the stars themselves—could match the brightness and beauty Raul saw when Yasmi stepped onto the stage.

He doubted that anyone else in the audience saw what he did. They cheered, of course, and raised their tankards high as she stepped out from behind the curtain, her whole body transformed by the magic of her masks and her shifting skills. Instead of a woman, there stood a lion, a monkey, a wyvern with a scaly body and its wings spread wide, a wonder that most of them would only have seen a few times in their lives, if they were even lucky enough to have a wandering theatrical troupe visit their home village. Now they got to watch a play every month or so, whenever the enemy was far away and the army of free Estis was celebrating a victory. Tenebrial, the troupe's playwright, had reluctantly abandoned nuance in favour of more monsters, more grand speeches, and more fanciful backdrops, all the spectacle that their audience loved. As several of the players had noted, what mattered most now was keeping people motivated. They could worry about high art later.

So the stories had been rewritten and Yasmi became even more the centre of the show. The story of King Balbianus no longer featured a wolf, since Yasmi had lost that mask, but the lion that now faced the ancient king in his final battle was as fearsome as the wolf had ever been, and while the string of monsters and animals that preceded it might not feature in the historical records, they kept the spirit of the old story, reminded people of the struggles that had founded the nation and the common bond that united them.

It wasn't as though truth was the rebellion's strength.

Still, when Yasmi stepped onto the stage Raul saw a different truth to everyone else. Instead of lumbering beasts and chattering imps, he saw the passion and energy that went into her performance. Instead of warts and claws, he saw the young woman who he'd known nearly his whole life and yet who still managed to surprise him in the best possible ways.

Right now, Yasmi was a heron, guiding Balbianus and his soldiers to the secrets of a mystical pool. As was traditional, the lead role was played by Efron Dellest, who seemed to find fresh energy playing alongside his daughter, his every third line drawing a cheer, a groan, or a laugh from the audience.

Next to Raul at the back of the crowd, Valens watched with an expression that Raul imagined was much like his own, wrapped up in more than the performance.

He nudged his da.

"Efron's on fine form tonight," Raul whispered.

"He is." Valens's tone was curt but a smile curled the corners of his lips.

"He looks good in that new doublet."

"He does."

"Have you ever thought about…" Raul looked down at his feet, then back up, taking a breath. He didn't normally feel awkward talking with his da, but this wasn't just about him. "About getting married?"

Valens blinked, long and slow. The lump of his throat bobbed as he swallowed.

"We've talked. I've said no."

"But you and Efron love each other."

"Loving a warrior is hard." Valens held up the stump where his hand had been. "Marrying them is harder. Fastest way to end up a widower."

"You won't be a warrior forever. Once we've freed the country, you can go back to running an inn, or travel the country and help Efron put up the stage."

"I was a terrible innkeeper and I'm a worse scenery hand. Besides, you'll still need warriors when this is done, to keep the country safe."

Raul frowned and plucked at a loose thread on his finely embroidered cuff. He hadn't thought about what came after, not properly. About what he was committing to by claiming the crown. About what that would mean for his future and the people around him. It wasn't as if their council meetings didn't come close to the topic, like weeds creeping across a field of grain, but he always tugged that conversation out and moved on to something else. Had he been purposefully avoiding it?

Valens, who seldom looked away from the stage while Efron was performing, looked down at his son.

"Something you want to tell me about you and Yasmi?" he asked.

"What?" Raul blushed as he looked up. "No! I mean, I would, but it's too soon, and..."

A warrior turned, finger raised, then saw who she'd been about to shush.

"Your Highness." She bowed. "I didn't know you was there. Would you like some cider?"

She smiled eagerly and held up an earthenware jug.

"Thank you." Raul took a swig. It had taken him a while to realise that people wanted him to say yes, even though he had so much more than they did—fine clothes, roofs over his head, the certainty of a meal when supplies were short. They wanted to feel like they were sharing with him, and like he appreciated it. This time, he turned his grimace at the vinegary cider into something exaggerated, one of Yasmi's tricks to turn awkward moments into shared amusement. "You're a braver soldier than I am, drinking the likes of this!"

She laughed and gestured uncertainly toward her companions. "Would you like to join us, Your Highness?"

Raul hesitated. The thought of relaxing with these people

was appealing, hearing about their lives and their adventures since joining the rebellion. But there were too many thoughts tumbling around his head; he needed to take a walk.

"Thank you, but I should do a tour of the camp. Maybe another time."

He handed back the jug, gave her the warmest smile he could muster, and turned away.

"You want me to come?" Valens murmured.

"Not tonight. I need time to clear my head, and I'll be safe enough by myself."

Away from the stage and the roaring bonfires, the spring night was cold as it could be. The clear sky that let the stars smile down meant there were no clouds holding in the land's warmth. Raul wrapped his cloak tight around him, hiding his embroidered tunic and tailored trousers as he headed out.

Though the rest of the encampment wasn't roaring like the crowd around the stage, it was never quiet. Warriors huddled at their fires, cooking whatever food they'd been given or gathered, talking about the day's fighting. Some of the civilians who accompanied the army joined them, spending time with the family they'd followed from home or the new friends they'd made along the way. Others were busy mending clothes, hauling supplies, rolling barrels from the barn where the Dunholmi had kept their supplies. Where the fields they were camped in met the edge of town, a fire blazed in the open front of a smithy and the clang of an anvil resonated through the night as blunted swords and spears were sharpened.

When the playwrights and chroniclers talked about war, it

was all battles and sieges, heroism and tragedy, but it was so much more than that. It was the routines people fell into, with all their boredom and familiarity. It was real life.

But as Raul wandered alone through his camp, the peace of the moment did little to ease his mind. Instead, the future gaped before him. Life in a palace, all plump pillows and politics, impossibly distant from the upbringing of a simple innkeeper's son. What would the routines of that life be? Was there space for Yasmi, whose craft took her across the country and beyond, performing in a new village every night? His ma would be fine, court politics was the life she missed, but what about his da? Could a life with Efron combine with life as one of Raul's advisors, and if not, what would Valens choose? Could Raul even place that decision on him?

Too many questions, each one stirring up a dozen more. What he did was too important to choose anything else, but he missed the inn in winter with Old Wellic grumbling by the fire and other locals sharing a meal while Raul bustled back and forth between them, fetching drinks and washing cups.

"Hey, you!" A voice broke through his reverie. From around the nearest fire, a man was waving. "Yes, you, raggedy cloak man!"

Raul looked down and laughed. His cloak was faded and frayed from long marches through the winter and camping out in the woods, its tears patched with whatever had come to hand because this wasn't a piece of royal costume but a practical thing to keep a warrior warm.

"Good evening." Raul smiled and nodded to the man.

Others around the circle turned to him and one shuffled up to make space.

"Do you know how to play seven stones?" the waving man said.

"Only a little."

"The best sort of opponent! I need someone different to beat for a while."

The warmth of the fire and of the company enveloped Raul as he joined the game, tossing one pebble in the air and trying to snatch up the others, shouting "Sevens!" any time he came close to a fistful. Others took a turn from time to time, but mostly they were happy talking, and playing the game meant that Raul didn't need to say much in return.

He soon learned that several of them came from Rianti, which they insisted had the finest crafting halls in all of Estis. Three were basket weavers, one a carpenter, another a mason. There were also farmers from near a place called Barrowblack, which they claimed had been a burial ground when the gods walked the world. Several around the edges wore clothes too poor to have been artisans or even farmers before the war, beggars and itinerant labourers who had joined the army as much for food as for the cause. A woman with a wooden flute didn't say much, too busy trying to learn the tune that the carpenter was teaching her.

"Thought you only knew seven stones a little, raggedy cloak man." Raul's opponent grinned gleefully, his eyes gleaming in the firelight. "But you're cursed close to beating me."

"I've been copying that thing you do with your wrist." Raul demonstrated as he tossed up a stone and plucked two more from the ground. "Trying to do the same. It works well, doesn't it?"

"What thing with his wrist?" One of the weavers leaned closer.

"Now, now, raggedy cloak." The man winked. "Don't go giving away all of my secrets."

"No, go on, show us." Another of the weavers leaned in. "Maldio here has been beating us all winter, I want my turn."

Raul smiled. It was nice to feel wanted without the pressure that fell upon a prince chosen by prophecy. Still, he looked at his opponent and raised an eyebrow.

"What do you say? I don't want to ruin it for you."

"Fine, raggedy cloak man." Maldio rolled his eyes, but he was still grinning as he grabbed for the stones. "You've forced my hand, but I'm going to show them."

There was more shuffling about, the group coming closer. The carpenter coughed and waved futilely at the smoke blowing from the fire. The woman with the flute squeezed up beside him and Raul saw her feet for the first time, both of them wrapped in bandages, torn strips of cloth stained around the gaps where missing toes should have been.

"Were you hurt in the fighting?" Raul asked, pointing at those sorry feet.

The woman shook her head and hunched over, wrapping herself around her simple flute.

"Some of Rina's toes got bit by the cold, had to be taken off," the carpenter said. "On account of marching through the ice and snow in these."

He reached past her and held up a pair of shoes. Their

leather had probably never been good and the crude stitching had been repaired in several places, only to fray the leather too badly to be sewn shut again. The soles had worn completely through in places, and parts of the upper had cracked apart.

Raul shook his head, trying to imagine what those poor feet must feel like, how it would have been to do the long weary marches they'd all endured without decent boots to protect him.

"We look around after every battle, don't we, Rina?" the carpenter said. "But good leather on your feet is as precious as gold out here, and half the fallen of Dunholm have boots as bad as ours." He touched a wooden charm of a goat that hung from his neck. "One day, we'll get lucky, and we'll all have better travels."

Forcing himself to exhale, Raul stared at those tattered shoes, then at the feet that had worn them, that were more comfortable exposed to the cold of the night than wrapped in such wretched leather. It wasn't fair for anyone in his army to be in this state. They deserved better.

"You can have mine," he said.

Rina blinked, then looked uncertainly at the carpenter.

"You've got spare?" the carpenter asked. "What you want for them?"

"It's fine, I've got others, and I don't want anything in return. I just…" His cloak fell aside as he reached down to start unlacing. "This is something I can make better, so that's what I'm going to do."

Damp had swollen his laces and the cold made his fingers numb, so it took a lot of concentration to even start unlacing the boots. He didn't notice at first that the group had fallen silent, but when he looked up they were all staring at his polished boots and at the embroidered tunic that had been exposed when the cloak slipped aside.

"Who are you?" Maldio asked, setting his gaming stones down.

Raul cringed and turned his attention back to his laces, bowing his head so that his blond fringe fell across his eyes.

Past the crackling fire, Rina whispered in the carpenter's ear. The man stiffened.

"You're him, aren't you?" he whispered. "You're Prince Raul."

Suddenly, they were all on their feet, boots and stones and flute forgotten, bowing and speaking the word "Highness."

"Please, sit, this is your fire." Raul waved them back down as best he could, but they were looking at him with awe and curiosity, not the companionable expressions of a moment before. "Yes, I'm him, but I'm one of you too, another warrior on the march looking to share friendship and a warm fire. We can do that, can't we?"

Yasmi took one last bow, luxuriating in the applause of the crowd. It felt glorious to be up here again, telling stories and raising cheers. The rebel army was a particularly responsive audience, especially for plays about the history of Estis and most especially on nights when they'd just won. She'd never experienced an atmosphere like it, and she had to force herself to ever step away. But if the players dragged this out too long, then the audience would get bored, the applause would falter, and the whole business would become embarrassing for everyone. Better to back out now amid a glorious chorus of approval.

She retreated through the scenery curtains and the other players followed suit. Backstage was mud and a pair of trestle tables on which props and changes of costume were laid, and it made her think fondly of the theatre they'd briefly occupied in Pavuno, with a clean and orderly backstage area, dedicated stores for costumes and props, even a small room of her own. And that mirror! The chance to see herself from head to toe, to check every last detail before she stepped out.

Wonderful as it had been, the raucous applause from beyond the curtains was even better, because here her performances meant something more than idle entertainment. The Company Dellest was helping change the world.

Valens was waiting for her father with a bottle of wine and an enveloping hug, but though she peered into every shadow she couldn't see Raul. Her smile faltered just a little, but there were so many other matters vying for his attention. She couldn't expect him to be here after every performance; the circumstances that made their performances matter were the same circumstances that kept him busy.

A cold wind wound its way between the players, fluttering the scenery and making Yasmi shiver. She picked up the black woollen cloak that Claudio had worn as the assassin in act four and wrapped it tightly around her. A simple grey outfit was both traditional and practical for a shifter performing onstage, but it wasn't warm enough for this weather, and the masks on her belt added no insulation at all. She straightened the fall of the cloak and forced herself to stop hunching her shoulders, but kept her arms wrapped tight across her belly, holding in as much warmth as she could.

"You were great," Valens said. He and her father stood with arms wrapped around each other's waists, both beaming proudly.

"Spectacular, even," Efron said. "Mesmerising. But then, you always are."

He kissed her on the cheek.

"Where's Raul?" she asked, more eagerly than she'd meant to. With the cold clawing ever closer, she wanted someone whose warmth she could cling to, a warmth that went beyond body heat.

"Gone for a walk." Valens gestured. "Needed to think."

"That boy thinks far too much," Efron declared. "To quote Viscount Guinekus in *The Wanderer's Lament*, 'Running at wisdom sweeps me in a dizzy circle back to ignorance.'"

"Of all Tenebrial's lines, I think that one makes the least sense." Yasmi tugged the cloak tighter. "But I'd better look for Raul anyway, just in case he's lost all his wits and fallen into a ditch."

Emerging from behind the stage wagon, she enjoyed the thawing walk around one of the bonfires where audience members had clustered following the performance. As in most plays, they hadn't seen the shifter without her mask for long, so few of them paid attention to the young woman passing by. Then she was out in the miserable cold again, walking between the small pools of light that were the army's firepits, looking for a distinctive figure.

When she spotted Raul, she was relieved to see that he'd abandoned his restless pacing and was sitting by one of those fires, talking with his companions while one of them played the flute. But then she noticed the awkward expressions on everyone's faces, the stiff back of the flute player, the gaming stones lying untouched on the ground. As she circled, observing from the darkness, she realised that Raul's feet were bare, toes exposed at the bottom of his cloak, but that the edges of his tunic and trousers were visible, courtly finery amid the mud and travel-stained cloaks. The flute player's eyes kept shifting from him to the fine boots on her own feet, and she was struggling with even the most basic elements of her tune.

It felt cruel to intrude, for him to know that she'd seen the awkwardness of the moment, but it would be even worse to leave him here.

"Your Highness." She laid a hand softly on Raul's shoulder and he looked around, expression caught between guilt and relief. "I'm sorry to distract you from your companions, but you're needed on council business."

"I see."

Raul rose, and the others jerked to their feet, then started a round of awkward bows as he said goodbye to each of them by name. Some were tongue-tied into silence; others said they'd been honoured to share their fire with him; only the man with the gaming stones managed something close to a normal farewell. Then she let her cloak fall aside, exposing herself to the cold so she could slip her arm through his and lead him hastily away.

As soon as they were out of sight of the fire, Raul's shoulders fell.

"Have you had a nice evening?" she asked, knowing Raul too well to think that he could hold back the truth.

"It was lovely for a while," he said. "Then they realised who I was, and then... I tried to make everyone relax, to just have a conversation, but it was strange and stilted, no one talked to anyone but me, I felt bad for being there but I didn't want them to think I didn't like them, and... and..."

And just like always, Raul wanted so badly for everybody to be happy, but was too innocent to see when the best he could do was not to try. Not for the first time, she wondered how in the world he could still be like this with everything he had gone through, all the lies and disillusionment, all the cruelty and struggles. All the power.

That wonder melted into something softer, a feeling that was the two of them together, arms intertwined, his footsteps in time with hers, a happiness less overwhelming but more powerful than anything she felt on the stage.

"You said there was council business?" he asked.

She stopped, turned him to face her, and wrapped her arms around him.

"Very important business," she said. "Keeping one of your councillors warm."

"The most important business," he agreed.

His arms enveloped her, bringing his cloak with them, and he pressed her close. In the distance, sparks flew from the fire, dwindling to darkness against the cold sky, but here there was only warmth.

Chapter Three

Leadership

Valens marched along at the head of the column, pack on his back and arms swinging, enjoying the steady rhythm of the road and the satisfaction of being part of an army again. When night fell and they made camp, everyone would moan about the mud on their boots and the blisters on their feet, about how cold it was, how small their rations were, how far they were from home. He'd do his best to make things better, to find good boots, more food, sheltered places to camp. But he would join in a little of that moaning too. After all, it was part of a warrior's life.

At least the weather was improving, spring finally offering the promise of warmth and light. For the past few days, since leaving their new garrison in Hewed and heading out down the vale, they'd had mild mornings and soft winds, though the rain still came often enough to keep the earth sodden. Decent marching weather, not too hot and not too cold, but lousy ground to march over.

The footfalls of the Imperial Legion—his legion—were a unified chorus in time to their marching chants. As the first troops in the column, apart from the scouts riding out to check the route, they would be the first to face any threats that appeared. Better that than being at the back, though, coming through after thousands of others, once the ground was churned into mud or throwing up clouds of dust and every step was a struggle. He'd served his years at the back and he wasn't ever returning to that.

Hooves thudded across the turf of a neighbouring field as Biallo galloped up, his cloak flapping in the wind. The actor had taken to war far better than Valens expected. They all had. Perhaps that wasn't good, but it was necessary. And if folk like Biallo brought a little more posing to the work than Valens would have done, then maybe that was needed too. A bit of showmanship to make them all feel like heroes. Same reason the Imperial Legion were kitted out in their matching red and black tabards. Same reason they'd remade the legion at all. This war was a matter of performance as well as substance. Maybe they all were, and he'd never known it, one more soldier marching in the column.

"General Valens." Biallo pulled in close so that he could be heard. "You're needed in the siege train."

The legionaries, well used to this routine by now, parted ranks to let their leader out.

"You're in charge until I'm back," Valens said, patting a captain on her shoulder as he passed. "Try not to lose the war."

Then he was out of the column and into a field of what

looked like onions, heading back past rows upon rows of soldiers with Biallo riding at his side.

"We could deal with these things more quickly if you had a horse, General," Biallo said.

"I'm a bad rider," Valens replied.

"One must practice one's lines to learn the script."

"I'm a soldier of Estis. All my scenes are played on foot."

"You're a commander, and a successful one. Perhaps your lines have changed."

Valens didn't have an answer to that. They'd used up too many words already, and he didn't know enough about theatre to keep up the comparison. Besides, he didn't want to face the feeling that wormed its way through his guts, the suspicion that Biallo might be right. He'd always marched with the army, and he wasn't going to change that now.

"What's the problem this time?" he asked as they passed the True Pavuno Company. Silvano Ironhead and his troops raised their fists in salute and Valens returned the gesture, careful to use his complete arm. These people didn't need reminders of what war could cost them.

"One of Quintae's war machines got stuck in the mud again. Drusil wants to disassemble it to keep moving."

"Sounds smart."

"Try telling Quintae that."

Passing the warband of the Withering Folk, with their rolling wicker huts and their woven armour, Biallo's horse gave a whinny and rose up, hooves flailing. A vast black bear, weighed down with tents and bundles of arrows, looked up at the alarm it had caused and opened its mouth to roar. The horse bolted, Biallo clinging on for dear life, and Valens shook his head as he kept walking. One more reason not to ride.

The war machines were near the back of the marching column, after the baggage but before the rear guard and the trail of assorted civilians following behind. Each piece was unique, the results of Quintae's increasingly eccentric experiments, and each had proved its value: the siege tower with its ratcheting bridge to reach different heights of walls; the ballistae with their complex arrangements of ropes and pulleys that gave them more range and power than any Valens had seen in the old days; the battering ram with its interchangeable heads and spiked wheels to hold steady on slopes.

Right now, all the fuss and activity was around the builder's latest creation, a towering trebuchet. With the bucket of its counterweight empty and the arm lowered, it was less intimidating than when in action, but it still had enough height to make it very obvious that the whole thing was leaning at an angle. It was also obviously being left behind as the army kept moving and the trebuchet didn't.

Valens muttered a prayer to Laughing Loftus and touched the swift talisman under his tunic, hoping for the god's guidance and a fast fix. Then he strode over to join the group around the base of the machine.

"General Valens." Drusil, the army's chief armourer, nodded at his approach. Even dressed in layers against the brisk weather, her muscles were as obvious as the hefty mallet in her hand. "I need to take this thing down so we can keep moving."

Around her, assorted warriors and labourers murmured

their agreement. They were spread around the base of the machine, covered in mud from their efforts to move it, most of them red-faced or sweating.

"No no no no no!" A scrawny, ratlike man clung to a beam halfway up the machine. His scraggly hair flew as he shook his head, revealing the scars underneath. "Good machine, precise balance, such work! Mustn't break it. Mustn't risk the balance."

"Surely you can rebuild it, Quintae?" Valens called up to him.

"The balance, such good balance." Quintae stroked the machine like he was comforting a pet.

"We've got the tools." Drusil tapped the mallet against her gloved hand. "That madman just doesn't want to, and he's more work to handle than any of these machines."

"Worth the effort, though."

Drusil snorted. "I suppose."

Valens knelt in the mud so he could look more closely at the trapped wheel. He didn't like the extra breath of time it took him to get down these days, but he liked the look of the wheel even less. It had sunk into a deep puddle of slippery mud, and when he thrust his arm through the ooze, he could feel a large, jagged lump of rock in there too, jammed between the axle and its housing.

"Might need a new wheel, Quintae," he said, oozing mud as he rose and looked around.

"New wheel, yes," Quintae replied, still clinging to his beam. "New build, no." He patted the side of his head. "Good boy. Good build."

"Sure, you did great." Valens turned to the lightest looking of the labourers. "You, run up to the Withering Folk, ask Ferra to bring their biggest bear and the hut that broke down yesterday."

The beasts of the Withered Hills always moved faster than Valens expected. It only took a few minutes for the massive, shaggy bear to arrive, accompanied by lean, grey-haired Ferra, dressed in straw-padded furs and with a bow strapped across her back. Behind it, the bear dragged a round wickerwork hut that rolled along like a giant wheel, but whose broken roof flapped as it moved, woven rods unravelling.

"Looks like yon tower's frayed as this here house," Ferra said in her slow, thick accent, peering at the machine. "You fixing to move it?"

"Yes."

"This one might be some help, so." She patted the bear's flank. "But I don't see owt we can do to stop this happening again."

"That's why I'm requisitioning the broken hut."

It felt strange to use a word like "requisition," as if he was giving one of the grand speeches from Efron's plays. But a general didn't just take a thing, even if that was the same in the end.

At his command, Ferra and one of the labourers set to breaking down the remains of the hut, cutting its outer wall into two giant woven mats. Meanwhile, Drusil and her team dug a sloped trench ahead of the trebuchet so that the mat could be slipped down in front of the sunken front wheels. Valens himself knelt in the dirt, threaded a rope down and around the rock, then set enough people to the ropes so they could heave it out.

"Don't think there's any lasting damage," Drusil said once she'd felt around the axle where the rock had been. "I can reinforce it later, just in case."

By now, even the army's civilian tail had mostly gone past, though half the rear guard hung back to protect the beleaguered war machine. Scouts with bows, a mix of locals from this region and veteran trackers from the Withered Hills, prowled around the surrounding woods and fields, watching for trouble. Their recent attacks had been designed to lure Dunholmi forces away from this area, but an army could only hide so well, and Valens wasn't taking chances when he didn't need to.

At last, they hitched the bear next to the oxen that usually dragged the trebuchet, with the human crew all on ropes at the sunken side. The oxen didn't look happy at their new company, and Valens wouldn't have done either given the saliva dribbling between those bared teeth, but he knew by now not to worry about the beasts from the Withered Hills—they were the least of his discipline problems. He surveyed the work one last time, then nodded.

"On my mark. One, two, three, heave!"

Together, they strained at the ropes; oxen and bear, warriors and general, all heaving. For a painful moment, it seemed like nothing was going to happen, the mud clinging too tightly onto the trebuchet to ever yield. Then there was a slow, wet sound like a blade being pulled out of a belly. The war machine groaned, wobbled, trembled, then began rolling out of the mud and up the wicker mat.

"Keep going!" Valens yelled. "For Estis!" That sounded too dramatic for the moment, making him feel like a pompous fool. "For the ale I'll give you all later!"

That got a cheer and an extra burst of effort. With more squelching and straining, the rear wheels rolled across the rut where the machine had stuck and up onto the mat.

"Now the other one," Valens called out, but Drusil was already ahead of him, rolling out the second mat with one of her team ahead of the oxen and the bear. As the beasts dragged the trebuchet onto that mat, the labourers picked up the first one and ran ahead, laying it across the next stretch of mud. Clear of the quagmire, the humans unhitched their ropes and left the animals to take the strain, picking up speed as they went.

"Going to be a long day, running to lay those mats ahead every time," Valens said as he watched them go.

"So's said." Ferra nodded her agreement.

"D'you think we could make smaller versions?" Drusil asked. "Small enough to fit around the wheels but strong enough to take the weight?"

"Could be." Ferra whistled and a couple of scouts ran over. "I'll send my folk out foraging, see what we can find to weave."

"And I'll look in the carpentry wagon, see what materials we have."

Just like that, they were done. No one needed Valens any longer, and all that was left to do was catch up with the marching column.

He smiled as he strode down the road, intent on getting

back to the head of the column. So far this spring, he'd outfought and outmanoeuvred the Dunholmi, and he would have bet that he was outdoing them at logistics too, keeping this column and all its machinery moving. If anyone had asked him back in the day, he would have said that he never wanted to be a general, but he couldn't think of a time he'd ever been more satisfied.

As the road ran through a stream, its waters flowing fast from the recent rain, he knelt at the ford and built a small cairn out of rounded stones, his own small tribute to Laughing Loftus, voice of the babbling brook.

"Thank you," he said. "If you did help me back there. And if not..."

He shrugged as he stood. Even if Loftus hadn't guided him, it never did any harm to be on the right side of a god.

As he galloped into the courtyard of Fort Fury, Count Alder felt the power of a god blazing through his veins. The heat of Jarrag was a fire inside him, a force constantly straining to burn beyond his control. But he was a nobleman of Dunholm, a descendant of queens and kings, while this was nothing more than a spirit from the wilderness, one more beast for him to ride, and he had never met a steed yet that he couldn't rein in.

Really? a voice sneered from the back of his mind. *You think you're in control?*

"I think I have royal blood," Alder snapped, "while you don't even have a body."

"You said something, my lord?" The chosen warrior riding beside him looked at Alder in confusion.

"It was nothing," Alder said.

He clattered to a stop at the base of the keep and swung out of the saddle, then paused to stroke Fellstride's mane.

"Good riding today," he said. "And you can rest tomorrow."

There was a wildness in Fellstride's eyes, and he leaned away from Alder instead of nuzzling into his touch.

"Stop that." Alder tugged on the reins, pulling Fellstride's head down to stare straight at him. "I command here, understand?"

The horse snorted and his eyes stayed wide, but he didn't try to pull away.

"Better." Alder raised his voice. "Where's a stable hand, curse you?"

"Here, my lord."

He spun around to see a girl dressed in Dunholmi blue, only two steps behind him. He thrust Fellstride's reins into her hand, then strode up the steps of the keep. A dozen of his chosen troop followed him, chainmail jingling and spurs ringing against the stone. Fort Fury had endured for centuries, since these lands had been a place of scattered fiefdoms, through the rise of the so-called Kingdom of Estis, into the days when that upstart land had made itself an empire, and now as part of the province it was always destined to be, the North March of Dunholm, a troublesome land tamed. A building could only endure this long through solid stonework, and Fort Fury was as solid as they came, barely a crack showing between the blocks even after centuries of wear. He should make more use of the place once he had crushed the rebellion. It might be useful to run the North March from a fortress like this, sitting harsh and forbidding astride the trade routes, instead of from the old royal palace, where he was surrounded by the distractions of Pavuno and all the opportunities for trouble the rebels could make there. After all, wasn't that where this had started, the fake prince and his newly forged ancestral blade, the wilful act of uprising that he had almost reined in before it began?

Fire flared between Alder's clawed fingers, heat licking his skin. He wouldn't just beat these rebels. He would burn them to ash and grind their bones, show every feeble one of them what the House of Alder could do. His would be the fury these fools feared and the punishment they deserved.

The great hall of Fort Fury was two floors up from the courtyard, looking out from the castle's clifftop position to the meadows where roads from five valleys met. A fire was blazing in the hearth, chasing back the cold, and Alder's closest advisors stood on either side of it, a study in contrasts. Ketley Tur was slender and stooped, his clerical robes bound with an embroidered sash belt that was meant to lend some dignity to the role of chamberlain, but that could only do so much to counter its owner's skulking, nervous indignity. Captain Brook, on the other hand, was dressed in chainmail and riding boots, with a sabre hanging from one hip and a silver dagger from the other, a shortbow across her back. Beneath her martial gear and blue surcoat embroidered with the white tree of House Alder, she was a deeply average-looking woman, only her muscles and steady stare hinting at the strength beneath.

"My lord, at last." Tur held his twig fingers toward the fire, then rubbed them around each other. "Were you held up on the road?"

"I was talking with my commanders." Alder strode to a table in the middle of the hall. "Doing my job. The question is, have you been doing yours?"

The map on the table told him that Tur had not been sitting idle. A selection of wooden counters showed which routes were considered passable and which unsafe in the current weather, as well as where the rebels had been reported in the past month, the past week, even recent days. Alder picked up more counters from a bowl and slapped them down onto the map, marking out what he'd learned on the road.

"Well?" he snapped. Brook had come straight to the table, but Tur lingered by the fire, grasping at a fragment of the warmth that was always in Alder now. "Get over here and show me you've done more than sit on your arse."

"Indeed, my lord, indeed." Tur reluctantly shuffled over and took a ledger from a stool. "Your main formation is currently supplied with a month's worth of food, three weeks of fodder, and sufficient arrows to fight two substantial battles."

"Why only three weeks of fodder?"

"Damp has damaged some of our supplies, and there was an unfortunate incident involving a supply train."

"Another rebel attack?"

"I'm afraid so, my lord. A small band slipped between our formations at—"

"Enough." Alder slammed his fist against the table, rattling the counters. "Brook, this is your territory. Find out who failed me and make them feel pain."

"My lord."

He didn't need more than that from her. Brook didn't waste time on excess words and vague promises, whereas Tur...

"My lord, if we might discuss the state of—"

This time, Alder silenced Tur with a glare. Could the chamberlain see the fire that Alder felt behind his own eyes? Probably not. It had never taken much to intimidate him, and a hint of this power would have left those robes stained with piss.

"The rebels have deceived us again." Alder slid counters across the map, then stood staring down at the pattern they revealed. He grimaced at what he saw. "Marching a reduced column north with so much noise, only to send the main force west and seize Hewed. Now Captain Reed's scouts report that they've regrouped and are heading toward Deladale, but I'm not riding into another trap."

There was a charred smell as he pressed his knuckles against the wood of the tabletop. He made himself step back and sit down, as he would have done before, to reach for the drink that a servant had set out for him. Milk, creamy and refreshing, in his favourite goblet, the one made from his grandmother's skull. He took a sip and smiled at her hollow eyes, taking inspiration from knowing that she had faced such challenges and beaten them all. He bared his teeth in imitation of hers and chuckled to himself as the two of them stared at each other down the generations.

"You would be proud of me," he whispered.

For a moment, he thought he saw her standing by the fire, nodding at him. A trick of the flames and his tired mind.

He blinked, felt the heat of anger rising again at those who opposed him.

"If I don't act, then my enemies pounce," he said. His milk was bubbling, steaming, or was that his imagination too? He set the goblet down, leaving a black streak on the skull. "They'll scuttle out of the shadows of the royal court and convince King Lorrin of what he wants to believe, that I've failed as badly as my father. Pathetic wretches, so scared to act they'll stop those with real courage."

Their faces swirled through his mind, and he shook his head like he could shake them from his life. It wasn't just the rebels who deserved to burn.

"If I do act and it's not the right action, then the same thing will happen," he continued, "an end for everything I've worked toward. North Marchers and their filthy magic running wild, while the House of Alder is put down. But with the right move, with the right strategy, with the right display of this power..." He opened his hand and willed a flame into existence, still captivated at feeling that power flare as if from nowhere. A promise of blazing light and terrible destruction. "I prove my worth, earn my place at His Majesty's right hand, and grasp a glorious future."

He looked up. Brook looked at him with satisfaction, but Tur's eyes were wide, his hands clasping and unclasping like a pair of insects mating.

"My lord, I don't believe that it is wise to... I mean, in front of the people, let alone the king... What I mean to say is..."

"You've said enough." Alder, scowling, jerked to his feet and stared back down at the map. He was smarter than these wretched rebels, had been bred for the hunt and raised in the saddle, a leader made for war. He would seize control of this situation and crush their pathetic revolt. He would have revenge for every embarrassment they had inflicted upon him.

"There," he said, jabbing at a clear spot between the counters. "And there." The counters jumped as his finger stabbed the map. "Two crossings connect all the routes they might use, all the places in this region where they might want to strike. We stop reacting to the rebels and press our spurs to their flanks. Set up camp between those crossings, where we can control their movements. Force them to a fight, thrash them in the open, and take their heads home dripping blood and terror, a gift for my royal cousin.

"Victory is there, for those with the strength to take it."

Heat rushed through him, glorious and furious, and he laughed out loud, the sound echoing from the fort's vaulted ceiling, becoming a chorus that cackled like flames crackling through wood, like the crack of a thousand riders breaking their opponents' bones beneath their hooves. Even Tur smiled a spider's smile as he looked at the map, and in the back of Alder's mind a voice spoke, the one he had been trying to quiet every day for a year, the voice that never left him alone.

Good, it said in a rasp like the crackling of flames. *Let battle come and let them all burn.*

Chapter Four
Old Friends and New Allies

Crouched behind the rocks on the top of a ridge, Raul looked south toward where the town of Bradda should have sat, straddling a crossing of the Doltano. He was met instead with a desolate ruin. The broad stone bridge that had been the heart of the town still stood, along with two large old buildings flanking the road on the far side: a temple of Yorl and a tollhouse. Beyond them, everything was ruins. The surrounding buildings had been pulled down to form a firebreak, then the rest of the town had been burned. All that remained was ash and the lingering smell of smoke.

Muscles tensed in his shoulders, hand gripping tight around the pommel of his sword.

"Why would anyone do a thing like that?" he hissed.

"For the crossing." Valens's tone was more measured, only a hint of anger breaking through the pragmatic assessment of a man who had seen far worse. "Easier to control it like this, fewer ways for us to get close and cause trouble."

"But it's still only two towers full of warriors and whoever's in that camp past them. If we bring the army up we'll easily outnumber them and fight our way across."

"That's the point. We can't sneak closer and torch their defences or sneak groups of people past in farmers' wagons. We have to fight for the crossing, which needs superior numbers, which means committing what we've got. I'd bet the hand I've got left that their main force is camped within two days' ride. The minute we martial what we need to do this, they'll send a messenger and bring up reinforcements. Alder's forcing us to face him head-on."

Raul slid back behind the boulder and looked at his companions. Aside from Valens, it was mostly Ferra and a band of her Withering Folk, fast-moving archers who could harass and delay, not the sort of troops who forced a gap or held a line. Yasmi was there too in her shifter grey, masks at the ready in case they needed to do something unexpected.

"We can't just leave," Raul said. "Prisca's message said she would meet us here. She could walk right into this."

"Don't underestimate your mother's cunning," Yasmi said. "I can't see a band of Dunholmi infantry getting the drop on her."

"But the bridge is the only safe way across, and her message said she had urgent news." Raul peered past the boulders again. "We need a way of getting her across."

"Not just her," Valens said. "Look."

A boat was coming up the river, powered by a pair of yellow

triangular sails. Raul had seen one or two like it at the docks of Pavuno, but never one as sleek as this, its dark prow cutting through the river like a knife. People were moving about its deck, most of them dressed in the same yellow as those sails, and flashes of sunlight glinting off metal said that they were armed.

"Corsairs," Yasmi said, smiling with glee. "Prisca's been making friends in Saditch."

It was hard to look away from the striking boat and the promise of help it held, but movement drew Raul's attention back to the ruins of Bradda and its long bridge of arched stone. If there was a way of lowering the boat's masts then it might possibly have fit through one of those arches, all things being equal. But all things weren't equal, and the Dunholmi troops were making sure of that. A score of them had run out onto the bridge and were heaving chain nets over the side, their links clattering down until they splashed into the water, blocking the way through. Meanwhile, other warriors were advancing onto the remains of the docks along the riverbanks. Even turning the boat would bring it close enough for the Dunholmi to board. They might not be a full army, but they were enough troops to hold one up, and they would outnumber whoever the boat held.

"We have to help," Raul said.

"We'll be outnumbered," Valens said. "Even with them on the boat."

"Not if we can control this end of the bridge and stop them getting across." Raul looked up at the sky, hoping for a flock of birds or a flurry of windblown leaves, something he could read the omens in, the slightest sign to tell him whether he was right. But in the end it came down to the need to act, nothing more and nothing less. "There are few enough on this side for us to take them."

Valens pressed a thumb and finger against his furrowed brow.

"Got to move fast," he said. "Before they see us coming."

"No time to waste." Raul drew his sword and pressed a finger against the flat of the blade. "Blood for luck."

"Blood for luck," the others echoed quietly, drawing their own weapons.

"No one loose until they turn to us," Ferra said to her archers. "So?"

"So's said."

Raul ran over the brow of the hill and down, letting gravity and the slope take hold of him, flinging his legs out as fast as he could to avoid losing his footing. Even so, he felt himself out of control, barely able to keep up with his own feet, the weight of his chainmail and his body pulling him on, constantly at risk of tripping over a bump in the ground and landing face-first. But that wasn't what a prince did, wasn't something a chosen saviour could ever been seen doing, so instead he kept running, kept his arms swinging, turned every almost-fall into forward motion and a perilous charge toward the enemy.

The Dunholmi were so focused on the boat that they didn't see the rebels until they were dashing through the ruins of the town. Ashes flew and grey mud spattered Raul's shins as he hurtled toward them, sword swinging. Valens was beside him, sword and shield at the ready, an unstoppable mass of muscles, and on his other side was Yasmi, bounding and gliding in the shape of a wyvern, scales and claws and leathery wings that almost made it seem like she could fly. He couldn't think of anyone in the world he would rather fight beside.

At last, one of the Dunholmi looked around and cried out in alarm. In response, Yasmi roared, a ripping, raging sound that sent half the enemy stumbling back in shock and fear. At the same moment, the rebel archers loosed, arrows hurtling toward the warriors at the near end of the bridge. Some hit armour, their stone tips shattering against steel helmets or chainmail, but others hits heads, arms, legs, and the first blood of the day flowed.

Raul wished that he didn't feel a thrill at the sight of it.

For a moment there was chaos amid the Dunholmi, caught between the unexpected attack from the hills and the boat about to reach the docks. But then someone on the far bank shouted an order and blue-clad bodies rushed for the bridge.

Raul kept charging. If they could beat the troops on this bank quickly, then maybe his people could hold the narrow end of the bridge while the boat unloaded.

Maybe.

Better than nothing at all.

The Dunholmi were infantry levies, dressed in plain blue tabards instead of embroidered surcoats, armed with spears instead of sabres. Their armour was nothing but thick leather and scraps of scavenged metal, a web of weak points stitched together with desperation. With his first swing, he knocked a spear aside, stepped inside its wielder's reach, and sliced into the soft gap between two of those plates. His sword, a thing forged to impress and sharpened to kill, severed leather and cloth, skin and muscle, and smashed through the bone beneath. The warrior went down howling.

Another one lunged at him. He caught her first attack on his shield, tried to get past her spear, but she was too fast, stepping back and stabbing again. Then the wyvern that was Yasmi came screeching into her from the side, ripping her open with jagged teeth.

Valens was already at the bridge, shield raised to protect him from Dunholmi arrows. The warriors in blue were charging across, but Ferra and her people loosed and loosed again, enough arrows to turn that narrow channel into a blockade of death and agonized cries, to hold the enemy back while their officers kept screaming at them to advance.

There were only a few left standing on this side. If they'd been braver or better equipped, they might have charged in, scattered the rebel archers, given their comrades time to get across. But they looked at Raul standing in his best hero pose, chest open, feet planted wide, blood dripping from this sword; they looked at the men and women groaning and clutching their wounds on the ground; they looked at the black-hulled boat as it banged against the dock, a fresh band of wild-eyed warriors waiting to leap over the rail. And like anyone with any sense would have done, they ran.

Raul let out a sigh of relief, as much because he wouldn't need to kill anyone else as because he wouldn't have to fight four of them at once.

While his comrades held the end of the bridge, Raul strode

down the dock. Half the Saditchi corsairs had already leapt out, some of them standing guard while others positioned a wide boarding plank. Nearly all had pale skin and hair, and they wore matching yellow arming jackets under black breastplates. Some had wide-headed hatchets on their belts, others short narrow swords, and the ones standing guard held sharply curved bows. Brightly coloured feathers rose from the backs of their ridged helmets.

"We need to move quickly," Raul said. "Before we lose control of the bridge."

On the far side of the river, some of the Dunholmi had found shields, while others were pulling boards from the windows of their fortifications. They wouldn't be the best protection to advance under, but they would do.

"Are you in charge?" asked the Saditchi with the brightest feathers.

"Of course he is," a voice called out.

Prisca Servita stalked down the gangplank, wearing the smile of a hawk who sees prey. She'd abandoned her tinker's outfit in favour of robes more suitable for a minister and ambassador, but still carried her flint-topped walking staff. Raul started hurrying over, ready to give his ma a hug, but a sharp look from her stopped him short. They had other roles to play for the moment.

"Your Highness." She bowed to him.

"Minister Servita," he said as solemnly as he could manage. "Let's save the niceties for later."

"Of course, Your Highness, but first..."

She gestured toward the two women following her down

the ramp. The first wore a red embroidered dress and a black lace veil, obscuring her strikingly blond hair. It was her movements rather than her appearance that gave away her age, moving cautiously with the support of one of the corsairs.

"Your Majesty." He bowed to Queen Junia.

"Your Highness." The former queen of Estis bowed to him in return. "Such a relief to see you safe, dear child."

To his surprise, she wrapped her arms around him, and he did the same, though it felt strange with a woman he had only met once before.

"And this is Her Royal Highness, Princess Nydia of Saditch," Prisca said.

This woman was closer to Raul's age, somewhere in her early twenties, perhaps. She was dressed in the same outfit as the rest of the corsairs, but her arming jacket had dark embroidery down its sleeves and her feathers were all black. Her eyes gleamed like the jewels in the hilt of her sword, and she greeted him with an amused smile.

"Should we bow to each other as well?" she asked, handing the reins of a pony to one of the corsairs. "Or should we get out of here?"

"What about your boat?" Raul asked as it drifted away from the dock, its boarding plank falling into the river with a splash.

"My brother can find me another," she said. "For now, I hear we have a war to fight."

Two of the corsairs helped Queen Junia into the pony's saddle, while others went to stand with the rebels facing the bridge. The Dunholmi had begun their advance, shuffling nervously forward behind their makeshift barricade, while the rebels arced their arrows high, dropping painful but poorly aimed volleys.

Raul whistled and waved his sword in the air. "Back to the hills," he called out. "We'll come back for this town another day, and when we do, we'll be liberating it for good."

The words sounded fine, and they got the rebels doing what he wanted. Still, as Raul joined them in the retreat, he shot a defeated glance back at the ash that had been Bradda. What good would liberation do for a place like this?

---•---

Even in the saddle, travel was a challenge for Queen Junia. By nightfall, they weren't even halfway back to the main rebel force, so most of them stopped in a village to find shelter for the night. Valens was itching to get back and make sure things were run smoothly, so he marched on into the twilight with two of Ferra's scouts for company, while Ferra and the rest of the scouts, well used to life outdoors, headed back along the road to watch out for Dunholmi pursuit.

Once the villagers realised who Raul and Junia were, they were eager to put them up for the night, though they looked more uncertainly at the bright and fearsome Saditchi. After a little negotiation by Prisca and a lot more reassurance from Yasmi, a barn full of straw and blankets was provided for the foreigners, while a family gave up their farmhouse for the Estian royal party.

"How have you been feeling?" Raul asked as he chopped

vegetables on a worn but sturdy table, his work lit by a cooking fire. After months of holding up the imagined dignity of a prince, it was nice to do something so ordinary. No need to keep up the lie in front of Prisca, who had created it; Yasmi, who he had confessed it to; or Queen Junia, who knew full well that her real grandson died at birth.

"I manage," Prisca replied, stirring a pot as it came to the boil. Was she looking for omens or just keeping the soup from sticking? "Though someone else will have to taste this, my tongue can't be trusted anymore."

She handed the ladle to Yasmi and took a seat next to Junia.

"So you've told..." Raul gestured to the queen, then realised that he maybe shouldn't do that with a knife.

"I have," Prisca said. "Words are weapons at the Saditchi court, and I needed someone to help when I couldn't find mine. My moments of weakness come more often, and I cannot rely on my own senses to perceive a change."

Raul reached across the table and squeezed her hand. It was thinner than before, flesh fading to weather-worn skin over a frame of bones. He found himself caught between relief that she'd had someone she could talk to about her sickness and a strange sort of jealousy. For years, she hadn't told her family how the work of divining was eating away her mind, but then she'd gone abroad and revealed it to Queen Junia.

"I saw the symptoms in my own husband," Junia said, toying with a jet mourning ring. "Prisca couldn't have hidden them from me if she'd tried."

"Don't underestimate her," Yasmi said. "No one can beat Prisca when it comes to weaving lies."

Raul glanced up at that, worried that old resentments might have given a bitter edge to Yasmi's words, but the smile she gave his ma seemed genuinely sympathetic, not just an actor's façade.

"Thank you." Prisca looked down at the scarred wood of the tabletop. "I appreciate that more than you might expect."

Raul tipped the vegetables into the pot and slid an arm around Yasmi. It was a welcome comfort to stand like that for a little while, watching her stir the soup and enjoying the warmth of the hearth fire, not thinking about much of anything. A break from all of the rest.

"We should talk while we're alone," Prisca said. "Princess Nydia's views will be valuable and the Saditchi are useful allies, but not every conversation is for their ears."

Reluctantly, Raul sat back down, facing his adopted mother and his fake grandmother. Sooner or later, duty always caught up with him.

"Tell me," he said.

Prisca and Junia looked at each other.

"I'm too old and too tired for the details," Junia said. "Besides, you're the mastermind behind all this."

Prisca smiled a thin smile that only a few people would have recognised as triumphant.

"We've mustered a substantial army," she said. "It has already crossed the border and is marching to meet your force, Raul."

"These are the exiles?" he asked.

"I have to admit, those Estians who fled the invasion have proved a disappointment," Prisca said. "Though some of them have hired..." Her voice trailed off and she scowled in frustration. "Other people's warriors, ones for money."

"Mercenaries," Junia said quietly.

Raul winced. Watching his ma's body fade away was painful; watching it happen to her mind was agony.

"That's it," Prisca said, and her voice grew strong again. "Some have hired mercenaries or armed themselves and come along, but others I counted on are reticent to fight. They've been away too long, established new lives in other climes.

"Fortunately, Saditch has been more supportive. Though they helped the Dunholmi defeat us a generation ago, that relationship has soured. Competition for influence around the Golden Ocean has placed them on the precipice of conflict, and we've used our influence to tip them over the brink. Our army contains a substantial force of Saditchi corsairs alongside the Estian exiles. Once our armies join up, we'll have the power to decisively defeat Count Alder and drive the Dunholmi out.

"This is it, Raul. The ultimate confrontation has arrived."

The intensity in her eyes was almost feverish. Was that the sickness again, or was he reading too much into the excitement of a politician seeing her plans fulfilled, plans that had been twenty years in the making?

There was a crude carving of a goat halfway up the frame of the front door, a charm to bring luck for anyone setting out on a journey. Its edges were worn smooth by generations seeking its power. Raul got up and ran his fingers across it. You could never have too much luck.

Besides, he knew enough politics to recognise what hadn't

been said, and asking about it felt like starting a journey of his own. Prince Raul stepping out for the first time as a diplomat.

"What do the Saditchi want in return?" he asked. "I won't give up land. I've promised to free all of Estis in a hundred speeches, and I won't break my word."

When he turned to face them, he feared Prisca might be frowning, but instead she smiled her narrow smile and Junia nodded appreciatively. Only Yasmi looked as wary as he felt.

"Nothing material has been offered," Prisca said. "Only a mutually beneficial arrangement that will strengthen both our nations in the years ahead, providing security in the face of the Dunholmi threat. A..." Her faced screwed up in frustration. "A..."

"A betrothal," Junia said. "The promise of two great nations bound together by blood."

Raul frowned. He'd learned a lot of long words from Prisca and her books, but occasionally it still took him a moment to work out what this sort of talk meant.

"Of course." The ladle clanged against the side of the pot, and Yasmi laughed bitterly. "What else could this act of the play demand?"

Then Raul accepted what some part of his brain hadn't wanted to understand.

"You want me to marry one of them?" he croaked.

Chapter Five
Whatever Follows

In the end, it took two more days for them to rejoin the main column, and another day of hard marching to reach terrain where Valens agreed they could safely rest. Three days in which questions hung over Raul and he couldn't bring the people he needed together to resolve them. Three days in which Estian rebels, Withering Folk, and the newly arrived Saditchi manoeuvred warily around each other while rumours spread like wrinkles across the skin of an old apple.

On the fourth day, camping on high ground north of the River Doltano, he ordered a day for rest, repair, and planning. Immediately, something seemed to ease, a thaw in the mood to match the warmth that spring had finally brought. Chatter and laughter sounded around the fires. Withering Folk sat with the Saditchi, both sides examining each other's arms and clothes with open curiosity. Improvised ovens rose at one side of the camp, and the smell of baking bread filled the air as warriors turned their flour rations into food for the next few marching days.

Not everybody got to rest. Any break from the march was a chance for the smiths to sharpen and repair, the clang of their work scaring away every bird within a mile. Drusil's and Quintae's crews set to work on the war machines, finally attaching the wider wheels they'd been working on. Efron's acting troupe arranged a hasty rehearsal to put on a new play.

For Raul, the work was politics.

"I'm not sure I should be here," Yasmi said as the two of them approached a wide tent at the top of the camp, guards keeping the space around it clear for a dozen strides in every direction. "Especially with Princess Nydia."

"You're part of my council," Raul said. "People trust you. They've been listening to your orders the whole way through. Half of them joined us because they saw you perform."

"I'd hardly call them orders." She smiled and brushed her hair back behind her ear. "But I'll take the compliments."

"Even if none of it was true, I need you there. It's so much easier to stand up for what I think is right when I know there's someone on my side."

"Always." She took his hand and gave it a quick squeeze, then let go again. He wanted to take hold of her and kiss her, to enjoy a calming moment to themselves before he entered the fray. But the guards around the tent included some of their new Saditchi allies, and the mere reminder of what that entailed made him hold back. One of those guards pulled a flap open as they approached and Yasmi took a swift step ahead of Raul, preceding him into the tent.

"His Royal Highness, Prince Raul Warborn," she announced with all the power and clarity she brought to speeches on the stage. Raul tapped his foot against the ground three times, like he'd seen her do for luck before a performance, and then followed her inside.

With a rustle of cloth, the inhabitants of the tent rose to their feet and bowed. The only exception was Princess Nydia, who nodded instead of bowing, a casual gesture among equals. Raul returned the nod, then waved the others into their seats.

"We can keep the formalities to a minimum while we're sleeping in fields," he said, crossing the tent. There was no council table here, where every ounce of weight was one more burden for their draught animals and the people who unloaded them. But there were folding stools designed by Quintae to be light and sturdy, which had been laid out in a circle. Raul had resisted the suggestion of a travelling throne, accepting a banner hung behind his seat as a more practical compromise: a small piece of showmanship without all the extra weight. He settled into that seat, facing the door, and Yasmi took the empty seat beside him, the masks on her belt clicking as she sat.

Raul looked around at the council. His council. The Royal Council of Estis, as it currently stood. Valens and Yasmi, of course. Silvano Ironhead and a couple of company commanders. Ferra and towering Ovida representing the folk of the Withered Hills. Drusil to discuss logistics and help with technical challenges. And now three new additions. Prisca returned from a year away, looking as authoritative as ever. Queen Junia in her finery, the voice of the exiles she had been hiding with since the failed first revolt. And Princess Nydia, who looked more comfortable in herself than most of the rest, despite being the one true outsider.

Someone had passed Raul a cup while he was surveying the room, and he took a sip. Weak ale for a working day, but better than they normally drank. Was that part of impressing the new arrivals? And who had given it to him while he was distracted? Were some of their guards playing at servant now? That idea made him shift in his seat, trying to shake a discomfort that came from more than the wood he sat on, but he supposed that sooner or later these things were bound to happen. He couldn't play the part of a prince without others playing the roles of a court.

"Thank you all for coming here," he said. "I'm sure there are many things to discuss, but if there's one thing we've learned over the past year, it's to settle the big decisions while we have time."

That drew blank faces from the new arrivals and chuckles from those who'd been with him so long. Before this, none of them had known how to lead an army, to organise and command so many different parts. They'd had plenty of costly mistakes and angry words before they'd worked out things that an established court probably took for granted, and what had been painful at the time was now part of a shared bond.

Princess Nydia smiled and raised a pale eyebrow. "It sounds like you've been on quite an adventure."

"More than one." Raul laughed. "But those stories will have to wait."

Beside him, bracelets jingled softly as Yasmi straightened her brightly patterned tunic and sat up straight. Around the tent, others joined in Raul's laughter. That was good. He didn't want them on edge already when they had such an important decision to make.

"As you all know by now, another column is marching toward us," he said. "A force of exiles and allies that will almost double our numbers. For the first time, we'll have the forces we need to face Count Alder in the field, not pick at the fringes of the occupation. We can advance on key towns and fortresses and besiege any that don't open their gates, confident that, when Alder comes to break the siege, we'll be ready to fight him."

His words were followed by cheering. Not as loud as when he stood in front of the whole army, but still heartening to hear.

"Before we do that, we need to make a choice," Raul continued. "General?"

Valens, who had already emptied his cup, set it down beside his seat.

"We've got two forces." He held up his clenched fist on one side and the stump of his wrist on the other. Raul was proud to see him wielding the stump so openly now, not hiding his injury from the world. "That gives us two choices. We keep them separate and try to trap Alder between them, or..." He wrapped his hand around the stump. "We unite their strength. We need to decide now while we've got time to act on it."

There was a long moment of silence. Clearly, everyone expected a general to take longer at explaining his thoughts. Equally clearly, Valens was done.

"If I may, Your Highness?" Queen Junia said, looking at Raul.

"Of course," he replied. "Everyone here is free to speak their mind."

"How enlightened." Queen Junia turned as she spoke, looking at each of the others. "As General Valens has said, there is strength in unity, and that strength is about more than raw numbers. The exiles I have gathered include many experienced commanders, veterans of our nation's past wars, some of whom have continued serving as mercenaries while abroad. By combining their leadership with the troops you have amassed, we can improve the performance of those troops in battle, while making better use of the skills and experience at our disposal."

Silvano Ironhead frowned. "You want your people to take over from us?"

"What you have achieved here is remarkable, given your lack of martial training and experience. Imagine how much more you can do with real officers in charge."

"You mean the old nobility."

"I do indeed mean the nobility of Estis, restored to their rightful place just as we are restoring the kingdom. What could be more natural?"

Silvano, a fist resting on his knee, jerked his head around to look at Raul. "Is this what you want, Your Highness?"

The tone of the conversation was already a long way from what Raul wanted, never mind the things they were saying. But he needed everyone cooperating, which meant letting everyone speak their piece. For all he knew, there might be wisdom in Queen Junia's words. Of all the people here, she had the most experience running a country.

"I want to hear what everyone thinks," Raul said.

"Fine, then I think that's crap," Silvano said. "My people

have spent the past year winning fights under the leaders they've got. Before that, they were the heart of Appia's work for the first revolt and they paid a price in blood for it. They've got experience and they know what this land's like now, not twenty years ago. More than that, they're the ones who didn't run from danger."

"I did not run, young man," Junia said sharply. "I remained in Pavuno until your failed first revolt. I gathered intelligence. I built connections. I prepared for this moment. I see things you have no concept of."

"That may be, but what I see is you throwing away an opportunity so your gang can throw their weight around. We'll only get one chance to catch Alder between the two sides. We should take it."

Outside, in the army camp, labourers were singing a work song to keep their movements in time. Mallets battered against wood. A chicken clucked.

In the Royal Council of Estis, silence filled the tent.

"If I may?" Prisca held out her hand like she was offering something to them all. "Your point about this opportunity is well made, but the opportunity cuts both ways. This is also a chance for the Dunholmi to attack the separate parts of our forces while they cannot support each other, to seize upon our geographical division, sever our forces, and destroy them one at a time."

The silence that followed was less brittle, more contemplative.

"Bringing the armies together doesn't have to mean changing who's in command," Valens said, one thick finger rubbing his temple. "Maybe we bring them close without putting your nobles in charge."

Prisca shrugged. "Once they're here, we might as well use their skills."

"Exactly," Junia said. "If we're rebuilding the kingdom, people might as well get used to what that means."

"Who says we're rebuilding it the old way?" another of the rebel captains snapped. "We've done fine without your nobles for the past twenty years."

"You've been suffering under the boot heel of the Dunholmi."

"So now we should suffer under your boot heel instead?"

That was when the shouting began, half a dozen voices slamming into each other, nobody being heard. Those shouts were joined by a pounding in Raul's ears. He wished that he'd put the tent further away from the rest of the camp, because he had a terrible feeling people might hear what was going on, their so-called leaders tearing into each other instead of the enemy.

"Enough." He rose to his feet. "All of you."

He spoke like a king was meant to speak, loud and proud, leaving no room for doubt or disobedience. He'd never done that before, never had to. He was surprised at how good it felt. His hand barely shook as he spoke, and his voice was steady.

"This is no way for a royal council to behave." He glared at Prisca and Junia. "You two should know that better than the rest."

Briefly, both woman glared daggers at him, but then they both bowed their heads.

"Apologies, Your Highness."

He wasn't sure who said it first, but it became a murmur that rippled around the tent. He sighed and settled into his seat. Maybe a throne wouldn't be such a bad idea, something with a back to hold him up when he felt like he'd spent all his strength in a single breath.

"We're all tired, we're all excited for what we could achieve, and we're all fearful of what might happen if it goes wrong." It wasn't a line he'd taken from Tenebrial's plays, but the rhythm felt close and it seemed to work. More of them looked up, every expression solemn and repentant.

He looked over at Ferra, who hadn't joined in the fight. She stared steadily back at him.

"What do you think?" he asked.

"I think you town folk put too much store in strength, piling all your rocks in one place and fixing to endure the storm that comes. Best to be deft instead, dodge the raindrops and stay dry."

"Manoeuvre rather than blunt force."

"Could be. More than that, you spoke of the future to the folk of the Withering, of not letting the road's teeth gnaw at our land again."

"I did." He didn't need to look at Prisca and Junia to know how they would respond to this. "The Withered Hills will be free to govern themselves, I promise."

"Word is word."

"It is." He laid his hand over the spiked moon stitched onto his sleeve and the supposed birthmark underneath. "I swear by my past and by my future, by who I am."

His chest ached at the act of swearing on a lie, but in some ways his destiny felt more real than it ever had before. He would be king of Estis, he would free his people and build a better land. If he did that through his own strength instead of the fulfilment of a prophecy, surely that made him more of a king, not less of one.

Ferra and Ovida placed their hands on their chests, weather-worn fingers on furs, and both nodded their heads.

He'd set out his position, but that didn't mean he had an answer to the question at hand, the important decision that he'd said they needed to make. Whatever the future held beyond this day, the armies needed orders now.

Looking down, he saw that someone had refilled his cup while he wasn't watching. He picked it up off the floor and took a sip. He needed guidance from somewhere, but he knew what everyone in this room said and none of that would help him cut through it when they had such powerful motives of their own. Bubbles spun in slow circles on the top of the ale.

Raul smiled, knocked back the contents of the cup in two gulps, twisted his wrist around three times to swirl the dregs about, then looked at the patterns they'd formed.

He hadn't been doing much divination lately. Estis needed a warrior king, not someone wielding the secret powers of the world. And the dregs of a cup of ale weren't the best of offerings to read the portents in. But Prisca had taught him that the signs could be found almost anywhere if you knew how to look, and it felt good to look again, to see what shapes were visible in those trails of dark liquid and the imperfections of earthenware.

He saw a hand, open fingers closing as the ale ran down the glazed clay.

He saw the shape of a horse collapse into foam.

He saw a crown, and that stayed.

"We'll keep the forces separate," he said. "Send some of our scouts to guide the newcomers and bring some of their nobles here to see how we work. Ferra's people will arrange messenger birds so that we can coordinate in ways the Dunholmi can't.

"Count Alder thought he could trap us by controlling the river crossings, but he has to stay in place to do that, which puts him inside our trap. He's about to find out how it feels when the hammer and the anvil meet."

He looked up and saw their smiles. That was the sort of language the Estians could all get behind, the language of hard work and martial steel. Ferra and Ovida looked pleased that what they brought had been acknowledged. Even Princess Nydia, sitting by the entrance, gave him a respectful nod.

"Well then." Raul took a deep breath. Fine talk was one thing, making it happen was another, especially when it meant telling people with more skill and experience than him what they ought to do. But he was the authority here, and he couldn't hold back from that anymore. "Prisca, you know the land, talk with our captains about the best routes for the columns to advance. Ferra, Ovida, please show Her Majesty your birds and work out how best to get the message to her followers. Drusil, you probably have another day here before we move, so talk to Quintae about any tricks that might give us an advantage fighting in the river lands." He rose and they all did the same. "Council adjourned."

As the others bowed and started to leave, Prisca came over to him.

"Very well done, Your Highness," she said, and those words from his ma made Raul's chest swell with pride. She lowered her voice. "But remember, we're fighting to..."

She faltered and her eyes went blank, gazing down at the floor.

"Ma?" Raul whispered. "Are you all right?"

She took a sharp breath, then shook her head before looking at him again, more intense than ever.

"You told people what you had to so we could get this far," she said, "but you need to prepare them for a return to the old ways."

"I'll think about it, Ma," he said, pride deflating at the realisation that she was on the other side of this business. It wasn't a big surprise, but it was a discomfort he wasn't ready to face yet, not when they'd worked so hard to find trust again.

"I've told you before..." she began with a thin smile.

"Don't call you Ma." He smiled back, and it only felt a little hollow. "But I'm about to become king, and that means I can call you what I like."

Still smiling, she shook her head and headed out.

"What do you want from us, Your Highness?" Yasmi asked. "I don't think Valens or I can fly a message anywhere, but we might dance more lightly around everyone's toes than Her Majesty does."

"That's why I need you to talk with Ma and Junia," Raul said. "Try to get them to understand how things have changed, that this place can't be the same as it was before."

"Of course."

"And Da?" He turned to Valens. "The Withering Folk like

you, and our captains are used to listening to your orders. Can you please reassure them that I won't let anyone take what they've fought for?"

"Aye, lad." Valens laid his hand on Raul's shoulder. "Don't worry. They all trust you."

As the two of them headed out, Raul sank into his seat. His mouth felt dry and his throat sore. He picked up his cup from the trampled grass on which the tent was pitched. Of course, it only held dregs.

One last figure stepped around the tent, jug in hand, and poured him a drink.

"Was it you doing that the whole time?" Raul asked.

Princess Nydia laughed as she sat down beside him. It was a beautiful laugh, but it couldn't match Yasmi's.

"That's what servants are for," she said. "Yours have decided to leave us in peace."

He looked around. The few guards who had been in the tent were outside now, only a couple of silhouettes visible through the canvas of the door.

"What do you think of all this?" he asked, taking a sip.

"When my mother was killed, I watched my brother rise to the throne, and I've watched his struggles over the past five years." Her lilting accent was a contrast with the shouting of his advisors, like listening to a flute play after the banging of a drum. "If you think your court is divided, you should see the squabbling of corsair admirals."

"What do you think of me?"

She looked at him sidelong, lips pursed. "Honestly?"

"Please. I have enough lies and evasion in my life already."

That made her smile again, and she pushed long white hair back behind her ear.

"No one in Saditch would ask so bluntly, but I rather like it." She poured ale into another cup and took a sip. "I think that you're less impressive than Queen Junia and Minister Prisca tried to tell my brother, but more impressive than they really thought once I peered past the bluster. I think you're innocent but eager to learn, and I like that in a man, or a woman from time to time." She traced the embroidered heraldry on his sleeve with a fingertip. "I think that you're the best hope your kingdom has, not because there is no other hope but because of who you are."

He swallowed. After that, his next question caught in his throat, though he couldn't have explained why.

"And what do you think of the deal that brought you here?"

"Marriage?" she asked. "You and me?"

She looked at him, her bottom lip caught between her teeth, eyes bright. Her finger was still on his arm, and it could easily have slid on around, signalling the sort of reassurance that a prince was meant to want. Instead, she drew it away, tossed her hair back, and raised her cup.

"I think we're a long way off having to think about that. In the meantime, here's to surviving the forces arrayed against us: your monstrous invaders, your miserable weather, and most of all your invigoratingly belligerent court."

Now he was the one laughing as he raised his cup to clack against hers.

"To survival," he said. "And whatever follows."

Chapter Six
Caught by Surprise

Valens knew that a proper general wouldn't be here, slipping out of a coracle in the predawn gloom and wading through the marshy ground at a river's edge, soaked to his waist and using the reed beds for cover. A proper general would have been with the main column, keeping troops in order as they marched down the vale, leading their triumphant advance into one town after another, not leading a score of silent veterans on a dawn raid. But then, he'd never had much time for proper generals, highborn folk with crisp accents, expensive boots, and clean clothes. You weren't a proper warrior without at least one shirt so bloodstained that it wouldn't come out no matter how hard you washed.

There were plenty of satisfactions to being a general, and Valens liked to think that he was doing it well, but he was determined to also keep being a warrior. If that meant a day or two away from all the politics, leaving Raul to get experience keeping the troops in line, then that only made it better. Especially if it meant time away from Prisca.

Pushing aside the reeds, he peered out at the village they'd come for. It was really just a cluster of grain silos built out of mud bricks, with three farmhouses standing watch around them, a place where farmers from the surrounding area could bring their tithes at tax time and store surplus for the tough winters. Right now, with Dunholmi levies standing guard by each of the houses, enemy supplies would be keeping their warriors fed. It was a shame to burn good grain, but it would be more of a shame to let it fill the enemy's bellies.

He looked around at the warriors he'd brought with him. With one exception, every woman and man here was from the Imperial Legion, his handpicked best of the best. Today they'd abandoned their red and black for murky ponchos borrowed off the Withering Folk, to go unseen for as long as possible before making their attack. The one exception was a Withered warrior herself: Ovida, a seven-foot giant carrying a spear broad as a small tree trunk. Having her along was almost as good as having Fabia with him, back in the old days. Not as good, but close, and it was better to look after the living than worry about the dead.

He checked the straps binding his shield onto his right arm. A stylised mountain was carved into the back of the shield, a charm for endurance, and all the legionaries' swords had eagles stamped onto the crossguards for ferocity. If the rest of the world feared Estis's folk magic, then they might as well wield that weapon.

Fingers splayed wide, he held up his hand. Along the reed bed, the legionaries touched the charms around their necks or touched their blades and whispered the words "blood for luck." As he curled those fingers in one at a time, Valens listened to the water flow past and offered a silent prayer to Laughing Loftus, like he and Fabia would have done back in the day, a prayer so short it was done with one finger left. Then that last finger curled in and they all moved.

Reeds rustled aside and warriors climbed up the bank. They wouldn't get to the silos completely unnoticed, so this was all about balance, stealth against speed, getting as close as they could before the alarm was raised. Following Valens and Ovida's lead, the legionaries hunched over and scuttled across the open ground, swords and shields in hand, a few with bows out at the flanks. The muddy riverside was followed by a field of broad beans, sodden boots trampling green shoots into the dirt. Valens drew his sword and picked up speed.

Outside the closest farmhouse a sentry turned, stiffened, raised his spear. An arrow whistled out of the gloom, thudded through his chest, and he fell without a word.

"Jeb?" someone called from the farmhouse door. "You say something?"

Another guard emerged, looked down, looked out. Two more arrows. One hit her in the arm, but the other slammed into the doorpost. She yelled in pain and alarm.

"Now!" Valens bellowed.

No more skulking. No more silence. They ran screaming across the last field, a noise to send the dread of war through these lowly Dunholmi levies, to make them think that they faced a whole army and not just twenty warriors soaked to the bone. Three more guards ran out of the first farmhouse and were cut down before Valens could get close. Others dashed from the other buildings, were struck by arrows or by panic, then fell or ran. A horse galloped from amid the granaries, a blue-clad rider low over its back, and raced away up the road. It didn't matter. Count Alder's army was hours away, and the rebels would be long gone by then. Besides, the idiot had ridden in the wrong direction.

Now that they didn't have to worry about who saw them, three of the legionaries unhooked lanterns from their backs and opened the shutters. These weren't normal lanterns, with flames the river could have put out. They were Drusil's work, powered by sun charms and just the right metal, their beams bright as day. Splitting into three teams, his warriors followed those lanterns into the shadows of the farmhouses and emerged with their shields piled high with firewood.

Working quickly, they opened the doors at the bases of the granaries, letting some of the grain flow out, then piled up firewood amid the spills of grain. The sun was rising, dusting the corn gold and the hills green, the granaries a warm orange brown. Shame to destroy them, but war was war. Jars gurgled as they poured lantern oil over the firewood, then there was the sharp scratching of flint and steel. Valens watched the first fire in satisfaction.

"General!" a sentry called out. "Company!"

Valens strode over, grinning in anticipation. Maybe that rider had found a Dunholmi patrol, and he'd tear another chunk off the invaders before the morning was done.

What he saw coming down the road was no patrol. At least fifty Dunholmi cavalry, blue pennants fluttering and spear tips blazing like flames in the dawn light, came cantering over the brow of a hill and down the road toward them. Riders on lighter horses rode out at their flanks, composite bows at the ready.

A small patrol, they could have handled. A score of riders, even odds, he might have stood against. This was far more.

"Road's teeth," Ovida growled. "Thought you said they weren't here, so?"

His instinct was to argue back, to point out that war always caught you by surprise. As if she didn't know. As if there was time for any of it.

"To the boats!" he bellowed.

There was no hesitation, no waiting to light the last fire. He'd trained the legion to fight like good infantry, all together and with instant obedience. Snatching up their weapons, they ran back across the farmyards and the bean field, heading for the water's edge, flinging up dirt and small green sprouts.

Behind them, the sound of hooves emerged from the dawn chorus and the spring wind. Those hooves grew louder, faster, accompanied by the jangle of harness and chainmail, the shouts of warriors urging their steeds to pick up speed. Arrows thudded into the dirt, not hitting yet but too close.

The distance to the reed beds seemed so much further this time. The fastest of the outriders had reached the riverbank and were galloping to intercept them, firing off quick shots as they went. Still none of them hit, but the threat slowed the fleeing legionaries.

"Faster!" Valens yelled. "It only gets worse if you slow down."

The two leading riders stowed their bows and drew their sabres, placing themselves directly in the path of the retreat.

That was their mistake. Valens ran screaming at one, waving his sword and shield. The horse reared, throwing its rider, then galloped off, dragging her shrieking through the dirt. Ovida took the other one, driving her spear through the horse's neck and into its rider, her powerful muscles punching fire-hardened wood through flesh and bone. Horse and rider went down screaming and thrashing, and there was a crack as a hoof slammed into Ovida's leg.

The legionaries ran past and into the water, wading out between the reeds. The first of them pulled coracles back for the rest, dragging them in on the ropes with which the small craft had been moored. Valens went with them, urging his troops to keep moving. The warrior next to him grunted as an arrow glanced off her armour. Another collapsed into the water as a shot burst through his chainmail.

Glancing back, Valens saw the last two legionaries helping Ovida to her feet. Her leg hung limp, bone jutting halfway down her shin. He wanted to go back but he could see the oncoming charge, the Dunholmi warriors with their spears lowered as they thundered across the final field. Too late for Ovida and anyone who had held back. The best he could do was to keep moving, not to get the others killed.

He flung himself into a coracle and paddled frantically into the current. Some of his warriors were ahead of him, some following. Behind them came crunches and screams, sounds he'd heard a hundred times before but that were a fresh horror every time.

At least the archers had spread out to make space for the charge. The arrows falling now barely hit the coracles, let alone their passengers. As the current grabbed hold, the tiny craft were carried into the middle of the river and away.

Looking back, Valens saw the cavalry massed on the bank and in the shallows. There was no sign of Ovida or the legionaries helping her. He hoped that whatever happened to them had been quick.

Beyond the riders, the granaries were burning, mud brick walls collapsing into the fire. That was something. Not worth the cost, perhaps, but compensation for the pain. Still, that wasn't what made his eyes go wide and his fingers clench tight on the coracle's side as he pressed his stump against the furrows of his brow.

Across the hill, more Dunholmi troops were advancing. Armoured cavalry. Light outriders. Infantry levies marching in massed blocks. The tops of supply wagons appeared over the ridge, not just a company this time but a whole column, an army advancing along a road where no army was meant to be.

None of their blue banners showed the white tree of House Alder. Their heraldry showed swords and seeds, beasts and boats, but most of all the royal crown, emblazoned in pure white across vast banners at the head of the infantry.

The rebels weren't the only ones whose reinforcements had arrived.

———————•———————

"Your Majesty." Count Alder bowed as deeply as he could without risking falling from the saddle. "It is a deep honour to receive a visit from you."

He was met with a scoff. "You think that I would bring all this for a visit?"

King Lorrin gestured toward the column of troops lined up along the road behind him. Thousands of them, cavalry and infantry and everything they dragged along in their train. Enough to fight a war on their own, perhaps, though not as many as Alder would have expected from a full muster in Dunholm. Some had to be held back to protect the homeland, of course, but was something more at play? Were the rumours of skirmishes with the Saditchi true?

He recognised the banners with a flush of bitterness. Many were people who had plotted against him and his family, who had publicly mocked his father and sneered when Alder was given this post. How dare they come here, playing at support. He should ride down the line and chase them from his territory.

Behind King Lorrin, the ghostly figure of Alder's grandmother nodded encouragement, but when he blinked she was gone.

The king swung his leg over the horse's back and descended to the ground, a sham of the monarch he had been, inches from humiliating himself and all of them. Everyone at court had seen nobles whose days in the saddle were behind them but who couldn't bear to face the truth. There was nothing more embarrassing than watching some red-faced and wheezing second cousin with their foot caught in the stirrup, trying to pretend they still mattered.

Nothing apart from having the monarch of the whole nation turn out to tear you down for your failings.

Taking deep breaths to calm himself, Alder felt another heat stir inside, one that had nothing to do with fear or shame, a heat that was more than human.

You're stronger than him, the voice of Jarrag whispered in the back of his mind. *You could have it all.*

Alder shook his head, trying to chase the voice away, then cringed as Lorrin gave him a disdainful look.

Following their monarch's lead, the surrounding nobles descended from their horses and handed their reins to assorted squires and pages. Alder had never been bothered with such things, so he clung on to his own reins after he had descended. Immediately, it felt like a mistake, not having the status symbol of some youth scurrying around to fulfil his whims. But status was about more than show. After the king, he was still the highest-ranking noble here, only three generations descended from the throne. If his grandmother had been the firstborn of her era, he wouldn't be bowing and scraping to his great-uncle now and the kingdom would have been stronger for it.

"Come, Brennett," King Lorrin said. "Walk with me."

Alder kept his face a mask of calm, despite his growing agitation. No one had called him by his given name in years, not in private, let alone in front of half the court. What some might naively have heard as a sign of intimacy was a reprimand, a belittling, putting an unruly child in his place.

"I would be honoured, Your Majesty," he said.

Lorrin walked away from the road with a ponderous pace that was just as likely to be about the stiffness of his age as it was royal dignity. He'd given up on dyeing his grey hairs since Alder last saw him, instead shaving his scalp bare, and his slender silver travelling crown looked more dramatic for it. But if he thought that hid the truth, then he was deluded. His face was a mass of wrinkles, the ruin of past glory collapsing in on itself.

Together, they walked up a hill at the edge of the army camp, followed by a small band of retainers including Brook and Tur. It was tempting to dismiss those two, so that no one of Alder's circle would see or hear whatever came next, but that would replicate his error with the lack of squires. Besides, if the king wanted word of this conversation to get out, then Alder couldn't stop it; by this evening, rumours of his humiliation would have run around the camp, everyone from bejewelled lords to the soldiers who dug the shit pits laughing at him behind his back. Heat flushed his cheeks and he rubbed at his neck, trying to chase the discomfort away.

At the top of the hill, servants had already set up a folding table and a pair of armchairs with their backs carved into matching pairs of horses' heads. The king sat and Alder joined him, looking across the camp and the new troops marching in.

"Very orderly," King Lorrin commented. "That's something I've always admired about you, Brennett. More self-control than your father. More discipline."

A servant poured wine into porcelain goblets and set them on the table.

"Your Majesty is too kind," Alder said, his nails digging into his palm at the reminder of his father's failings.

"Which raises the question, what has been going wrong?"

Lorrin sipped his wine and nodded in approval. A single silver ring set with black pearls glinted on his finger. "First that trouble in Pavuno, our monument torn down, riots, prisoners escaping. Then that trip into the wilderness, noble warriors lost on some fool's errand. And now, after a year of war, you haven't managed to put down this pathetic rebellion. From what I hear, they've been burning our forts and even seizing our armouries. This was not what I expected when I sent you north."

The fire blazed bright in Alder's chest, the urge to lash out, to fight back, to destroy. He imagined reaching across the table, wrapping his fingers around the saggy skin of Lorrin's throat, watching his flesh bubble and char as he burned the life out of this pompous pig. He grinned at the thought. But then he would die as surely as the king did, and for what? A fitting tribute to his father, destroying House Alder for good. A fresh failure adding to a line of indignity.

"The North Marchers have proved more resourceful than anticipated," he said, forcing his voice level. "They've been cantering across the high hills, avoiding a real confrontation. But we have them penned in now. Whatever they do next, they will have to use one of two key river crossings, and we're positioned to catch them when they do."

"You don't think that, in all this time roaming their own country, they might have been recruiting more troops, training them, making weapons? That while you sit here grazing the meadow, they might be growing in strength?"

"I'm sorry for any disappointment I've caused Your Majesty." Alder's hand tightened around his cup. The glaze blackened beneath his touch and the wine began to steam. "Or any alarm I might have caused your more nervous advisors. But might I remind you that I already put down one rebellion less than two years ago, and that I have been here long enough to understand these people in a way that no one else in Dunholm does? I've even fought their leaders up close, taken a hand off one, and humiliated the others. They're not a threat you need to worry about."

"I decide what is worthy of alarm," King Lorrin said coldly. "And might I remind you that you serve at my pleasure? When that pleasure ends, so does your governorship."

And perhaps much more than that, his tone implied, though he at least wasn't saying it out loud. Just the hint of it made Alder's breath rasp in his throat, and the cup cracked in his hand.

"I bring other strengths to this fight," he said. "Things that can counter the northerners' abominable magics."

He could feel Lorrin's servants watching him, sneering at their betters. He would show them. He laid his hand palm up on the table and finally let the heat inside him flow. Flame rose, bright as the sun, its heat rippling the air around them, and he grinned at the gasps of shock from the courtiers and servants. Let these weaklings gasp and shiver; they didn't understand real power.

King Lorrin's hand clamped around Alder's wrist.

"Stop this at once," the king snapped.

Alder bared his teeth and stared at the king.

"I said stop it!"

Alder almost laughed in the king's face, but that would have ruined everything. Reluctantly, he forced the flame back down, pulling his power in. He trembled as the king's nails dug deeper into his flesh. He should have known better. Lorrin was one more old fool, scared of the possibilities that the world presented, too weak and complacent for the power that Alder had found.

But he was still the king, and everyone there was sworn to obey him. Everyone including Alder.

"My most humble apologies," Alder said, bowing his head. "That was foolish and inappropriate."

"It certainly was. We marched into this land twenty years ago to bring their foul experiments to an end. I will not have my own courtiers, my own family, reviving the dark arts that brought the Empire of Estis infamy."

It was laughable. These things might have brought Estis its unpopularity, but they'd also brought it success. The magic was an excuse, a moral screen behind which others could bring down an overreaching empire, reclaim what they had lost, and take more in compensation.

But then, what did Alder know about politics? According to this wrinkled old has-been, he couldn't even govern the Northern March right.

Lorrin let go of Alder's wrist, then clicked his fingers.

"We found this on the march here," the king said. "Do you know her?"

Four infantry approached, leading a woman in chains. She was the tallest person Alder had ever seen, bulging with muscles under bloodstained furs and a broken imitation of a breastplate made from woven reeds. There were bandages around her thigh, her arm, and her head; one of her shins was bound in a splint. Two of the infantry had to hold her up just to bring her a short distance. Pale skin and trembling lips indicated shock and blood loss, as he would have expected from those wounds, but when she stared at Lorrin there was a blaze of hate in her that Alder almost admired.

"One of the rebels' wild supporters from the Withered Hills," Alder said. "Hardly worth your consideration."

Lorrin gestured to one of his captains, who drew his slender silver dagger. Quick slashes of that charmed blade cut away armour and furs, revealing the powerful body beneath.

"Are they all like this, these hill people?" Lorrin asked.

"Hardly."

"Shame. With a hundred like her, we might have started a breeding pool, raised some truly magnificent labourers for the forests and the mines. But just one, in such sorry shape..."

The woman pursed her lips, then spat. A thick gobbet of phlegm landed on the king's tunic, right under his chain of office. Alder pressed a hand to his mouth, suppressing vicious laughter at it all: the perfect position of that moist mess; Lorrin's look of fury at something so small; the glorious gall it took to do a thing like that in a moment like this. His humiliations felt infinitely more bearable after seeing Lorrin receive one of his own.

"You might think that your war is over," the king said, staring in fury at the captive. "But you're wrong. Your head is going on a pike, and it will go ahead of my army as I trample this rebellion into mud. The last thing your friends will see before I slaughter them will be your cold dead eyes staring down at them. What do you think of that?"

The woman's smile was a horror to behold.

"Nowt you do to me will stop what's coming for you and all the rest of these filthy road's teeth," she said, her imperious gaze taking in Alder, the surrounding courtiers, and the thousands of troops mustered below. "A new moon rises, and there's nowt you can do about it."

"Take her away," Lorrin hissed. "I'll deal with her later. And as for you..." He turned to Alder. "You will continue to serve me as I lead our forces to victory. If you can stop screwing up for the rest of the campaign, then maybe you have a future, whether here or at court. But note this well, Count Brennett Alder—fail me again, and I'll have more than one head on a pike."

Chapter Seven
Moonrise

Sitting on the bedroll at one side of his tent, Raul watched Yasmi finish dressing, her hands straightening the line of her loose tunic, lining up the masks neatly on her belt, artfully draping a scarf around her neck, putting on a selection of bracelets and then, after careful consideration, taking one off. She never took off the one he'd given her, but even if she had, he would have smiled at every little gesture. His heart swelled just watching her.

He was living in a tent, sleeping on wet ground, exhausted from marching and from the hammering rain that had kept waking him through the night. Half the people he loved most were arguing with the other half about their every move, with all their lives and millions of others' at stake. He'd never been more anxious about saying the right thing or more worried for the safety of his friends and family, the weight of a whole nation weighing down on his shoulders like a pack the size of a mountain. And yet in this moment he'd never been happier.

Life was funny sometimes.

"Are you laughing at me?" Yasmi arched an eyebrow.

"I'm laughing with how happy I am." He got up and took her hands in his. "Here in this tent, with you."

"I've never met anyone as sweet as you," she said, smiling up at him. "Or as utterly ridiculous."

"Is that any way to talk to a prince?"

He tilted his chin back and puffed out his chest. Yasmi burst out laughing, which only made his chest swell more.

"I've taught you that role far too well."

"Of course you have. You're the best actress in the world."

"As if you'd know, ridiculous boy." She stretched up and kissed him. "But we should get going, the council will be waiting for you."

That should have been enough to deflate him, given how their recent meetings had been. But today he was determined. He was going to show them what a prince could do, even without a script.

"I want them to wait," he said. "Just a little. I want them to start arguing before I get there."

"Are you sure that's wise?"

"No, but when I'm there the arguments grow around me and I'm never sure when I should cut them off. It looks like I'm part of the problem. This way, I'm coming in from outside, maybe that could make a difference."

"You're developing a delicious sense of drama." She straightened his tunic, ran a finger down the embroidery on the chest. "Will Princess Nydia be there?"

Her tone didn't change, nor did her expression, but Raul

felt like some undefinable thing was amiss. Normally, if he didn't understand what was happening with people, he went to Yasmi for help, but he could hardly ask her for advice about herself.

"I hope so," he said. "If we're going to make decisions about how to fight, then we need someone representing the Saditchi."

Yasmi let him go and pulled the tent flap back, revealing an army camp draped in drizzle.

"That's good," she said. "Nydia seems smart, she'll help find the best option."

"I hope so." He passed her a cloak, pulled his own on, and headed out with her into the damp.

"She's beautiful too."

"Not as beautiful as you." At least that was something he knew how to answer, and the answer came from his heart.

"Hmm."

Or perhaps he hadn't got that quite right.

Raul's tent wasn't far from the big one where they held council meetings, but even on this short walk he was accompanied by warriors of the Imperial Legion. Prisca had insisted upon it, both for security and for the look of the thing, and it did add a swagger to Raul's step knowing they were there for him. It helped that matching armour had arrived for the legionaries, forged to Drusil's specifications at Hewed, finished off with charms hammered into the edge by the royal armourer herself. A bull for strength, a mountain for endurance, and Raul's symbol of a dagger-pierced moon for loyalty. The legionaries had been armed with swords as well, though many of the army were equipped with cheaper axes and spears, a sign of their prestige. They marched proudly along, hands always ready on their weapons, straight-backed and alert.

The bustle of the camp was muted, warriors hiding from the rain in their tents, the noises they did make muffled in the heavy air. That made it easier to hear the raised voices as he approached the tent.

Yasmi paused at the entrance.

"Do you want me to announce you?" she asked.

Raul shook his head. "Not this time."

There was a pole in the middle of the entrance, a charm of a crossed-out eye carved into it to turn away the attention of spies. Above that hung a rabbit's foot—lucky for the hunter, not so much for the rabbit. Raul touched its worn and rain-sodden fur. Today, he was hunting for solutions and could use all the luck there was.

Raul pulled back the flap and walked into the argument.

The council had been growing. Exiled nobles and a mercenary commander, brought covertly through occupied ground from their other army, sat alongside Prisca and Queen Junia. Local captains had been added as more volunteers flocked to their banner, most of them sitting with Silvano Ironhead and his allies. Ferra brought Lestavo with her now instead of Ovida, whose loss weighed heavy in their expressions. Even Princess Nydia had a pair of corsair captains at her back. Not everyone was shouting, but as Raul crossed the tent, he felt like they were.

He settled in his seat and leaned over to speak quietly with Valens.

"How bad is it?"

"Worse than last time." Valens rubbed his forehead with his thumb and forefinger. "Sorry, lad, this is my fault."

"No, it isn't."

"I lost—"

"You brought news we needed to hear."

"I suppose." Valens took a deep breath. "You want me to shut them up?"

It was very tempting. The roar of his da's fury could put fear into even the hardiest of warriors, and some of these people, especially the nobles, were soft as unshorn sheep. But much as Raul wanted to see their reactions, what he needed was for them to react to him.

"No, they need to hear from their prince."

He stood, planting his feet as firmly as Efron readying to deliver a big speech, and took the deepest breath he'd ever taken.

"Enough!" he bellowed.

The reaction was instant and amazing. They froze like early flowers caught in a snap frost, all hard edges and the sort of stiffness that would wilt in a beam of sunlight. None of them had seen their prince like this before, loud as his da, stern as his ma, regal as any royal role Yasmi had ever performed. Even Raul had only practised a few times, far from camp and with only Yasmi to see. The reality of it, trapped within the confines of the crowded tent, left everyone stunned.

Cautiously, they turned their heads to look his way.

"I don't know which is worse." Raul treated them to his ma's cold judgement, not one of his da's angry growls. It seemed more fitting for a prince. "That you are all still clinging to the same arguments you wasted yesterday on, or that you treat each other, treat my most loyal subjects, with such disrespect."

He turned slowly as he talked, jabbing with his finger as he pointed at each of them in turn.

"I chose every single person here because I want to hear your wisdom." And because he needed their influence, though now wasn't the time to admit it. Given a real choice, he would have made some different choices, but he was learning that real rulers made more compromises than the ones in books and plays. "When you do not take the time and care to listen to each other, you are not listening to the insights I have chosen. You are not listening to me."

He softened his tone. "You disrespect me, and worse yet, you disrespect each other."

Yasmi and Tenebrial had insisted that he should reverse that line when they were planning for this the previous night. The playwright in particular had said that Raul needed to focus on himself, to assert royal supremacy. But while he valued the guidance of the people around him, sometimes he needed to be himself, and as he watched his council glance at each other, he felt that he'd got it right. Some still frowned defensively, but enough looked embarrassed to achieve what he needed.

Raul clapped his hands twice. Some newer members of the council flinched as the tent flaps flew back, then they relaxed as a pair of servants appeared, carrying trays loaded with cups of wine. Serving the drinks gave them all a pause, time to soften the edges of shame or defensiveness, time to appreciate the good wine they'd taken after liberating Lower Charn. Raul settled in the high-backed chair Quintae had carved for him and graced them all with an indulgent smile.

Beside him, mirth sparkled in Yasmi's eyes. She loved a good performance.

"Now," Raul said, "let's talk like adults. Is this about bringing the armies together?"

"Your Highness." Prisca bowed her head. "As General Valens reported a week ago, the enemy has been reinforced. Our scouts have since established that this is no mere column of reinforcements dispatched from the plains of Dunholm. The..." Her hesitation was brief but painful to see. Raul hoped the others didn't hear it as more than a pause for thought. "The expedition is led by King Lorrin himself and its core consists of his chosen, the supreme embodiment of Dunholmi chivalry. Alongside them are companies led by some of his most battle-hardened noble houses. Their intention is clear: a short, sharp shock to terminate our endeavours so that he can turn his attention south."

"By turning his attention south, you mean..."

"Invading my nation." For the first time since Raul had met her, Princess Nydia looked stern. "Apparently, Lorrin needs to attack us to defend himself."

"An argument we've heard from him before," Junia said.

The response from around the room mixed bitter laughter with growls of anger; their country had supposedly lain under the yoke of Dunholm to keep the rest of the world safe. Raul silenced those sounds with a wave of his hand. It wasn't just that he needed to control the mood of the meeting. He was uncomfortably aware that other countries had followed this logic before Dunholm, and that the cloth of Estian history was as stained as any other.

"I thank their royal personages for their wisdom," he said, "but please remember, when I want to hear from any of you, I will ask."

Was that going too far, given that the assembled council included a princess and a queen? Or had he been too soft, using the word "please"? He would ask Yasmi about it later so he could do better next time. For now, he had to keep playing the prince.

No, not playing the prince. Being him.

He sat straight-backed, drink set aside, hands resting on the arms of his seat, the only one in the tent with its own back. His throne, with the symbol of his birthmark bright red on the banner hanging behind it. The place he had earned through his struggles.

"Continue," he intoned, looking sternly at his ma. He felt a little better when, instead of stifling a glare, Prisca twitched the corners of her lips into something close to a smile.

"With their weight of numbers, we can't risk remaining divided," she said. "We need a large enough host assembled in one place to counter them wherever we clash."

"Captain Ironhead, you can speak for our other option?" Raul said.

Silvano took a deep breath and glanced around, checking that none of the others wanted to speak instead. It wasn't a mark of respect that Prisca had shown the nobles of the old court, but it suited the docker captain and his care-worn compatriots.

"Thank you, Your Highness."

Silvano cleared his throat and took a deep breath, ready to take the fight to the old guard. Then he caught Ferra's eye. The Withered Hills war leader gave a small shake of her head. Silvano closed his eyes for a moment, let that big breath out, and looked at Raul.

"You know the argument by now," he said. "We've one chance to catch the enemy between two forces and we shouldn't waste it."

Raul appreciated his restraint almost as much as he appreciated Silvano consulting with the others, taking time to listen and learn. Yasmi had said that if Raul set a good example, then others would learn from it. And despite Valens's reservations, it seemed to be working so far.

Was this what it felt like to be a prince, or even a king, every moment tangled in complicated calculations? He wished King Lorrin was in the country as a guest rather than an invader so that he could ask another monarch how it was done. But if Lorrin had been here on friendly terms, there would have been no need for war or for a fake chosen one to unite a shattered people. Perhaps he could ask Nydia instead; she'd seen how her mother and her brother ruled, and as Yasmi had said, she was smart.

"There's one thing I'm sure we can all agree on," he said. "It's better to make the wrong choice than to make no choice at all, leaving our enemies to dictate the course of this campaign."

To his relief, they all nodded at that.

"Before King Lorrin arrived, the argument for manoeuvre and trapping the enemy was convincing." He took a deep breath. "Now things have changed. We need the safety of numbers. We'll bring the armies together, and General Valens will be in charge." He laid a hand on Valens's shoulder and his da straightened in his seat, his fierce expression adding to the commanding presence of his bulk. "Anyone who disagrees with his orders can take it up with the general; he has my absolute trust, as well as some anger to work out."

As instructed beforehand, the servants had poured more of the good wine while he was talking, and laughter eased some of the tension in the room. Valens helped, pushing his scowl to a comedic extreme. Raul wondered whether he'd also been taking acting lessons while he and Efron were alone.

Still, some of the nobles had resentment in their eyes at this upstart warrior raised above them.

"Princess Nydia, the organisation of your troops is up to you and your people," Raul said. "But as long as you fight with us, you answer to the general, understood?"

"In your country I am yours to command, Your Highness," she replied with just a hint of a smile.

"On that note, I believe we're done for today. You all know your roles, but General Valens and I will be available to talk about practicalities, Drusil for logistics, Prisca and Ferra for route planning and intelligence gathering. Unless anyone has anything else?"

He stood, ready to round out the meeting and get rid of them before they remembered how they'd felt about each other at the start. But before he could speak, Silvano beat him to it, jumping to his feet and raising a fist in the air.

"A new moon rises!" he declared.

The others surged to their feet, even Princess Nydia and stiff, old Queen Junia.

"A new moon rises!" they shouted as he strode past, and their voices seemed to lift the tent.

As Raul stepped out, the cry was carried up around the nearby camp, then rippled out through the army as others heard the call. Looking across his forces from the hillside, watching the sun break through the morning's rain and paint a rainbow across the sky, Raul found that even he believed in himself now. Thousands of his fellow countrymen, all the warriors of a trampled kingdom rising up to make themselves free, that chorus compelled him and lifted him up.

He raised his fist and shouted one more time, leading thousands in their heartfelt battle cry.

"A new moon rises!"

Chapter Eight
Parts to Play

Yasmi took the books from Tenebrial's slender hands and set them back down on the ground.

"We're travelling light," she scolded. "You can't bring those with you."

"We're going on tour," the playwright replied. "What if I need them for inspiration, to write something new?"

"You found plenty of inspiration during the occupation, when we couldn't carry books through Estis at all. And besides, you know what play we're performing. We've been rehearsing for days."

"I can do better. So many people have seen *Sisters in Sorrow* already."

His hands twitched toward the books but withdrew at her slap to his wrist.

"We need to leave before midday," she snapped. "If you can't be trusted with packing, I'll send you to harness the horses instead."

Tenebrial muttered something about the tyrants of history, but he got back to packing the costume bags. Pretending not to hear, Yasmi turned stiffly to another corner of the players' tent and started bundling fake swords together with a sharp crack of wood on wood. More and more often, the players needed her to take charge if they were going to achieve anything at all. She remembered her mother playing the same part when Yasmi was young, herding people into the wagons even as she planned out their route, and her father's efforts had never matched that efficiency, even when he was in his prime. It seemed that, just like Raul, her time had come, but she was struggling to accept it with the same good grace. She wished that she had her mother back so that she could be the one resentfully packing props, slacking off whenever the opportunity presented, joking with the others about the unfairness of it all. But then she turned quickly, felt the masks shifting at her hip, and was caught in a moment of guilty relief that her mother would never know she'd lost two of those precious faces. At least she'd lost the ogre protecting Raul, but she'd cast the wolf into the flames rather than overcome her own weakness, and some days the guilt of it gnawed at her.

"Yasmi?" someone called out. "Are you around?"

She emerged from the tent into a bright day, the warmest of the spring so far. She could hear birds singing and smell the flowers in the nearby meadows, though both were nearly obliterated by the sounds and smell of the army camp, thousands of voices and the sweat of as many bodies, the creak of siege wagons and the stink of mass latrine pits.

"What is it, Biallo?" she asked.

He whirled around like the leading man he'd always wanted to be and thrust a bundle of costumes into her arms.

"Here," he said. "These all came from the company wardrobe."

The clothes were freshly cleaned and folded, a recent tear in a sleeve neatly sewn up, as she expected from a company member whose offstage duties included laundry and costume repairs.

"You're really not coming?" she asked.

"Claudio knows my lines."

"Claudio bungles your lines, you say so yourself every time he steps up."

"He's been getting better."

"So have you."

He shuffled back a step, tugging his lopsided collar out from under the edge of his chainmail, a costuming flaw he never would have allowed onto the stage.

"There's a war on," he said. "I need to be here fighting, to do my part for our freedom."

"This tour is how we do our part." She bundled the clothes up under one arm so that she could grab his hand and force him to meet her eye. "Our side is outnumbered. Even when we manage to meet up with the exiles, that's still going to be true. But if we can whip up support, then we can get more people into the fighting line and give ourselves a real shot at freedom."

A company of infantry tramped past, shields at their sides and battle axes resting on their shoulders. Their commander shouted an order and they started to wheel, but the movement was messy and uncoordinated, warriors stumbling over each other's feet and knocking shields. There was no lack of courage in this field, but experience and discipline took more rehearsal to get right.

"It's easier for you," Biallo said, watching the unwieldy manoeuvres rather than meet her eye. "You're the shifter, you've found your purpose on the stage. I've been with the Company Dellest my whole adult life, building my way up to the big roles, waiting for my chance to be the leading man. But this is Efron's company, and your father will still be acting long after he dies, coming back to haunt us every night with his acclaimed turn as Count Valderest. As long as I'm with you, I'll be living in his shadow, waiting for my turn until my hair turns grey."

"How is serving as one of Raul's captains different?"

Another band of warriors marched past, Withering Folk dressed in wickerwork armour, two bears and half a dozen wolves mixed in among the humans. Their leader bowed her head respectfully to Biallo.

"I feel like I'm making a difference," he said.

Yasmi gave a small nod. After all, wasn't making a difference her reason for dragging the actors out on tour, risking their lives by roaming a nation at war? One of her reasons, at least.

"Good luck," she said. "Try not to get hurt too badly, you were always terrible at death scenes."

"None of the rest of you commit properly," he said. "You've got to really lean into the scream."

They hugged, the bundle of costume an awkward

encumbrance between them, and then he hurried off through the camp, leaving Yasmi to her work. She looked up, saw the sun further across the sky than she wanted, and carried Biallo's bundle into the tent for Tenebrial to pack.

"I'll be back shortly," she said. "I need to check on the wagon."

She walked out, around the corner of the tent, and straight into the other reason why she had to get away.

"Your Highness," she said more loudly than she'd meant to, bowing from the waist.

"Mistress Dellest." Princess Nydia flicked her fingers as she usually did to dismiss such formalities, a gesture that Yasmi was determined to steal for a future performance, either despite or because of the way it made her flinch. "I hoped to find you. I hear that you're leaving us?"

"Indeed, Your Highness." Yasmi wished that she couldn't feel her cheeks flushing. "We're going out recruiting, a patriotic play to rally more troops."

"I thought *Sisters in Sorrow* was a civil war tragedy? I saw it performed once when I was young, and I found it very moving."

Yasmi wondered whether that performance had been by the Dellests or one of the other companies Tenebrial had taught the play to for a fee during the off season. If she asked, would the princess even remember?

"The tragedy is part of it, but as you saw there are some stirring speeches, and Tenebrial has made changes to fit the occasion. I hope Your Highness would find this version equally worthy."

"Please, enough with the Highnesses. Call me Nydia, and I hope I may call you Yasmi."

"Of course you may, Nydia." Yasmi put on her warmest smile, but she was certain that the woman saw through her performance just as surely as she saw through the mask of benevolent royalty. They might be united by a shared interest, but they were divided by it too.

She tried not to stiffen as Nydia slipped an arm through hers and took the two of them strolling down the side of the tent, as casually as a courting couple wandering through a summer glade.

"I'll be sorry to see you go," Nydia said. "It's good to have someone closer to my own age among all these old people with their scars and their oaths of vengeance for the wrongs done a generation ago. Someone sensible too, able to find the compromises we need for the future."

Yasmi watched the princess from the corner of her eye. She really was beautiful, her face slender, skin flawless, blue eyes shining like stars. Was this a Saditchi thing, the lure of the unfamiliar, or had the royal line got lucky in the bait they could cast into diplomatic waters? Whatever he said, Raul had to see that beauty, had to recognise that what had been promised to him was better than what he had.

"You're far too kind, Nydia," she said, the words snagging on her guts as she forced them out.

"Someone who knows Prince Raul as well, who understands his motives, his ambitions, what pleases him."

There was an ache in Yasmi's chest, as raw as burned flesh. Her arm tightened around Nydia's and she tried to pass it off as a gesture of friendship, but the grip was steely rather than affectionate. Was this woman really saying what she seemed to be saying? Did she expect her to share the things she knew about Raul, the things that no one else could or should know about, the small secrets threaded between the two of them?

"I..." For perhaps the first time in her life, Yasmi was at a loss for words.

"Don't worry, I'm not going to snatch him away from you. As I said, I value people who understand how to compromise. It's what politics is built on. There's no need to upset what the two of you have, at least not until he and I are married, and after that we can work something out for as long as it entertains him." Nydia smiled a hungry smile that made Yasmi feel utterly sick. "He's very good-looking, isn't he? And young enough that there's still time to shape his tastes, as well as to teach him some tricks."

The crash of a cart upending gave Yasmi the excuse she needed to look away. She was trembling, barely able to hold back the scream swelling from deep inside. These were words she might have used herself when young men were just a source of entertainment, something to play with on an idle night. But Raul was so much more than that, and now this woman was laying claim to him, this woman with her cheekbones, her exotic accent, her extra years of experience and self-assurance. This woman whom Prisca had offered Raul up to in marriage, for the sake of politics.

When she was younger, Yasmi had never thought about marriage. That was an abstraction, something that happened to other people when they grew bored and boring and decided they wanted children instead of wine and song and late nights dancing through the streets of a strange city. Marriage was for her parents. Even in the past year, with Raul in her arms and in her bed, she hadn't given it the slightest consideration. They were simply doing what people did when they enjoyed each other's company, and if that meant she was no longer interested in the company of others, then that was fine. It was no big decision, just a long series of moments, of pleasures shared and hearts beating together in the night.

But now he was meant to marry someone else, and apparently the best she could hope for was a few more years as his compromise. The feelings she had been trying to avoid came charging over the hill of her heart and chased her hopes from the field.

"Excuse me," she croaked, extricating her arm from Nydia's. She forced the best smile she could manage upon the princess and gestured toward the sun still progressing across the sky. "I need to make sure my people are ready to exit this stage by midday."

"Of course."

Nydia's smile offered something, but what? Friendship, sympathy, gloating? Yasmi, for so long the master of her own masks, couldn't calm her mind enough to decipher it. She gabbled a final few words, bowed to the princess, and hurried away.

She'd meant to head for the wagons, to make sure that the stage was properly stowed, but she could already feel herself bracing to argue with all the things the others had done wrong, as the bubbling cauldron of her frustrations threatened to boil over. Instead, she flung aside the flap of her father's small tent and stormed in.

At the sight of Efron's and Valens's bare torsos, she immediately regretted her choices. As least the two of them were dressed from the waist down and seemed to be putting clothes on rather than taking them off, but still, she could think of at least three strong reasons why this wasn't what she wanted to see, and a hundred smaller reasons more.

She closed her eyes and took deep, calming breaths while cloth rustled frantically.

"You are meant to be packing the scenery," she said, somehow managing to place emphasis on every single word.

"Don't fret yourself, my queen of the boards," her father declared. "Claudio has it in hand."

She risked opening her eyes. They both had shirts on now and Efron was helping Valens lace up his boots.

"That's no excuse," she said. "Claudio is as appalling at packing scenery as he is at remembering his lines."

"You're too hard on the dear boy."

"And you're too soft on him, at least outside of rehearsals."

"Don't worry, I'll get there before we need to leave and tidy up any mess he makes."

"We need to leave now! It's nearly noon, half a day's ride from here to Barrowblack, never mind Giontona. We can't push the horses any faster with all these wagons, and we can't afford to be out at night in a war zone. We talked about this yesterday, we talked about it this morning, we've been talking about it all cursed week, and yet here you are and instead of packing, you're—"

She forced herself to stop, catching the last of her words between clenched teeth. How could she keep going in the face of these two, half-dressed and with their heads hanging, twice her age and bowed down by the hurricane of her fury. It wasn't like her anger was even meant for them. Not most of it, at least.

"I'm sorry," her father mumbled as he bent to put on his boots. "It's just that we're not going to see each other for a while and, well..."

"I'm sorry too." She sighed, took his cloak off the cot, and hugged him before she draped it around his shoulders. "Now go and get that scenery packed. There'll be time for a kiss goodbye before we leave."

Efron tweaked up the corners of his moustache, then bustled off out of the tent.

Yasmi sat on the edge of the cot, her head in her hands. For a few minutes there, her anger had taken over, and while she didn't like that feeling she truly dreaded the ones lining up to take its place.

"How are you doing?" Valens squatted in front of her, their faces level.

"Fantastic. Brilliant. Utterly sublime. Never better. Can't you tell?"

He rubbed his stump across his scalp, eyes lowered and face crumpled into a look of strained concentration that she'd sometimes seen when he was trying to work out how to talk to Raul.

"Your father's a good man," he said, looking at her again, all seriousness. "I'm going to miss him a lot."

"I know." She reached out to squeeze his hand. "I'm sorry, that was lousy of me just now."

His brow furrowed again. "I expect you'll miss Raul too."

She burst out laughing, but then the laughing turned into sobbing, and when that subsided she could breathe normally again for the first time since Nydia had taken her arm.

"Of course I'm going to miss him," she said. "But do you really think I'd fall apart over that?"

When Valens shrugged, it was like mountains moving.

"Thought *I* might," he said. "It's a war. I say goodbye now, I might be going to die. He might. We might never see each other again." He pressed thumb and finger against his forehead, like he was pressing the words from his brain. "I've lost people before, but I never had anyone where it mattered this much. No one except Raul, and that's different. He can take care of himself. Efron, though..."

He swallowed. Was he almost crying? She'd never seen him like this. Not with her, not with Efron, not even with Raul. She didn't know if he'd ever made himself this vulnerable, and that moment gave her permission for her own feelings.

Surprised by the impulse but unwilling to resist, she flung her arms around the big man. After a moment, he put his arms around her too. It was a stiff, awkward hug, and all the more moving for it. Her cares drained away through the ridiculous muscled mass of the one person in the world who might love Raul more than she did.

"Now you're going to make me miss you too," she said, drawing back so she could look him in the eye, hands resting on his shoulders. "But that's not why I'm upset. It's this business with Nydia and the diplomatic marriage."

Valens nodded and frowned again, face furrowing like a freshly ploughed field.

"Don't assume that the lad will follow Prisca's orders," he said. "He's told her where to stick her schemes before."

"That was when Prisca was directing us toward disaster. This time she brought an army, and half of it's only here because she offered him up. Do you really think that Raul would throw that away when we're already outnumbered?" She sighed and even that breath made her throat feel sore. "Do you think that he'd give up on the freedom of Estis for the sake of his own happiness? You raised him better than that."

"And Prisca raised him smarter." He squeezed her knee. "He's surprised us before, he could do it again."

"Does he even realise where all of this is heading?"

"Sometimes I think he hides thoughts from himself, when they're too hard to face." He touched a charm that hung around his neck on a worn strip of leather, a disk stamped with the stylised smile of Laughing Loftus. "I'll pray for him, and for you."

"Do you think that will help?"

"It'll help me." The cot creaked as he sat down next to her and started lacing up his boots, hooking one lace around his stump while his fingers threaded the other lace through. "You should get back to packing. From what I hear, the others will get it wrong."

"You've been talking about me with my father," she said as she got up, feeling a little defensive and a lot touched.

"'Course I have. I expect you talk about us too."

"Strange, isn't it, our little family?" She stopped behind the tent flap and tapped her foot against the floor three times, bracing for her performance.

"Aren't they all?"

Yasmi's smile felt more real as she hurried away from the tent, heading for the sound of Efron's voice and the thud of boxes and bags being loaded into wagons.

"There you are!" Raul was helping Tenebrial manoeuvre a large crate, his tunic discarded and sleeves rolled up.

"You're meant to be behaving like a prince," she said as she picked up the.

"I wanted to help out." He gave the box one last heave, sliding it into place. "Like old times."

"I remember old times, and we don't need any more of your wonky scenery or terrible singing."

"I made that brilliant tree!"

"You made one tree, and half the branches fell off on opening night." She held the tunic opened toward him, sleeves hanging loose and ready for his arms. "Come on. A proper player needs to wear his costume."

She helped him into the tunic, then fastened the lacing up the front and straightened the collar because, no matter how hard he tried, Raul never quite seemed to get that part right. As her hands fretted around the back of his neck and she felt the warmth of his body only a finger's breadth from hers, she remembered what Valens had said about how this might be the last time he and Efron saw each other, and she realised that if she never had a chance to make Raul presentable again, it would break her heart. But if she stayed to watch him with his princess, that would break her heart too. Besides, she'd promised to go and find people who could fight for him.

She tapped her foot against the ground three times, movements so small he wouldn't see, then smiled up at him.

"If you're going to die in battle, make sure to do it dramatically," she said. "Take down ten warriors with you, or an enemy general perhaps, something heroic for the final act of the play. Don't worry too much about your last words, though, Tenebrial can write those for you once you're gone."

"I'm hoping it won't come to that," he replied.

"Me too, but it is a war. I hear they don't always end well."

He opened a pouch. "This is for you."

He pressed a charm into her hand, a perfectly round bronze disk, its edges smoothed and its surface polished to a high shine. A symbol had been stamped in the centre, a stylised image of a house.

"Home, for safety and support on the road," he said. "I'd come along myself, keep you safe, help move scenery, but..."

"But we all have our parts to play." She pulled her hair back so that he could hang the charm around her neck. "You made it, didn't you?"

"Drusil let me use her forge at night, when no one could see me doing unprincely things."

"It's wonderful. I wish I could give you something to bring you luck."

"You already do just by being in the world, your special and unique self."

Her eyes prickled as she looked up at him. She wanted to talk about princesses and politics, about marriage and children, about a future that seemed impossible when they might die any day but that had to be imagined to make sure that the horrors didn't devour it whole. But he had to go lead an army, while she had to go out and perform, and if they started on that conversation, she wasn't sure she would be able to stop.

"I'll see you soon," she whispered.

"You will," he said confidently.

Then their arms were around each other, his lips on hers, someone was cheering and Tenebrial of all people whooped, but it wasn't embarrassment that made her flush as the handsome prince of Estis led her to her wagon and helped her up to her seat. There was a thud as they raised the tailboard, a crack of reins, a creak of wheels, and the wagon lurched beneath her.

With the sun not yet at its noon peak, the Company Dellest headed out to spread the word.

Chapter Nine
Reading the Signs

The hammering of boots, hooves, and wheels against boards was like a roar of continuous thunder filling the valley around Raul. The sound of a single traveller would have been lost in this place, drowned out by the noise of the spring-swollen river rushing through the heart of Estis, watering fields and washing merchant barges down toward the ports of the Golden Ocean. But today those barges were moored in place, turned into the struts of a temporary bridge, and the sound of people crossing smothered the voice of the water. When thousands came together, they became stronger than they could ever be alone.

"Excellent work, Quintae," he said, raising his voice so that he could be heard by the man next to him.

The builder's beaming smile made him splendid to look at, scarred head, clumps of hair, weathered apron and all. He waved his hands excitedly toward the bridge he'd planned and created with the help of Drusil's growing company of artisans.

"Good boy, yes." Quintae patted the side of his own head. "Very good."

It was a relief to have this moment with Quintae, to appreciate the achievement of getting around Dunholmi control of the crossings, to spend time with someone who was simply happy in his work and his world. Not to worry about the arguments and resentments that only grew deeper as the armies united, the issues that Raul would have to face after this moment of ceremony.

The warriors and their supply wagons marched past Raul and on across the river meadow, to a gap between the hills and the army camp beyond. Some of them paused for a moment to add a stone to the small cairn Valens had raised by the end of the bridge, an improvised shrine to Laughing Loftus and whatever other gods they wanted to thank for a safe journey. Others turned their heads the other way to see the banner that had marched ahead of them all the way from Saditch, faded by time and frayed at its edges but still flying proud.

At a gesture from Raul, Prisca stepped out of the cluster of courtiers behind him.

"Your Highness?"

He still couldn't get used to the way she bowed her head. It was absurd, like if Raul had offered the chickens a selection of dishes before feeding them their dinner at the inn.

"Is that really the Blazing Banner?" Raul asked. "The one Queen Padelli flew during the Days of Lead?"

Pages from history books and tales told around fires came back to him. The heroic deeds of the early Estian monarchs, defending their people against monsters and invading armies, creating a land that was stable and safe. Stories of service and sacrifice, in which small setbacks were always the precursors to great victories. Ages in which every leader was a figure of legend.

"What do you think, Your Highness?" Prisca replied, both of them speaking too quietly for anyone else to hear.

"I don't see how the real banner could have been saved from a Dunholmi bonfire at the end of the last war," Raul replied. "And if you can forge swords and prophecies, why not an ancient flag? It would have to be close enough to the original to fool older soldiers who saw it at a distance, but you probably had a chance to examine it up close back in the day. And it would be an inspiring symbol to rally half-hearted exiles around."

Prisca's smile didn't reach her eyes, but then it seldom did.

"If it leads our forces to unity and victory, then surely it must be the real Blazing Banner," she said.

"I suppose it must."

The last supply wagon rumbled past, its driver tossing a small coin onto the roadside shrine for luck. Then all that remained was a rear guard of archers on the opposite bank and Drusil's team swarming across the bridge, stripping away the boards for future use, freeing the barges to be returned to their rightful owners, along with the money that Raul had insisted they would be paid. Apparently, a royal army had the right to requisition what it needed in order to protect its people, but he didn't think those people would remain his for long if he didn't treat their livelihoods as things that mattered.

"Your Highness," Queen Junia called from among the

councillors. "Now that's dealt with, can we get to the matter in hand?"

Raul turned to face the group, though it was really two groups, clutches of courtiers acting out the divisions between them. On the one side stood the likes of Silvano, Ferra, Biallo, and Drusil, commanders who had fought under him for the past year and more, turning hope, desperation, and a handful of nervous rebels into the sinews of war. On the other stood Queen Junia and her noble commanders, surviving earls from the old days and their heirs. Raul wondered how many of them had really marched across the country in their chainmail, war axes at their hips, and broad shields slung across their backs. The mercenary captains behind them didn't bother with such symbols of the hardy infantry, sitting comfortably on their horses, but they had nothing to gain by grasping the trappings of Estian military tradition.

Only Valens and Nydia stood in the middle ground between the two groups, his da too stubborn to acknowledge what was happening, the Saditchi princess safely detached from it all.

"We'll deal with practicalities shortly, Your Majesty," Raul said. "First, I need to seek guidance."

While their commanders watched, Raul and Prisca walked down to the riverside. Though the army had marched over rather than through them, the waters had been disturbed by all the activity, turning them a silt-heavy brown at the river's edge. Prisca took a bowl from her pouch, its sides decorated with symbols including an acorn and a tree. She held it out to Raul.

"You know what you're doing," she said.

It was a small thing, but it made him smile even as he reluctantly shook his head.

"I'm a warrior prince, remember? I need to be all action and command, not studying books and signs. Using your insights, not squinting into the royal tea leaves."

It was a shame. He enjoyed the challenge of divination just as much as he enjoyed losing himself in books and manuscripts. There was so much satisfaction in seeing the pieces come together, in discovering that there was more to the world than he had known before. But he had his place in all of this, so he stood proud, one hand resting on the jewelled pommel of his sword, while Prisca did the work.

She crouched in the shallows, water soaking up the front of her scholarly robes, filled the bowl with murky water, and swirled it around. At least Raul had been able to contribute to planning this part, talking the previous night about what omens they could best interpret, how to connect them to the army and its fate, any practical steps that might make their message clearer. While the two of them waited for the silt in the bowl to settle, Prisca waved her fingers over it and chanted nonsense words, a bit of display for the more credulous commanders, a way of reminding them that this campaign rested on more than military might. Then she tipped the bowl abruptly, spilling the water back where it came from, and flipped it up again, revealing the muddy shapes clinging to its inner surface.

"What do you see, Ma?" he asked quietly.

"I've told you before, don't call me Ma, especially not in front of the court."

"They can't hear."

"You don't know that." She tilted the bowl and squinted. "I see waves breaking against a shore."

"The Saditchi corsairs?"

"Or the collision of one great force against another. Our army against that of Dunholm."

Or our own armies against each other, Raul thought for a moment, glancing at the expectant commanders. But Prisca was right, the biggest forces moving across the land right now were those of Dunholm and Estis, and when they clashed, something really would break.

"I see a sword," Raul whispered.

"Of course you do."

"What does that mean?"

She tapped a finger against the edge of the bowl.

"The art of divination is about nuance, unexpected connections, affiliations within the world that an untrained eye would miss. Your attempts at interpretation are becoming too...too..."

Her face scrunched up in frustration, eyes closing as if in pain.

"Too literal?" Raul asked softly. He wanted to reach out for her, a show of support and reassurance, but that wasn't how Prisca liked the world to see her, never mind how a prince and his royal minister should be seen.

"Close enough." She held the bowl out between them. "Tread more softly with your thoughts. Look for what's in the bowl, not what's around you in your life. That connection will come next."

"I shouldn't be treading at all," he said, to remind himself as much as her. "You're the diviner here."

"True." She pointed at the mud on one side of the bowl, where it had separated into small clumps. "I see droplets, rain or blood or tears. Possibly bad weather or the coming battle, more likely a warning of pain."

"Pain is guaranteed for someone, given the war."

"True, so what else is it?" She watched as two of the drops merged. "Forces coming together, growing strong as one. A promising omen."

"That's good, but we need something more to guide us." Raul paced back and forth, mud squelching around his boots. "I wish Holy Cirillo was here. He could ask Yorl what he thinks."

Prisca snorted. "The last thing we need is to start listening to a half-blind god. Besides, Cirillo is of more use keeping his head down in Pavuno, sending us news from the city and coordinating our agents."

"They'd be safer out of the city, and so would he. What if the Dunholmi arrest him?"

"You think he hasn't acquired some subtlety along with his wrinkles?" She glared at Raul. "Fire and fury, will you stop that pacing? I'm trying to concentrate."

"Sorry." Raul returned to his spot facing her and pointed into the bowl. "What does that look like to you?"

"A dog."

"That's what I thought."

"A symbol of guarding. You should send out more scouts, perhaps there's something in the enemy's movements we've missed. And look..." She pointed at other, smaller shapes next to the dog. "Footprints. Movement toward the dog."

"Hound's Gap?" Raul asked. "It's not too far from here. We weren't heading toward it because there are places that matter more, but if we got there first, then we could use the hills to our advantage."

Prisca looked from him to the shapes in the mud to the rear of the army marching across the meadow. Her finger tapped against the edge of the bowl and she nodded slowly.

"Hound's Gap. I should have seen that. It's a useful choice even if we find out that we misread the signs."

"Are you worried about that?" The thought of Prisca doubting herself shook Raul to his core.

"Of course not," she snapped. "But we need to be ready for all manner of contingencies."

Prisca crouched once more to rinse the bowl in the river, but as she did so she swayed, then toppled, falling on one side in the water.

"Ma!" Raul hauled her to her knees. "Are you all right?"

Her gaze was soft and vacant. She laid a dripping hand against his cheek and smiled.

"Raul, tell your father to bring a barrel up from the cellar, we'll have more travellers tonight."

"Ma, what are you talking about?"

"I..." She looked down, saw the water running across her soaked robes. "Where am I?"

Then she blinked and her usual sharpness returned. She wrenched herself out of his grip, snatched up her bowl, and stood.

"We should get back to the others," she said. "There's no time to waste."

"Ma, what was that?" Raul asked. The empty look she'd given him made his heart ache.

"It was nothing."

"But you fell, and then—"

"Nothing, I tell you." Her words were a blade.

"You should see a physician."

"You think they can help?" She laughed bitterly. "Whatever you saw, it was the price I pay for our freedom, and it's no one's business but mine."

"Not even your family's?"

"No one." She strode up the bank, then paused to wring the water from her robes. "Are you coming?"

Raul felt like the weight of the whole river was pressing down on him, but so were the expectations of the people he led. He walked back to where the others waited, talking in tight little clusters, bodies turned to each other but eyes turned out. Valens pointed across the river, the smaller meadow on its far side, and the hills beyond.

"Smoke," he said. "Lots of it. The Dunholmi are close."

"And we'll be ready to face them," Raul said, forcing himself to focus on this. His ma might not want his help, but these people did. "We're marching to Hound's Gap."

There was a pause, the commanders looking to each other's reactions while they thought through their own. A flock of geese honked as they flew past overhead. From the river came the shouts of the work crew and the clatter of boards as they disassembled the bridge.

"It's a solid spot," one of the earls said.

"We can use the hills," agreed another.

"And the woods." This came from Biallo. "I've seen them when we were touring that part of the country. It's ideal for Ferra and her people to get around the Dunholmi flank."

"That's certainly an interesting idea." The earl who'd spoken exchanged a look with Junia. "We should take every advantage we can."

"Speaking of which…" Junia took a step forward. "Your Highness, Earl Tordesse held these lands before the invasion, he knows the terrain better than anyone. If we're to make the most of the opportunity Prisca has guided us toward, then it would make sense to put the earl and his people in charge of formations, which might be less familiar with the ground."

"You mean in charge of us?" Silvano growled, glaring at the queen.

"It's a matter of pragmatism. We can't expect captains from Pavuno or the Withered Hills to understand the lay of the river lands."

"Which by coincidence puts you lot in charge."

"I've made the case before for using that authority and experience, but this time I—"

"Authority my—"

"How dare you speak like that to our—"

"He can say whatever he—"

"Enough," Raul snapped, and the dozen voices shouting over each other all fell silent.

He took a deep breath. He hadn't needed omens to know that this was coming. Junia's faction had kept prodding at him to let them take charge, and the arrival of new commanders among the reinforcements gave them an excuse to bring it up again, as well as more people to make their case. Watching the supposedly wise and experienced Estian nobility jostle for position felt like the first time he'd seen Valens make a mistake fixing something around the inn, then cursing as he clutched the thumb he'd hit with a mallet. This wasn't the way adults were meant to behave.

But it was the reality of politics and of who he was fighting alongside. If compromises needed to be made, then he would find them.

"I appreciate your expertise, Earl Tordesse." Raul nodded to the man. "I look forward to being guided by it, as I'm sure my other commanders do. Please select some of your experienced leaders who can serve as assistants to the other captains, to help them understand this land."

"Your Highness?" Tordesse scratched at his grey beard and looked at Raul with something like genuine bafflement. He didn't wear gold jewellery like some of the others, just a black mourning ring. "Are you suggesting that members of the nobility should serve as lieutenants to actors, dockhands, and rootless wanderers from the wilderness?"

It seemed that the incoming nobles knew a lot about the people they were joining. What they didn't seem to understand was the value of those people, how they would feel about being treated this way, or the respect that they'd earned. Glancing across the faces of his commanders, Raul could feel the argument about to break out again.

Labourers from the bridge walked past, carrying heaps

of long planks to a wagon waiting further up the meadow. Some of them had been with the rebellion since its earliest days, women and men with whom Raul had foraged for food, fought Dunholmi patrols, raised buildings to house their friends and families in the forest. As they walked past, laughing and chatting, he wished that he could go and help them, could enjoy some simple work and camaraderie instead of negotiating politics and fragile egos.

"Silvano, are you happy to take advice from the earl's people?"

"I'll take advice from anyone, as long as I'm still making the decisions."

"Then yes, that is exactly what I'm suggesting, Earl Tordesse." Raul wanted to point out that he himself had been a poor orphan raised running an inn on the outskirts of nowhere, and if they could follow him, then the nobility could follow anyone. But that wasn't a thing he could say out loud; it wasn't something that most of them even knew. "Our successes so far have been earned by the likes of Silvano, Ferra, and Biallo. You owe them just as much respect as me."

The earl, his face red above the grey of his beard, looked to Queen Junia, who made a small, placatory gesture.

"We can discuss this later, my lord," she said, then bowed to Raul. "Your Highness, we should catch up with the rest of the army. I don't want to make the rear guard's work any more difficult than it already is."

"I'll bow to your experience." Raul smiled. "Perhaps you and Earl Tordesse could lead the way?"

He didn't think that his captains would mind which order

they marched in as they followed the trampled trail of the army, but letting those two lead the way might feel like a concession to their former importance, which might, he hoped, make things a little easier later.

It wasn't a strong hope, but it was something.

As the captains and nobility of Estis tramped across the meadow, flanked by their guards, Prisca stood next to Raul, wringing the remaining river water from her robes.

"You're going to have to put them in charge sooner or later," she said.

"Why?" Raul asked. As often happened with his ma, he felt like he must be missing something, that vital connection that she was smart enough to see but he wasn't.

"They're nobility. They run the country, and that means they run its wars. They're raised for this from birth. They have the skills, they have the experience, and the longer you hold them back from their natural position, the more frustrated they will become."

"We've managed without them in charge. Our other captains have skills and experience too."

"I know, you achieved marvellous things with the limited resources you had." She gave him a serious look. "But, Raul, this is all about restoring the nation we lost. Its crown..." She squeezed his arm. "...and its nobility. Use the resources you have to prepare for the future as well as win the present."

Raul frowned. All the bits made sense, but when they were put together the picture was unsettling, like the scenes of a play acted in the wrong order. He was fighting to free Estis, and all the stories he knew showed Estis being run by the monarch and nobility, but still...

"They're not the only ones with a stake in this," he said. "Or the only ones who know how to fight. After the past year, some of our captains might have more experience than them. I'm not saying there isn't a place for Junia's people, but they need to make compromises, like everyone else."

"You can't expect nobility to compromise with the people they rule. That's no way to run a country, and frankly it's beneath their dignity. Don't let your naive tendencies ruin everything."

Raul thought of all the things he'd learned from Prisca, from reading and writing to divining, even the little he understood about politics. But he also remembered that he'd been manipulated by her, led along by a lie that got people killed. Drawing back from her touch, he straightened his back and stared down at her.

"I'm not the one being naive," he said. "And if anyone's dignity has been hurt here, it's my captains'. I suggest that you have a talk with your courtier friends, remind them that they're not the only people fighting for this country."

She glared back at him.

"I did not raise you to play the recalcitrant fool, and I will not be spoken to as if—"

"As if you were a minister and I was a prince on the verge of becoming king?" Raul raised an eyebrow. "Yes, you will, and you'll remind the others to do the same. This is my court, my army, my country, and we're going to run things my way. Do you understand, Minister Servita?"

Her expression was as hard and pale as midwinter ice, lips pressed so tight that they almost disappeared.

"Yes, Your Highness," she hissed. "Or perhaps that should be Your Majesty."

Her footsteps slammed hard against the meadow grass as she stalked away. Looking around, Raul realised that the only people left were him, Valens, and half a dozen rear guard archers landing a boat on the near shore.

"Well done, lad." Valens grinned. "That must have been satisfying to say."

Raul laughed, but it was just relief, releasing a tension he wished he didn't have to feel.

"It was," he said. "But I've divined the future, and I predict that she'll make me regret it."

Chapter Ten
Where We Make Our Stand

There was something spectacular about the army on the march. The tramp of feet. The beat of drums. Hundreds of voices joining together in battle songs to keep their pace along the road. The way the light reflected off their weapons like jewels scattered across the land. Like when he'd first arrived in Pavuno and witnessed the scale of the city, something that seemed impossible to a boy raised in a rural inn, Raul found that it took his breath away. And joining in with it, marching at the head of the column to the rhythm of the songs and of those marching feet, becoming part of this incredible beast made up of thousands of individual lives, all of them sharing the same sense of excitement and determination, he couldn't think of anything better in the whole world.

Of course, not every day could be like that. Over the winter, marching through a horizontal wind that found all the gaps in his clothes even as it soaked them through with sleet, that had been misery that multiplied itself, thousands of pains and moans uniting. That was one of the most dispiriting experiences ever, when maybe it might have been better to suffer alone. But they'd got each other through it, they'd gained more warriors to fight alongside them, and now they were marching toward glory. Or at least toward the dip in the hill line at Hound's Gap, and if they'd read the omens right, then that was where glory lay.

He looked up, saw birds overhead, long V-shaped flocks migrating north now that the winter was over. Looking down from the point of one of those flocks, he saw an inn at the foot of the gap. A tavern for locals and travellers to rest in, just like the one where he had grown up.

Birds returning home had pointed him straight at an echo of his own home. That had to be an omen, didn't it? Not one that Prisca could have identified, perhaps, rooted in abstract forms and theories about how the world connected together, which signs and symbols could possibly mean which things. But he'd learned in the Withered Hills that divination was more personal than that. The magic was personal. It flowed through him. He shaped it and was shaped by it, understanding coming from where they met.

The moment he started looking around, his companions turned to him.

"You seen something?" Valens asked.

"Maybe. Where's Earl Tordesse?"

"Here, Your Highness."

Tordesse emerged from the group immediately behind

them, the members of Raul's council who were walking rather than riding. Raul had been determined that they were the ones who should lead the way. Not that he objected to anyone riding, especially given how sore his feet had got in the early months of the campaign, but this fitted the myth of Estis and its stubborn infantry. Plus it was a good example for the thousands of warriors who marched after them. Raul thought it reflected well on Tordesse that, unlike some of the other earls, he joined in the march.

"These were your lands," Raul said. "Do you know that inn?"

"No, Your Highness," Tordesse said. "Not my sort of place."

Raul looked around, then waved. Biallo, mounted on a light horse and with a bow across his back, broke off from the flanking cavalry column and galloped over to join them.

"Take a couple of your warriors and ride ahead to that inn," Raul said. "Send my compliments to the innkeeper and apologies in advance for the damage his fields are about to sustain." He tossed a pouch of coins to Biallo. "Ask him if he's seen the Dunholmi recently, and whether there's anything about this territory we should know."

"Yes, Your Highness." Biallo whistled, waved three fingers in the air, then galloped off with a small group of riders following him.

"I assure you, Your Highness, I know this land well," Tordesse said with a pinched expression.

"And you showed us the best marching route to pass through it," Raul conceded. "Now we need the small details, the things that only people living on this dirt would know."

A chorus of honks drew his gaze up again. A flock of geese parted, flew in two curving arcs then together again, like lines of dancers at the harvest fair. It seemed like a good sign.

———————•———————

From his place at the head of the second Dunholmi column, Count Alder watched Captain Brook gallop out of the dusk and across the ford to him. She'd been riding at the front, one of his minions amid the king's company while he was stuck back here, swallowing the dust of half the army. He seethed at the very idea of it.

Ketley Tur tutted and shook his head.

"The upstart returns, my lord," the chamberlain rasped. "No doubt here with some fresh demand."

"No doubt," Alder growled. "But we serve at the king's pleasure."

For how long? a voice whispered in his head.

That was dangerous talk, but Alder didn't argue. The only answer he could give was *too long*.

Brook wheeled in beside them, her horse matching pace with Fellstride and Tur's inelegant steed. She stroked her horse's neck and bowed her head.

"Brook." Alder nodded curtly.

"My lord. I'm sorry that the current of life has swept me away from your service."

"A terrible burden, to have King Lorrin's attention."

"Not one I asked for."

"Of course not." He laughed bitterly, and Brook flinched as his hand flicked her way. "I'm sure you wept and wailed at the prospect."

"My lord, if you would prefer that I—"

"I would prefer my own servants to show some loyalty." He jabbed a finger at her. "To remember who raised them up."

"My lord, I haven't forgotten."

"Oh no?" He snatched the sash that hung from her saddle, a white crown against Dunholmi blue. "This is my sign, is it?"

From the riverbank, a ghost of his grandmother seemed to gaze at him again, nodding and urging him on.

"I'm just following orders."

"Whose orders, Brook?" The sash burst into flames, then fell from his hand, ashes scattering in the dirt. All around, heads turned to look at him. He lowered his arm, hiding his soot-stained and smoking hand, and forced himself to take deep breaths.

This wasn't how he was meant to be. His grandmother had been cunning and ruthless, showing him the path to success. He pressed his fingers to his forehead and the ache growing there.

"You have a message from King Lorrin?" he asked through gritted teeth.

"Indeed, my lord."

They'd reached the ford, their horses' hooves splashing through the shallow waters. Alder pulled his cloak tighter around his shoulders as a chill swept through him, a breeze blowing in along the valley, or perhaps the power that warmed him from inside withdrawing, Jarrag's strength waning when they were over water instead of dry land. The image of his grandmother faded as they passed.

It wasn't only the cold that made Alder frown as they crossed the ford. This was one of the two crossing points that he'd based his strategy on, that he'd been sure the rebels would have to use to get across the river, that would let him control their movements and pin them in place. The assurances he'd given the king, and the extent to which he'd been wrong, were part of why he was back here. He had made an idiot of himself, giving Lorrin an excuse to beat him down.

But he still knew this land better than the rest, so the king had deigned to deal with him again. Alder needed to seize his moment, and this time he needed to be right, whatever it was about.

"Our scouts have found evidence that the enemy have turned from their path, heading east instead of toward Pavuno." Brook glanced at him nervously as she talked, her hand pointing toward gaps in the hills ahead, their upper edges harnessed in gold by the setting sun. "Some of the others think that it's a bluff, false trails to distract us. His Majesty would like to know what you think."

Alder looked out across this wretched land, which he knew better than any of the old fools around King Lorrin, most of whom hadn't been here since the North March was first conquered. Splashing sounds were replaced by a comforting clop as Fellstride stepped out of the ford and onto the far bank.

"Give me a map, Tur," he snapped.

"Of course, my lord."

The chamberlain rummaged in his overcomplicated saddlebags and pulled out a large roll of parchment, almost falling from the saddle as he tried to unroll it. Alder suppressed a scathing comment. Tur might be pathetic, but he had his uses. Alder snatched the map out of his hands and unrolled it for himself.

Two options for where the rebels were going, one toward Pavuno and the political heart of the North March, the other toward... what, a few small towns and a stretch of woodland? What else was there? Some place called Hound's Gap?

And then he remembered riding through it once before, a single notch cut from steep hill lines controlling the road in that direction. Those hills could protect an army's flanks and funnel cavalry into a narrow gap, giving the advantage to an army heavy on infantry. An army like the North Marchers.

But what if he was wrong? One more mistake and Lorrin would have his head.

Fire stirred within him, a blazing voice demanding attention. He closed his eyes to quiet it, but instead the voice became an image seared across his vision, an army's worth of campfires lit against the coming dark. When he opened his eyes and looked at the map, bright spots lay over Hound's Gap. Jarrag was a power of the land as well as of fire. It felt the places where those two powers met, and it was showing him.

Alder grinned.

"It's not a feint," he said, leaving a sooty mark as he tapped the map. "The rebels are at Hound's Gap, and the longer we leave them to prepare for battle, the better it will be for them." He handed the map to Brook. "Tell His Majesty that if we march hard east, we can catch them tomorrow, rob them of their chance to prepare the ground."

"Are you sure?" Brook asked, looking at him with something closer to concern than he would have allowed most subordinates.

"Oh, I'm sure." He curled his fingers and let fire flare between them. Brook smiled. Tur cringed. Alder reluctantly drew that glorious flame back into himself.

"I'll let His Majesty know," Brook said, and galloped away.

———————— • ————————

The innkeeper's name was Esvali. She'd inherited the place from her parents and lived in it for nearly fifty years amid the comings and goings of brothers and sisters, nieces and nephews, all of whom helped run the place between tending their neighbouring farms. But while her siblings had settled down to raise families, Esvali had stayed married only to the land of Hound's Gap. No one could have known it better than she did. Raul learned all of this at her fireside on the night he arrived. Esvali was the sort of innkeeper who delighted in talking with passing strangers, and once she got over playing host to royalty, she was happy to sit up for hours talking about the land and its hidden ways.

Raul's omens had been right. This was the place for them.

It was too dark to explore the ground properly that night, so they rose early in the morning so that Esvali could show him some of the places she'd spoken about. He brought Ferra and Valens along but left everyone else to sleep for another hour. They'd had a long march and there would be plenty of hard work for the rest of the day.

The other two were most impressed with the woods that ran from one of the hillsides down past the inn. Ferra rested her hands across the trees like they were old friends, rubbed the loam between her fingers, watched fragments of earth fall, and smiled.

"Best place I've seen in all your town lands," she said in her low Withering drawl. "Put me and mine in here, we'll fix to fray anyone yon road's teeth send this way. Maybe come out at them once the fighting gets thick, rip some holes where they're not expected."

"Good straight trees." Valens tapped one with his knuckles. "We'll cut some down and build barricades on our flanks, force the Dunholmi to fight where we want."

But it was the drainage ditch of the other side of Hound's Gap that got Raul's attention. A hidden slit in the landscape, something an attacker wouldn't see until after they'd ridden past. Especially not if his followers had a day or two to cover it.

And when he looked down into that ditch for the first time, the bold light of early morning broke through a clump of nearby grass, making a pattern like flames on the surface of the water. Fire for the fight, for the destruction they would carry to the heart of the enemy. A good omen.

That hour of roaming the countryside with two old friends and a new one gave him time to relax, to feel like his old self. But when they got back to the army sprawling around the inn, he had to set that aside. They probably only had a few days before the enemy caught up, and he couldn't afford the distraction of more politics, of wearing himself out and wasting time on squabbles over status.

Sitting on his high-backed seat, which was placed on a table in front of the inn, he looked down at his commanders and advisors, old and new, Estians and foreigners, nobles and humble labourers.

"There will be no council today," he declared. "Only orders. This is where we make our stand. The very land here is on our side, but complacency won't bring us victory. We need to prepare. So, starting with Earl Tordesse's company..."

By the time Hound's Gap came into sight, Alder was back where he belonged, among the commanders at the front of the army. A few seemed pleased with his return; the rest he treated with sneering disdain. A minor lordling flinched as Alder bared his teeth in a ferocious glare. Fools and cowards, the whole herd of them. Opportunists he would crush if they crossed him.

This was how the court had always worked, vipers hiding in the long grass between the hooves of honest men. Now they were all trying to work out the implications of his ups and downs, the political opportunities, whether this was the time to be seen talking with him. If his success in predicting the rebels' moves paid off, then House Alder would be back to its position of old—preeminent among the nobility of Dunholm, a house second only to their royal cousins. If it went wrong, he would be relegated to some backwoods fief, an abject lesson for anyone with real ambition. Caught between peril and potential, most of the nobles offered him no more than a half-hearted smile, and he was left riding alongside the North Marchers who had stayed loyal, representatives of good trading families who could see that their future lay with Dunholm, not some pathetic rebellion.

"Mother bought it for me." The young man's name was Senius Tisco, and as well as looking too young for war, he was too boring for words. He waved a sabre through the air, coming dangerously close to his own horse's ears. "Just like the ones you chaps carry. She wants me to learn a proper martial tradition, to prove myself to King Lorrin."

"She sounds wise." Nobody who compared a clumsy blade like that to a proper Dunholmi sabre could be called wise, but the elder Tisco was one of the most reliable military victuallers in Pavuno. However tedious her son was, he wasn't worth offending, at least not until Alder had a firmer grasp of his position.

"You're so right. She said there would be trouble, that we couldn't trust the priests or the peasants, and look where we are now."

"Indeed." Alder smiled a half smile, safe in the knowledge that the boy wouldn't even know he was being mocked. Beyond him, Captain Brook rolled her eyes.

"That's a splendid dagger." Tisco pointed at the silver-handled weapon hanging from Alder's belt. "How do I get one?"

"By being an officer of Dunholm."

"I am leading a company, you know."

"But you're not Dunholmi."

"Perhaps in time, I might—"

"For all the gods' sake, shut up." The fire of frustration became too much, burning away the last of Alder's patience. He snarled in satisfaction as the quivering wretch finally fell silent, and ignored the small voice in the back of his head asking if this was wise. He'd listened to that voice for too long.

"Count Alder!" a voice called from the very front. "Count Alder to the king!"

With a tap of his heels, Alder set Fellstride into a quick trot, past other nobles to the head of the column. Brook followed him. The sun was at its peak and now would have been a good time to rest the troops if not for the view up ahead.

Alder's memory of Hound's Gap had proved accurate. It looked as if a giant horse had grazed on the hill line, taking a curve out of a long ridge. In that gap, amid scattered farmhouses and a stretch of woodland, stood an inn. Camped all around the inn was the rebel army.

For all that he sneered at their fake prince and his first failed revolt, Alder knew better than to underestimate the North Marchers, and looking at the army felt like vindication. This wasn't just a few hundred rebels hiding out in the forest, as it had been when he was hunting them the previous winter. It was thousands of warriors, a baggage train, artillery mounted on the slopes behind where their main line would stand. Small movements in the surrounding fields would be skirmishers, unless any of the local farmers were fool enough to dig turnips between two armies, and even the North Marchers weren't such stubborn mules.

A pair of mounted servants parted to funnel Alder through

the courtiers and into his new position, right next to the king. The army's greatest banners were carried right behind them, flapping in the wind.

"You were right, Count Alder," King Lorrin said, stroking his chin. The surface of the black pearls on his ring seemed to swirl. "And right to encourage a fast march. They're digging in."

"We should attack straight away!" a voice piped up from behind Alder. He turned to see that Senius Tisco had ridden up with him, like a tick clinging to a horse's flank, and now the boy was set on making a fool of himself. "Scatter these wretches to the wind!"

King Lorrin didn't even spare the boy a glance. "Do you share this bold strategy, Alder?"

"No, Your Majesty. It will take the afternoon just to bring up the rest of our forces and arrange them for the fight."

"You're not as impulsive as your father was."

"And I hope to serve Your Majesty better than him."

"Good. Tomorrow, you will serve me by commanding the right flank. I'm sure these rebels will have some unpleasant surprises in the woods, and I want someone who has shown he can fight in difficult terrain."

"Your Majesty is too kind." His Majesty was a pompous relic of past glories, but Alder maintained his subservient smile and bowed his head respectfully.

"You had better earn that kindness." Lorrin turned stiffly in the saddle and looked to his standard bearers. "The attack can wait until dawn, but for now let's remind them who they face."

"Bastards," Valens growled as he stared across the fields.

The other army lay less than two miles away, far enough not to start a battle yet but close enough to ensure that the Estians wouldn't march away. If they did, then the Dunholmi cavalry would descend on their rear and the army would be ripped open, then pinned in place while Dunholm's infantry levies marched up to finish the job.

Not that anyone was planning on retreating. This was the moment they'd been preparing for. They hadn't brought just Count Alder and his troops out into the open but King Lorrin as well. There would never be a better chance to strike the decisive blow and ensure their freedom.

In the west, the sun was sinking behind the Dunholmi column as the last of their troops fell out of line and made camp. But it wasn't the army that held Valens's attention. It was the spear that their scouts had planted in the middle of the field, a blue pennant flapping beneath its head and something worse spiked on top.

"It is her, isn't it?" Once, he could have spotted a face at this distance, but that had been when he could march all day, drink late into the night, and still be fresh for the next day's fight. Now the features of the head on the tip of the lance were a blur, if a horribly familiar one. "Ovida."

"Aye." Ferra's calm was terrible. "So's said."

"Once night falls, we'll go get her, give her a decent burial."

"Aye."

"And tomorrow, we'll get them back for this."

He half expected her to respond by telling him about the ways of the Withered Hills, about how life came and went, about how you had to focus on the future, not worry about getting revenge for the past.

"Aye," she said instead, her voice as steady as her gaze. Steady as the ancient trees of the land where she lived. Steady as the Withered Hills beneath them. Steady as the certainty of death. "We'll fray the road's teeth but good for you, Ovida. Word is word."

Chapter Eleven
Future by Firelight

The inn's fire blazed brightly, as did the lanterns hanging along the walls, muddying shadows and warming the place until sweat beaded Raul's brow. Back home, this would have seemed excessive, using too much fuel for the sake of a single night. The only time they would have done it was midwinter night, when it was important to bring the light out to send the darkness away, to bring the spring sooner and ensure a bright year ahead. Perhaps that was the value of this, to chase away the shadows of the occupation and shine a light for their glorious shared future. Raul liked to think so. He suspected that, in reality, it was the work of servants overeager to please the nobility, worried that some ageing earl might complain if he had to squint.

Raul hadn't wanted to take over Esvali's inn, to become the invader occupying someone else's home for even a day or two. But a ruler needed to reinforce their authority, and that came as much in costume and displays of status as in the real matter of what they did. So he had a high-backed chair placed on the small platform in the corner of the room, normally a stage for travelling storytellers and musicians, and sat there looking out across his assembled court.

Times like this were when he most wished he had Yasmi with him, offering suggestions on how to impress and reassuring him that he was doing well. She didn't even need words; her smile was enough. But she was out on the roads of Estis, spreading his story and rallying support, sending back the idealistic bands of freedom fighters who had been swelling their ranks.

Valens would have been a good alternative, always ready to back Raul up or to stare down a troublemaker. But his da was doing a general's work: positioning troops, checking defences, talking through tactics and arranging signals with the commanders of the battle lines.

Apart from those commanders who were in the inn, making the same determined case as before.

"It's one thing to stop and offer advice on the march," Earl Tordesse said, "another to do it in the heat of battle. It would be easier to respond swiftly and decisively with our people in charge."

Raul sat stiff-backed, his lips pinched together. It was the same argument again, day after day, just phrased differently. He glanced at Prisca, who understood these nobles but knew the rebels as well. The pragmatic politician, the woman who had spent decades making connections and weaving schemes. Surely, she would have something to say.

But she stood silent, a sharp-faced shadow at the side of

the room, occasionally looking away from the people to the flames flickering in the fire. He hoped that she could divine something useful there.

"My own daughter was assigned to those Withered Hills barbarians," another noble piped up, "and they laughed when she tried to teach them how a battle line is formed. Actually laughed!"

Raul sighed and rose to his feet. They were wasting precious time while the enemy prepared for battle.

"All of you," he said. "Listen. Since the moment you arrived, you have belittled and berated good people. You have done more to destroy the morale of this army than all the Dunholmi riders burning supplies ahead of our advance. I offered a solution and, in spite of your behaviour, your comrades accepted it. It seems that you will not.

"If you will not compromise, then you will bow to my command. The next one of you to raise this topic will prove their incompetence and give up any position of authority, whether commanding or advising." He paused, letting his words sink in. "Now go make sure your warriors are ready for the fight."

He pointed across their heads to the entrance of the inn. The warrior standing guard, a veteran from Silvano's company of sturdy dock workers, pulled the door open. Estian nobles swept out of the room, buoyed along on a wave of indignation. To Raul's disappointment but not his surprise, Queen Junia was among them, treating him to a look of pure venom before she strode out in a swirl of embroidered skirts.

The person who did surprise him was Tordesse. The earl

stood for a long moment, tapping a finger against his mourning ring and looking up at Raul, then bowed. Not a curt bow, nor an overeffusive one, but a gesture that seemed like real respect.

"I apologise, Your Highness," Tordesse said. "Things aren't as I expected, and that's difficult to accept. I hope that, with time, I can adjust."

"I hope so too." Raul didn't mean to sound curt, but the blood was pounding in his ears and he could barely keep his hands from shaking. The only way of making his voice steady was to make it hard. "If I don't see you before the fight, then good luck."

"Thank you, my prince."

Tordesse strode out, leaving only Raul, Prisca, and the guard at the door.

"Pellius, isn't it?" Raul asked, looking at the guard.

"Yes, Your Highness." The guard stood taller, chest out.

"I need to talk with the minister alone. Could you please step outside, close the door, and make sure that no one is listening."

"Of course, Your Highness."

Filled with the seriousness of royal responsibility, Pellius stepped smartly out of the inn and slammed the door behind him. Voices were raised in the yard as he ordered people away from the shuttered windows.

Releasing a long breath and a deep, jagged store of tension, Raul slumped into his seat.

"Power should never be an easy thing to wield," Prisca said, stepping away from her place by the wall. "You're doing well with it, but don't be surprised when it wears you down."

"Thanks." He tried to remember how good praise from her had once felt, but childhood memories were no match for his frustration. "Wielding power is harder with my own mother and minister undermining me."

"I didn't argue with you this evening."

"Your silence spoke."

She shrugged. "I would be a poor mother and minister if I didn't challenge you to do better."

"There's a difference between challenging and undermining."

"And that difference lies in your response. You need practice."

"I need support."

"You need to listen to those with real political experience."

He took a deep breath. This was adding to his frustration, and it wouldn't help him to lead. Better to provide a peace offering, to show that he valued her advice even if he didn't agree with all of it.

"Have they always been like this?" he asked. "The nobles, I mean."

"For better and for worse, yes. Don't worry, they'll be more manageable once the Dunholmi are defeated and they can settle down in their hereditary estates. That's when they'll remember all their old grievances and start arguing with each other instead of just you."

He shouldn't be looking forward to something so petty, but it did sound like cause of relief, right up until he wondered who else they might have grievances with.

Prisca was staring into the fire again, her expression blank.

"Do you see something there, Ma?" Raul asked quietly. She didn't respond. "Ma?"

Still nothing. Her face, so alert a moment before, was slack, her lips hanging open. Raul felt as though a knotted rope was stuck in his throat. It was as if his mother had gone away and only an empty set of robes remained.

"Ma?"

He stood, wanting to touch her but afraid she might crumble. Instead, he reached for a jug of wine and poured out a cup, then pressed it into her hand. Ordinary actions, everyday kindness, trying to bring her back.

Prisca's fingers tightened around the cup. Suddenly she was back in the room, frowning at the wine. She swallowed a mouthful and grimaced.

"This tastes like dirt."

Raul sniffed the jug, then took a sip.

"It's better than I'm used to," he said.

"Everything tastes like dirt now." She set the cup aside. "If it tastes of anything at all. One of the prices I pay."

Was that why she looked so thin, skin stretched between fingers that were little more than bone? The lamplight cast shadows across her sunken cheeks.

"Perhaps you should find somewhere to rest," he said. "You've brought us this far, let others carry the weight."

"There's too much to do." She shook her head. "And it has to be done right."

"What we need to do is win a battle, and that's other people's work. Surely, you can give yourself a few days while the generals lead."

She waved him off and stepped away, robes swishing across the fresh rushes covering the floor.

"We need to start thinking beyond tomorrow's battle," she said. "Assuming that we win, you will have a small opening, a brief period of praise and adulation in which you can act without resistance. It will be an ideal opportunity for a coronation and to establish the lines of authority that flow from you. Issues of local governance, taxation, organisation within your court. Things that might sound like tedious minutiae but are vital to the good running of a kingdom and are best established at the point of greatest compliance."

The two of them paced back and forth across the inn, like they were on the road again. Raul enjoyed stretching his legs and letting his arms swing, not worrying about posture or dignity. Not being seen by anyone but his ma.

She was right, of course. It sounded cold and calculating to make political schemes when people they knew would suffer and die tomorrow, but that pain had to be worth something. A fresh start for Estis. A future they could all be proud of.

And if his ma's mind was working again, then he should respond: ask questions, seek advice, draw out the learned and insightful woman who had raised him. How else could he keep her from sliding into blank oblivion?

"The nobles are going to be trouble, aren't they?" he asked.

"If you mishandle them, certainly. But they can be your greatest asset. In peace as well as war, they have the experience and insight to ensure that the nation is effectively run, to..."

She held herself in one of those frozen moments that were becoming all too familiar, body and face tensed as she looked for a word she had lost or a thought that had run away from her. He wondered how many of the nobles had noticed, whether they whispered about it behind her back.

"It's all right, Ma." He laid a hand on her shoulder. "I get what you're saying. We can use what they know."

"Exactly. The quicker they are returned to their old authority, the more smoothly everything will go."

He started pacing again, the fire warming his face on one side and then the other depending upon which way he went.

"They can't just have their old authority back," he said.

"What?" She twisted her head. The hunch of her shoulders and the fall of her robes made her look more than ever like a hawk, about to tuck in its wings and drop upon some innocent prey.

"Like you said, there are things about the peace that will be like the war. Lots of people have had a chance to organise themselves and shown that they can do it well. Even if they hadn't, their people have fought, suffered, and died. They've earned their reward."

"Their reward is a country freed from the Dunholmi yoke."

"It's not enough."

Her foot stirred the rushes and she stared down at the patterns it made. Slowly, she nodded.

"I suppose there is something in what you say. A few noble families were lost in the fall, and two or three don't plan on returning. We can elevate the best of our humble-born commanders to lordships. Who knows, generations down the line one of their families might provide an earl of its own."

Raul shook his head. He'd been afraid of this, the way she'd aligned herself with Junia's people since she'd returned, the assumptions she brought to the council tent. His ma had always been the smartest person he knew, but maybe this was the divination sickness taking its toll, or maybe he just saw her differently now. As her son, the cause mattered to him, but as the crown prince of Estis, all that mattered was the result. Minister Prisca Servita had a complex, sophisticated view of the world and where it should go, but that view was rigid and people who didn't agree with her existed to be persuaded or ignored.

"There are going to be real compromises in peace as well as war," he said. "No more trying to bend the Withered Hills into obedience. Dockers overseeing their own work, setting the rules and managing the tithes, not someone from court telling them how to do their business. The same for other trades. More army captains taken from the ranks instead of the nobility."

Prisca scowled at him. "What is this nonsense?"

"It's the way I want to run a country."

"It's... it's... it's..."

Her fingers curled, clawlike, as she grasped for some word he was glad not to hear. When that failed her, she wheeled around and stalked across the floor like she was stamping the rushes into submission. Now the two of them paced like warriors preparing for single combat, eyeing each other up, readying their weapons. All they had tonight was words, but they both knew how deeply those could cut.

"It's no way to run a country," Prisca said.

"It's my way." He forced himself to stay calm and quiet, not to rise to the bait of her agitation.

"You'll be a laughingstock."

"I always enjoyed comedies more than tragedies."

"You'll undermine your own authority."

"I'll reinforce it by having good people working around me. It just won't be the same as before."

"And that's the whole problem!" She waved a hand, thin fingers scything at the air. "We know that Estis worked as it was before. Your... your... your experiments risk undermining good order in the country."

"There is no good order in the country, only Dunholmi order. Whatever we do next means building something out of what they leave behind, and I've promised something new."

"You've promised?" She stopped in her tracks and pointed at him. "When this started you were nothing but a baby, a mewling pink mess that would have died if we'd left you behind. Two years ago, you had no concept of any future beyond a... a... a crumbling inn in a backwater vale, so far from the heart of power that not even the street rats would notice it. I made the promises. I wrote the legend. I forged a future for all of us, and I will not have it brought to ruin by a boy who suddenly thinks that he's... he's... he's..."

"A prince?" Raul asked, raising an eyebrow. "About to be crowned king?"

There were few people in the world he knew better than Prisca. Now that he understood her sickness, the way that divination had worn grooves through her mind, he could see the difference between when she was stuck for words, angry at herself, and when she was organising an argument, angry at someone else.

She was angry at him now. Let her be. The anger was about to become worse. For the good of his country, there was a wound he needed to bleed, and the sooner they got past the pain the sooner they could recover.

"There will be a place for you in my court, of course," he said. "Your insight will be invaluable. But I'll be choosing someone else as royal chamberlain and head of the council."

Her mouth fell open again, just a little, her lips parting enough for a few quiet words to slip out.

"Your Highness?" Her tone was incredulous. "Raul, I know you're angry, but this is no time for childish games."

"This isn't about my anger. At least, not the anger I have now. I made the decision days ago."

She turned from him but stopped halfway to the door. Straightening into a posture of pride but not facing him, she spoke.

"Is this because of my sickness?"

"No."

"You don't trust me anymore."

"That's not about you being sick. It's about the fact that you don't listen to anyone else, don't take their views into account. Some people might call that a strength, but I think it's a weakness. I need my council to be led by someone who hears what others have to say."

"You think that I'm just some belligerent old woman?"

"I think that you're my mother. I think that you're the mastermind who built the scaffolding for our liberation. I think that you can be the most insightful person I know. But I've seen how you talk to others, and it's not good enough. I'm sorry."

"So am I."

With that, she flung the door open and stormed out.

Raul stared into the fire. Flames had seemed like a good omen when he'd seen their image on the water of a ditch, but now they felt oppressive, like the heat of Jarrag's fire in the Withered Hills. Had he made a mistake, talking about what came next before the war was even won? Not that it had been his choice, but still...

Too late to change it now. When dawn came, so would battle, his greatest test yet as a prince.

He walked out of the inn, guards falling in behind him, and set off into the camp, to see his warriors and to be seen by them.

Chapter Twelve
Blood and Flames

By the time dawn broke, Raul had been standing in the infantry line for an hour, waiting for the moment to come. That was as expected. They had to be ready before the Dunholmi attacked, and some parts of the army took longer to coordinate than others, but it was unlikely that the enemy would advance before the sun rose, especially not when the Estian army had been able to prepare the ground. So they waited and they watched the darkness turn to grey, then to the pale predawn light, and finally the glowing warmth of the sun rising in the gap between the hills behind them, illuminating an open expanse of pasture and fields full of sprouting crops, all of which were about to be trampled. Until yesterday, it had been farmland. Now it was a battlefield.

"You should be further back, lad," Valens said quietly. He stood next to Raul in the line, carrying a shield just like his and just like all the hundreds of others beside them, with the rebel symbol of a blade through a crescent moon painted in red across black. The new moon rising. Estis reborn.

"I need to take the same risks as everyone else," Raul said, shifting his shoulders to better settle the weight of his chainmail.

"You need to give orders and to respond when things go wrong."

"I will. But first I have to show them that I'm here to fight."

As expected, the Dunholmi had been waiting for dawn. As its light slid down the lances of the armoured cavalry on their flanks and gleamed off the helmets of the infantry levies in the centre, a shout went up.

"For Dunholm!"

"For Estis!" Raul's forces bellowed back, and his voice joined theirs. "A new moon rises!"

He'd wondered about giving a speech. He used to do that sometimes in the old days, when they were a few hundred rebels, then a thousand, two thousand. Most of them could hear him then. But now his voice would have been lost across the crowd, and getting them close enough would have meant disrupting the battle line. Any good he might have done for morale would have been undone by the damage to their fighting formation. So instead, he'd been around the camp the previous night, talking briefly at as many fires as he could, and now he was in the line with them, where actions would speak more decisively than any words.

The Dunholmi advanced. Raul's heart raced at the sight of them coming, but his body couldn't keep up the tension. Time wore by and they didn't seem much closer, the distance still too large for a charge. He wriggled his shoulders, trying to get rid of the itch where a seam from the padded doublet under his armour rubbed against his skin; checked that his sword was loose enough to draw quickly from its sheath; hefted the battle axe that rested against his leg; put on his kettle helmet with its curved dome and the brim that ran around the outside, matching those of the men he stood with.

In denial of all common sense, he kept expecting the Dunholmi cavalry to come hurtling at them. After all, that was the Dunholmi way of war, the swift and decisive charge. But as Valens and Earl Tordesse had explained, that charge wouldn't come until the rest of the army was close, ready to capitalise on any breakthrough the cavalry achieved. Until then, the only action on the field was skirmishers shooting arrows at each other on the flanks, and even that was limited. Hound's Gap didn't leave much flanking space, or much need to cover it.

The silence that had filled the ranks after the battle cry became a mutter of conversation, grim laughter, the clink of equipment being adjusted. Not quite enough time for people to became bored and complacent, but too much for them to keep standing at the alert, shields raised, weapons in hand. To Raul's left, a warrior pulled a bread roll out of her pouch and ate a hurried second breakfast. Someone else sang a song about lost lovers and a monster in the forest.

The Dunholmi were halfway now, perhaps more. Banners flew above their heads, a range of white heraldic devices on backgrounds blue as the sky, so that it almost seemed as though the ghosts of crowns, swords, and lions were flying free above the oncoming horde.

"Close enough," Valens said. "You want to give the word?"

Raul turned to a warrior in the row behind him. "First signal."

"Yes, Your Highness."

The warrior raised his spear and waved it back and forth, a long yellow pennant flying underneath. Among the artillery devices on the hillside behind them, someone flew a black pennant in response. There was movement among the machines, then a hiss.

The first shot fell short, a rock smashing into the ground just ahead of the advancing line, throwing up dirt. An arrow the size of a lance followed, missed the first few cavalry on the right but punched through two behind them. Then the arm of the vast trebuchet swung and the whole world seemed to pause. The Dunholmi infantry levy could surely see what was coming, but there was nothing they could do as a stone sphere three feet across smashed into their centre, shaking the ground.

"That stuff's more use against forts," Valens said, "but it'll give them a fright."

Raul was sure that he was right. How could anyone see what those machines did and not feel fear clench them in its icy fist? But only a few warriors had been hit, and it was too early in the day for fear to become panic. The forces of Dunholm came marching on while something shifted in their front line.

"Shields up!" Valens shouted, and the cry went down the line, a moment before arrows came thudding down. Two of them punched into Raul's raised shield, but didn't break through its boards. A few got past their defences and one warrior went down screaming, while others withdrew cursing and bleeding from the front lines.

The Dunholmi cavalry started picking up speed, cantering ahead of the infantry line.

"This is it," Valens said, then raised his voice. "Ready!"

Raul looked back over his shoulder. "Second signal."

As he drew his sword and adjusted his stance, another pennant flew above his head. There was clattering and whirring as warriors turned the handles on more of Quintae's machines, then a hiss from the ground beneath their feet as ropes rushed like long snakes. Like at Hewed, sharpened stakes jerked up into the Dunholmi cavalry's front ranks. Several horses fell, taking their riders and one of the war banners with them. But the enemy had seen this before and they were ready. Several warriors in the front rank were carrying longswords instead of lances, and they sliced through the ropes between the stakes. A few horses got tangled and fell, but most galloped on, their hooves like the sound of an avalanche as they plummeted toward the Estians.

Arrows flew. Rocks crashed. Stakes rose. Raul ignored it all and kept his eyes fixed on the cavalry charging straight at them, shields raised and lances lowered, an onrushing mass of muscle and steel.

"Brace!" Valens bellowed.

Hundreds of shields clattered as they formed an overlapping line, while knees pressed onto the padding at their backs and everyone leaned in.

The charge hit.

A lance slammed into Raul's shield, almost knocking him

off his feet. The tip burst a hand's breadth through the layered boards before the shaft behind it splintered. A steel spike glinted inches from his shoulder. The horse reared and Raul slashed at it with his axe but didn't hit. The rider dropped his broken lance and drew his sabre, the blade coming down at the same time as the hooves of his steed. Raul raised his shield and was almost flung to the ground again as blade and hooves hammered home, shaking the shield so hard that the lance tip fell out. He lowered the shield just enough to see what he was hitting and swung his axe. The head gleamed as it descended in a long arc and hit the rider's outstretched arm, ploughing through armour and flesh to shatter the bone beneath. The impact juddered from Raul's wrist to his shoulder, but his opponent came off worse, blood spraying as he wheeled away.

Others were pulling back too. The Dunholmi cheered and jeered at their retreating backs. Valens snorted.

"That was just the test," he said.

"Which we passed," Raul pointed out.

"True, but there's worse to come." Valens slid his own axe through a loop on his belt. "You've made your point, lad, now we both need to be elsewhere."

Raul frowned. He felt exhilarated, his body buzzing from the moment of action, his head ringing with their celebratory shouts. He was part of something here, one of the warriors in the line, a hero like he'd always dreamed of being.

"Your Highness," Valens said, leaning in close. "I don't like it any more than you, but our job today is to lead."

Reluctantly, Raul followed him back through the lines, past fresh warriors moving up to take empty places and labourers carrying away the winding drums that had raised the stakes. As they passed, warriors cheered and chanted Raul's name. He cheered them in return and waved his axe above his head.

"A new moon rises!" he shouted.

"A new moon rises!" they shouted back.

———————— • ————————

Count Alder had never liked woodlands. They were treacherous ground for both mounts and riders, the sort of place where legs got broken if you rode anywhere above a brisk trot. No room to cut loose and feel the wind rushing through his hair. No space to let Fellstride stretch out and show what he was worth.

Today, though, the woods were a sign of something good. King Lorrin had trusted the right flank to him, given him a chance to prove himself. The woods were with House Alder, and he would do his grandmother's memory proud.

He stopped at the edge of the trees and braced himself. He hated the order he had to give next, which went against the dignity of the nobles and knights who rode with him. A battlefield was a place for honourable charges, not descending to join the common mob. But there was more pride in victory than in an unforced defeat.

"Dismount," he commanded.

He'd told his captains the plan, so they knew what was coming. Still, Brook had to ride back and forth getting stragglers out of the saddle and making sure they tethered their steeds at the edge of the trees, while Alder did his best to form a line in the woods. They would be back, and perhaps this battle still had time for a glorious charge, but only if they could do what was needed first. Only if they could get around the North Marchers' flank.

Armed with sabres and shields, they advanced into the shade of the trees, trudging through heaps of old leaves and climbing over fallen branches. Lady Maple, high seneschal of the royal court, cursed as she slipped on a damp, rotten heap. Count Burrow's squire sank halfway up his shin in some hidden rabbit hole.

Unseen creatures scurried away as they approached, disappearing beneath the bright, fresh leaves of spring. Birds burst away in fluttering flocks, disappearing across the treetops. But where were the enemy? He couldn't see a single North March warrior, not the slightest flash of red, not a gleam of a lone blade.

Branches creaked. A shadow shifted. Bright spots vanished from the sun-dappled ground.

Alder looked up. There was a mass above him, twigs and leaves like a nest but far too large. It shifted.

"Above!" he shouted.

Too late. Arrows hurtled down. Plenty of them shattered as their obsidian heads hit metal armour, but some found gaps. Count Burrow fell against his mud-stained squire. Maple cursed again and broke off a dozen arrows protruding from her shield.

"Archers!" Alder shouted. He would have been a fool not to prepare for this, but as his own bows moved up, there was a rumbling and cracking from the hillside ahead of them.

Two shapes rolled through the gaps between the trees, picking up momentum as they came. Vast wicker wheels decorated with spikes of fire-hardened wood, each twice as tall as he was. Faced with a choice between moving or being crushed, the flower of Dunholmi chivalry leapt out of their way, and a mob charged into the gap.

They didn't look like real warriors, not even infantry levies. Their armour was nothing but woven sticks, their weapons crude clubs and stone blades. They would have been comical if not for the beasts that fought beside them, towering bears and slavering wolves, giant cats with fangs like daggers.

One of the archers dropped from the trees, straight onto Alder's back. Abandoning his shield, he got his arm up quickly enough to stop them from cutting his throat, but they kept squeezing in, a long black blade inching toward his face.

He staggered back and slammed his attacker against a tree. They grunted but clung on. Alder raised his sabre, slashing wildly above his head. They twisted and writhed, clinging fiercely on. Then metal met flesh. Blood flowed down his neck and a fur-wrapped body slumped to the ground at his feet.

The battle line had descended into chaos, every warrior for themselves. Bodies tumbled between the trees, armoured knights lumbering across uneven ground while forest beasts and their equally uncivilised owners darted and lunged between them, light on their feet and the forest ground.

A bear was towering over Captain Brook, about to crush her between its brute paws. Alder snatched up his shield and charged. A slash of his sabre severed the beast's forearm, and its moment of pain gave Brook the opportunity she needed. Holding off its other paw with her shield, she darted in and sliced across the beast's belly. Blood and guts poured across the forest floor. The beast wobbled, let out a spine-shaking moan, then thudded into the dirt.

Brook looked at Alder, her eyes wide, panting in exhilaration. This moment was a victory worth the telling.

But all around them, the chaos continued. Alder's shot at redemption was collapsing into defeat.

———————•———————

Valens felt like a fool, standing on a stool they'd taken from the inn, craning his neck to stare over the heads of his warriors. The sound of battle echoed off the hills behind them, the drumming of hoofbeats and the shriek of signalling whistles, screams of anger and pain, steel crashing and bones cracking. Sounds of real work, real endurance, while he wobbled and tried to stay upright as he looked around.

But he was a general now, and apparently that didn't guarantee a proper view. Not unless he wanted to fight from horseback, trusting his fate to a beast that might panic and carry him away. At least his stool had its wobbly legs planted on the ground, even if he didn't.

On the Estian left, the trees were rustling as the flanks clashed. He couldn't see what was happening in the overgrown ground beyond the inn, but that wasn't part of the field he worried about. One thing he knew for certain was that Ferra's people could fight in the woods.

In the centre was the sort of battle he would have liked to fight in, the Dunholmi infantry against the foreigners fighting for Estis, paid mercenaries and Saditchi corsairs with their round yellow shields and viciously hooked spears. Those troops weren't as loyal to the cause, which was one reason not to line them up against the shocking impact of cavalry charges he expected on the flanks, where he needed warriors he was sure would stand their ground. But they were good fighters, experienced and well-armed. Given time, he was confident that they could push back Dunholm's infantry levies, reluctant warriors fulfilling obligations to their lords, poorly equipped and barely trained. That was where victory was most likely, so he had to buy them time.

He'd never had to worry about things like these before he was a general. Holding it all in his head was exhausting and holding back from the fight was frustrating, especially now that he'd learned to fight properly with his left hand. But he had to do this, and maybe he was even getting used to it. It was a matter of endurance, like being in the shield wall, just of a different kind. So here he stood, back behind the troops gathered on the right flank under Estis's Blazing Banner, watching the main mass of Dunholmi cavalry gallop toward them, a fist striking their vulnerable face. What little cavalry the Estians had were led by Biallo on the edge of the fighting, harassing the enemy with bow fire, but the artillery had fallen still now that the sides were so close. All that counted was their ability to endure.

The Dunholmi hit and the whole line seemed to reel. At first, he thought they'd withstood the shock of the impact, and it would come down to the grind in which stubborn Estian line fighters excelled. But then he saw a wedge of Dunholmi blue advancing, sabres slashing to the left and right. Two Estian companies—Silvano's dockers and Tordesse's household guard—peeled away from each other as startled warriors drew closer to those they knew.

Valens's fingers clenched the haft of his axe. This wasn't good, but they'd prepared for it. Another company lay in reserve, waiting to fill the gap when they were needed. He'd chosen them for the task, an exile company run by a young noble eager to prove her worth. As soon as word came back from Silvano, they should advance.

Why weren't they advancing?

Valens jumped from his stool and stormed through the ranks, pushing aside anyone who got in his way. Sure enough, there was the reserve company with its commander at its head, with one of Silvano's lieutenants gesticulating frantically toward the front line.

"Why aren't you moving?" Valens asked.

"I'm sorry, general," the noblewoman said. "I was waiting for a command from someone with real authority. If I respond to every demand from some unknown warrior, my troops might end up in the wrong place."

Valens narrowed his eyes. This sounded a lot like excuses, a lot like politics, a lot like the nobility not wanting to be bossed around by dockers. He should have planned for it, but too late now. All that mattered was the fight.

"I'm the last authority you ever need to hear," he growled. "So get in there, and pray to Yorl that it's not too late."

Alder wheeled around a tree, sabre raised, and pulled his blow aside a moment before it would have hit Brook.

"I thought that you—"

"Look out!" She lunged past him. Sticks snapped, there was a groan, and a wicker-clad warrior dropped her spear as she fell bleeding from a bush. Brook slashed across her neck, finishing the job.

Fire flared inside Alder, fury and thwarted power.

"Well done, Captain," he hissed, holding back the urge to lash out at everything in sight, to destroy for the sake of destroying. To burn it all down. That was what Jarrag demanded, but he had to concentrate.

He glanced around, trying to make sense of what was happening. Warriors of both sides, living and dead, were scattered through the woods, along with the beasts these barbarians had brought. By rights, the savages should have lost far more people, with their weak armour and brittle weapons, but at least as many Dunholmi lay fallen with last autumn's leaves.

At least they were holding their ground, but there was no pride to be had in any of this. The rebels weren't trying to push them back, weren't even forming a line like a proper army. Instead they struck and ran, vanished into the greenery, drew the Dunholmi after them before appearing out of nowhere to strike again. They couldn't possibly win like this, but neither could he. The whole business was making his head ache. Heat crept through his fingers and charred the handle of his shield.

But what if these people weren't trying to beat him? Perhaps all they wanted was to hold him in place while the real battle was fought elsewhere. Tying down a whole wing of Dunholmi warriors while leaving the best of the rebels free to fight.

As long as he held this ground, he was letting them win. But if he pulled back, he would leave a flank exposed, weakening the whole army and giving King Lorrin one more excuse to humiliate him.

With an animal screech, three more of the savages charged at him and Brook. He dodged a thrust from a jagged-bladed spear, blocked a club with his shield and lunged, but his target jerked aside. He tried again, almost hit, but they parried, twisted, knocked the sabre from his grip. A calloused hand grabbed him by the throat and he gasped as they squeezed, choking him while a huge, fanged cat forced Brook away.

He couldn't get a good blow in with his shield, and his fist just cracked against their wicker armour. Black spots appeared. The terror of failure closed in on him, of a defeat like the one in the wild.

No. Never again.

Let me free, the fire roared from inside him, the voice that called itself Jarrag. *Let me burn it all.*

Alder pressed his hand against his attacker's chest. The world was turning dark, but suddenly there was a brightness at its centre as the heat and fury flowed from his heart down to his arm and through his fingers. The wicker armour became a cage of flames, and his attacker staggered back screaming.

Gasping for air, Alder sank to his knees. He pressed both

hands into the mass of fallen leaves. Steam billowed as the spring's moisture evaporated, then flames ran free, igniting the leaf litter, the bushes and trees, the bodies scattered across them. He caught a glimpse of a grey-haired woman aiming a bow, but when the arrow flew, the flames reared up, turning it to ash.

"My lord!" Brook, her blade bloody and shield abandoned, put a hand under his arm and hauled him to his feet. "We have to get out of here."

"Wait."

Alder bent into the flames. The heat inside him was already so intense, he felt no pain. He plucked his sabre, glowing hot, from the blazing ground.

No need to guard this flank now. The fire would do it for them.

———————•———————

Raul waded along the drainage ditch as quietly as he could while bent over and thigh deep in water from the spring rains. Down here, the sounds of battle were muffled. He didn't know what was happening out there, but the Dunholmi didn't know that he was here either, and that could make all the difference.

He stopped and forty of his best fighters stopped in a line down the ditch behind him, silent and expectant. Raising his head as little as he could, he peered out.

From this low down, it was impossible to understand what was happening in the battle. He could hear the mayhem and see the backs of the Dunholmi forces, and had to hope that Valens could hold them long enough for the plan to work.

The plan depended on other things too, but fortunately the character of the Dunholmi king hadn't failed them. Lorrin sat on his horse well back from the fighting, a few courtiers and servants around him. He was impossible to miss, dressed in the finest armour and surcoat, a silver crown on top of his bald head. It was a huge risk, but taking him out would be a huge shock to the Dunholmi. Enough to leave their forces shaken, perhaps even enough to convince them that they should withdraw from Estis. Hopefully, enough of a shock for Raul and his chosen warriors to get back to their lines alive.

It was one of those plans that Valens hadn't liked, but there was a drama to it that Prisca and the rest understood. Burning the heart out of the enemy, like the image of flames had shown him. A prince taking down a king and so earning his birthright. The sort of action that wouldn't just shake the enemy but would secure Raul's position whatever came next.

He drew his sword, with its engraved blade and its jewelled pommel, the symbol of the kingship he would inherit. Solemnly placing his finger on the flat of the blade, he mouthed the words "blood for luck." Down the ditch, the other warriors clutched their charms and whispered the words back.

Then they scrambled out of the ditch and ran.

No war cries. No battle songs. Even their armour had been carefully bound to minimise noise. Of course, it didn't keep them from being seen. A servant running from the king's party toward the supply wagons stopped and stared, trying to make sense of the rushing figures. A wounded soldier pulling back from the lines pointed his sword, but his shout was lost amid the battle noise.

Raul ran as fast as he had ever run, despite the weight of armour and shield. Half his warriors ran with him, while the others fanned out to the sides, bows drawn, shooting at anyone who came close, trying to buy them a little more time.

He was only ten yards out when one of the courtiers around King Lorrin turned. Their cry of alarm was cut short as someone flung an axe into their chest, but it was enough. The king and his entourage turned, drawing their weapons.

Then Raul and his people were in among them, attacking horses and tack instead of riders, making sure they couldn't get away. Some horses went down, kicking and thrashing, while others flung their riders and galloped off. The king tried to turn, to escape, but Raul cast his shield aside and grabbed a stirrup. The two of them battered at each other, swords clanging, sparks flying, while Lorrin tried to jerk free. Then someone else hit the horse and the king went down.

By now, more of the Dunholmi had realised what was happening. Warriors were pulling from the main fight, turning to protect their king. Infantry levies shouted in panic at seeing enemies to their rear.

As the line loosened, the Estians and their allies advanced. The fighting surged back toward Raul even as he fought for his life, fending off the mounted nobles who charged to their monarch's aid. Dodging and parrying, slashing and stabbing, hacking opponents down and heaving others aside. King Lorrin was scrabbling away across the dirt, dragging an injured leg, and Raul couldn't let him escape.

A brightness caught his eye. Flames at the far side of the battlefield, consuming the woodland and stalking toward Esvali's inn, their smoke staining the blue sky black. From out of the inferno, cavalry galloped, dark against the brightness except for the warrior at their head: Count Alder, fire blazing from his upraised blade.

The battle line wasn't a line anymore but a surging mass of bodies, the two sides tangled together, warriors desperately fighting for their lives. It was a wildfire of its own that swept across Raul and his chosen fighters as the Dunholmi were driven back. An armoured woman bumped into him, then someone swung a mace at his head. By the time he fought them off and looked around, he'd lost sight of the fallen king.

A circlet of silver caught the sunlight. Lorrin's crown. The king was back on his feet, shouting commands, trying to rally his guard only a few strides away. Raul hacked his way toward him, the remains of the raiding party at his back, one last push for the victory that had come so close. The currents of combat parted and empty space opened between them. The king's eyes went wide as he saw Raul charge.

A horse slammed into Raul, black as night and making hideous noises. A blade of fire cut an arc through the air, and then Alder leapt from the saddle. Fire blazed in his eyes and rippled across his armour, burning the grass at his feet. The horse bolted, as did half the warriors around them, trying to get away from the inferno in their midst.

As Alder came at him, Raul rose to his feet. He couldn't wait and let the count dictate the fight. He lunged at him, was parried, made a second stroke and a third, a succession of attacks like he'd learned from his da on a riverbank back in the Vales. *Feint, feint, make your real strike. Regroup, riposte, go on the attack again.*

The air sizzled with heat as the two of them fought, pushing back and forth across a growing gap in the heart of the battle, the clang of their blades somehow louder than everything else.

The Estians fell back while some of the Dunholmi held, realising that this blazing thing was on their side. But Raul had taken Alder down once before and he could do it again, could prove that they had nothing to fear.

He deflected one of Alder's attacks, knocked the flaming blade aside, lunged with his whole body, committing everything. Alder dodged, not quick enough to avoid being hit, but his pivot meant that Raul's blade hit at an angle, scraped across armour, didn't penetrate. He brought his sword up in time to block Alder's next attack, their blades catching above their heads, he and the count pushing against each other with all their strength, so close they could touch.

Then came the pain, sudden and agonising. He looked down to see the hilt of a silver dagger pressed against his body, blood flowing around it. Alder pulled it out and thrust again, fire flashing. Raul staggered, open-mouthed. The pain was too much, fire and blood and a scream from inside that faded as his world fell into darkness.

Chapter Thirteen
An Aftermath of Ashes

The last time Yasmi and the players had come through Lellingpool had been three years ago, when they were just actors trying to make their craft pay and to fill people's lives with delight. It was easy to forget these places, towns so small they barely earned a name, but she'd been struck by the beauty of the cherry trees that ringed the green at the settlement's heart. Their scent had filled the air like the soft breath of a kindly god, blossom-draped branches wafting in the breeze like low pink clouds.

Her heart broke as she rode up the track and saw what remained. Half the trees had burned down, along with several houses close to them. Blackened remains of branches trailed into one side of the pond where ducks perched on their skeletal blackness, staring into water that had once been clear and full of life. A chill wind blew ash across the green as she leapt from the wagon and forced herself to walk into the devastation.

Men and women emerged from the surviving buildings,

holding pitchforks, mallets, and scythes. Their expressions didn't become any less suspicious when they saw the wagons, but they huddled together for a few minutes, then one of them walked over to her.

"You're the actors, aren't you?" The man was thin, his cheeks sunken, eyes red raw. "What are you doing here?"

"We're touring." Yasmi pressed her hands together to keep them steady as she looked across the ruined village. "Performing plays to keep people's spirits up."

"Keep their spirits up?"

"Because of..." Now she felt absurd. "Because of the war."

"Well." The man rubbed his chest like he was rubbing salve into a wound. "You can see how our spirits are."

One of the ducks had descended into the water. It poked its bill through the ash-slicked surface, shook its head, and climbed back onto the bank.

"What happened?" Yasmi asked.

"Dunholmi warriors came, demanding food. Third time this winter, between them and the others. We couldn't spare anything, needed grain to feed ourselves and for the spring planting."

"When you said no, they attacked."

"You think we said no?" The man snorted. "No one says no to folk with swords. We found enough to appease them, piled it up in one of the houses while they sent someone for a wagon, on account of they'd taken ours the last time.

"While they was waiting, the rebels came. There was more of them. The Dunholmi set the food on fire rather than let them have it. Food set the house on fire. That house set the rest on fire. We couldn't put it out because they was fighting all around."

He rubbed his hands across his face. Other locals cautiously approached, looking at Yasmi with a mixture of fear and longing. A teenager laid her hand on the man's shoulder and he leaned into her, face still hidden, shoulders shaking.

"It's all right, Pa," the young woman said, then looked at Yasmi. "My aunt took a bucket and ran out, but..."

She gestured to a shrine at the edge of town, a low mound with wooden boards on its front carved with the signs of various gods: Yorl's one eye, Loftus's smile, the split face of Kialla. The field around the shrine was full of burial markers. Several stretches of dirt had been recently dug.

"Are those all your people?" Yasmi asked.

"Some of us, some of them."

"Which them, the Estians or the Dunholmi?"

"Does it matter?"

To her, it did. One side were the people she marched with, shared meals with, fought alongside. They might even have been people she helped to recruit. But to these people, they were the destroyers who brought violence into their town, and she couldn't blame them for not sorting red from blue, fellow countrymen from foreigners.

The wind grew colder. She was terribly aware of its whistling through the branches of the remaining trees, a mournful performance for a place shrouded in sorrow. The edge of her tunic was askew and she fought not to straighten it. How would that look to these people, trying to make herself look better when they had such devastation to deal with?

How would a story about patriotism and a civil war play out in front of them?

"We're proud folk." The man recovered himself enough to speak. "We wouldn't normally ask, but it's not just our stores. Foragers from both sides have hunted all the deer and boar and taken most of what else the woods offered. We were hungry even before this. If you have anything..."

"All we can spare is yours."

The man took a deep breath, like he was bracing himself for a feat of strength.

"Not all," he said. "Word is they're going hungry at Six Bells too, and the folk at Follia had half their homes pulled down to build war machines. Spare us a meal, but keep some for them."

He looked so gaunt, so exhausted, she was amazed that he could manage such generosity. It seemed more heroic than all the fight scenes she'd ever played out on the stage.

Efron and Tenebrial were sitting on the board of the first wagon. Other players stood staring at the state of the village, whispering to each other and shaking their heads.

"We're staying here tonight," Yasmi said to them. "And we're going to feed these people. As grand a banquet as we can manage, big portions for everyone."

"My sweet," Efron began, "we only brought enough victuals for a brief tour, and you've seen how challenging it has been to find more."

"We're feeding them, and we'll see how we can help repair the less damaged buildings. The good thing about making scenery is that we're all experienced carpenters."

"But the play..."

"Will be a comedy tonight. Tenebrial can work out which one."

"A comedy?" Efron's moustache twitched at his snorted breath. "We've been rehearsing *Sisters in Sorrow*, one of our best performances in years. So visceral. That shouldn't go to waste."

Yasmi waved toward the locals standing beneath their charred trees.

"Do these people look ready for a tragedy about civil war?" she asked, then pressed a hand to her chest. "Do I?"

It almost felt like cheating to win Efron around this way, using the sort of theatricality that he could never resist. But she wouldn't abandon these people, and she wouldn't rub salt into their wounds for the sake of art.

"We could do *Two Chamberlains and a Barrel*." Tenebrial tapped a thin finger against the wagon. "Everyone knows their parts, and the house over there has the perfect doorway for the stuffed-sheep scene."

"Fine." Efron deflated dramatically, then waved a hand in surrender. "True art can wait for another day. Never let it be said that the Company Dellest left an audience less than delighted."

Yasmi doubted these people had it in them to be delighted right now, but if a play distracted them for an hour, maybe raised laughs from people who hadn't smiled in weeks, then that would be the most good she'd done in months.

A selection of pages and equerries stood in the yard outside the inn, waiting on any nobles who came to talk with King Lorrin. Alder rode Fellstride right up to them and dismounted.

"Be careful with him," he said. "He's been agitated since the battle."

"Of course, my lord." The closest page took the reins and led Fellstride toward where other horses were hitched. Was it Alder's imagination or were the other servants standing further back than usual, looking less eager to serve than they should when facing a count of Dunholm?

He strode across the inn's yard, its ground blackened by ashes blown from the woods. The fire had burned out during the night, but he felt its heat as if it was still there, flames blazing inches from his face. The memory made him smile and walk proudly. He'd saved the king, saved the army from disaster, brought them the victory they'd needed. True, the outcome had been too chaotic for a proper pursuit, and many of the North Marchers had got away, but the important thing was that they were beaten. Once again, their upstart prince had tried and failed. Once again, Alder himself had beaten the boy in combat. There could be no doubt of who the champion was here.

Thanks to me, said a voice from inside him, crackling like flames.

Alder ignored it. This was his triumph and he was going to enjoy it.

As always, the royal court was a place of bustling activity, even when it was far from home. Smoke billowed from the inn's chimney, and the air was filled with smells of roasting and baking. Servants hurried back and forth across the yard, while others polished armour and weapons to one side. Messengers and advisors went in and out of the front door, some of them carrying letters and accounting books. As Alder approached, the crowds parted, making way for the hero of the hour. Many of the ordinary people looked at him with wonder.

There was a carving of a goat at the top of the doorframe, one of those cursed Estian charms. Alder reached up and pressed his hand against it, let the fire flow. The smell of smoke grew sharper as the wood charred. With a flick of his fingers, he brushed away the ash where the goat had been.

One of the warriors guarding the doorway looked at him in amazement. The other stared resolutely away.

King Lorrin's travelling throne had been assembled on a stage in the corner of the room, a platform barely big enough to hold it. Several countesses, counts, and other nobles stood around the edge of the room, drinking from painted clay cups. Lady Maple, her arm in a sling, raised her cup to Alder, but no one else met his eye.

"Your Majesty." Alder bowed to King Lorrin before accepting one of the cups from a servant's tray. Even far from home, the court worked like clockwork, Lady Maple's impeccable coordination setting everything in its place.

"Count Alder." One side of King Lorrin's face was bruised and his left leg was fat with bandages. "I trust that you are rested from yesterday's engagement?"

"As rested as one can be with the enemy near to hand." Alder ran a hand through his thick hair and offered up his most confident smile. "I've been talking with some of the lords I led into battle yesterday, and with captains who know the terrain. If Your Majesty will permit us, we believe that we can cut off most of the rebels before they reach a substantial town, scatter the remnants before they regroup."

He wanted to say more, but had already pushed the limits of what he should say to the king uninvited, relying on his achievements the previous day to see him through. Lorrin's face, though wrinkled by age and bruised by battle, revealed nothing about what he was thinking, no invitation for more and no judgement on what had been said. Others, though, looked at Alder with hostility.

"You have my thanks, Count Alder," Lorrin said. "Your decisive action was a crucial part of our victory."

It was the whole victory, and Lorrin had to know it, but Alder gritted his teeth and kept smiling.

"Your methods, though..." Lorrin frowned. "A generation ago, we conquered the North March to stop their sorcerous ways. We have worked hard to prevent them from twisting folk magic into something darker, but yesterday you embraced it. You unleashed something that should not be."

The heat rose in Alder again, hearing how he was being treated after all he'd done.

"I saved us from disaster."

"Disaster? That's your perspective on how my armies fought?" Lorrin leaned forward, and there was more than anger in his expression. There was disgust. "What you did was not needed, it was forbidden."

"I saved your life!" Alder snapped, and it was all he could

do not to curse the king out for his ingratitude. Anger boiled inside him and he felt the flames flash across the fingers of his left hand. Courtiers gasped and stared.

Burn them all, the voice inside him said. Alder's sneer was meant for that voice as much as for the king. This was all Jarrag ever wanted to do, and tempting as it was, this wasn't the place.

While the others had stiffened, even reached for their weapons, Lorrin sat back in his throne, shaking his head in disdain.

"Perhaps I misjudged you all this time, Alder. Perhaps your judgement is as flawed as your father's, your behaviour as impulsive as his. But a man cannot hide his true self forever."

The desire to argue back, to fight his corner, to defend his honour and that of his family was almost impossible to resist. But Alder swallowed the fire and the fury, though it felt like smoke in his throat. He let experience slide the mask of respectful restraint across his face and bowed to his king.

"I apologise, Your Majesty," he said. "I took a blow to the head yesterday and am clearly not as rested as I thought. I should not have come into your company in this condition."

"Indeed. Countess Yewgrove will lead the pursuit of the rebels; the last thing you need is another hard ride." The king waved a hand, the black pearls on his silver ring gleaming. "You are dismissed."

Alder bowed again, then strode out of the inn. The crowds parted for him again as he crossed the yard, and he couldn't help seeing the contrast between the so-called nobles, sneering as they practised to impress the king, and the common warriors, who looked at him with wide-eyed awe. They understood what Alder had done, what it took to win when nations were on the line.

Captain Brook was standing by the equerries, her own horse's reins in her hand.

"How was it, my lord?" she asked.

Alder looked around. Too many people might overhear him. Anything he said in anger could be taken as treason, and the king might not mind an excuse to put his head on the block. Of course, Lorrin claimed that it was about the taint of magic, but more likely he had decided to end the Alders once and for all, the grasping, ungrateful wretch. With no heir yet born, His Majesty could seize the house's lands when its head fell, adding to his own power.

There was no space for mistakes here, but little time for timidity. He had never been in greater danger and there was no easy way out.

Brook stiffened and nodded past Alder. He turned to see Lady Maple walking toward him.

"Count Alder." Her bow was small and respectful, the exact correct etiquette for a noble of her station facing a count. It gave nothing away. "I wanted to thank you. You saved us in the woods yesterday." She lowered her voice. "I'm not the only one who thinks so. I doubt you'll be feasting with the king this evening, but perhaps you would join some of us in my tent. Other nobles who appreciate what you did." She glanced down at his hand, ash darkening the fingers. "And what else you could do."

Alder watched her walk away. He might not have an easy way out, but perhaps he had more options than he'd realised.

Past Lady Maple, Alder's grandmother stood by the side of the road, hand resting on her sword, her expression stern. She gave him a slow, steady nod, then faded to flames.

The world was black as ashes, fever hot and featureless. Raul wondered whether he'd been swallowed by some vast monster, except that he couldn't feel the sides of a throat or a stomach. In fact, he couldn't feel much of anything.

He remembered feelings from before, discordant and overwhelming.

Shock.

Disbelief.

Agony.

The terrible dread of feeling his own life pour out between his fingers, of knowing that this must be the end.

Some omens couldn't be wrong.

Nothing hurt. Or maybe everything hurt but he'd left it behind, cast his burden into the distance, come to a place where he was safe. Somewhere he didn't have to bear it anymore.

Was this death?

"Not yet," a familiar voice replied.

Raul wiped his brow. He had a brow again. Had that been there a moment ago? Had his hand?

He was hot, aching, drenched in sweat. That was more than he'd had.

He wasn't sure that he wanted more.

"Where are you?" he asked.

Not "who are you." He knew *that*, even though it didn't make any sense. It was easier not to think about things that didn't make sense, just like it was easier not to think about the pain, where it had gone to, whether it might return. Best not to think about where a fever came from if he was only half convinced he still had a body.

Best not to think about heat.

Or flames.

"I'm here." The figure didn't move out of the darkness, but came into perspective as if they'd always been there, waiting for Raul to notice. "Where else would I be?"

Raul looked his other self up and down. That Raul was dressed in armour over a red tunic, with the symbol of blade and moon stitched into its collar. He carried the jewelled sword that Prisca had prepared for them and a scroll in his hand. If someone had asked Raul what a legal proclamation looked like, he would have pictured that scroll with its heavy wax seal, and perhaps he was simply picturing all of this now. If he was, then he had a splendid imagination, because the other Raul's crown was spectacular, gold strands woven into intricate spikes, each one holding a ruby as wide as his thumb.

Blood dripped into the darkness. Raul thought it came from the other Raul's sword, but when he looked down he saw that it was dripping from him too, seeping through his simple shirt and spattering across boots speckled with chicken shit and mud from the yard of the inn back home. Just seeing that wound made him wince, and clutching a hand to it made it worse.

"You don't have to worry about that." The other Raul

touched the wound and Raul's skin rippled as it sealed shut. No more dripping. The pain was still there, but at least now he wasn't dying.

Was he?

"Is it over?" he asked.

"It's saved for later."

"But what's for now?"

"Now, you have to make a choice. Are you going to get up off your bed and live, to become the person you were meant to be?" The other Raul gestured up and down his own magnificence, straight-backed and splendid. "Or are you going to give in and die, taking the rebellion with you? Are you going to be the chosen one?"

The other Raul took a step back and stared at him, expectant.

"None of that's real," Raul said. "The sword, the prophecies, the birthmark..." He tapped his upper arm and it stung. Was that a memory of the original pain, being branded as a baby, or was he just imagining himself into the gaps where pain should be? "There is no chosen one."

"It's as real as you want it to be." The other Raul pointed the sword at him. "The rebels need a leader. Someone strong. Someone special. Someone to inspire them. Who cares who wrote the prophecies or forged the word? What matters is whether you have that strength." The crown rang out as he tapped it with the edge of the sword. "Whether you have the makings of a king."

Raul took a step, then another. The darkness was surprisingly solid. His footsteps echoed as he paced back and forth.

"Someone else could do it," he said.

"Could they? Who else has your skills? Who else can fight and divine the omens and act the role needed to inspire the troops?"

"Who else is as big a liar as me?"

"King Balbianus, for one."

Raul stopped, blinked, looked at the other Raul. "What do you mean?"

"Oh, come on, you saw the temple in the wild, you heard what Jarrag had to say. Balbianus lied and so did the stories about him."

"Then the whole kingdom is a lie."

The other Raul shrugged. "Maybe that's all a country is, a stretch of ground bound together by comfortable lies."

Raul's stomach tightened, bringing a fresh wave of pain. That couldn't be true, could it?

"No," he said. "A country is a community. It's people standing united, looking after each other, building more together than they can alone."

"Maybe it's both."

The tension in Raul's gut worsened. He bent around the pain.

"No," he hissed, straightening. "That's not how it works. There are good things in the world."

"There are things in the world, and they all have some good and bad in them. Even you."

He swallowed. It was terrible and it was true. However hard he tried, he got it wrong sometimes. He'd lost the sword twice. He'd failed when he faced Count Alder. He'd lied to people who believed in him because he'd told himself that was what had to be. Guilt bore him down as heavily as the pain, but it could all go away if he accepted the darkness, if he stayed here and let it all fade.

"Stop that," the other Raul snapped. "You can't give up."

"Why not?"

"Because you're special, remember? You're the chosen one." The other Raul puffed out his chest like Efron about to give a speech. "I'm the chosen one."

Easing himself carefully upright, Raul looked at the other Raul again. The Raul he'd been raised to become. The Raul he'd been working toward. The Raul he could still be.

"It doesn't matter whether you were chosen by fate, by chance, or by Prisca." The other Raul laid a hand on his shoulder. "You were chosen. They need you to save the country."

Raul licked his lips, which were as dry as his throat and swollen with fever. Maybe the other Raul was right. After all he'd done, was it so bad to admit the truth?

"You're special," the other Raul said. "You're unique."

Raul blinked. Special. Unique. He'd used those words himself not long ago, but about someone else. Who had it been? Who else was there in this dark, blank world?

He ran his fingers through the air, felt soft hair, remembered the sunlight shining through it.

"I am," he said. "So is Yasmi."

He thought of Valens, fighting on with only one hand.

"So is my da."

He thought of Prisca watching the flight of birds, reading secret messages from the world.

"So is my ma."

He thought of the inn back home.

"So are Old Wellic and Young Wellic and Longa, whose plough got stuck."

He thought of his journeys and his struggles.

"So are Efron and Tenebrial, Quintae and Drusil, Silvano, Biallo, Ferra, Lestavo, all the rest." He took a deep breath and his chest ached even though he knew that the breath wasn't real. "So are Appia and Ovida, even though they're not with us anymore."

The other Raul frowned and seemed to diminish. The crown didn't shine with reflected glory anymore but was just a band of soft metal and stones. The proclamation crumpled in his hand.

"No one else is like me, that's true," Raul said. "No one's like Yasmi either, or any of them. If I've been chosen, then so has everyone. We've chosen each other. We've chosen who to become."

He looked the other Raul up and down, this puffed-out man who hadn't cleaned his sword, who clutched at written words as if they mattered more than the ones he spoke, who still wore his armour in the dark, far from the battlefield.

"I don't want to become you," Raul said.

"Then you'll become nothing."

"If I must."

"Just one more nameless peasant like all the rest."

"Making me like the people I'm fighting for?" Raul smiled. It hurt, but that was fine. "That sounds good."

Then he was alone in the dark, with only his fever and his pain.

Chapter Fourteen
Scattered Pebbles

A bat fluttered out of the south, across the marshland at the foot of the hills, a black shape against the grey of dusk. Valens watched it like he'd watched every other shape flying their way over the past three days. At first it had been exhausting, expecting any passing sparrow to be a messenger sent by the Withering Folk's scouts. After a while, it had become a matter of resignation, watching without real hope or expectation because watching was all he could do.

He finished eating a turnip they'd roasted in a fire at the back of the cave, then licked its flavour from his fingers. At least this was something he knew how to do, making the most out of every scrap of food that came his way while campaigning. Learning not to starve when his supplies were lost along with everything else.

"One of yours?" he asked as the bat came closer.

"So's said." Ferra whistled shrilly. The bat swooped down and settled on her outstretched hand. The hand was red where she had been burned in the woods, but she didn't flinch as the creature landed. She stroked its fur, then uncurled a strip of leaf from around its leg and squinted at the marks on it.

"Lestavo's found Earl Tordesse," she said. "This side of the marsh. He's fixing to bring him along."

"Is Tordesse in one piece?"

"Aye."

"Has he got many with him still?"

"Aye."

"How many?"

"We'll see when we see." She shrugged. "Lestavo's never been one for details."

"With Tordesse, that's half the earls found, and the Saditchi, as well as the captains we've accounted for."

Not that "accounted for" always meant good news. Three captains had been lost in the battle and two more spotted strung from trees by the pursuing Dunholmi.

"Aye, they've not frayed us as hard as we feared."

"Still..."

Still, they were scattered, separated by strong Dunholmi patrols, every fragment of the rebel army desperately evading pursuers while they tried to regroup. Without Ferra's folk and their winged messengers, there would have been even less hope, and right now hope was most of what they had.

Valens had always preferred solid steel to hope, but he would take whatever Laughing Loftus gave him and still keep praying for more.

Back down the cave, they'd lit a fire behind a pile of boulders, hidden from anyone passing outside. He didn't like seeing fires after what they'd seen at Hound's Gap, but they needed the warmth, especially for the wounded. The light of the flames threw shadows across the walls, and he couldn't escape the feeling that others might see them through those flames. Jarrag had reached inside his own head to toy with his soul once. They'd weakened the would-be god, but the power Alder wielded looked a lot like Jarrag's tricks, and that was going to bring someone pain.

As if there wasn't enough pain already.

"You and Lestavo, you've got a kid, don't you?" he asked.

"Aye."

"What happens to them if you two don't make it back?" He wouldn't have raised the prospect of death with the likes of Biallo or the earls. Even Silvano, solid with muscles from years of labour, wasn't steady enough for this sort of talk. But Ferra could face reality.

"Community's helped raise him his whole life," she said. "They'll finish well enough. It's the Withering way."

"And what would you do if you lost him? Your son, I mean?"

Ferra's reddened fingers rasped across the grey stubble on the shaved side of her head.

"Reckon I'd fray who done it all the way dead, then water the trees with their guts." She placed her hand on Valens's arm and looked him in the eye. "Best not to think on it before you must."

"I might have to soon enough." Her gesture was meant well, but he couldn't bear the closeness of touch, the sympathy that came with it, the grief that he could only hold back by bolstering his own strength. He stood. "I'll tell them about Tordesse."

They'd chosen the cave because it was larger inside than at its mouth, meaning plenty of space for shelter and less likelihood anyone would notice. In the cavernous chamber at the back, Prisca, Drusil, and several others sat around the fire. Past them, bodies lay in the dark, wounded or resting or both.

Valens crouched between Prisca and Quintae. The builder of secret compartments and siege engines was rocking back and forth, clutching the scarred side of his head and muttering to himself. The sound made Valens twitch in annoyance, but they'd given up on trying to soothe him after the first day. Quintae would have to find his own way back to something like peace.

"Tordesse's turned up," Valens said.

"Does he have troops with him?" Prisca asked, dropping a handful of small pebbles on the floor in front of her crossed legs.

"That's your first question, not whether he's alive or dead?"

"Don't be unnecessarily obtuse." Prisca peered at the pebbles for a moment, then scooped them up again. "Your tone told me that he's alive and the question of martial resources matters."

The pebbles clattered down.

"Martial resources? You mean people's lives?"

Prisca's face froze, contorted, as if she'd tasted something so awful that it froze her in place. For a long moment, she seemed to stare at nothing, then she shook her head and glared up at him.

"You understand full well what I mean."

"I do, and it's not good."

"Trust me, keeping a distance from terrible consequences is part of what keeps leaders sane. I expected you to have learned that by now, General."

"Trusting you is what got us into this mess."

"If our leader had trusted me more, accepted the wisdom of my experience, then we might have emerged victorious at Hound's Gap, instead of being scattered to the winds."

Valens snatched the pebbles from in front of her and flung them across the cave. They cracked against the far wall, a sound sharp as snapping bones.

"Our leader, as you call him, is our son," he bellowed, towering over her. "And while you count off human lives like they're coin, he's dying."

He gestured across everybody else's heads, toward the back of the cave.

She jerked to her feet, chin jutting, thin finger raised. "At least one of us is trying to redeem this situation."

"Because only one of us gives a shit about other people."

"I've spent my life trying save our people."

"You've spent your life trying to get your power back."

"Enough nonsense. We can talk when you've calmed down." She turned her back on him.

"You cold-hearted..." Valens raised his arm between them, trembling with rage. If he'd still had that hand it would have been a fist.

Everyone else in the cave was silent, staring at them.

"Da, please don't," a voice croaked from the back. "She's hurting too."

At the sound of that voice, Valens choked with relief. He

stumbled past the fire, almost kicking Quintae over, and wrapped his arms around Raul.

"You're alive," he said, squeezing his son tight. "You're awake. You're standing."

"Not for long like this," Raul mumbled into his chest. "Sorry."

Valens let go and tried to take a step away, before realising that he was the only thing holding Raul up. The boy was dressed in trousers and the improvised bandages wrapped around his middle, one of Valens's field poultices seeping yellow and green through strips of a torn shirt. Technically, he was standing up, but his back was bent, head hanging, knees buckling. His skin was somehow both pale and hot, eyelids flickering. While one hand clung to Valens's shoulder, the other clutched his wound.

"What happened?" Raul whispered as Valens lowered him to sit on a rock.

"Count Alder."

"I remember. But after that?"

"Biallo. He rode in and snatched you while others were fighting the count. Got you out of there before the whole thing fell apart. Turns out he was a better rider than he looked."

"Was?"

Valens swallowed. If he'd ever been good at this part, he'd forgotten how.

"Like I said, he got you out, but then he went back to cover the retreat. We'd have lost all the engineers and more if he hadn't held the gap for them."

Raul ran a hand across his brow. "How bad is it?"

Valens thought about how much they'd pieced together over the past week, while the unconscious Raul clung to life by the thinnest of feverish threads. Even now, he looked most of the way dead.

"Bad enough," Valens said. "We'll tell you more when you can sit up straight."

"I can..." Raul tried to straighten but slumped back down. "I suppose."

Crouching beside his son, relief and fear waged war for dominance in Valens's heart. Relief that Raul hadn't slipped away in his sleep, like so many other injured warriors. Fear for how his injury might weaken him and for what lay ahead.

Since when had he faced fear with anything other than bloody-minded determination?

He glanced across the fire. Quintae had stopped rocking and was smiling at Raul like he was the most precious thing in the world. That was something they could agree on. Prisca watched him too but stayed where she was. Perhaps she did have the good sense to shut up once in a while.

"We've started regrouping," Valens said. "Finding survivors. Bringing them together."

"That's good." Raul raised his head. "Is there water? My whole throat feels dry."

Drusil held out a cup and the boy reached for it with a trembling hand. Water spilled over the edge as he tried to raise it to his lips, so Valens wrapped his hand around and held it steady while Raul drank.

"More?" he asked when the cup was empty.

"More."

By the third cup, Raul was holding it up himself, though it took both hands and he winced when his elbow brushed against his bandage. Drusil dug some dried fruit out of her pack, which Valens handed to Raul a little at a time.

"You've not eaten in a week," he said, seeing the eager plea in Raul's eyes. "Too much too quick won't do you good."

It reminded him of when Raul was young and needed him for all the little things—eating, drinking, keeping warm, finding comfort when the world scared him. That tiny body pressed against his own. Fond memories but not good ones to have when they needed a grown man leading them.

"It's good that you're awake," Prisca said. "We can start summoning commanders and other key contacts to discuss what comes next. It will be easier for them to motivate people once they see that their prince is alive and preparing to return to the fight."

"Return to the fight?" Valens rubbed at his forehead. Holding back his frustration at Prisca was giving him a headache, but the boy's first words on waking had been to stop the two arguing, and he wasn't going to let down his ruler or his son. "Look at him. He's pale as bones. He's got wounds in his gut that would have killed most people, burns running from there down half his leg and up his chest. Sitting up long enough to drink water has exhausted him. He's not returning to the fight anytime this year."

"We'll find a way. Careful costuming to hide the wounds. Position him in a high-backed throne to give speeches. As long as he's near the battlefield wearing a sword they'll assume that he's participating in combat, and who knows, after a few months he might—"

"You're going to kill him!"

"Fire and fury, don't you understand? If we can't pull this rebellion together right now, then King Lorrin will kill us all." He'd seldom seen her so genuinely angry, her face curling into a vicious snarl, a cornered beast turning on its predator. But in the space of two breaths she had it back under control, face stern, voice cold. "We need a leader, someone to muster people's courage, to channel their hopes, someone they can commit to. That's Raul."

"No." Raul's voice was so faint, Valens had to pause for a moment to be sure of what he'd heard. The others seemed to be doing the same, their expressions shifting through confusion to concern.

"Raul." Prisca moved closer, robes swishing, hands clasped in front of her. "Your Highness. I understand why you might have certain reservations, given the ordeal you've suffered through, but replacing you with another figurehead at this juncture would be challenging, possibly even counterproductive. If necessary, we could substitute some other figure, but your return, even delayed, remains infinitely preferable."

"General Valens is right." Raul raised his head, showing a determination greater than the pain. Even weakened, he was the prince they had followed to war, not the vulnerable child of so many years ago. "I'm in no state to fight. I might never be."

Prisca stared at him, then into the fire. Was she making

frantic calculations, or did she already have a backup in mind? No one in their right mind should underestimate the schemes of Prisca Servita.

"Give yourself a few days to be sure," she said. "I'll begin preparations in the meantime. Preemptive abdications are not unprecedented, and if we can track down the Company Dellest, then I can consult with Tenebrial on how to tell the story to draw out sympathies for a new hero."

"No." Raul shook his head.

Prisca blinked and the corner of her mouth twitched. "Excuse me?"

Valens laid a hand on his son's shoulder, willing his own strength into him. He didn't know what Raul was thinking, but the lad had a sharper mind than him and a better heart than any of them. One good thing Valens had made in his life, and he trusted that goodness to choose right for everyone.

"Hanging all our hopes on one person is how we got here," Raul said, resting a hand against his wounded side. "If something happens to them, then it all falls apart. It doesn't matter if they make a mistake, lose their sense of right and wrong, or get cut down in battle. They fall and everything falters around them."

"Without that leader, there's nothing to fall," Prisca said, as if she was teaching a lesson to a small child. "I fear Your Highness's mind may still be weak. We should leave this until you've recovered."

"Princes. Kings. Chosen ones." Raul put his hand on Valens and pushed himself to his feet. Through that hand, Valens could feel a trembling, but Raul held himself too proudly for anyone else to see. "No one gets it right forever. If we hang our hopes on one person, then we invite disaster. We weren't strong because people were following me. We were strong because they stood together, because they all brought what they had to the fight. All I did was help get them there. So now, we're going to do things differently. No kings. No figureheads. Shared authority."

"That's a touching idea, Your Highness, but hopelessly naive. This is how the world has always worked."

"What's naive is doing the same thing that has failed so many times and expecting it to be what we need."

The fire crackled. They all looked at him. The others were smiling for the first time since Hound's Gap. Quintae giggled and clapped his hands together, then slapped them across his mouth. Drusil laid a hand on the hammer hanging from her belt, the charm on its side that she'd carved to give it extra strength. Only Prisca was frowning, the flickering firelight casting sharp shadows across her face.

"Your Highness," she hissed through clenched teeth, "there are plans in place, not just for this war but for what comes next, assurances and expectations holding this together. The stability of the country, the diplomatic marriage to Saditch, these things are built around a king. You must be realistic."

As Raul stepped away, Valens had to fight the urge to leap up and support him. Now was the time to trust his son's choices. Raul's legs trembled and he clutched one arm across his bandages, sweat dripping from his feverish brow as he walked unsteadily but purposefully to Prisca, then took her hand in his.

"We must have hope," he said. "Real hope. Strong hope.

Shared hope. A hope that can endure the battering the world throws at us. It might be harder to build it my way, but it's better. "There will be a court, but we will share responsibility, not lay it on one person. There will be renewed relations with the world, but I won't marry anyone to make it happen. No one's heart should be shackled like that, not mine and not Princess Nydia's."

He let her hand go, took a deep breath, and stood as straight as Valens had ever seen him. The lad was going to regret that later, when they had to restitch his wounds, but in the moment he was a perfect tower of strength.

"A new moon rises," he said. "New. That was the promise, Minister Servita, and I intend to deliver."

Prisca stared at him, stone-faced. A log cracked in the fire and sparks whirled toward the ceiling.

"Word is word." Ferra slapped a hand against her chest. "A new moon rises."

"A new moon rises." Quintae leapt up, waving his arms.

"A new moon rises." Drusil rose, hammer at the ready, steady as a statue.

"A new moon rises." Valens stood, his remaining hand resting on the pommel of his trusty sword.

The other rebels in the cave rose, joining in the cry. Pride filled the air and with it a confidence that had seemed impossible an hour before.

Raul trembled and Valens stepped forward, easing him to the ground. As he did, he caught Prisca's eye, saw the sternness behind her silence. This conversation wasn't over any more than the war was.

Chapter Fifteen
Burn Them All

Count Alder strode through the camp. All around, warriors were returning with the dying light, ending another day of half-hearted pursuit. If the court had listened to Alder, he could have told them what he had learned of the land and its people in his time as governor, which ways they were likely to go, which towns and villages were least loyal to the crown. He could have told them which thorns needed to be dug out of the hooves of the North March and their remnants burned so no one would feel their pain again. But while some ears at court were receptive, they weren't the ones who mattered to King Lorrin.

"My lord." Ketley Tur stalked crane-like beside Alder, head tucked in as if he expected a lash to fall upon him. "I don't wish to question your judgement—"

"Then don't," Alder snapped. Tur might have his uses, but he had no spine and this was no night for cowards. "Wait outside until I'm done."

Captain Brook, walking at his other side, took a step forward and pulled back the flap of the grand marquee housing the royal court. Guards stood alert around the inside, smart and attentive. Servants hurried back and forth with trays of cups and bottles, occasionally stopping by Lady Maple for instructions. Maple herself stood with the other senior nobles around a rectangular table in the centre of the tent. There was a gap at the near end, but Alder ignored it. Leaving Brook by the door, he walked up the table, noting which nobles flinched from his presence and which held his gaze. Arriving so late, he wouldn't normally have been able to take a place near the king, despite his house's seniority, but one of the nobles jerked aside rather than stand near him.

Cowards.

The heat rose, flames of fury roaring in his ears.

All cowards.

They were what was wrong with Dunholm. He had been given an extraordinary power and they rejected it rather than embrace what he could do. But then, what could he expect? He had held himself back for too long, afraid of upsetting the good order, of forcing their hands.

No more.

He took the place beside King Lorrin, his rightful place, and bowed respectfully.

"Your Majesty."

"Count Alder."

A servant set a wooden cup in front of Alder, small but carefully carved and richly varnished like those the other nobles had. The scent of apple brandy was sweet, sharp, and heady, a rich combination for powerful people and important decisions.

One of the other counts pushed wooden tokens across the map on the table, showing where the rebels had been spotted. Some of it made sense, but other parts were clearly misinformation, scouts who didn't understand what they'd seen or where they'd been. Even the talk of skirmishes was disappointing. The advance parties, like the army itself, had been trotting along when they should have galloped, held their hands high when they should have brought the whip down. He felt the fire again, heard the voice in the back of his mind that might have been Jarrag or just his own frustration at this pathetic display.

"That village," Alder said, interrupting one of the reports. "It's leaned toward the rebels from the start. Search the cave in the woods beyond. If you don't find rebels there, then burn the granary and get the nooses out. The peasants will tell you where they're hiding."

He took a sip from his drink. All the others had set theirs down and stared silently at the king.

"I command here, Count Alder," King Lorrin said. "And I'm starting to suspect that your mind has been addled by dabbling with dark forces."

"Commands are only as good as the advice they are based on," Alder said. "You've been listening to the wrong advisors."

It was as close as anyone would ever dare come to saying that the king was wrong, and the shock of it rippled around the table. Wrinkles piled up on Lorrin's face, disdain turning into fury.

"You go too far."

The hands of the guards settled on their swords.

"You don't go far enough." Alder held out his hand, flames dazzling bright within the cage of his fingers. "I have been granted a gift like no one else, the power needed to bring us victory, and you squander that power along with my insights."

Lorrin snorted. "I knew that I would need to deal with you sooner or later, but it seems the matter will not wait."

"No, it won't." Alder leaned over, hand on the map. "It's time for stronger voices to make themselves heard."

Fire rushed from his hand across the map, consuming the image of the North March. As it hit the wooden cups, brandy flashed into pillars of flame. The nobles jolted back, crying out in alarm.

The guards leapt forward, drawing their swords, but Maple's servants knew their signal. Narrow daggers appeared from beneath serving trays and plunged through gaps in the guards' armour, into their sides and backs. Around the table, nobles drew their weapons, some looking around in alarm. But others, the ones Alder had dined with, those as frustrated as he was, were on the attack already. As the light of burning spirits flared and fell, blades clashed and bodies thudded to the floor, blood sprayed red across Dunholmi blue.

Lorrin drew his sword, but Alder grabbed his wrist and squeezed. Skin blackened and the king screamed, dropping the sword amid a stink like burning meat. Alder wrenched Lorrin's arm down, bringing him to his knees.

"Now, Your Majesty, you will listen to your true advisors," Alder said.

As swiftly as it had begun, the fighting was over. The guards were all dead and the servants had their swords, standing by the entrances to the tent in case trouble came. A good third of the nobles were down as well, dead or injured, while others had their hands raised. Not all had even drawn their swords, whether out of pragmatism, cowardice, or simple indifference. Alder could work with people like that if he had to, but he preferred the ones with blood on their blades and the fire he had unleashed reflecting in their eyes. The ones who understood real power.

Captain Brook crouched near the entrance, hand pressed to the neck of one of the fallen. She shook her head.

"Lady Maple, my lord," she said. "We've lost her."

It was a shame, he needed more people like Maple, competent and decisive. But there were casualties in any campaign.

Brook leapt up as the tent flap shifted, but it was only Tur, shoulders hunched and hands raised, his eyes wide. Through the flames, Alder saw him shudder and shuffle his feet.

"My lord, I have word from your officers," he said. "The camp is secure, though there is some muttering, some uncertainty."

"His Majesty will give a speech tomorrow laying that to rest." Alder twisted the king's burned arm. "Won't you?"

Lorrin whimpered and nodded.

Alder held out his hand to receive a fresh cup from one of the servants. He blinked, felt the heat behind his eyes. Did the others see it when they looked at him, as he saw it when he looked in the mirror? He blinked again and the brandy ignited. He tipped it into his mouth, flames and all, and it burned down through him like the sweetest satisfaction. Then the cup crumbled to ash.

His grandmother's face appeared in the flames rising from the table. She smiled proudly at Alder, and he smiled back.

"His Majesty will be embracing the strength needed to deal with the North March. From now on, this is our strategy." Alder tapped a finger in the warm black dust that had been a map. "Burn them all."

———————————•———————————

A storm was coming in as the Company Dellest approached Rollway, a logging town on the edge of the Grey Hills. The black of the clouds above matched the smoke rising from the town. If that wasn't an omen, then Yasmi didn't know what was.

Over the past few weeks, she'd seen some dreadful sights. Trampled crops. Burnt orchards. Houses torn down. Rollway had all of that and more, with a string of bodies hanging from trees along the road into town. She hadn't seen a display like this since Count Alder put down the rebellion in Pavuno. It had sickened her then, but the lurching of her stomach was even worse now. The people she fought alongside would never do a thing like this, but she had helped start the fight. Did she bear some responsibility for what she saw?

"We should turn around," her father said, his voice hollow, moustache drooping. "They might still be here."

"If they were, we'd be surrounded by lances and blue pennants by now," Yasmi said. The horses had slowed as they smelled the wrongness in the air, the smoke and rot. She gave a flick of the reins to urge them on.

"The place is still burning. They can't have gone far."

"That's not the town," Tenebrial said. "It's the forest behind." He shook his head. "Fire like that can go for days, though this weather should end it."

"By Yorl's blind eye, what sort of heat must it take to burn a forest in the spring?" Efron asked.

That seemed like the sort of line Tenebrial should have leapt upon, scribbling it down ready for use in one of his plays, but he sat silent, head in his hands. The wheels of the wagon creaked. So did the bodies swinging from the trees in the rising wind.

Yasmi nudged Tenebrial.

"Go back to the other wagon," she said. "Ask them to stop here. They're the burial detail today."

Tenebrial shuddered.

"I see them in the night," he said. "Cold and stiff, the ground swallowing them like a vast maw. Lives smothered as a fire at the end of the night, but with no hope that the embers will be stirred to life in the morn."

Yasmi swallowed. She'd seen too many bodies herself in the past few weeks, helped lower many of them into the cold ground. It would wear at anyone's soul, and a vivid imagination was part of Tenebrial's gift. Apparently, it was his curse as well.

"Catch up with us once you've told them," she said. "You don't need to wield a spade."

"No." He swung down from the wagon. "I will not look away."

Leaving him behind, they rolled on along the rutted dirt road. The houses here were mostly ruins, either burned out or torn down. Smashed pots and broken furniture littered the ground. Some buildings were deserted. From others, people peered at the passing wagon with haunted and terrified expressions.

"My queen of the boards, what are we even doing here?" Efron asked, laying a hand on hers. "We are a wandering theatrical troupe, and these people are far beyond wanting what we have to offer the world."

It was the same small, sad speech he made every time, and she tried not to let it bother her, to extend the same kindness to her father that she extended to these people. He wasn't built for what he was enduring here. He'd barely been built for running a theatrical troupe, had relied on her mother as long as she lived and after that upon the habits that held his company together. As long as he could navigate the world through extravagant gestures and florid speeches, he was fine, but they didn't live in that world any longer. They weren't even rallying the troops or inspiring new recruits. They were riding through the ruins of towns where they had once brought tears and laughter, knowing that only one of those would do now.

"We stopped being a theatrical troupe five massacres back," she said. "We've become something else."

They stopped in the middle of the town and started to unload. The edge of the storm had reached them, a hard wind rattling loose boards on broken buildings, fat drops of rain bursting in the dirt. More people appeared, not coming close but peering at them from among the ruins of their lives. A young boy tried to run forward but his mother held him back. The players mostly worked in silence, aside from the thud of sacks and the clatter of planks.

"You deal with the food," Yasmi said to her father. "Claudio and I will look at the houses."

That was usually how they split the labour. Seeing a few smiles as desperate people ate was a way to keep Efron's spirits up. Maybe it would have helped the others too, but he was her father and on some level he was still the heart of the company. It mattered that he kept going, and it was harder to keep him going since these attacks had got worse, the Dunholmi more indiscriminate in the damage they did. It was as if they didn't care about the state of Estis anymore, as if they would rather destroy the place than risk it becoming free. She couldn't imagine what it took to see the world in that way, didn't want to imagine it. But a month ago she couldn't have imagined developing a routine to deal with devastated villages, and now here she was.

She pulled the hood of her cloak up against the rain, not worrying what it would do to her hair. She still wore the masks around her waist in case she needed them, but her only jewellery was the silver bangle Raul had made, her only charm the bronze one he'd given her for the road. She touched it with her fingertips, took strength from the promise of home. That was what she would bring these people, a chance to start rebuilding, a hope that the place they lived could survive.

They always started with lightly damaged buildings, looking for where they could make enough difference to be useful. That usually meant places that had been attacked with mallets or had their roofs torn off with hooks and ropes, not those that had been burned. A woman emerged as they approached one of them, a felling axe in her hand. Behind her, children and old people huddled beneath a roof that couldn't hold off the rain.

"Who are you?" the woman demanded, planting herself in front of the new arrivals.

"My name is Yasmi, this is Claudio. We're here to help."

"Who sent you?"

"Does it matter?"

The woman took a better grip on the axe. "You can see what our last visitors did."

"I'm sorry."

Yasmi pushed her hood back so that the woman could more clearly see her face. When they'd first done this, part of it had been a performance, summoning the spirit of all the tragedies she had ever acted out. After what she'd seen, she didn't need to act the part of sorrow anymore.

"If you're worried that we might hurt you, we can leave," she said as the rain ran down her face, plastering her hair to her cheeks. "But we have food, all that we've managed to gather since the last town like yours. We have tools and timber and carpenters who can help fix your homes."

The woman hesitated, then lowered her axe, suddenly looking unutterably weary.

"It could have been worse, I suppose," she said. "If we hadn't heard about trouble at other places. If we hadn't been ready to run and hide. Still, some folks didn't believe it, and there's only so much you can hide."

"I'm so sorry." Yasmi gestured toward the town square.

"My father's set up a shelter and there will be food once it's cooked. Take your family. We'll look into whether we can save your house."

"Thank you."

The woman waved and her family came timidly out. At her direction, they headed between the ruined buildings toward where Efron stood. She waited until they had all gone past, standing next to Yasmi in the rain.

"Is this because of Hound's Gap?" the woman asked.

"We've been on the road for a while, not keeping up with events," Yasmi said. "What happened at Hound's Gap?"

"They say there was a battle. That Estis lost. That Prince Raul almost died." She looked at Yasmi. "Some folk say he's dead, which is why he can't protect us from the Dunholmi. Others say Count Alder's hunting him and that's why they're doing all this. Did you really not hear?"

Yasmi felt like someone had dropped a boulder through her, ripping out her heart and flattening it in the dirt. She took a step back and clutched the bronze charm in her hand, squeezing it so tight it dug into her palm.

She remembered the last smile her mother had ever given her, lying amid sweat-soaked sheets, and then she remembered Raul lying in a hidden glade, smiling across a book.

Not again.

She wanted to run back to the wagon, to unhitch a horse and ride like fury, to gallop through days and darkness until she found someone from the army, someone who could tell her what had really happened, whether her beautiful, innocent innkeeper's son was lying dead.

But there were bodies hanging by the road, friends and families grieving them, children who needed to be fed. The certainty of what they had been through mattered more than her maybes.

It had to.

Still, she turned away from the woman, away from Claudio, away from the work she had insisted that they do. Shedding her cloak as she went, she walked away through the buildings. Her hands unhitched a mask from her belt. She didn't even look to see which one, what shape she would take on. All the mattered was not to be herself, to run off into the woods, to cower and tremble and hide from the world even if that wasn't fair on everyone else, to let out her feelings until she was ready to be herself again.

Chapter Sixteen
Routine Pain

Raul didn't know much about how bodies worked. As an innkeeper's son, he hadn't seen all the things that his neighbours had while working the land. A lamb stuck on its way out of its mother, leading to a desperate struggle to keep both alive. The accidents and diseases that afflicted sturdy highland cattle, and which couldn't just end on the butcher's block when the prize bull was at stake. Experience with the bodies of other animals that gave farmers an instinctive idea of how the human body worked, or didn't, as well as a string of fixes and formulas passed down the generations in a community where everyone's livelihood was interlinked. He hadn't seen the years of war his da had either, the hundreds of different ways a life could hang in the balance in the aftermath of battle, the devastating injuries and desperate cures. Even in the past year of struggle, he'd been too busy leading to take the time to learn these things, though he'd wanted to. After all, what could be more useful than knowing how to keep someone alive?

But even with his limited knowledge, he felt like he should be able to move, just a little, without it hurting. That didn't seem right. How could lifting his arm trigger an ache in his stomach? How could every step cause him to catch his breath? How could each shift of the bandages feel like it was scraping at his burned flesh despite the poultices between them? However tightly he clutched the flower charm that Drusil had given him or pressed his fingers against a lucky rabbit's foot, the pain persisted.

He tried to tell himself that he would get used to it, like he'd got used to sleeping in caves and under trees, like he'd got used to the weariness of long marches. But the weeks were passing, the weather growing warmer, and everything still hurt.

It wasn't fair.

"I suppose life never is," he said to himself. "No more fair than we make it."

"What's that?" Valens turned to look at him. All his da's movements seemed sharp at the moment, twisting about at the slightest sound from Raul. Dealing with that was tiring in itself.

"Nothing." Raul leaned on the staff that Quintae had made for him, cutting a fallen branch to just the right height, trimming away the protrusions and carving the head into a pierced moon. A substitute for his missing strength and for the sword he'd left on the battlefield. "Just thinking out loud."

"Easier than keeping it in your head sometimes."

They emerged from the trees where their current shelter was built, out into the open ground beyond the forest's edge. Deciding where to camp was different now than it had been before. They still had to think about water supplies and how they'd get back onto the roads, about having enough space for everyone, but they had to think about running and hiding as well, about where their cover would be and how the leaders would get away if Dunholmi raiders appeared. Thinking about that felt like looking at his wounds, vulnerability and past defeat laid bare, hope for the future feeling slimmer than ever.

Not gone, though. They'd first built the rebellion from a handful of people hiding out in a theatre, and they were still far stronger than that. Not the full might they had been, but thousands once more, bands of survivors following the directions Ferra sent out in the claws of bats and birds, finding their way back to the army. Some would never return, too hurt or scared or captured by the Dunholmi, mercenaries deciding that the pay wasn't good enough. And there were the dead. But more survivors were approaching now up the road from the river lands, a Saditchi company in their black and yellow, and others would follow.

"You don't need to come out for this." Valens leaned toward Raul and lowered his voice. "I can send the leaders to you once I've shown them where to camp."

Even in the aftermath of defeat, Valens was setting everything in order, arranging training, patrols, and sentries, planning for how and where they would march out so they never stayed in place for too long. It was heartening to see how quickly the rebels fell back into obeying his orders, instinctively knowing that he would get the work done. If only everything was that easy.

"They need to see me," Raul said. "To know that I'm still here for them. That I'm alive."

Valens rubbed his brow, wrinkles doubling up as he squeezed them between finger and thumb. His frown didn't fade, but he nodded.

"Come on, then."

They walked down the meadow, past rows of tents and improvised shelters, past warriors who stood attentively as they passed. Taking a hand off the staff would have slowed him more, turning their sedate procession into an obviously pained hobble, so he nodded and smiled, called out the names of as many as he knew, did his best to keep smiling.

The rebels had known that the Saditchi were coming and set aside space for them. Prisca was already there, one hand on her own walking staff, greeting Princess Nydia and her captains. They all turned and bowed as Raul approached, while behind them the corsairs started pitching camp.

"Your Highness." Nydia looked him up and down, then nodded approvingly. "My people say that scars are the measure of a man, and you must look very manly under there. Something for me to look forward to."

One of her captains grinned, and passing corsairs jeered encouragingly. Raul fought to keep his composure even as heat rushed through his cheeks. Yasmi would have been able to hide a reaction like that, could even have taught him how, but it was probably a good thing that she wasn't here.

"It's good to see you, Your Highness." He bowed as best he could and hoped that the movement hid the flinch of pain it caused. Straightening was worse, but he was braced for that, and it helped him keep his expression serious, as befitted a ruler rallying his allies in desperate circumstances. "I see that you've come out with souvenirs of your own."

"This?" Nydia's fingers brushed the dark stitches trailing across her pale cheek, but paused before the dressing on her ear. Judging by its size, a chunk of that ear was gone for good. "I would tell you that my opponent came out worse, but who could tell amid the chaos of combat? I'd always been told that battles on land were more orderly than boarding actions, but it seems you northerners have embraced our ways." Her hand went down to her thigh, drawing attention to a bulge beneath her loose trousers. "I'll save the others to show you later, but right now I have a gift."

She waved toward a horse-drawn wagon that was rolling up the meadow, one corsair at the reins and another standing on top, waving a black and yellow flag, drawing cheers from the rebels he passed. The canvas covering bulged around boxes and sacks.

"Produce liberated from a Dunholmi supply column," she said. "We would have brought more, but oxen are slow and our pursuers were persistent."

"Pursuers?" Valens got the word out before Raul could. "What have you led here?"

Raul laid a hand on his da's arm. "I'm sure that Her Highness wouldn't make such a mistake."

"Be careful with your certainties, my prince." Nydia winked. "What my people call a bold adventure might be labelled rash and reckless in some quarters."

"I knew it." Valens raised his voice to shout across the camp. "Drusil, we need to—"

"No." Tightening the hold on his da's arm hurt Raul, but it quieted him. "My princess, for the sake of the love between our two countries, please stop teasing General Valens. It's hard to see the fun in life when it's your own home at stake."

"Fine." She sighed and fluttered her eyelashes. "For the sake of love." Then her voice hardened into one of command as she turned to the wagon. "Yisprani, find Drusil and get that added to the supplies. Harito, make sure the camp's set straight. Tollosa, head count, make sure we haven't lost anyone on the road." Then her attention was back on Raul, her voice soft again. "Perhaps we could retire to your tent. You could tell me about who remains and what you have planned for us next."

Sheer relief made him want to say yes. Of all the people fighting here, Nydia was the one who could most easily have abandoned them in the face of defeat, separating her nation from the stink of failure and hurrying south for the battles that were coming there. But here she was, and even if he didn't know her reasons, he still understood the value of reinforcing them, of showing consideration and tightening their alliance.

But the moment he took a pause in the business of leading, caught a breath or a moment to think, that was when the pain grabbed his attention, a stiff wind that whipped away his energy. And if the gaps in the pain, the moments of attention, were growing longer every day, they were still too few and too short. He needed to get out of sight before it became too much, reducing him to a trembling, weeping ball of agony. Who would keep following a leader like that?

"You should see to your people first," he said. "We can talk later, once the other commanders are free."

"No time to ourselves?" That spark in her eyes was irrepressible. "What a shame, but we'll make up for it once the war's won."

This time he didn't blush, too busy standing up without shaking. They bowed to each other, then Raul turned to head back up the meadow, leaning hard on his beautifully carved staff.

"I should come with you," Valens said quietly. "Change your dressings."

"Don't be daft, Da," Raul said. "You've got an army to lead."

"I've got a son to look after."

"Other people can do that. Besides, these dressings were fresh this morning."

"An infusion then, to deaden the pain."

"Those things deaden too much of my mind."

"Maybe I could—"

"General Valens, as your prince I'm ordering you to focus on the army and not on me. Do you understand?"

Valens's scowl deepened.

"You wanted me to be a warrior and a leader," Raul said. "Let me be that, with everything it brings."

"All I wanted for you was to be happy. This..." Valens gestured at the camp around them. "This was meant for someone else. Someone we imagined twenty years ago."

"Well, that person's not here, and I am." In the shadows at the edge of the woods, Raul let himself sag against the staff.

"Fine." Valens looked across the camp, gaze moving from one challenge to the next. "You rest and recover."

"And you do the same once the work's done."

"I'm not the one who needs rest."

"We all do." Raul didn't have the strength to reach out, just to cling to his staff and hobble forward one step at a time.

"It gets better."

Raul managed to look back over his shoulder and see his da standing framed by the trees. The fingers of his remaining hand touched the stump of his wrist.

"Not just the pain," Valens continued. "The defeats. They get bearable. Give yourself time."

Past him, more new arrivals were approaching the camp, the skin of the injured rebellion closing over its wounds.

"Thanks, Da."

Raul hobbled on into the woods, feeling wearier than ever. He hadn't even tried bearing the burden of defeat yet. First, he had to learn to cope with the routine pain, then he could face something worse.

———————•———————

Valens was used to the last night in a camp, that moment before an army marched out, leaving behind whatever comfort and convenience they'd built up over a few days, weeks, even months. Favourite tree stump seats. Improvised shelters that kept the rain out better than moth-eaten canvas. Bread ovens built out of logs and mud. A warrior's life was a string of goodbyes, but that didn't stop it having meaning, especially when you weren't sure where you'd be resting next.

He knew, of course. He'd made that decision, something

he couldn't get used to yet. And he spread the word as he made his way around the camp, discussing logistics with other leaders, but there was a difference between being told where you were going and understanding what the place would be like. He had scouting reports and the knowledge of why he'd chosen the place. All the ordinary warriors had was a name.

Campfires drove back the darkness, staining faces in fiery shades. Around one of them, Saditchi corsairs were finishing a barrel of beer rather than have to carry it or leave it behind. At another, a company drawn from the crafting families of Deladale were singing a song about weaving hope. It was the first time he'd heard the song since Hound's Gap and it tugged at his chest, made him want to sit and sing with them, to sink into the bittersweet message. But he remembered the awkwardness of a captain joining him and his comrades around a fire back in the day, the strained laughter and stiff shoulders. Instead of sitting, he raised a hand in acknowledgement and walked on.

Hundreds of fires, thousands of warriors. An army again. Diminished, but still singing. Sturdy farmhands from the Winding Vales who now worked with shields instead of ploughs. Barge hands from the rivers, their pole hooks turned into spears. Mounted scouts from the border plains, the ones Biallo had ridden with.

Poor Biallo, one more to mourn. For the first time in a while, Valens felt the absence of his hand, of his fingers, of the ring he'd worn in memory of Fabia, the first death in this campaign back when the other war was ending. He wished she was still with them. She wouldn't have minded having him by her fire no matter how high and mighty he got.

He passed the other fires with little more than a wave and a nod. Some raised cups or wineskins in his direction, cheered his name. He let himself smile. It wasn't so bad, being a general. On balance, he'd earned more respect than resentment, which was as good as any commander could do, and he didn't have to tolerate anyone else's terrible decisions.

At least there was one fire where he could sit, up at the top of camp by the edge of the trees. The fire where Drusil and Prisca sat sketching in the dirt, while Silvano and Earl Tordesse exchanged accounts of how they'd survived Hound's Gap and found their way back to the rest. They all nodded greetings as he approached, and no one stiffened or stopped their conversation.

Valens took the seat by the fire that had become his place in the short time they'd been here. He rested his stump against the end of the log where they'd carved a crossed-out eye, like many more across the camp. There was a goat next to it now, cut in Quintae's precise, angular style, ready to grant them a safe journey the next day.

Someone had left a bowl of food for him. Bread, roasted meat, an apple. He set it in his lap and started to eat, working quickly and methodically through it all. Sure, his next meal was more certain now that he was in charge of the supplies, but his body responded out of habit as much as hunger, fingers reaching for one piece after the next.

Nights like this had been what he lived for once, the moments where the hard work and violence subsided but camaraderie remained. Now he felt the absence of something else. Of Efron's hand in his, of their quiet conversations, of the actor's voice suddenly rising into a joke or a song.

Nydia emerged from the woods. Prisca shifted along the log where she sat, making space for the Saditchi princess, but instead Nydia walked around the fire to Valens. Prisca's eyes narrowed for a moment before she turned back to her conversation with Drusil.

"You've been with him?" Valens asked quietly.

"Only to talk." Nydia added a log to the fire, then sat down beside him. Disturbed by the new arrival, other logs scattered sparks into the night. "He's not ready for anything else yet."

Watching her from the corner of his eye, Valens took a bite from his apple. Had that just been about Raul's wound, or something else? Did all Saditchi love this sort of conversation, full of layered meaning and innuendo, or was it just their princess? Either way, she would have been better off taking that seat with Prisca.

"Too much pain to talk?"

"Oh, he tried." She shook her head. "He's stubborn, your prince, but I suppose he was raised to it."

"Got to be stubborn to survive this."

He waved the half-eaten apple, a gesture that could have been meant for the camp, the conflict they were caught up in, or the whole world. Maybe he could manage Saditchi conversation after all.

Across the fire, Prisca glanced their way, then turned her attention to the flames, probably looking for signs to guide them again. Her cheeks were sunken, the skin under her eyes sagging, and her finger trembled as she sketched a shape in the air. Eighteen years together, living in that inn out in the Winding Vales, and he'd never seen her look as sick as this. Rough living and the shadow of defeat had worn them all down, but Prisca showed it more than most. He hoped she saw something helpful in the fire, because she needed it right now; they all did.

"Wasn't sure you'd stick with us." Valens turned his attention back to Nydia. "Thought your brother might call you back."

"He still might, but I think it would be a mistake. Your stubborn, charismatic prince will be back in action sooner than he thinks, and you people are all smart enough to learn from your mistakes."

"You think we'll win?"

"I think you might, and if not, then I can be called home later. But on our way back to you, we saw the way the Dunholmi have changed. They fight with bitterness now and no mercy, hurting the people they want to rule. That won't go in their favour."

Valens chewed up the core of the apple, spat out seeds, and tossed the stalk into the fire.

"You talked with Raul about this?" he asked.

"No, and I doubt you did either, though your scouts must have told you."

"They did."

"Still you wait and regroup."

"The Dunholmi want us to charge to the rescue without thinking. That's a sure way to lose, which hurts people more."

"But you don't think His Highness would see it that way."

"I don't think he's ready to make that decision yet."

"Then when?"

Prisca stood, her legs trembling. The firelight cast her face into harsh shadows, eyes vanishing into darkness.

"I see three crowns," she said, finger tracing peaks against the flames. "One." She pointed into the woods. "Two." She pointed at Nydia. "Junia makes three. We'll find her tomorrow. Then it's time to stop licking our wounds and make a council of war."

Valens stood too. He wanted to argue back, not just because Raul needed more rest, not just to keep Prisca in her place, but because he was the general and the orders should come from him. But like it or not, she was right. She often was.

"We're three days' march from Barrowblack," he said. "It's a good defensive place. We'll have our council there, whoever we pick up along the way."

It wasn't exactly agreeing with what she'd said, or disagreeing either. He waited to see whether she was in a mood to push back. If she had the will for a fight, then she was saving it, because she just nodded curtly.

"They say the ancients buried people under Barrowblack, back before the founding of Estis." Earl Tordesse twisted the black ring around his finger. "Is it wise to make camp somewhere haunted?"

"Don't tell me you're more afraid of ghosts than of Dunholm," Silvano said.

"I don't fear either as much as your cooking." Tordesse tapped his plate. It was good to see the earl and the docker captain spar like this, desperate circumstances forging a warrior's sort of friendship. "But superstitious might cause disquiet."

"Remind them that it's their ancestors buried at this place," Nydia said. "Surely, any ghosts will be on their side?"

Valens nodded. It was a good story and that mattered more than who was really buried there, if anyone was at all.

"Barrowblack, then." Prisca picked up her staff and hobbled away.

As if they'd all been waiting for that decision, people started rising from around the fire, heading off to sleep. Valens would have liked to do the same, but the absence that left him feeling hollowed out was making it hard to sleep. He'd wait a while longer, until his eyelids properly drooped, then let the night claim him.

As he sat back down, only Nydia remained.

"Now will you tell him?" she asked.

"In two more days."

"Such splendid stubbornness." She laughed. "I came north ready to make the most of whoever my brother was set on marrying me to. I didn't expect to like them, but your prince has won me over. Your son."

There was a whole other conversation to be had here, about things Raul had said in her absence, about what would happen to their alliance if he really turned down the marriage. But that wasn't what weighed on Valens's mind now. Her words touched something inside him, a tension he'd been trying to ignore. Whatever Raul meant to him, to the rest of the world he was the heir to the royal family, and that had to be how he was seen.

"I just looked after the lad for a while," he said. "A humble warrior doing his duty."

"I don't believe that for a minute." To his surprise, she took his hand. "I hope that I can be good enough for him. Good enough for you."

She let go, stood up, and bowed good night. As she walked away, he looked down at his hand and thought of another hand holding it, not Efron's this time but that of a little boy so full of love and wonder that it had touched a weathered old heart.

His eyelids drooped. Time to sleep.

Chapter Seventeen
The Prince

Nobody knew for certain where the great earthen ring of Barrowblack came from, though many had stories. According to some, it had been created just after the dawn of the world, when Laughing Loftus cried for the first and only time, his single tear so huge that it scattered the soil, creating a circle of raised earth. Others said that it was an animal pen built by ogres when the world was theirs, a place for holding monstrous cattle the size of houses. One line of scholarship argued that it was a fort built long before the founding of Estis, a place local people retreated to in times of war and where they buried their dead to keep them safe. Now that he'd seen its earth ridges standing proud from the surrounding meadows, grass rooting their steep sides in place, Raul had a theory of his own. He liked to think that it had been a theatre, its sloping walls once lined with seats, with plays performed in the centre. The actors would have needed supernaturally powerful voices to be heard from one end to the other, but there was probably a charm for that. Maybe they'd bound sound into jewellery like Drusil bound sunlight into the metal of her lanterns; stranger things had happened in the world.

Those walls were several times Raul's height, and from their top he could see for miles across the surrounding countryside. The Dunholmi wouldn't catch them by surprise here, and if they came, then they would be attacking one of the toughest positions the landscape could provide. Nothing short of a castle would give them the same defence, and no castle was large enough to hold the whole rebel army, not now that they were regrouping in earnest.

But the Dunholmi didn't have to find them to cause terrible harm. Pillars of smoke beyond the woods and hills signalled the devastation taking place across Estis. The country couldn't afford for him to sit and wait.

Using his staff and a supporting hand from one of his bodyguards, Raul pushed himself upright. His da had been right, the pain was getting better. He just needed to be patient with the pain and with himself.

That would have been easier if there wasn't so much pressure. He'd managed to postpone the council meeting for a day after they arrived at Barrowblack, giving himself time to recover from the journey and from what Valens and Nydia told him about the Dunholmi's destructive acts. Even a day was probably more delay than he should have taken.

Halfway down the slope, he spotted a pair of birds overhead, the two of them darting around each other as they rose and fell through the sky. At times, they seemed on the verge of flying apart, but then they would find each other again, their paths synchronising for a while, finding harmony in the shared journey. It seemed like a good omen for what he was facing, and he stood watching for a little while, hands tight around his staff, enjoying one last moment of peace.

"Your Highness." One of his bodyguards stepped uncertainly forward. "General Valens said it was important not to be late."

The script really had changed. Before Hound's Gap, arriving after the others was a way to assert his dominance and prove who was in charge. But now everyone was warier, less willing to accept disagreement or disrespect from each other, possibly even from their king. The army had come back together out of hope, but keeping it united would take more care. That was what today's council was all about.

He hobbled on down the inside of Barrowblack and through the army camped there, past the flicker of cooking fires, the crack of training weapons, the clang of a hastily assembled forge. Between teams of engineers raising wooden palisades, sentries stood on the earth walls, silhouetted against the blue sky. Two of the rebels with the best eyesight were positioned on the crenellated roof of a tower in the centre of the ring, surveying the countryside beyond their defences. Unlike the rest of the place, the tower wasn't a mystery. It had been built by the local earl three generations back, supposedly to watch for bandits but really as a way of asserting himself on the landscape. Like the wooden forts of the Dunholmi, it was as much about what it showed as what it did. Walking up the steps and through the double doors into the ground floor, Raul imagined what it would be like to enter as one of the earl's subjects with this stone edifice towering over you, rising to meet your master.

Across the camp, one of the bears from the Withered Hills roared, and another roared back. Raul smiled. Compared with them, nothing made with human hands seemed quite so intimidating.

The rest of the council were waiting one floor up, sat on a circle of stools around a cavernous audience chamber. Raul's high-backed chair was near the top of the stairs, saving him a walk across the room, and he sank into it gratefully, leaving his staff leaning against the side. After a moment to catch his breath and loosen the muscles he had clenched against the pain, he looked around a selection of silent, expectant faces.

They were a little diminished since the last time they'd met, but not as badly as he'd feared. As usual, Prisca and Queen Junia sat on one side of the room, surrounded by noble war leaders, while the new guard sat around Drusil and Silvano on the other side. Ferra and a couple more from the Withered Hills sat at the fringe of Silvano's group, a pair of ravens perched on their shoulders. Opposite Raul, Valens and Nydia sat with one of her captains, a borderland between the factions. He wished he had Yasmi here, to steady him when he was uncertain and to guide his performance in his role as leader and royal prince. She would have been so much better at this than he was, but he had to perform without her.

"Thank you all for coming," he said. "Both coming back to me after Hound's Gap and coming here today to talk."

"Where else could our honour take us, Your Highness?"

Earl Tordesse said. "And what greater honour could there be than to fight alongside you after you almost gave your life for our country?"

Servants came around pouring drinks. Nothing strong this time; they all needed to keep their heads clear. Third ale, the last brew of the grain, better to drink than water but not as fortifying or as tasty as what came before. Even after a long gulp, Raul's mouth still felt dry. A lingering remnant of his fever, or something else? Everything seemed to make him uncomfortable today, including the fact that someone was serving him. Once he could lift a full jug without his hand shaking, and once the political situation was stable enough to let a prince escape expectations, he would start pouring his own drinks again.

"Your Highness, if you need more time..." Silvano's voice trailed off, his expression uncertain. However well-intentioned the start of that sentence had been, the end couldn't go anywhere useful.

"I appreciate the sentiment, Captain," Raul said. "But the country needs our time and our attention. The Dunholmi are calling out for it."

That brought uncomfortable laughter from some and muttered curses from others. Queen Junia sat stone-faced. Was she waiting for something?

"Our forces fought bravely at Hound's Gap," he said. "We fought with skill and determination, and came close to victory. But in the end, we couldn't stand against the power that was unleashed.

"Jarrag," Ferra said solemnly. She held a doll made out of

grass and leaves, the sort of puppet the Withering Folk used in important discussions. "Felt it when the fire came, so."

"Who's Jarrag?" Earl Tordesse asked.

"A spirit from the wilderness," Raul said. "A force of fire and destruction that pretends to be a god. We went looking for magic to help our cause and found Jarrag instead. I thought we'd left it behind, but apparently Count Alder had other ideas."

"You came back empty-handed," Queen Junia said. "Alder didn't. It seems that one of you knew what you were doing."

People stiffened in their seats. Several glanced from her to Raul and then back again.

Should he react with anger, as a king who had been disrespected in his own court? Even if he'd had the strength, he wasn't sure that he would have had the will.

"We brought back friends, Queen Junia," he said. "Just like you did."

"He brought back magic more powerful by far than anything we can do, and now we have to face him on those terms, all thanks to your jaunt into the hills."

Raul took a deep breath, tried to imagine where this new attitude of Junia's came from. She was hurt and frightened, just like the rest of them, desperate and lashing out. It was only natural, especially to a woman who was used to being in control of her own destiny. Best not to pick a fight, but to give her time to come around instead.

"Alder is just one man," Raul said. "He can't be everywhere at once."

There was a restless energy in his legs, but he didn't have

the strength to stay up for long. Instead, he tapped his fingers against the arm of his seat.

"We tried fighting the Dunholmi head-on using old, familiar ways," he continued. "It didn't work and now we're weakened, so we need to try something new."

"Of course." Junia looked at him with disdain. "You want to change everything, don't you?"

Raul looked at Prisca, whose lips pressed tight together as she met his gaze. He'd wondered how much she shared with Junia about the conversation in the cave and his plans for the future. He hadn't meant it to be a secret, but there was a difference between that and telling the person most likely to take offence, the one most invested in the country as it had been. After all the effort Prisca had put into planning a revolt with him as its figurehead, he hadn't expected her to take such a risk, but it seemed that winning her way was as important as victory itself.

"Your Majesty," Tordesse said quietly. "Have a care for who you're talking to. This is your grandson, our rightful king."

"No, he isn't."

Raul sucked in a sharp breath. His whole body felt tight, like her words were a fist crushing him. He'd expected arguments, resistance, fierce debate over how best to fight, but he hadn't been ready for this. So much was built around one lie, it hadn't occurred to him that Junia might tell the truth and risk shattering the movement for which she'd waited a generation.

Except that this wasn't the movement she'd been waiting for. She was looking for the restoration of an old order, everything back as it had been, while he was aiming for something else.

The air was heavy with confusion, council members exchanging uncertain glances. He felt sorry for Prisca, sitting beside the queen, her careful scheme unravelling. Her hand trembled in her lap, but somehow her expression remained calm.

"What do you mean?" Tordesse asked, his brow furrowing.

"My grandson died at birth alongside his mother, Princess Aemiria, days before the fall of Pavuno. This boy who makes pretensions toward the throne is nothing more than an orphan, snatched up at random as the city fell and raised to fake his way into this role."

Raul sank in his seat. For months, he'd barely felt the weight of his own lies, his mind swept up in the urgent needs of war. Now that burden slammed down upon him again, and with it dread at how his friends and comrades would respond.

"He's got the birthmark," Silvano said. "Like in that play about Balbianus."

"That so-called birthmark was branded onto him, and you might want to think about who arranged the play."

"His sword..." one of the nobles said.

"Another falsehood, no older than he is. Do you really think that an ancient sword of our royal line would have been kept all these years and not seen around court? I would invite you to examine it and judge the true age of its steel, except that it was lost during our recent humiliation."

"He fits the prophecies," Drusil said, but the uncertainty in her voice matched the mood of the room.

"Prophecies can say whatever you want, especially when

the prophet is a politician. Ask Minister Servita, who did such a careful job weaving fact into fiction that no one could tell the difference. But she raised this boy to be a symbol, a tool for our nation's restoration, and if he can't do what he's meant for, then it's time for things to change."

The room was silent. Raul felt the weight of countless eyes on him—the false prince for whom they had fought, bled, and mourned. Shocked gazes turned betrayed, and even angry, as it sank in how much each had lost in the service of a lie. Raul felt as if the ground had been swept out from under him and he was teetering on a cliff edge, ready to fall. But strangely, he felt a wave of relief as well, finally free of the guilt that rose like bile each time he lied to friends' faces. While he knew that he should deny it, keep up a myth they all wanted to believe and that could hold their rebellion together, he also knew that he couldn't.

"I'm sorry," he said to them. "At the start, I thought it was real, and once I found out the truth, I couldn't see another way to make the rebellion happen."

"Excuses." Junia shook her head. "Your fraud is at an end. As King Cataldo's widow, I am the closest survivor to the throne. I will dictate our strategy, in war and in peace. We will see the true Estis restored, not some twisted child's dream built upon a lie.

"To ensure the continuity of good governance, Minister Servita has agreed to act as my chamberlain and first minister. Whatever mistakes she has made in the past, she steered us to this point, and she will redeem herself by ensuring our victory."

At last, Prisca couldn't meet Raul's gaze anymore, and he

was glad of it. He couldn't face her himself, hearing that she was part of this, that she'd abandoned him rather than let him build something better. She'd told him before that she loved him, but he was starting to think that maybe she only loved what she could control.

"You." Valens, his voice ragged with fury, stormed across the room.

Tordesse leapt up, hand on the hilt of his sword, standing between him and the queen, but the old warrior's rage wasn't directed at Junia, it was for the woman sitting next to her.

"You betrayed that boy twice," Valens said, spittle flying from his lips, finger jabbing past Tordesse toward Prisca. "Once by raising him in a lie and now by turning against him. I helped you the first time, but I won't do it again."

He strode over to Raul and sank to one knee.

"There's only one monarch I'm fighting for."

He bowed his head for a moment, then rose, as solemn as a priest in temple, and went to stand at Raul's back.

Raul swallowed and fought back tears, seeing that even now, with the rest of the country against them, his da was there for him.

"You disappoint me, General," Junia said scornfully. "But you don't surprise me. I trust that the rest of you will show loyalty to the true throne?"

Stools scraped across stone as nobles got to their feet and went to stand behind her. The two remaining mercenary captains, bought and paid for by the former exiles, exchanged a wary look before they joined in. Raul's heart sank as he watched the people he'd led walk away from him.

"Now," Junia said with a satisfied smile. "Let's get down to—"

"No." Drusil stood. Dressed in her leather apron, hands soot-stained and clothes charred by sparks from the forge, she couldn't have looked more different from the nobles, finely dressed in their embroidered tunics despite weeks on the march. With her strength, she could have crushed any one of them barehanded, but she shook, a blacksmith facing down a queen. "I'm here because I believe in Raul. I don't care who anyone's descended from or what the prophecies say, I care about actions. Without him, we'd still be living under the Dunholmi. That's my prince right there."

If her words left Raul reeling, the bow she gave knocked him back in his seat. Then she was standing behind him alongside Valens.

"We'll manage without the blacksmith and the cripple," Junia sneered.

"Is that how you see it?" Silvano stood. "If I can choose between a leader who listens and one who wants to put me in my place, I know what I'll choose, and all the other dockers with me."

As he walked over to stand with Valens, other captains followed, every one of them bowing to Raul as they passed. He felt elated, bewildered, not sure what to say or to do.

Ferra didn't even spare Junia a glance, just looked at Raul. "You still fixing to keep our deal?"

"I am."

"Me too. Word is word."

Then she was with the others beside Raul, and though the

nobles and mercenaries were important for their armed companies, he found that he didn't care what any of them thought. He sat straighter even as his injuries screamed in protest. Across from him, Prisca and Junia glanced back and forth, eyes darting as they tried to count the sides. Perhaps that was their problem, that they could only measure things in how to win, not whether it was worth winning.

Junia looked past Earl Tordesse, who still stood protectively in front of her, his hand on his sword.

"Princess Nydia," the queen said. "I trust that, as the voice of Saditch, you will see sense in this matter."

The princess pressed a hand to her mouth, but her laughter still burst through. Junia stared, a picture of shock at the younger woman.

"You think this is seeing sense?" Nydia asked. "Having this argument right now?"

She laughed again and Raul found himself laughing with her, swept up in the unravelling tension and the absurdity of it all. Here they were, desperately fighting for their lives, yet their elders, the people who supposedly had the breeding and experience to make the right choices, had descended to infighting. The stupidity of it was tragic but it was funny too, right up until the laughter made his stomach shake and he buckled over, wincing and clutching his wound.

When he looked up, Nydia was looking at him, wiping an imagined tear from the corner of her eye.

"I would declare the engagement over," she said, "but my brother loves a bold adventurer as much as I do. We can work out who owes what once the waves settle, but in the meantime, the forces of Saditch will fight alongside whoever takes charge, and we won't be taking a side."

There it was. Raul looked at the commanders assembled behind him, then across the room at those clustered behind Junia and his ma. Weighing up their followings, it was as close to an even split as things could be. Now what?

At last, Prisca looked at Raul.

"I understand your resistance to surrender," she said. "But you're an intelligent young man and I taught you better than this. Without the façade of legitimacy, you cannot retain your... your..."

Raul could have spoken into that hesitation, but whatever his ma had done, she deserved the chance to speak for herself.

"You cannot continue to lead," she said. Even with her fingers clasping her knee, she couldn't hide her trembling. "If you try, you will bring disaster on us all."

Part of Raul wanted to give in for the sake of unity, to hold together what he'd brought this far. But that would mean abandoning the people who had fought for him all this time and who believed in a new Estis. There was a better way to run the country, and it didn't come from reverting to the past.

"Hold," a low voice said. It took Raul a moment to realise that it was Earl Tordesse, still standing alone in the middle of the room, arms folded across his chest. The earl looked steadily at Raul. "When this is over, are you still planning to claim the throne?"

Raul shook his head. Why would he? He'd only done that to keep up the lie, inspiring people and binding them together.

Now that lie was ripped open, its rough edges threatening to tear them apart, there was no more reason to play the role.

Tordesse turned, and though he looked at Junia he was clearly addressing all the nobles.

"Your Majesty," he said, "my loyalty remains with you and with the royal house, and I will serve you once this war is won. But Princess Nydia is right—this, here and now, is foolishness. This young man bound an army together, he led it from one victory to another, and a single defeat doesn't undo that. If you try to replace him while we teeter on the brink, you could plunge us into disaster. I won't take that risk, for our country or for your noble house.

"Until this is over, I fight under the command of Raul Warborn. Once we're free, my sword is yours."

He crossed the floor to stand behind the stunned Raul. With a movement that seemed more embarrassed than decisive, several of the nobles made to follow him. Junia let out an affronted scoff before she rose from her stool and swept out, past Raul and down the stairs, leaving her commanders with him.

Trembling in his seat, Raul tried to take it all in, but too much had happened too fast, and he needed time to think. Better to wait another day here in the safety of Barrowblack than to rush into the wrong strategy while everyone was distracted by politics.

"We'll gather again tomorrow," he said. "Here, an hour after dawn. Until then, go and rest, tell your people what happened, they're going to hear about it anyway."

He wanted to raise his fist and lead them in a uniting cry,

to call out the new moon that rose, but that was tangled in the lie. Instead, he gave a dismissive wave.

"I've got to go," Valens said, squeezing his shoulder as the others hurried past. "Tell the legion my way before someone else does it theirs. You going to be all right?"

"I'll be fine," Raul replied.

Prisca hobbled past, hiding in the wave of nobles and mercenaries rushing for the stairs and for a chance to gossip about what they'd seen.

Once he was almost alone, he reached for his staff.

"Allow me, my prince." Nydia took the staff from where it rested and held it out to him.

"I'm not anybody's prince," he said.

Nydia laughed once again. "After today's display, you most definitely are."

Chapter Eighteen
A Royal Coven

Inevitably, there were desertions, small spaces within the earth walls of Barrowblack that had been occupied one day and were empty the next. Tents that vanished in the night. Faces missing from around campfires. Awkward exchanges as people left their comrades behind.

The surprise for Raul wasn't how many people left, but how few. Like the nobles following Junia, the ordinary people who had followed him into rebellion had been lied to from the start. That sort of revelation should have shaken their faith into dust.

"Is it true?" a man fletching arrows asked as Raul limped past. "Were you really an orphan from Pavuno?"

"I was."

"My mam died when the city fell." The fletcher carefully pressed a feathered flight into the glue around the arrow's end. "Bad business. We'll get them back for it though, eh?"

Raul walked on, aware of all the eyes on him. That wasn't

new in itself, but the mood was different. Subdued in some places, excited in others.

"I don't care where you come from," a young woman said as she ground a whetstone along the blade of her axe. "I saw you fighting at Hewed and a dozen other places. You stand your ground, so will I."

He wished that he could take credit for these displays of loyalty, but he knew how hard the other commanders had worked to keep people in place. Valens had told the Imperial Legion straight after the confrontation with the council, given them a handful of heartbeats to decide if they were staying, then set them to training, marching back and forth in time to a song about the rising moon. Silvano had taken his cue from Valens, and soon half the companies in camp were training while Drusil set her people to making swords and raising palisades. No time for them to gossip until the first shock of the news had passed. No acknowledgement that the day was different from any other. They prevented the rebellion from being swept away in the first rain of a strange season, which gave Raul time to work out how he would hold them together as the waters rose.

After an evening in which the camp bustled like an anthill and agitated conversations filled the air, the following day seemed almost normal. A little louder, the atmosphere a little more strained, but not a place that had been turned upside down. If anything, they were more productive than before, people putting their all into their work, whether as a distraction or as a sign of their commitment.

After the drama of the previous day, the council of war was

a muted meeting from which it was hard to draw opinions. They settled on a few more days of preparation, time to train and to arm while their scouts mapped out Dunholmi movements. In an ideal world they would have been swinging into action, but time to regroup meant time for Raul to work on some other changes. He limped through the camp, picking out people he'd noticed over the past year and more. A few who paid particular attention to the patterns of the world or had a gift for putting the pieces together. A handful of others who made particularly effective charms. He made sure that a couple of them came from among Junia's exiles, although he didn't know them so well, drawing on people from across the rebel forces, a show of unity.

Wanting to impress on them the seriousness of the moment, he set his stage carefully, leading them into the stone tower where only the council normally went, sitting them down around a table with cups and jugs of ale but also with a bag of sand, a pile of feathers, odd pieces of string. Drusil waited with a pile of books in the seat next to Raul's.

"Most of you don't know each other," Raul said, "but you will soon. We're going to work together."

No one even reached for a cup. All twelve of them sat staring at him with varying degrees of admiration, uncertainty, and suspicion. Picking up a full jug was more strain than Raul was used to. He clenched his teeth to keep from trembling, but he managed to pour for himself, Drusil, and the people either side of them, then passed the jug on. He couldn't conjure comfort out of nowhere, but the gesture made them all a little less stiff, a little less wary.

"How many of you know what a coven is?" he asked.

The hands that went up included both of the people he'd picked from the exiled forces. That was good, a chance to show that he valued them. He nodded to the one with the short-cropped curls, a woman named Cloia.

"It's a group of diviners," she said. "Working together to read the world."

"And to reshape it," her companion added. He was a round man named Ivus, wearing the robes of a scholar or senior servant, and he gestured at Drusil with his cup. "Is that why you're here? I've heard about your sunlight lanterns and the shields enchanted to be hard as stone."

"Not quite stone yet," Drusil said. "But we're getting there."

"The late King Cataldo had a coven," Raul said. "It was one of our country's greatest strengths. On ordinary days, they offered guidance on where the world was going, how he could best influence it. On their most extraordinary day, they made the ground open up and swallow an enemy charge.

"We need to do that again, bringing together the knowledge that's spread through Estis, the skills in reading signs and crafting charms. That's why I've brought you here, to be the beginnings of a new coven."

At the far end of the table, a man was shaking his head.

"No, I..." He stood. "I'm sorry, Your..." The word "Highness" hung like a possibility before its promise disappeared. "This is what got us invaded. I won't do it."

"It's important that you only do this if you're happy with it." Raul looked around the table. "Would anybody else like to leave?"

A couple looked uncertain but none stood up. After a few moments the man headed for the stairs and disappeared from view.

"I don't know much divination," Ivus said, straightening the sleeves of his robes. "Just some things to look for in the birds and the wind."

"I'll teach you what I know about divination, and Drusil will teach you how to forge powerful charms." Raul patted the pile of books. "We'll learn from these together, and from each other. I've never been in a coven before, but people do their best when everybody's skills play their part."

"Will we be able to do like Count Alder?" Cloia asked. "Summon fire? Burn down our enemies?"

There were excited expressions at that thought, and frightened ones too. Some of them must have seen terrible things at Hound's Gap. For better and for worse, he couldn't live up to that.

"Count Alder was using a different sort of power," he said. "Maybe one day, we'll be able to match it. For now, it's going to be a lot more mundane. Charms for protection or to keep blades sharp. Signs to guide our strategy. I have one big thing that I want us to work on together, but—"

Familiar footsteps on the stairs made him stop. Prisca appeared and looked across the group like she was assessing animals to take to market. Judging by her sneer, she didn't think they would fetch much of a price. Scooping sand out of the bag in the middle of the table, she let it run through her fingers.

"So it's true." Her face was pale and her movements jerky, but her voice was as strong as ever. "You're forming a coven."

"I am," Raul replied.

"Without me."

"Without you."

"Without the one person in this whole army who knows more about charms and signs than any other."

Drusil snorted at that.

"Oh, please." Prisca shook her head. "Your crude endeavours at the forge are pure trial and error. Even your lanterns work less than half the time. What you have to teach is nothing compared with what scholarship encompasses."

"That's true," Raul said. "And if you want to form your own coven, then you should. Anyone around this table is welcome to join you if they prefer."

"You're splitting our resources?"

"I'm offering you a chance to do things your way. I just don't want to be part of it."

It was hard to say these things to his ma at all, never mind to say them in front of strangers. Knowing that this confrontation had to come, he'd spent as long preparing his words as choosing who to recruit, and now those words had to be forced out. The urge to get up and pace about was stronger than ever, but he needed to conserve the energy he had, the small part of the day where he could function properly despite the pain, so instead he wrapped his hand around one of the books and clutched it tight.

"Is that Osulwa's *Universe of the Heart?*" she asked, peering at the book. "No wonder you're making foolish decisions, if you've started taking his word seriously. This philosophy of a personal relationship between the diviner, the signs, and the world is misguided at best. We must be objective in our assessment, must cut through the clutter to the most..." Her eyes flickered like she was looking around for something. "To the correct understanding."

"Correct as decided by who?"

"By the most experienced diviner present, of course."

"Meaning you."

"Around here, yes."

"And that's why you're not part of this."

Raul took a deep breath. His fingers were white from clutching the book tight so that they wouldn't tremble, but was it really so bad if others saw his moments of doubt? He wasn't playing the role of a chosen saviour anymore. That way of leading the rebellion, one man providing all the inspiration and the orders, was a weakness he wanted to move past. Collaboration. Cooperation. A multitude of voices sounding together. That was how they were going to win.

That was one more reason Prisca couldn't be here.

"I value your wisdom," he said, "and everything you've taught me. But our country's strength was never in the one voice at the top, the robed diviners of the royal court. It was a long tradition of charms common folk could use, of patterns they saw in the world. Bringing those things together let the court coven achieve greatness, but it wasn't about them, it was about the thousands whose understanding they drew on.

"Making the most of that means making sure that everyone is heard, that those who understand the magic can trust each other as they collaborate. You don't listen, and you showed me yesterday that I can't trust you. That's not going to change until you change."

"Foolish child," she hissed. "You saw what Alder unleashed at Hound's Gap. Do you really think that people like this, sitting around and...and...and..." Her sunken eyes twitched and her hand trembled at her side, but all the sickness in the world couldn't curb Prisca Servita's wounded pride. "That they can gather and manage such power?"

Raul ran a hand down the side of his body, felt the pain of burned skin under layers of poultices, bandages, and carefully arranged clothes. He didn't hide his grimace. No one knew what Alder had unleashed better than he did. No one who had survived it.

"Alder is using that power to burn down towns and villages," he said. "To kill and destroy. To vent his hate on innocent people. Do you think that a coven of a dozen good Estians would give anyone the power to do that?"

"I think that all your high-minded talk of collaboration is worthless if we cannot win."

"And I think that winning is worthless if we become the thing we're trying to defeat."

"That is..." Prisca gritted her teeth, failing to hide the way her jaw trembled, the wild flicker of her eyes as she sought words that had deserted her. "It is..."

There was a creaking and thudding, someone awkwardly manoeuvring through the tower's doors, then footsteps on the stairs. Silvano and Quintae appeared, carrying a bundle of cloth and wooden rods between them.

"Delivery for Raul Warborn," Silvano said. "You want to see it now?"

Prisca snorted and waved a hand. "Go ahead. It's not as if

we were holding a critical conversation about the future of our entire nation."

"You think anyone's asking you, after the crap you pulled?" Silvano turned his back on her. "Your Highness?"

"No more of that, please," Raul said.

"Not sure that's your choice. You want to see this now or not?"

"Yes, please."

While the would-be coven watched, Silvano and Quintae unrolled the bundle. In Quintae's deft hands, rods clicked together at carved joints, quickly forming a frame. The last piece went onto the top, wrapped in cloth, and once it was in place the cloth unravelled, revealing a freshly stitched banner: a green circle in a black ring against a red background, some continuity in the colours to balance out the change.

"Seriously?" Prisca shook her head. "In the middle of all this, you're worrying about changing your heraldry?"

"Not my heraldry," Raul said. "The symbol of what we are. We lost the Blazing Banner at Hound's Gap, so it's a good time for something new." He got up from his chair and limped over to look more closely at the banner. "This is good stitching."

"There are seamstresses in the Rianti company," Silvano said. "They were glad of a change from mending torn trousers."

"Fire and fury, can we please return to matters of more urgency?" For years, such agitation from Prisca would have jolted Raul into action. Now her ranting left him time to examine the banner, the way the green stood out.

"Red is for blood and fire," he said. "Destruction. If we must have it, then it should be the background, not the thing we're focused on. I think we'll soon have had enough of blades, so no dagger this time, but the black of a mourning ring, to commemorate the people we've lost. And in the middle of it all, a full moon instead of the crescent, made from green for growth." He turned to the people around the table. "What do you think?"

They looked at each other uncertainly, at the man who they had thought was a prince, at the minister fuming next to him.

"A new moon rises," Cloia said at last.

"A new moon rises," someone agreed.

"Can we stitch charms into fabric?" Ivus asked. "Something for courage, perhaps, or direction."

"Gah!" Prisca flung her shaking hands in the air. "Imbeciles wasting time. When these foolish experiments are over, you'll come running back to me, if you haven't lost us the war along the way."

Raul looked at his coven instead of her, at faces filled with a growing curiosity, at Cloia carefully reaching for the stack of books.

"A new version of the new moon," he said. "And a new sort of coven."

Prisca snorted one last time, then stomped off down the stairs and out, slamming the doors behind her. Quintae, craning his neck to peer after her, shook his head from side to side.

"Not good." He stroked his scarred scalp. "Not nice."

"She's certainly a charmer, your mother," Silvano said.

Raul flopped into his seat. He felt guilty, and only half of that was the habitual angst that flared up when challenging his parents. The other half was knowing how he'd left Prisca exposed, short on words, displaying a temper she used to control. She'd brought her arrogance to the conversation, but he'd let them see signs of her sickness and that wasn't fair. He would apologise when he had a chance. Maybe she would accept it, maybe she wouldn't, but he would do it anyway.

In the meantime, most of his coven had stuck with him, just like most of the army. He had hope for a better future, and a plan to secure it.

"Today, we'll start with small signs and charms," he said. "Tomorrow we'll talk about something bigger, about how we might deal with the power that Count Alder brings."

Chapter Nineteen
Missing Faces

The wagons of the Company Dellest rolled through a ford and up the shallow bank on the far side, through mud churned up by many travellers and along a track that was unusually worn for the countryside. If Yasmi had any doubts that they were heading in the right direction, those faded away. If there wasn't an army nearby, then there was a city hidden for generations, and that sort of thing only happened in the wildest of Tenebrial's plays. No ancient wizards this time, no fickle folk from other realms who lived in trees and granted twisted wishes. Either they were riding into the arms of their friends or straight into the teeth of the enemy, and while they'd pieced together the army's location based on rumours, she didn't think even the most confused farmers would mix up the destructive Dunholmi with the people fighting them.

She straightened the scarf that hung across her masks, thought better and lifted it so that she could adjust the masks themselves, then carefully replaced the scarf again.

"Almost there, my sweet," Efron said, giving the reins a small flick. "You'll see your prince soon enough."

"Or not." She wrapped her arms around herself, feeling a chill despite the sunshine, and clutched the charm Raul had given her.

"That boy is indestructible. Remember the spring when we rode into town and he'd broken his leg falling from a tree? Didn't even slow him down."

"Trees don't carry as many swords as Dunholmi warriors."

"True, but there are fearsome oaks up in the Vales."

"I wonder which face is most appropriate for mourning." She pulled the scarf aside to examine the masks again. "The bear has dark fur, but might cast too large a shadow at the funeral, and the monkey is hardly…" Her hand tightened around the charm and she closed her eyes, taking a breath that seemed to scrape its way down her throat. "Is hardly…"

Her father laid a hand gently on her shoulder. "If there's one thing I've learned from loving a fighting man, it's not to borrow worries ahead of time. As Gatrio says in *Three Lovers at Leisure*…"

"'There might not be a cloud in the sky tomorrow,'" the two of them recited together, "'so why let a rain of tears fall today?'" Yasmi let out a wet laugh and squeezed Efron's hand.

The road turned around a stand of trees and the landscape opened up in front of them. On a wide expanse of meadows, between forests on one side and a river on the other, stood the earth circle of Barrowblack. The smoke of campfires trailed into the sky before fading on the breeze. Tiny figures roamed the tops of palisades that crowned the earth walls. Closer by, a column of troops was marching along the trail toward them, flying banners that showed a bright green disk in a black ring against a red background.

Yasmi frowned. That wasn't the symbol she was used to, but she didn't see who else's army this could be.

"Out of the road!" There were riders ahead of the column, one of them waving a hand as she shouted at the players. They did as they were told, turning onto meadow land that wasn't much less solid than the dirt road. The wagons kept moving, bumping over lumps in the ground, watched by a lone brown cow with large, curious eyes. Yasmi watched the riders for any sign of Biallo. Were they his company or someone else?

The column that marched past was thousands strong. They looked the part of Estian infantry, most of them armed with large shields and battle axes, some with spears or bows. A few companies had the flamboyant uniforms of mercenaries and were armed with other sorts of weapons, including halberds and crossbows. There weren't many cavalry, and apart from the scouts, they mostly accompanied the supply wagons jolting along at the back.

"It seems we're here just in time," Efron said. "The whole rebellion is marching out."

"Not all of them." Yasmi pointed at warriors practising manoeuvres in the meadow and standing sentry on the walls of Barrowblack. "But who's stayed and who's gone?"

By the time they passed the column, the players' wagons were almost at the walls. They steered up onto the track and toward a pair of huge wooden gates that stood wide open, framing a fraction of the bustle of bodies within. A sentry waved at them, one of the rebels she recognised from the early days, and it was all she could do not to leap up shrieking, demanding to know what had happened with Raul.

Then she saw him, hobbling hurriedly out of the camp, a staff in his hand and a delighted smile on his face. She slapped a hand to her mouth, trying not to let the relief overwhelm her.

"Didn't I tell you?" her father said, but even he was beaming fit to burst.

She vaulted down from the wagon and Raul rushed up. They flung their arms around each other and his lips met hers. She clutched him tight, thrilling at the feel of him against her, afraid that if she let go, he might vanish like a character whose scene was done. For a long time, he was all that mattered.

"They said you might be dead," she managed at last.

"I almost was," he admitted, pulling up the hem of his tunic. The smell of a medicinal poultice wafted from the bandages around his stomach, and the flesh around them was badly scarred, the skin reddened and unnaturally smooth.

"What happened?"

"I was run through by Count Alder, and by the power of Jarrag."

"It's healing?"

"Slowly, but yes."

"Good, because if you die in battle, I will bring you back just so I can kill you again, understand?"

He laughed. "I missed you too. But I'm glad you were somewhere safe instead of with us."

She swallowed, not knowing what to say. Was there a

safe place in the whole country? From what she'd seen, she doubted it. The settlements that weren't being pillaged by the Dunholmi were plagued by bandits or starving to death thanks to stolen food and stalled trade. Perhaps she had been safer than Raul, but plenty of people she had seen weren't.

Efron was down from the board of the wagon, wrapped in a hug from Valens. It was lovely to see, but their wagons were blocking the gateway, the sentries looking agitated as people waited to get past.

"Let's get inside," she said. "Then we can catch up properly."

With some harrumphing and snorting through his moustache, her father got back onto the wagon and set it moving again. Yasmi and Raul walked along beside him, hand in hand.

"This is impressive," she said. "Based on the rumours, I thought we'd find five people and an injured mule, with Prisca in a corner telling everyone why they should do better."

He laughed. "That last part's true enough."

"Some things are unstoppable. The fall of night, the arrival of a storm, and Prisca's disapproval."

"Ma's easier to ignore than the other two."

"You wish."

She paused, pushed her hair back behind her ear, and looked around at the rows of tents and shelters, watching for familiar faces. There was Ferra training a band of wolves, and Lestavo heading up the walls with a hawk perched on his hand. She couldn't see Drusil, but she could hear her shouting instructions. Quintae ought to be around here somewhere, and

Biallo of course. She looked forward to teasing him with how well Claudio had filled his shoes, threatening that the world of theatre might not need him again. But even with half its occupants gone, the camp was too big to spot everyone.

"We saw the column marching out as we arrived," she said, still peering around. "Why did you send half your forces away? Or to look at it the other way around, why are half of them still here?"

"It seemed prudent." Raul tugged at the edge of his tunic.

"Wouldn't it be more prudent to keep them together? King Lorrin beat you while you had them all in one place. Surely, he'll have an easier time of it picking you off separately?"

"There were some tensions in the camp."

"Ah, people finally snapped at Prisca's scolding."

His laugh was weary and a little bitter, not at all like the Raul she knew. When she turned, he was looking down, hair hanging across his eyes like a veil.

"I can explain properly later, but the simple version is that the exile faction didn't get on well with our people. I found a way to stop it from bubbling over, but the tensions remained. There were arguments, a couple of fights in the evenings. Separating the factions seemed like the easiest way to stop things from getting worse."

"You've sent Junia's people to get lost in the woods? I approve."

"We needed to split our forces for strategic reasons anyway, so this fixes two things at once." He let go of her hand and started pacing back and forth in the dirt. "Hopefully."

Surveying her surroundings like she would assess an

audience on opening night, Yasmi spotted a group in yellow and black. She stiffened but maintained her smile.

"I see Nydia's still here."

"She's been very helpful."

"I bet she has."

Normally, Raul was an open book to her, but she couldn't read his expression now, or perhaps she didn't want to. It was hard enough dealing with the fact that he'd almost died, with the scars he bore and the responsibility that weighed him down. Talking through those things, and her own feelings around them, would make for a tough evening without factoring in his royal fiancée.

"Nydia and her people could have left," he said. "It might have been better for their country if they had. She's taken a risk on staying with us, even after our losses."

He took Yasmi's hand and with it a deep breath, like he was building up to something. Before he could start a conversation she didn't want to hear, she squeezed his fingers and spoke.

"It's good. We need all the help we can get, whatever it is you're planning. And believe me, I'm going to ask about that plan, just as soon as I've washed and changed into fresh clothes. I've been in these for days, getting showered with dust from the road." She swept her hair back and tilted her face to best catch the light. "You should be grateful. Not many women would travel so far for an innkeeper's son, not even one covered in scars."

"Yasmi, I..." He rubbed his forehead, a gesture so much like his father's that she almost laughed. But the strain of his expression froze the breath in her chest. What was he trying to tell her? She looked around, half expecting to see Nydia triumphant, gloating over the spoils she would be taking out of the war. But the Saditchi were marching out through the gates, curved composite bows over their shoulders, half of them carrying archery targets of wound rope, and Nydia wasn't evening glancing back.

Instead, Yasmi saw her father standing next to the wagon, dragging a hand down his pale face. He shook his head, waved his arms like he was trying to fling the world away, until Valens wrapped his arms around him and he slumped into the hug.

Then it all came together. What she'd seen, what she hadn't, Raul's strained effort to say something he couldn't get out.

The Company Dellest was a family. They travelled together, performed together, lived together. Those same voices and faces had been part of her life for as long as she could remember. Tenebrial fussing over every word of a script. Claudio painting scenery and bungling lines. Biallo strutting the boards, proud as a real king.

Biallo, who wasn't here.

"I'm so sorry," Raul said.

Chapter Twenty
Needs

"Why do I even need to think about this place?" Alder asked.

Trestis lay in the bend of a barely navigable river, such a pathetic little town that passing merchants might not even bother stopping to trade. The only reason it had a wooden palisade was the threat of wolves from the nearby woods and the need for something to keep livestock safe in winter. If not for the pigs in their streets, the locals would have been entirely defenceless, which might have kept them from indulging in acts of defiance.

"Troops from our advanced column chased a party of rebels here," Captain Brook said. "Savages from the Withered Hills. If we can capture them, we might find out where the rest have regrouped."

The two of them stood in what passed for a road, looking along the last few hundred yards of dirt to this so-called town. A hundred Dunholmi cavalry were spread across the surrounding fields, tending to their horses and their war gear, waiting for orders. This was one of the raiding parties he'd let off the leash, with the intention of sending a message to the North Marchers: accept the reins of Dunholmi power or face the consequences. The response hadn't been as weak as he expected, but the North Marchers only had so much strength between them, and one by one these communities were seeing sense or seeing their lives turned to ash.

"Do we know how the locals feel about these savages putting their town in danger?" he asked.

"Seems like this was their choice," Brook said. "They gave the rebels shelter and barred the gate against us."

"Do they think their fake prince is going to rescue them?" Alder sneered. "Unlikely, given the state I left him in."

"Half the towns around here were in open rebellion before Hound's Gap. Makes it harder for them to back down."

"Then let's teach them why that's a mistake."

He'd handed off Fellstride the moment he dismounted. The stallion had been agitated lately, faster to flinch from sound or movement, often snorting and shifting, ready to take flight. It was infuriating to see his best horse turn bad, especially when there was no obvious cause. Once this was over, he would have to train him again from the start, as if he hadn't already wasted enough time reining in the Dunholmi nobility and dealing with these wretched rebels.

Or perhaps he should find another, less wilful steed.

For now, being on his feet suited him. Those walls meant they couldn't make a cavalry charge against the town, and it was often better to be on foot for street fighting.

"Tur!" he shouted.

His chamberlain emerged from among the chosen guard who had come with Alder. Of course he'd dismounted as soon as he could. Good horses were wasted on a man of his breeding.

"My lord?" Tur rubbed his hands together as he bowed obsequiously. "Would you like me to return to the main column and gather reinforcements, some siege weapons perhaps?"

"That won't be necessary. I just want you to hold this."

Alder took off the large gold bracelet that had once been a token of status for some North March earl. Its edges weren't as neat as they had been, some of the decorative details obscured, a consequence of the heat last time he'd used his power. With it went the ring he'd taken off King Lorrin, three black pearls set in silver. He didn't want to ruin either of them.

"My lord." Tur clutched the jewellery. "Is it appropriate for you to put yourself in danger this way?"

"What danger?" Alder snorted. "It's nothing but a band of scruffy rebels."

"Those scruffy rebels almost..." Tur's voice trailed off. "I mean, that is to say..."

"Wait here." Alder raised his voice. "The rest of you, follow me."

He strode straight toward the town's gates, drawing his sabre as he went. Somewhere in the back of his head, a voice that might or might not have been his own wondered whether he should have taken the time to strategise, to minimise casualties and make sure the targets didn't get away. But a far louder voice, his own true voice, the voice of fire and strength, urged him to stride straight in, to burn and tear, to use the strength Jarrag had given him. To show what a leader looked like.

So he stormed toward those wooden walls, a hundred armoured warriors following him.

These people probably had bows to hunt with, but the walls were too crude for ramparts or shooting platforms. Nothing threatened him as he approached, hand extended, and called power from inside. He pressed his palm against the rough surface of the wood, then felt the rush of heat, the flow of flames, wood crumbling to ash as fire swept up.

The gates groaned, then crashed down.

There were screams as he strode into the town, shrill voices slicing through the smoke and the smell of warm ash.

Facing him were what had to be the rebels, a score of archers dressed in poorly cut furs and armour made of woven sticks. One of them shouted and they loosed, arrows hissing through the air.

Unlike his forces, Alder didn't have a shield. Instead, he spun his sword, fire arcing behind it. As the arrows hit the flames they flared and vanished, stone heads shattering and falling amid the dust. Another round of arrows flew, followed by thuds against shields and flesh, some yells of pain from behind him, and then he was on them.

His first swing almost sliced straight through a wooden club with chunks of stone. The next took the head off the weapon and half the head of its wielder.

Already, the rebel line had disintegrated, faced with the overwhelming number of attackers and the fury of his fire. The fighting spread through the village, a chaotic mess in which some of the locals took up arms and others were caught in the conflict even as they tried to hide. Blades clashed, blood flew, bodies fell. A bear charged, roaring from between the buildings, and was hacked down. He killed another of the locals himself, felt the satisfaction of hearing their last breath, of watching defiance die. As he advanced, flames rose from his footsteps, took hold of a mound of straw, spread into nearby buildings. By the time the fighting stopped, half the place was ablaze.

He stalked back out, leaving warriors to oversee the locals as they tried to quench the fires. Tur was waiting, long fingers twisting around each other.

"Should we let the whole place burn, my lord? I don't think there will be much left anyway."

"Yes," Alder said, then heard the voice in the back of his head, the one calling for calculation, for reason. Hadn't that been the voice at the front of his mind once? "No. We need places like this to supply our people while we fight."

"Indeed, my lord, indeed." Tur stared at the flames that leapt from Alder's sword. "But many of the towns we've taken have gone back to the rebels as soon as we move on, or their people have fled, leaving no one to tend the land. We're taking places, but are we truly conquering them? I merely ask, of course. Whatever you decide, I will do."

Flames crackled. Smoke swayed in the wind. There was a creak and then a crash as a building collapsed. Someone was sobbing, more than one of them perhaps.

"We'll string some of them up," Alder said. "Let the others know what happens if they don't stay here and obey."

"Of course, my lord." Tur backed away.

"Is something bothering you, Tur?" Alder took a step after him and held up the flaming sword. "This, perhaps?"

"My lord, I..."

"Don't you like it when we win, Tur?"

"Of course, my lord."

"So your problem is with my methods?"

"I just... I think... I want..." Tur closed his eyes and took a deep breath. Soot blown on the wind blackened his cheeks. When he opened his eyes, there was a steadiness that Alder had never seen in the man before. "We came north to stop these people and their abominable sorcery. Now we use it ourselves. This is not right."

His arms hung motionless by his sides. His gaze was steady.

Alder was used to people disagreeing with him, offering different perspectives and information. That was an important part of decision-making, of governing a province or leading an army. But those perspectives should come from his equals, from his fellow nobles and warriors. Where had this snivelling peasant, a man who could barely stay in the saddle, found the temerity to tell him that he was wrong?

"Take that back," he hissed. This couldn't be stood for, not from Tur of all people.

"No, my lord." Tur swallowed. Tears ran down his cheeks, drawing pale lines through the soot. "I'm sorry, my lord, but this..." He pointed at the blazing sword. "This is wrong."

"Take it back." Alder grabbed him by the scruff of the neck. That voice was in the back of his head again, reminding him that Tur, wretched as he was, could be useful. But the voice of the flames was louder and the voice of the flames was right. Allow words of dissent and you would find yourself opposed. Allow folk charms and, in time, you'd face a rebellion.

"No, my lord." Tur closed his eyes.

"Take. It. Back."

"Never."

Fire ran across Alder's fingers, blackened Tur's robe, scoured the skin beneath. Alder breathed the stink of burning hair and scorched flesh.

Then he let go.

For a moment, he wasn't even sure why.

"You aren't worthy of dying by this power," he said.

Crumpled on the ground, Tur patted at the smouldering remains of his robe, trying to smother the lingering flames. Exposed skin on his chest and shoulders was red, his eyes streaming. He looked up.

"Please, my lord," he said. "You're better than this."

Alder turned to his warriors.

"Let this place burn!" he shouted. "We ride back to war."

With that, he stormed away, leaving his former chamberlain to tremble in the dirt.

Valens raised his axe high, then swung it down with all his strength. The impact as it slammed into the shield sent a judder up his arm. But though it shook, the shield held steady, not even a dent in the iron band around its edge.

"Well?" Drusil asked. "What d'you think?"

There was a nick in the axe blade. Valens would deal with that later, a chance to work with his hands instead of telling other people what to do. For now, he took a step back and swung the axe, this time hitting the shield near its centre. He struck again and again and again, the sort of blows that would have reduced a door to splinters. The shield shook, almost falling off the tree it was strapped to, but its boards were barely scratched.

"It's good." Valens slid the axe through the loop on his belt, then ran his fingers over the charm carved into the shield's front. A mountain, to endure. "Thought you worked metal."

"Quintae might not be able to forge a straight sentence, but he knows wood. Working with him's like having a thistle up my arse, but it's been worth it."

From further into the woods came the sound of chopping and the crash of a tree coming down. Birds flung themselves into the air and flocked away. There was probably a sign in that, but Valens wouldn't know how to read it.

Drusil took the shield off the tree and turned it around. Another charm was carved into the back: a heart.

"Not sure this one does any good," she said, "but warriors should think of courage."

"How fast can you make more of these?"

"Not fast enough. It needs planks from the heart of an oak, iron from the highest mountains, and masters of both crafts. Even for me, the charms don't work on one shield in three, and I'm cursed if I can work out why."

"Two in three are this tough?"

"That's the other way of seeing it."

"Better than your lanterns."

"I've been learning."

"And even when the charms don't take, you're making solid shields?"

"You think I'd stand for shoddy work in my armoury?"

"You think I'd employ an armourer who did?"

"Not like it's your choice anymore, General Valens." Drusil slung the shield over her back, leather straps resting on her muscular shoulder. "Council decides things together, and my vote hits as hard as yours."

"I don't see us coming to blows."

"Not with each other. Junia, though..." Drusil snorted. "If anyone younger than her showed me that sort of sneer, I'd slap it off their face."

Valens looked down at the stump of his wrist. He'd had a hand there once, before he lost it to Prisca's schemes and the hope of freeing Estis. He'd had a ring on that hand too, a reminder of an old friend who he'd fought alongside for King Cataldo and Queen Junia. He might not like the queen much, but it was hard to shake off a loyalty whose hooks had been in his heart for decades. If she was still around, would Fabia have sided with Raul over Queen Junia? One thing he knew for sure, once she picked a side she wouldn't have doubted for a moment.

When he closed his eyes, he could still feel that ring around his finger, a long-gone thumb rubbing across it.

"We need Junia's people," he said.

"I suppose."

They set off from the edge of the forest back toward Barrowblack. A mile of open ground lay between the two, meadow that would have been grazed by the herds of local farmers if not for the army sitting inside the earth walls. A few stray cattle still nibbled at the lush grass, tails flicking away flies in the warmth of a spring now edging into summer. It was good ground for cavalry, not a place Valens would have wanted to fight if not for Barrowblack itself.

The two of them walked in companionable silence. Giving so many orders in a day used up more words than Valens even knew he had in him, and Drusil had always preferred action. With Efron back, Valens's life once again overflowed with words, speeches from plays and tales about the actor's life on the road. He loved every minute of it, not least because he didn't have to talk much, but he was happy to enjoy a chance for silence as well.

There were more banners flying above the walls than they'd had before, and proper gates barring the gaps in their defences. An attacker could still advance up those earth banks into the camp, but only where the palisade wasn't complete. Even if they managed it, they'd be tired and facing defenders with the advantage of high ground. The banners that flew above those walls bore their new symbol, the green circle of a moon full of life and hope, Raul's promise for the future. Seeing them made Valens smile with pride. Whatever else he'd ruined in his life, he'd raised the lad right.

Raul himself was on the walls with his coven, very different figures from the sentries with their helmets and bows or the engineers working on the palisade. The coven pointed and waved at what looked to Valens like ordinary patches of dirt, huddled together for excited conversations, scattered along the walls and then regrouped.

"Shouldn't you be part of that?" he asked Drusil.

"Don't have time," she replied. "I answer their questions when they come, get them making charms when I can. I'd like to join them for the books and talking, but there are shields to make. Maybe when this is over."

That maybe was a lead weight between them. Maybe when this was over he would be leading the palace guard and she would rebuild her smithing business in Pavuno. Or maybe they'd be strung up along a roadside, crows feeding on their cold flesh.

"What are they doing up there?" he asked, watching as coven members crouched and touched the ground. He was nearly at the foot of the walls, close enough to make out their faces and hear fragments of excited conversation, the wind shredding the words too finely to follow.

"Some sort of charm."

"What sort?"

"Told you, I don't have time for that."

They headed up the steep earth slope and Valens felt the strain in his knees. One good thing about dying in battle: you didn't have to put up with getting old.

"Da!" Raul waved. "Drusil! How are the shields?"

The lad was looking better than he had since Hound's Gap, standing straight with only one hand on his staff, the colour back in his cheeks. His tunic didn't bulge so much around the bandages, and his lips no longer curled into a grimace every time he moved. For that alone, Valens could have wept with relief.

"The shields are good," he said as he reached the top of the wall. "Could use more of them."

Down the far slope, the interior of Barrowblack was filling up again. Survivors of their defeat were still finding their way back as the weeks passed, as well as new recruits, people determined to throw out the Dunholmi. Those recruits were grimmer than they had been before, many of them bringing stories of villages burned down and communities driven out, of whole families strung up because one daughter or son had joined the rebels. Aside from their injuries, many of the survivors wore mourning rings in memory of those they'd lost. No carved jet for them, but simple bands of wood or wool stained black with soot. If Valens had thought the occupiers were bad before, that was nothing compared with the blade they'd now drawn.

In the middle of the camp, the rebels had built a wooden crane next to the stone tower, and pieces of a great trebuchet were being hauled onto the roof. Quintae's original had been lost in the retreat, but he seemed even happier with this one, and from that raised position it could fire out across the walls, threatening anyone who approached. Sure, it was slow to shoot and slower to load, but it was intimidating, and nervous opponents made mistakes.

Near Valens, one of the coven was crouched with a trowel in her hand, burying something in the top of the wall. He was about to ask Raul what this was, but then Yasmi came striding over.

Valens had expected Yasmi to struggle more than her father with Biallo's death. Efron might not have been a warrior, but he'd lived long enough to lose a few friends as well as his wife, to have the sharp corners worn off of grief. But to think about it that way was to forget that Yasmi had known death at far too young an age. Seeing her mother pass away put all other loss in its place, or perhaps gave her scars to hide behind.

She stopped in front of Raul, arms folded, expression determined. "We need to talk."

"Here?" Raul asked.

"Now. No more delay."

"If you say so."

At first, Valens wondered if Raul had managed to offend Yasmi, but she didn't seem angry and he mostly looked confused.

"You two as well," Yasmi said, nodding to Valens and Drusil.

Raul's coven stood around them uncertainly, some of them holding scraps of parchment, others half-made charms.

"Carry on around the walls," Raul said. "You know what you're doing."

With obvious relief and a few curious backward glances, the coven hurried away, leaving the four of them.

"We need to go on the offensive," Yasmi said.

"We're still preparing," Raul replied. "Pulling our forces together, letting people recover from their wounds, arming and training. If we rush to attack the Dunholmi, we risk losing everything."

"People are losing everything already." Yasmi waved across the walls, across the meadows, across the woods and river and the country beyond. "The Dunholmi are destroying communities while we sit here doing nothing."

"That's war," Valens said.

"That's your answer?" Yasmi glared at him. "That it's war?"

"It's true."

She raised her foot, and he thought she was going to tap it three times, the actor's lucky charm before beginning a performance. Instead, she stamped down hard, shoving herself in his face.

"You think I don't understand what war is?" she snarled, and though he had to bend his neck to look down at her, her anger was intimidating. "I've been out there travelling Estis, seeing what this war does. I've seen bodies strung up along the roads, faces contorted by their dying screams. I've seen whole towns razed to the ground, nothing left for shelter but stumps and ashes. I've seen stick-thin children slumped with hunger because they've nothing left to eat. And I've seen the looks in their eyes—the living, the dead, and the dying, the desperate and the hopeless, the people we're meant to protect.

"You've seen the war that warriors live through, but I've seen the one they inflict. The longer we sit here licking our wounds, the worse it gets."

Valens didn't know what to say, barely even knew what to think. When he'd just been a warrior, none of this was his to worry about. He marched where he was told to march and killed who he was told to kill. Now that he was a general, he'd been thinking about strategy, resources, and manoeuvre, about their path to victory. Not this.

It wasn't that there had never been moral choices before. Becoming a warrior was one. Joining Prisca's scheme instead of surrendering was another. How to treat defeated opponents had come up from time to time. But he'd never had to face a choice on this scale, for such high stakes.

"What good are we if we let our people die?" Yasmi asked, her expression softening as she turned to Raul.

"It's not my decision anymore," he said. "This has to go to the council."

"Then we'll take it to the council, and I'll look them in the eyes and dare anyone there to tell me we can keep delaying."

"What do you think?" Raul asked, looking at Valens.

Valens pressed his thumb and finger to his brow, took a deep breath as he did his best to balance their choices. He was a general; he knew more than anyone about their warriors and what they could do. He couldn't dodge his part in this decision.

"She's right," he said. "It's time to draw them in."

"I agree," Raul said, "but we'll need everyone to decide." He whistled and several of his coven came running. "Please find the council members and ask them to gather in the tower."

The trainee diviners bowed their heads, then hurried off down the slope.

"I'll stow the shield, then join you." Drusil followed, taking long strides down the trampled grass.

That left three of them, standing in the gap between two sentry positions.

"Thank you," Yasmi said, her voice softer than before, shoulders sagging. "For listening, and for agreeing."

"I should have acted sooner," Raul said quietly, hanging his head. "Should have pushed myself into action, got us back into the fight. Now we're only half-prepared and we're all out of time."

"We're acting now, that's what matters."

"If the council agrees."

"They will," Valens said. "Maybe not Junia and Prisca, but

most of their earls have marched off leading the old guard, and they'd have lost the vote anyway."

"I'll help spread the word." Yasmi detached herself from Raul. "See you at the tower?"

"See you there."

She rushed off down the inner slope of the walls. Her clothes weren't as bright as they'd once been, but she stood out like a beacon amid the mud and weariness of the camp.

Raul sighed. "I should have got ready for this."

Valens laid a hand on his son's shoulder.

"You pushed yourself as hard as you could without pushing yourself over," he said. "We need you as much as we need any of this."

"I'm not a prince anymore, not even a fake one."

"True, but you made it so everyone matters, and you're part of everyone." He took a deep breath, calling up words that he usually let rest inside him, where they were safe from the judgement of the world. "And to me, you're so much more than that. You always will be."

"Oh, Da." Raul flung his arms around him, and Valens hugged him tight. It was only when Raul took in a sharp breath that he realised he'd gone too far.

"Sorry," he said, letting go of his wounded, wonderful son. Caught by an impulse he hadn't felt in years, he ruffled the lad's floppy blond hair. "I'm proud of you."

"I'm proud of all of us."

"And that's why we need you."

Chapter Twenty-One
Light of Dawn

Crouching in the bushes by the riverside, Raul watched the sky. It was starting to lighten, the deep black of night fading into grey, but the stars were still visible, bright gems for all to see. When he'd been young, his ma had told him stories about the shapes in the stars, the heroes and monsters whose bodies were outlined against the void, tales that left him eager for more as he settled to sleep every night. Then he'd grown older and he'd learned to look for other shapes, in the stars as much as in anything else around him, to see a deeper reality reflected in the world. Now his thoughts had turned again and he wondered whether what he saw really had been something deeper, something truer, something universal, or whether it had simply been the things that he himself thought and felt. And if it came from inside him, did that make it any less true? Perhaps that was how the universe spoke, not by bending the world but by guiding his eyes as he gazed upon it.

"Looking for omens?" Ferra whispered from her place next to him.

"The omens brought us this far, helped us find the perfect spot. Now I'm looking for the dawn."

Ignoring the camp of the Dunholmi army on the far side of the river, he turned to look behind him, to the east and the moment he was waiting for. Beyond these low bushes, there was nothing else disrupting the view until the hills that made up the horizon. No shelter. No place to hide. No way that anyone could miss seeing which way someone went as they ran from this riverbank.

The pain had been almost absent over the past few days, apart from the ongoing ache in his side and the sharp twists if he moved his arm too fast. Nothing he wasn't getting used to. Nothing he couldn't ignore when he had to, for a while at least. Still, he took a breath and rolled his shoulders, paying attention to where the strains were, what might distract him or slow him down. Everyone else would be faster than him regardless, and he knew they wouldn't leave him behind no matter what he said. But he needed to be here to make sure things ran smoothly, so he would have to make sure he ran as fast as he could, as fast as it took to avoid putting them at risk.

At last, the first hint of red bled its way into the grey of the eastern sky. Raul turned to Ferra and nodded.

She raised her hands around her mouth, and if he hadn't seen her moving he would have sworn that it was a real owl he heard call out. A matching hoot came from the far bank, somewhere beyond the Dunholmi sentries. A third rose from upstream, close to the bend where the river disappeared from view. In the bushes alongside Raul and Ferra, warriors mouthed prayers or kissed their battle charms. Estians and Withering Folk, with a few Saditchi mixed in—they were the best archers he'd been able to find, and now they all raised their bows, arrows nocked.

Across the river, past the Dunholmi camp, a glow appeared like an echo of the dawn. For a moment it was a faint flicker, but then it flared as jars of oil shattered and burst into flames. The dawn chorus started, a strangely beautiful counterpoint to the fire that snatched at dry grass, rushing across open ground toward tents and supply wagons.

"Fire!" Half a dozen voices shouted almost as one. The sentries by the river turned, and some of the archers in the bushes twitched at oblivious targets silhouetted against the blaze, but they knew the plan and they knew when their moment would come.

The Dunholmi leapt into action, some tearing out of their tents so fast that they got tangled in ropes or tore the canvas down. Half-dressed warriors rushed about like ants whose hill had been kicked over, dashing this way and that, uncoordinated.

Unnoticed amid the chaos, low dark shapes drifted around the river bend.

Commanding voices rose from the camp, the voices of women and men raised from birth to expect obedience. Order started to emerge, some of the Dunholmi grabbing blankets to beat at the flames, some running with buckets down the riverside, while others led away their precious, panicked horses, out of the smoke and firelight that was causing them to whinny and kick in fear. Through it all, sentries stood a twitchy watch, because this was a well-trained army and the last thing they would do was let their guard down.

The ones with buckets reached the river. Some waded in, forming a chain.

Raul tapped Ferra's arm. She hooted.

Along the east bank, archers rose from amid the bushes and shadows. Bowstrings creaked and a single Dunholmi looked up, catching the sound amid the shouted orders, panicked horses, and roar of flames consuming supply wagons. Arrows hissed through the air and that warrior fell, others with him, thudding onto the bank or sinking into the shallows, almost every shot finding its mark. All the sentries on that side fell dead or injured, then a second volley focused on the bucket carriers, and a third after it. Bucket chains dissolved as some of them rushed for cover, some ran for their armour, and others stood exposed, staring around in confusion.

The dark shapes shifted down the river, accompanied by the soft splash of paddles. Raul took the end of a string lying by his feet and tugged until it was tight. Behind him, in the east, the sky lightened.

All was chaos in the Dunholmi camp again, and out of that chaos a score of figures came running. Most of their bodies were bulked out with armour, buckets in their hands, but one was smaller than the rest, a monkey bounding along with its tail outstretched.

One of the warriors by the riverbank turned to welcome them, another to warn them. The monkey shifted briefly into a woman and then a lion, flung herself at one of the warriors and ripped him apart. Her companions tossed aside their buckets and their last jars of oil, then smouldering rags. The oil flared into flames.

Illuminated by the fire they'd lit, the Withered Hills scouts drew their weapons and charged down the riverbank. One injured Dunholmi sentry tried to raise a spear, but her weak thrust was knocked aside. Still in her lion shape, Yasmi tore another of them down.

The Dunholmi from the bucket chain, half of them wounded by arrows and almost all of them unarmed, scattered out of the way. Behind them, orders were being shouted from the camp, armed warriors rushing to pursue the saboteurs.

The rebel archers shifted their aim, shooting over the heads of the scouts and into their pursuers. These volleys weren't as accurate as the ones before, but shots still found their marks. Warriors screamed and fell. A body writhed in the flames.

The scouts reached the bank at the same moment as the low boats rowing down the river, Saditchi corsairs at their tillers and oars. The scouts scrambled aboard and the boats turned, heading for Raul's bank, moving slower beneath the weight of their passengers. The lion became a crocodile, weaving through the water as fast as the boats.

Out of the inferno, a man emerged, sword in hand. Flames rose higher around him. Even across the river and half the camp, he was unmistakable, mouth hitched into a viscous half sneer beneath dark, wavy hair.

Count Alder had arrived.

He strode toward the river, shouting orders as he went. The half-dressed troops that rushed to his side carried bows, some of them waving fistfuls of arrows, others with quivers over bare shoulders.

Around Raul, rebel archers kept shooting, arrows hissing over their comrades in the boats. Alder spun his sword and fire rippled through the air. The arrows falling closest to him disintegrated into ash; others flew off course as their fletching flared away; only those at the edges found their marks. The Dunholmi archers formed a line and drew their own bows, aiming at the fleeing warriors in the boats.

The sun rose over the horizon. At the same moment, Raul yanked hard on the string in his hand, pulling back the shutters on charmed lanterns planted along the riverbank. Bright magical light joined the glare of dawn itself, shining into the eyes of the Dunholmi archers. Most turned away, covering their faces. A few loosed where they'd been aiming a moment before, but their arrows splashed into the current, the only hit slamming harmlessly into the wood of a boat.

Alder bellowed furious orders. His archers squinted, trying to find their aim, while groups of riders saddled up to gallop north and south, looking for crossings.

The boats were over the river now, thudding into the east bank where Raul stood. Their occupants clambered out and rushed up through the riverside bushes, away from the water and the enemies on the far side. Each Saditchi pilot in turn kissed the prow of their small vessel then pushed it out, letting the current carry it away. Yasmi scrambled up the bank beside them, back in her human form, dripping wet and grimly satisfied.

"Come on," she said, touching Raul's shoulder. "I'm not leaving you behind."

At Raul's command, the archers pulled back. Half held in place, giving covering fire while the others scrambled up the bank, then those who'd retreated took their turn shooting while the rest hurried after them. Raul was among the last to leave, running as fast as his wounds would allow him, Yasmi and Ferra at his side.

They left the lanterns. Precious as those were, lives mattered more.

Out of sight of the river, wagons were waiting. By the time Raul reached them, most had set off already, wheels whirring and hooves hammering, going as fast as they could with full cargoes of fighters. Not as a fast as a rider on horseback, but faster than an army could march.

Other hooves could be heard in the distance, following them from the river. Some of the Dunholmi had got across.

Raul flung his staff into the back of the last wagon and tried to pull himself up, but the strain ran from his arms down through his body, pulling at his wounds. Pain flared as bright as the distant flames.

Ferra reached down to grab him under the armpits while Yasmi pushed him from behind. The hooves were getting close as he lay on the boards, his face a finger's breadth from someone's muddy feet.

"Go!" Ferra snapped.

The driver cracked his reins and the wagon jolted into movement, sending another burst of pain through Raul. He dragged himself upright and looked back to see Yasmi unhook a mask and press it to her face. Her body twisted, bent, fell, and then she was a fleet-footed deer dashing to catch up.

Past her, Dunholmi riders appeared. Only half a dozen of them, but all armed and armoured, galloping after the wagon, gaining ground fast. The rebel archers started shooting, using the spare arrows they'd stashed in the wagon. Even after the previous day's practice, they struggled to aim straight as the world lurched under them, but one hit a rider in the shoulder and others glanced off shields. The Dunholmi slowed, falling back out of range. There was a shout. The one with the injured shoulder peeled off and headed back, but the others kept going, following the wagon along the road toward Barrowblack.

A dove swooped out of the sky and landed on Ferra's shoulder. She took a string from around its leg and ran it through her fingers, reading the pattern of knots.

"From our hidden lookout," she said. "Alder's given up on fighting the fires. He's got his troops crossing the river, ready to come after us."

A small twinge of guilt bit at Raul. How far would the flames spread? What meadows, crops, even woods might burn down before they ran out of fuel or rain came? It was awful to realise that the rebels couldn't fight without harming the country they called home, but worse yet to think about what might happen if they didn't fight back.

"As long as they're coming," he said, "it's all worthwhile."

———————•———————

The day was almost over by the time they returned to Barrowblack. After the first rush to get out of the Dunholmi army's range, they'd slowed to a pace the horses could keep up, and their pursuers had done the same, always staying far enough out of bow range but never falling back so far that they would lose sight of the rebels. Raul wondered whether those Dunholmi warriors thought they'd achieved something noteworthy, preventing the rebels from disappearing into the countryside, discovering vital intelligence on where they were based. Perhaps they realised that this was deliberate but kept coming anyway, risking a trap to bring back valuable information. In the end, it didn't matter as long as the army came.

Riding across the meadow around Barrowblack in the last light of the afternoon, he was pleased to see that someone had moved the cows. It was such a small thing in the scale of death and destruction they faced, but for the sake of both the cows and their owners he didn't want them caught up in what was coming next.

As the wagons approached the gates, rebel riders came galloping out. Normally they would have been badly outnumbered by the enemy cavalry, but today they only had to worry about a handful of pursuers. They could give them just enough time to see what was gathered here: the earth walls reinforced with wooden palisades around the top and stakes protruding from their slopes; a tower with a trebuchet rising above those defences; enough scouts and banners to imply an entire rebel army inside, not just the part that had stayed. Let the Dunholmi get an eyeful and then they could be chased away, leaving the rebels free to prepare the ground.

Valens was waiting at the gates.

"It went well?" he asked, eyes shifting across the riders in the wagons, checking who was there.

"Perfectly." Raul reached out and his da helped him down. Next to the wagon, the deer raised its hoof and turned back into Yasmi. "We didn't lose anyone, and they definitely know where we've gone. The birds from Ferra's scouts said that the army's heading this way already."

He couldn't help grinning. They'd tried something bold and so far it was working. A lot more risk was about to follow, but it felt good to see the enemy pivot around their plan.

Valens ran a hand across his head. "If they've marched today, we might only have tomorrow to prepare. Better get Quintae's people out there now, use what light's left."

"Is there any word from the others?"

Valens shook his head.

Leaning on his staff, Raul clutched the wood tight. He was aching and exhausted. Since his injury, it was harder to keep going through long days and difficult journeys. He wanted to collapse in a corner and sleep, but there was still too much to do.

"Do you think they'll come?" he asked, too quietly for others to hear.

"If it was just Prisca and Junia, I wouldn't bet on it," Valens replied. "They were still angry when they rode out to join their troops. Turning up late, forcing you to withdraw instead of fighting, that could work for them. Makes you a failure, puts them back in charge."

"And if we stand our ground without them?"

"Wouldn't cross their minds. We'd be too badly outnumbered to risk it."

"Except that we have to risk it, or keep leaving people helpless."

"Not how Junia thinks, Prisca either." Valens took a deep breath. "Fortunately, Tordesse's with them."

"You're right, he wouldn't abandon us."

"He spoke up for you while he was here, but he's still one of the old earls. Less likely to abandon us than Junia, but it's not certain."

Yasmi, her mask back on her belt, laid a hand on Raul's arm.

"Come on," she said. "You're exhausted."

He shook his head. "There's an hour of daylight left for me to work with the coven. After that I'll rest, I promise."

All around them, the camp was bustling with activity: armourers sharpening blades, warriors fetching supplies, engineers heading into the meadow. There would be work long into the night, and all through tomorrow, the things that were needed for them to stand a chance against an overwhelming foe who had beaten them once before.

Yasmi and Valens exchanged a look. If they'd decided to manoeuvre him by force, Raul couldn't have resisted, and might have ended up in bed against his will. But there was a reason they were the people he loved most in the world. They understood why this mattered.

"Do you think this magic of yours can work?" Valens asked. Though he tried to hide it, Raul could see his uncertainty as he looked up at the trainee diviners carving circles into the gateway above.

"In the Withered Hills, I made a charm from nothing but

snow, one big enough for us all to stand inside, one that drove back the wolves." Raul poured what energy he could find into his most confident smile. "This is the same, landscape as magic, just on a bigger scale."

"You're sure?"

"I'm sure."

"Then I'm looking forward to this." Valens grinned. "But right now, I need to get to work."

He strode off, shouting orders as he went.

Yasmi slipped her arm through Raul's.

"If you won't rest, then at least let me help you up the walls."

"Thank you." He leaned on her and on the staff, and it was a relief. "I'm really glad you're back."

"So am I. But remember, I taught you how to put on a performance, and I can see through it. Show Valens all the false confidence you want, but you're not fooling me."

Chapter Twenty-Two
The Battle of Barrowblack

Alder stood in the entrance to King Lorrin's tent, flanked by a pair of his chosen guards. Behind him, the camp was coming alive in the predawn gloom.

"It's time, Your Majesty," he said.

Lorrin stared with bloodshot eyes, the folds of his face exaggerated by the flickering light of a torch. He'd been sleeping on his throne again. The physician said it was to avoid rolling onto his bandaged arm and triggering pain from the burns, but Alder could see the truth. This was about the injury to Lorrin's pride, not his body. Sitting up all night in his crown and his arming jacket, only ever half-asleep, he could delude himself that he still led the army, that his authority was something more than a sham.

Alder flexed his fingers, small flames flickering between them, dancing across the ring he'd taken from the king. Lorrin clasped his injured arm.

"I should don my armour," Lorrin said.

"It's traditional before battle."

"And what part will I play in this battle?" Lorrin looked coldly at Alder. "Are you going to let me give orders, maybe join the fighting line?"

"You will be seen by your people, and that's what matters." Alder leaned in over the king, placed his hands on the arms of the throne, and let the wood char under their heat. Again, a voice in the back of his head insisted there was a better, smarter way of dealing with a man of Lorrin's pride and stature. That voice was weak. "Remember what I can do if you are less than cooperative, Your Majesty."

An hour later, the two of them were at the front of a column marching the final mile from their overnight camp to where the rebels waited. There had been skirmishes in the night as scouts from both sides surveyed the opposing armies, and foragers had reported attacks by wild animals. But nervousness and rumour were to be expected. Everybody knew that they would fight today, and while victory was assured, so was death. Some of them, especially among the infantry levy, wouldn't make it through. That was the price Dunholm paid for strength and security.

Thousands of hooves clopped against the dirt road. Thousands of feet tramped in their wake. Smells of dust and sweat drove the freshness from the early morning air.

They marched out from a gap between woods and river onto a wide stretch of meadow land. On a low hill in the middle of that open ground stood a ring of earthworks as wide as any castle, topped with a wooden palisade. At a gap in the wall, tall gates stood between a pair of crude wooden towers. Banners fluttered in the wind, a green circle in a black ring against a red background. Was this meant to trick him into thinking that some new force had joined the rebels? It didn't matter. He had them at last, backed into a corner from which they couldn't retreat.

Captain Brook had ridden ahead with the scouts and was waiting at the edge of the meadow.

"Your Majesty." As was fitting, she bowed her head to Lorrin before turning to address Alder. "My lord, the rebels withdrew their last troops inside the walls when they heard us coming. I have scouts searching the woods for whoever they've left hidden."

Around them, commanders peeled off from the column, ready to order their troops into position for a battle line. Veteran captains and experienced nobles found their positions with ease, focusing on the business of logistics rather than the sorry excuse for a fortress they faced. The less experienced moved uneasily back and forth, heads twitching, hands uneasy on their reins.

"You," Alder called out to one of them. "Tisco, isn't it?"

"Yes, my lord." As the son of a North March merchant, Tisco had more need to prove himself, less certainty of his place in the battle or after. It showed in his every movement.

"You're on the other flank."

"Sorry, my lord." He tugged at his reins and galloped away, an unnecessary speed that would wear his horse out. Not that it mattered; people like him were little better than the infantry levy, fuel for the fire of war.

Looking out across the meadow, Alder felt an almighty urge to charge, to cut straight to the destruction. But the quiet voice was right this time; he needed the whole army ready if he was going to crush the rebels. Besides, there were probably traps waiting to be sprung. For all their flaws, the rebels had shown ingenuity in the way they fought, and he didn't believe they would have taken this position without some idea of how to use it.

Give the whole army time to catch up, then they would put an end to this once and for all.

———————•———————

Valens stood at the top of the central stone tower, looking out across the walls and the meadow to the Dunholmi army unfolding under grey skies. These days, it was hard to make out details at a distance, but he saw enough for a rough count. There were already as many of them in line as there were defenders inside Barrowblack, and plenty more were marching up the road, spreading out to take their positions, banners flapping in the wind.

Beside him, the vast trebuchet creaked and groaned under the tension of its strained ropes and beams. Quintae stood by the machine, drumming fingers against the scarred side of his head, muttering to himself. That ought to have bothered Valens, but he felt a strange sort of calm. Within the walls, everything was as he'd ordered. Tents and shelters cleared away to form killing grounds. Wagons and logs piled up into secondary defensive lines. Archers and spear troops on the walls.

Shield warriors behind the gates. Reserves held ready to counterattack. Everything in order. Everything understandable.

Everything except Raul and his coven, who were spread around the top of the earth mound, backs to the inside of the wooden palisade, wearing robes in a green that matched the banners. The more Raul had explained, the less Valens had understood. He just had to trust the lad and pray that he lived.

Not for the first time, Valens found himself missing Fabia. He hadn't felt the absence of his hand in a while, but thinking of her, he looked down to where the mourning ring had been. So much was lost; how much could they regain even when the fighting was done? That is, if they were even here at the end. She would have mocked him for thoughts like that, told him that he needed to live in the moment if he wanted to survive it.

Across the meadow, Dunholmi warriors shuffled forward to make space for their second line.

"Can you reach them from here?" Valens asked.

"Yes, yes." Quintae grinned. "You want now?"

He wrapped his hand around the lever that released the counterweight. Spots of drizzle darkened the wood.

Valens looked at the enemy lines again. Enough of them had arrived to make an assault, but they hadn't finished forming up. It was time to force their hand.

"Do it."

Quintae pulled the lever, flinging his whole body into the movement. The counterweight fell; the vast arm of the trebuchet swung in an accelerating arc; it slammed against the restraining beam, the force of the impact shaking the whole tower. Valens watched a rock as big as he was hurtled through the air toward the Dunholmi lines.

The rock slammed into the first line of the Dunholmi army, smashing dismounted warriors, ploughing into the infantry levy beyond. Bones cracked. Flesh spattered. Whole bodies were flung aside, limp as rag dolls. The injured screamed in pain while a horse ran wild in panic.

Across the rebels' defences, Alder saw the arm of a trebuchet swinging back down, ready to be reloaded.

He looked along the line. As long as they waited here, that thing would keeping flinging death down among them and he had no way to respond. In theory, he would get more troops in line by waiting than he would lose to that cursed machine, but every hit would send a ripple of shock through another formation, and he'd seen what helplessness could do to an army's morale.

It's time, the fire inside him urged.

"All companies!" Alder bellowed, waving his sabre in the air. "Advance!"

Shouts and whistles went up all along the line. Commanders waved their own weapons or pointed toward the fort. Within moments, the meadow was filled with the sounds of tens of thousands of footsteps as the armed might of Dunholm marched to battle.

In a proper fight, with open ground and an accessible opponent, Alder would have started with a cavalry charge. The might of a mounted attack was Dunholm's greatest weapon, a surging wave of steel and muscle that left the enemy reeling. But the North Marchers had chosen their ground well, using the earthworks to counter Alder's advantages. Horses would be a hindrance here, so they advanced on foot, a single solid line, shields raised, banners flying.

Another rock hurtled through the air and smashed through the line, tossing broken bodies into their comrades. He was proud to see that those around them didn't falter, despite the screams and the wails. Perhaps it was steadfast courage, or perhaps they simply understood that they would be safer close to the earthworks, too close for the trebuchet to hit.

A cry of pain came from a different direction. Down the line, a warrior had tripped in a hidden hole and lay clutching her broken leg. Others stumbled, some falling, some keeping their feet. One vanished entirely, plummeting into a cunningly concealed pit.

The front lines faltered, slowed, warriors pausing to prod the ground ahead of them. Alder scowled. This wasn't how the brave troops of Dunholm were meant to advance, but what else were they meant to do? The rebels had ruined the ground ahead of them, and it was impossible to tell where holes might be hidden in the grass.

Another rock struck a different part of the line. Nearby troops moved faster, then stumbled into each other as they hit a hidden ditch.

This was ridiculous, to be held up by nothing but spadework and the ground they walked across. It wouldn't stop them from crossing the meadow, but if it meant that his troops crossed cautiously and uncertainly, then that was how they would approach the fight. He couldn't have that.

One way lay open: the road directly to the gates, a broad stretch of dirt trampled by the rebels' comings and goings, too bare to hide a trap or pitfall. Senius Tisco's company from Pavuno was there, a timid band raised from merchant houses, half of them barely out of childhood. He would have to put some courage into them.

"Brook!" he shouted as he strode down the front line. "I need ten of your best."

"Yes, my lord." Captain Brook hurried to his side, waving some of her warriors to follow.

"Not you, though," he said. "Funnel reserves up the road behind me, as fast as you can."

"My lord?" Brook knew better than to challenge him, but she raised an eyebrow.

"I'm going to show these rebels how little their walls are worth."

Valens clambered up the tower by the side of the gate as fast as his one hand would allow.

"What is it?" he asked as he reached the top.

Ferra pointed.

A column had emerged from the centre of the Dunholmi line and was advancing up the road at a fast march. The banners of Estian merchant families flew above the company at its head, the symbols of people who had chosen the occupiers over loyalty to their own, and the very sight of them sent fury boiling through Valens. Leading them were a dozen Dunholmi warriors in full armour, carrying sabres and shields.

"Thought they might do that," Valens said. "Shoot them full of arrows."

"Look who's at the front."

He squinted, made out a dark-haired figure with a sword that shone in the sunlight. Except that there was no sunlight, just grey skies and drizzle dampening his face. That bright line along the edge wasn't reflected light; it was fire.

Alder.

Valens's hand clenched around the hilt of his sword.

"Make sure you've got plenty of arrows for him."

With the column in range, the archers started to loose. The Dunholmi and their local allies raised their shields. Valens couldn't hear the thud of arrows against boards or the wet sound as they pierced flesh, but he could remember what it was like to make an advance like this, knowing you might get hit but had to keep marching anyway. Poor fuckers.

When Alder raised his shield, it was bright with flames. The air around it shimmered. An uneasy feeling settled like stones in the bottom of Valens's belly, watching arrows flare and fall into ash.

Arrows flew. Troops marched. The column strode toward the gates while the rest of the Dunholmi advanced more slowly across the meadow. Behind him was the creak and thud of the trebuchet hurling its heavy load, punching new holes in the opposing line.

Still, there were far more of them, and they kept coming.

The column reached the gate. As Valens watched, Alder pressed his shield against the wood, which blackened at its touch. Flames stretched from the shield along the beams of the gate. Dunholmi warriors raised their shields to protect their lord from arrows. Some of them fell, but others took their places. With mounting dread, Valens watched smoke billow.

"Form a line!" he shouted to the warriors waiting behind the gate. He'd thought they would have longer than this, while the Dunholmi brought up a ram or built a fire of timber and oil. Some general he was, not counting on Alder. He would have to do better next time; for now, all he could do was provide their best response.

The bar holding the gates gave way, and with a groan and a swirl of ashes, their remains swung open. The Dunholmi surged forward and slammed into the Estian shield wall, the defenders holding the gap with their courage, their resilience, and their charmed shields.

Bodies pressed against each other, swinging and stabbing, pushing and shoving. The sound of fighting was an old friend inviting Valens down. That was where he should be, using skills learned over long years, risking his life to take those of his enemies. He half drew his sword, then Ferra caught his eye and shook her head.

He slid the sword back into the sheath.

There were thousands of warriors here, but only one general.

"Archers, target the press outside!" he shouted. "Silvano, more shields to the gate. Yasmi, Nydia, bring up the first reserve."

His hand twitched to his sword as clangs and grunts rose from below, but he resisted the urge.

This was going to be a long day.

From the narrow walkway near the top of the palisade, Yasmi watched the Dunholmi forces advance up the earthworks. They were all around Barrowblack, coming up the slope with ladders and ropes. The stakes planted in the dirt slowed them down, as did the slipperiness of grass in the lightly falling rain and the heavier fall of arrows from the walls above. But they kept advancing, and there were far more of them.

"'A storm of shot shall not fell him, but the calm thereafter brings him to his knees,'" she said.

"What?" Princess Nydia glanced over, bow drawn.

"It's a line from Earl Endimeer in *The Falling Land*, just before the final battle."

"Then you're a little late with it." Nydia turned her attention to the slope below, then loosed. One of the Dunholmi infantry fell, arrow flights protruding from her throat. "Unless there's another battle coming after this one?"

The hook of a grappling iron clanged onto the wall close to Yasmi. She grabbed it, but whoever had flung it already had their full weight on the rope, holding it in place. If she donned her bear mask, she would have the strength to throw it off, but she doubted the walkway could take that weight. Instead, she drew a dagger and leaned over the parapet to saw on the rope. Arrows thudded into the woodwork a hair's breadth from her arm and she jerked back into cover, the rope untouched.

Nydia, an arrow nocked to the string of her curved bow, rose from shelter again, aimed, and loosed. Yasmi thought she heard a scream in response, but there was a lot of screaming, a lot of clangs and thuds and angry roars. Around the curve of Barrowblack, she saw the packed fighting around the gate, bodies wedged in tight together. Drusil's shields had let the defenders stand for over an hour against relentless attacks, fresh waves of Dunholmi fighters coming against them over and over, but the line was creeping back now, the Dunholmi close to breaking into open ground beyond the gate. Meanwhile, others were at the walls with ladders and ropes and climbing spikes, starting to ascend.

She felt so useless, not an archer or a shield fighter, doing little more than watch the fight and carry arrows back and forth. In some ways, it would be a relief when they broke through. In others…

She stared across Barrowblack to where Raul stood against the palisade at the back, wrapped in the same green robes as the rest of his coven. All of them, at their different positions along the wall, were drawing circles in the grass over and over. Every few minutes, a pair of bearers would leave a body at the base of the bank below one of them, some poor soul the physicians hadn't been able to save, their arm hacked off, head smashed open, body pierced by an arrow. Estian blood flowed into Estian dirt while above it the diviners chanted and drew their signs. More than anything, Yasmi wanted to believe that Raul knew what he was doing, that this could work, but in the moment, it looked like madness.

There was a thud, then another, and her section of the parapet shook as ladders slammed against the wall. Any moment now, she wouldn't be useless any longer, and that wasn't a good sign. Reaching for her masks, she turned to peer over the palisade.

What caught her eye wasn't the warrior halfway up a ladder, or the body of a Saditchi corsair falling with an arrow through his eye. It was movement at the edge of the woods, people emerging from a trail that ran into the hills. A few at first, then more, riders galloping out to the edges, warriors forming lines along the outskirt of the meadow. Banners flew above their heads: those of the earls of Estis alongside a green moon.

The other army had arrived.

———————•———————

Alder stood back from the gate, sheltered from the North March archers by the shields of his guard, wiping blood from his sabre and taking reports from his commanders.

"We're all around their flanks," one reported with glee. "Up the walls in several places."

"And almost through the gate." That was Tisco, far too pleased with himself for someone who'd looked as pale as he had when the lines closed. "One more push, that's all we need."

Alder almost laughed at the unwarranted confidence coming from a boy who'd barely even fought in his life, but he was right. Despite all the defences and all the losses, they were almost in, and once that happened the rebels were done for. No walls to protect them. Dunholm would water the land with their blood and burn the ruins of their fortress to the ground.

"My lord!" Brook ran over. An arrow thudded into her shield as she ran, but she ignored it. "More rebels are coming out of the woods."

Alder scowled. He didn't need distractions. "I thought your scouts swept the trees."

"They did. These must have arrived since, and they're not just scouts or ambushers. There's a whole army coming."

"So." Alder looked at the fortress. "They split their forces and hoped to trap us between them."

"Looks likely, my lord."

"Or to put it another way, they left half their army exposed during a fight against the pride of Dunholm." His commanders might not have flames flaring from their fingertips, but feral grins showed their ferocity. "The levy can fight for the fortress. Everyone else, mount up. We're going to show them how a real battle is fought."

Chapter Twenty-Three
Mourning Ring

The first of the Dunholmi came over the wall, an axe in his hand. Yasmi flung herself at him, teeth bared and claws outstretched. The man had a moment of frozen terror as a lion slammed into him, and then he was gone, flung to the ground below.

The next one held her sword ahead of her as she emerged, then swung a shield off her back. Her full attention on Yasmi, she never saw Nydia's hatchet before it sliced through the back of her neck.

Parts of the parapet were still lined with archers shooting at the approaching Dunholmi, but others were chaotic battlefields in which the two sides grappled, slashing and hacking and shoving. There was barely space to stand on the narrow walkway, never enough for anyone to get past. No chance to dodge or manoeuvre. Shuffling back, one of the defenders lost her footing and fell. Another swung a club that knocked a Dunholmi flying, to crash through the roof of a storehouse below.

It wasn't enough space for Yasmi either, with her broad body and heavy paws. Her growling presence slowed the attackers as they came up, but it wasn't enough. She needed space to fight.

A shout of command drew her attention to the space below. Too pressed to hold the gate, Valens was finally pulling the shield wall back, reforming at their next line of defences, rows of overturned wagons and roughly cut logs with spears thrusting from behind them.

Pulling off her mask, Yasmi reverted to human form just as another Dunholmi appeared across the wall. He swung his sabre. She ducked, slapped the monkey mask on, and rolled off the parapet as she shifted. With the long fingers of one hand, she grasped the edge of the walkway, swung herself around, grabbed a knot in the back of the palisade, and went scrambling down.

Even in those brief moments, the shape of the fighting shifted. Dunholmi warriors, pent up for so long behind the gates, came surging in. A wave of steel and battle cries crashed against the second line. Some of them went scrambling up the barricades, carried by momentum and the rush of the crowd, to be skewered by spears as they went over the top. Others fell back before advancing again, while arrows arced over their heads from both sides. At one end of the line, the barricade collapsed and infantry ploughed through, only to be met by the folk of the Withered Hills and their allies, the beasts of the wild. A bear grabbed two warriors and smashed them together while wildcats tore another down.

The lines were collapsing, descending into a messy tangle in which knots of warriors stood together against whatever came their way. Spears stabbed. Sabres slashed. Axes hacked. Shields slammed against one another. Roars and screams and battle cries echoed from the wooden walls that fenced them all in.

Then she saw him, the scholarly exile who'd become part of Raul's coven, standing on the mound beneath the barricade. The rest of the coven were safely away from the fighting, but it was about to wash over him as he worked at his task, drawing the same circles over and over again. He believed in what he was doing so much that he would stay there and be overrun rather than give up. Maybe Yasmi had been spending too much time with Raul, or maybe she needed something to cling to after all the hurt she'd seen, but that man's faith and his courage were things she could believe in.

She scampered across Barrowblack, dashing along the top of a barricade, swinging from a spear, running across the roof of the smithy, her tail keeping her balanced. Near the end of the roof, she whipped off the monkey mask and pressed the lion in its place. As her body stretched out into that muscular form, she leapt, a streak of golden glory through the rain, to crash into the blue-clad warriors ascending the bank. She tore one of them open and slammed another down the bank, so that he knocked his comrades over as he fell. Then she pressed her claws into the dirt and ran up the slope to stand by the green-robed man.

He looked at her, eyes wide. "Thank you."

With a growl, she took up station beside him, ready to fend off anyone who came for him. She only hoped no archers looked this way.

"Not long now," the diviner said. "We're almost done."

At the bottom of the slope, two Dunholmi had been added to the pile of dead bodies. All around more were falling, the brave and the foolhardy of both sides. More death wherever she looked. Yasmi hoped for all their sakes that the diviner was right.

With a heavy heart, Raul watched the destruction paying out within the ring of Barrowblack, heard the fighting outside its walls. He had made this happen, him and the rebellion he led. So many lives. So much loss. Appia. Ovida. Biallo. A thousand others who he couldn't even name.

He raised his hand. Around the fort, his coven imitated the gesture, signalling that they had seen. Each of them drew a black mourning ring from their belt and slid it onto their finger. Then they took up smouldering rope matches and touched them to the ground.

A ring of lantern oil ignited around the inside of the palisade. For a moment, in that flash of fire, Raul thought of Alder and of the destructive force of Jarrag, unleashed from the Withered Hills. This was his symbol, his power. But like any symbol, it could mean many things. What mattered wasn't finding the right meaning, but finding a meaning people could share. Symbols like that bound people together, bound the world together. Hopefully, if he'd understood what he'd read, they could bind this magic too.

Fire could be destruction and death, but it could also be

warmth and light. It could be the inferno itself or its aftermath, the smoking dirt left once that brief flash of flames burned out, a ring of ashes around the top of Barrowblack.

A mourning ring.

Loss and grief signified by darkness.

Barrow. Black.

Prisca had told him there were thin places in the world where its deeper power bled through. He'd felt that in the Withered Hills, when he'd reached into the power of the land and turned a snowy field into a charm. But from what he'd seen, power wasn't found where the world was thinner. It didn't lie in some eternal meaning from which humans were cut off, leaving them grasping for scraps. Whether he was reading signs or making charms, power arose when people connected to the world and to each other. It was in the places thick with meaning, where they could draw the threads together and make something new. Threads of history. Threads of rebellion. Threads of a nation.

Threads of loss.

Around the circle of earth walls, Raul felt himself connect with the rest of his coven, with the land beneath them, with the people who had reshaped it centuries before. Had those people really built this place to commemorate their dead, in the same way modern Estians wore mourning rings? It didn't matter whether it was true or not. What mattered was that it let him connect to Barrowblack, to its past, and to the people there now.

He took a deep breath and thought of the parents he had never known, dead when he was a baby. So far lost from him that he didn't even know their names. A part of him he could never touch.

One heartbeat, his and the coven's. Then he exhaled, and so did they, each of them thinking of their own loss.

Grief swept like a torrent of tears across the heart of Barrowblack, rolling out of this vast mourning ring and soaking the armies that fought there. The fighting faltered, cries of anger subsiding, shouts of pain fading to whimpers. The sensation hit the Estians hardest, Raul could see that. It was as it should be. This was their land and their tradition of death, so the connection was deeper. But it hit the others too: Withering Folk, Saditchi, Dunholmi. Faces fell. Someone sobbed.

Like the dark of the moon, everything was blackness.

Raul thought of his other parents, the ones who had loved him and raised him, who in their own ways had tried to do what was best. Without the deaths of his first parents, he never would have known them. Was the price worth paying? It was impossible to know, but without it he would never have known that love. Without death, there could be no life. Without all the risks and suffering of their war, there could be no freedom.

Without a night of darkness, there could be no new moon.

He let out a breath of hope and renewal, his heart beating harder. The banners on top of the palisade fluttered in a brisk wind that drove the rain away.

The bright burst of hope hit the Estians hardest. Their land. Their tradition. Their connection. Every one of them stood straighter, their weariness wiped away, moons closing, battered blades sharp. For a moment, they stood so proud that they seemed to glow.

Then they surged forward, voices raised in a battle cry as Raul raised his fist and led the shout.

"A new moon rises!"

The rebels rushed the shaken Dunholmi, sent them tumbling in the dirt, staggering back toward the broken gates. The desperate grind of combat became a surge of movement, a flood of furious action, a storm wind sweeping the enemy away. In the time it took Raul to sink to his knees, the invaders were driven across the bloody ground of Barrowblack and out onto the meadow beyond.

"Raul, are you hurt?"

He looked up to see Yasmi crouching in front of him. Nydia and a half dozen Saditchi stood around them, bows and cutlasses at the ready, watching for anyone who came close. How long had he been slumped like this, staring at the ground, his hand clenched to his chest?

"Raul, please, talk to me. Is it your wound? Can you stand?"

"I..." He tried to find the thing he wanted to say, but his mind was an empty chamber, nothing there he could connect his thoughts to. However hard he grasped at them, he was lost for words.

———————— • ————————

Valens stormed through the gates of Barrowblack, waving a banner over his head and roaring orders.

"Silvano, form a centre, every company with shields! Ferra, left flank, all your beasts and bows! Nydia, right flank! Every other fucker, find a place!"

He took a deep breath, smelled blood and smoke, felt the heady rush of victory. They'd held the line, like the shield wall of Estis always did, and the enemy had broken against it, had shattered and stumbled. Now they would seize the moment and show what true warriors could do.

Thousands of them streamed past him, bloody but determined. Ranks formed and swept across the meadow, catching the Dunholmi between the defenders of Barrowblack and Queen Junia's old guard. The hammer and the anvil, a strategy as old as war. He howled with wild laughter and thrust his arm into the sky, punched at the heavens with his stump. Who cared if the world saw what he'd lost? That loss had forced him to become stronger, to find his new self, to be a leader and not just a warrior. A new moon was rising, and so was a new Valens.

"For Estis and a new moon!" he bellowed. "Advance!"

On the flanks, Dunholmi infantry were running for their lives. Valens ignored them and shouted at his commanders to do the same. Those ones didn't matter anymore. The ones who mattered were the warriors still fighting.

Across the meadow, a furious combat was underway. Wave after wave of Dunholmi cavalry charged against the battle lines of the former exiles and their mercenaries. Pinned against the woodland, the Estians had little space to manoeuvre and the Dunholmi had caught them before they were formed up. Reduced to individual companies and small clumps of infantry, it was a desperate fight, the sort that Valens had seen go badly more often than it went well.

Not today.

Silvano fell into step beside Valens, grinning as broadly as he did.

"That was strange," the docker captain said. "Back there, I mean."

"What did you expect?" Valens asked. "Fireballs and lightning bolts? A hole in the ground that would swallow them up?"

"I heard there was a field of teeth once."

"Would you expect that from Raul?"

"I never know what to expect from our prince anymore." Silvano laughed. "Except for victory."

Valens waved his banner, the new moon fluttering in the wind. The clouds above parted and the sun shone down as he charged his army into the rear of the enemy.

The chaos of combat broke out again, and this time it was on their side.

———————— • ————————

Count Alder swept his sword down with all his strength, a blow full of fury and frustration. Weary from the fight, he struck too slow and the rebel brought her shield up. Alder's flaming sabre bounced off its edge, barely even leaving a black mark. Where in the names of all the gods had the North Marchers got these shields from?

He swung again, then thrust, got past the woman's defence and pierced her shoulder. She grunted and staggered, but another took her place. Fellstride lashed out, hooves smacking against those cursed shields.

This was meant to be his hour, breaking the last army of the North March and driving them from the field, shattering their dreams of rebellion for generations to come. An hour of glory. An hour of triumph. An hour that would secure the status of the House of Alder and make sure no one questioned what he had done.

An hour of blood and fire, of crushing everyone who stood against him, a thought that made his heart swell.

"My lord!" Captain Brook was shouting across the heads of his warriors, trying to push her steed through. "My lord, we've been attacked in the rear."

"Don't be ridiculous." But when he pulled Fellstride from the front line and stood in his stirrups, he could see that she was right. Half the infantry levy was shattered, cowardly peasants fleeing for their lives, tossing weapons aside as they ran. The other half was caught in a fighting retreat against rebels advancing from their fortress, a retreat that was pressing his forces into a fast-shrinking space.

He looked around. There had to be something he'd missed, some part of his army not yet engaged or a place where the enemy was weak. But somehow they had turned the beast of war against him, and if he stayed, it would end in ruin. There was a pulsing in his ears like a second heartbeat racing to matching his own. His throat constricted around the order he didn't want to give but that was vital if he wasn't to lose everything.

"Pull back!" he shouted, and his commanders took up the cry. "Head for the road."

As least the rebels hadn't seized the way out of the meadow, and he would make them regret that mistake. He wheeled his cavalry around, forming up in the swiftly diminishing space. Whatever else might have happened, the knights of Dunholm were the glory of the world, strong and disciplined, courageous and obedient. The ranks drew in, ready for his order.

"Charge!"

Spurs pressed against flanks and they galloped again, heading for the flank of the rebel army and the road beyond. For a moment he could forget the shame that burned his cheeks, the frustration that tightened his fingers around the handle of his shield. He was a noble of Dunholm riding with his finest warriors, humans and horses moving as one, an unstoppable force.

The rebels tried to hold their ground, forming a hurried line. But these weren't the disciplined Dunholmi infantry that had once mastered half the continent. The line shattered as the charge hit, some of them trampled in the dirt, others swept aside.

A bear reared up in front of Alder, roaring loud enough to shake the sky. Fellstride swerved and Alder's sabre slashed out, carving a great red wound down the beast's shoulder as he passed. Looking back, he saw it stagger and slam into the ground, blood spraying into the grass. He bared his teeth and laughed. If they couldn't beat the rebels today, they could tear some of them down as they went.

Then he was past the last of the rebels, only a few scattered arrows pursuing him. He slowed to let more of his riders catch him, not to leave the infantry so far behind they gave up. The battle was over, but the war wasn't. He clenched his teeth and shook his head, like he could shake off these northerner fleas who had caused him so much trouble. He would make them pay for what they had done to him.

Fire flared again along the blade of his sabre, so bright the warriors around him looked away. He could feel the same heat blaze in his eyes and in his heart.

He was going to burn Prince Raul Warborn's whole world down.

———————•———————

Clinging tightly to his staff with one hand and Yasmi's shoulder with the other, Raul stumbled out through the gates of Barrowblack. People were cheering from the walls, from the towers, from all across the meadow. Some of them cheered his name. Some of them cheered that a new moon was rising. Some made wild, inarticulate noises, cheering for the sake of cheering, to let out the dread and pain of the morning and their exultation at how it had ended.

He staggered beneath that sound, his whole body threatening to give way. He felt as if all his energy had been sucked dry, leaving him so hungry it hurt.

"You should lie down," Yasmi whispered, while keeping up her own smile for the crowd.

"I'm fine," he said, smiling as best he could.

"No, you're not."

"I'm not, but people need to see me."

"And I need you to live."

"It's not that bad."

"Less than an hour ago, you could barely speak. Don't you dare tell me it's not that bad."

Her words were such a furious hiss, he thought that smile might collapse, but she held it in place, the professional performer at every turn.

They kept walking onto a field littered with bodies and abandoned weapons, its grass trampled and stained with blood. He blinked at the carnage, shook his head, tried to remember why he was here, where this terrible destruction had come from.

A battle. A stand against Dunholm. That was it. He lifted his head, watched prisoners being rounded up while enemy stragglers were chased from the field.

"Your Highness!" Silvano marched over and sank into a bow.

"I shouldn't use that title anymore," Raul said.

"Really?" Silvano rose and grinned, waving at the exultant crowd that was gathering around them. "That's not what this lot thinks."

Like ripples on a river forming a current, the cheers came together into a chant.

"Warborn! Warborn! Warborn!"

Raul blushed. "Not sure that name works anymore either."

Silvano shrugged. "We can work on it, now that we've won."

Raul took a deep breath. He didn't want to spoil the celebrations, but he doubted that all this was done. A single battle wouldn't stop Dunholm.

Orders were shouted and the crowd parted ahead of them.

Through the gap came Valens, along with Prisca, Queen Junia, and Earl Tordesse. Prisca and Junia stood stiffly, their smiles restrained.

"Raul, there's someone here you should meet," Valens said. "He let us catch him instead of galloping off with Count Alder."

"Alder survived?" That was bad. Worse that he'd got away. By tomorrow, he'd be gathering the remains of his army, just like Raul had done, and then he would be back to burning and pillaging, trying to punish Estis for the crime of wanting to be free.

"Raul Warborn, head of the council of Estis," Tordesse said, the formality of his voice setting Raul on edge. "May I introduce His Royal Majesty, King Lorrin of Dunholm."

He stepped aside to reveal a man Raul had only seen once before, in the desperate fighting at Hound's Gap. He had looked proud then. Now he looked battered, exhausted, one arm pressed to his chest and the other clutching the silver circlet of a travelling crown.

Maybe this single battle would do more than he thought.

Chapter Twenty-Four
Greater Good

Raul closed his eyes and took a deep breath, luxuriating in the scents of the woodland, so different from the lingering stench of blood and smoke that still draped Barrowblack two days after the battle. If he focused on the scent of nature on the breeze and the whistling of the birdsong, instead of the people shouting at each other across the meadow behind him, then he could almost believe that he was back home in the Vales and this was just another walk out from the inn. Except that he hadn't been followed by a pair of bodyguards from the Imperial Legion in those days, travelling companions whom Valens insisted he keep with him now. They might have beaten the Dunholmi, but many of their forces were still out there, and who knew what they had planned.

He opened his eyes and walked deeper into the woods, leaning on his staff. It was almost like an extra leg now, he was getting so used to it, instinctively swinging it ahead to lean his weight in before lifting his good leg. Queen Junia's personal physician and the ship's surgeon from Princess Nydia's warband both agreed that his pain would lessen over time but never entirely go away. Now he was waiting to see where the balance between wound and recovery lay. How much pain would remain? How mobile would he be when this was over? It seemed unlikely that he'd ever go running up the steep slopes of the Vales again, but it would be nice to walk through the woodland without help.

"Prisca?" he called out. "Where are you?"

"Over here," came an answering shout from deeper in among the trees. He followed that voice, hobbling over roots and around clumps of ferns. In among the madness of war, he'd lost track of time passing, but somewhere along the line spring had reached its end. Was this the first real day of summer he'd seen, a world soaked in warmth and light, nature in full bloom? Or was it only the first one that he'd noticed?

He emerged into a small clearing. Prisca sat on the trunk of a fallen tree, watching the patterns on the ground as light filtered through the leaves. She patted the wood and Raul went to sit beside her while his guards took up positions at the edge of the clearing, adopting the same stance as the warriors who guarded Prisca, watchful and ready.

A part of him wanted to enjoy this moment, to cling to memories of time spent with his mother in the past, to find again the connection they'd had, whatever part of it had been true. But in the struggle for control of the rebellion, she had sided with Junia, and that was a hard thing to let go. Her reasons were understandable—everything she'd set in motion had been meant to restore Estis as it once was—but understanding wasn't the same as forgiving, however much he wanted it to be. When he needed all the support he could get, his mother had turned against him, and that memory stood like a wall between them.

"What do you see?" she asked, pointing to the patterns of light on the ground.

Laying his staff aside, Raul let himself relax and watched those patterns shift. The longer he did this, the more he understood how to read the signs. Part of it was about becoming unfocused, not so much his eyes as his mind, releasing his own preconceptions so that the world could reveal itself.

Preconceptions. There was a word that showed how much he took after his mother. His da never would have come out with a word like that.

"Fragments scattering, then coming together," he said. "Not all of them, though. What remains is diminished."

"The Dunholmi army."

"Most likely, yes."

"Not a staggering revelation."

"True, but it's a starting point. Didn't you used to encourage me to be patient?"

"So you're teaching me now?" She treated him to one of her slender smiles, and he couldn't help smiling back. This was as close as she came to saying she was proud of him.

"I'm reflecting your own wisdom." He nodded to the dappled ground. "In which spirit, what else do you see?"

Prisca's eyes narrowed as she surveyed the shapes, then raised a thin, trembling finger to point them out.

"A house and a crown. The monarch coming home, perhaps? A promising omen."

"It could symbolise Pavuno and the royal palace there." Raul clenched up at memories of that place, of being at Count Alder's mercy, learning the lies of his life, seeing Valens lose his hand. Not a place he wanted to go, but sooner or later he would have to face it.

"Something to do with King Lorrin, perhaps. Whatever happens next, he will be key." She looked at Raul. "What do the reports from the scouts say?"

"That Alder's retreating, gathering his remaining forces as he goes. That he's significantly diminished, half his army dead or deserted."

"We should follow and..." Her voice faltered and her fingers twitched as if they could grasp at whichever words escape her. "We should finish him off."

"That's what Tordesse and Nydia say, but Valens and Drusil aren't convinced. They think we still need time to recover from the battle, and there are logistical challenges to moving such a large army. Then there's the option of talking, using control of Lorrin to pressure Alder into leaving our lands."

"What do you think?"

He blinked, then looked at her. Was his mother actually asking his opinion?

"I'm considering it. My mind's still fuzzy from the magic we worked during the battle, but I'll decide in time for this afternoon's council meeting."

More shapes revealed themselves to him on the forest floor. Chains. A heart that broke in two. A circle beside a star.

Those could be connected to his magic and the coven; the circle symbolising what they'd done and the star as a representation of brightness and power, as well as a tool of divination.

"It was impressive, what you did in the battle," Prisca said. Had she seen the same signs and drawn the same conclusion, or was this just an obvious conversation for them to have?

"Thank you."

"You turned away from magic before."

"We both thought the rebellion needed a warrior king. Besides, I saw what divination was doing to you."

"Yes, well..." Prisca held her own hand in front of her, staring as though willing it to change. Her fingers were trembling again. "I expect that you'll be setting it aside soon."

"I..."

Raul pushed himself to his feet, turning away from Prisca as he rose. He reached for his staff, then decided against it. He could do this. With slow, tentative steps, one hand outstretched and the other pressed to the ache of his belly, he started walking across the clearing.

"This war isn't over," he said. "We came back from a defeat and Alder could do the same. The fighting could drag on, and while that happens more people will suffer."

"A definitive victory is required."

"Exactly." He took a deep breath. This much walking without support left his whole body shaking. Was he proving something to himself, or to her? "We have to hit them with everything we've got."

He turned awkwardly, started walking back toward Prisca and the fallen tree.

"Everything we've got includes my coven." His coven, not theirs. He trusted Prisca with this conversation, but not yet with his people. "Hopefully, it includes more of what we did at Barrowblack, though I don't know exactly what yet. It certainly includes a lot of divination to give us an edge over Alder."

"Even though..." Prisca tapped the side of her head.

"Others have paid with their lives for our freedom. Part of my mind doesn't seem such a high price."

He stopped at the log, turned, lowered himself back to his seat. Prisca laid her hands on his elbow and back, steadying him, easing the strain.

"Thank you." He wiped sweat from his brow. "The others aren't going to like this, Yasmi and Da especially. I'll need your support when they try to argue me down."

"You'll have it."

"I thought I would, this time."

She didn't flinch at the allusion to her past behaviour, but she had the decency to look away.

"That was..." She hesitated. Was that a sign of shame, or were the words she needed eluding her again? "I love Estis. I have committed my whole life to its well-being. I need to see it run..." Her eyes flitted from side to side like she was following a fly through the air. "...competently, efficiently, for the greatest common good. I understand that this sometimes places us in opposition to each other, and that grieves me, but I can't let it weaken my decisions."

An angry, bitter part of Raul wanted to ask if it was so bad to be human in her decision-making. But he didn't love his mother for who she could be, he loved her as she was, even on the days when he didn't much like her. For that reason alone, he would keep this civilised, not air his grievances in front of their guards.

"How do you think we should deal with King Lorrin?" he asked.

"Don't you want to save this discussion for the council?"

He shrugged. "We're here now, we might as well talk. Then I'll have time to think before the meeting."

Prisca looked up, watching a swift dart across the sky.

"We can move quickly now to end this," she said. "Between King Lorrin's demeanour and the state we found him in, it's clear that he and Count Alder are no longer in alignment, but legitimate authority rests with the king. If we can..." One of those pauses, Prisca blinking as she gathered her words. "If we can agree a peace with Lorrin, then I think many of the Dunholmi will happily ride home, and we'll be free of further intervention while we root out the count."

"You don't think Alder will leave with the king?"

"I've seen the look in Lorrin's eyes when he talks about Alder, the burned skin peeking out from under his bandages. As long as Lorrin rules, returning to Dunholm would mean the headsman for Alder."

"So we make peace with Lorrin and war with Alder."

"Indeed."

Moments like this reminded Raul why it was valuable to have his mother around, despite their disagreements. Perhaps because of them. He didn't have to share her whole world view to learn from it.

A squirrel scrambled down a tree, stared at them both for a moment, then ran off into the undergrowth. Twigs snapped as one of the guards shifted her weight. This far into the woods, Raul could still distantly hear voices from Barrowblack, but for the most part the world was calm and still.

"We can bring Lorrin to the council," he said. "Negotiate a peace for everyone."

"Negotiate, that was the word." Prisca ran a hand across her face. "And no, that won't work. Lorrin is a monarch, he'll expect to negotiate with someone of equal stature, one ruler to another. That could mean Queen Junia, or it could mean you if we set the council aside and position you as a prince. Now that you've shown strength through your victory, Junia would accept that, I think. It's not as though she has another heir waiting in the wings."

Raul took a breath and took the time to consider what she was saying. He owed her that much, even if he'd known before she was halfway done that he wouldn't agree. She didn't see Estis or its people the way he did.

"Lorrin is on the losing side," he said. "He'll negotiate with whoever he has to."

Silence fell, the two of them sitting stiffly on the fallen tree, a small and yet infinite gap between them. So much for the comfortable feeling of sitting with his mother, spending time from her, learning from her.

"This is your final word on the matter?" she asked.

"It is, and if you've been paying any attention, then you know the council will agree."

Another squirrel scurried past the tree, or perhaps the same one from before, then come back for whatever lay in those branches.

"I see." Prisca sighed and hung her head. For a moment, she seemed like one of the puppets that people made in the Withered Hills, lying idle before its maker animated it. Then she lifted her head and waved a hand at one of her guards. "Remto, could you fetch my pack? I left it by that stream when I was studying the current."

"Yes, Minister." The guard headed into the trees.

"Apologies." Prisca looked at Raul, her slender smile and steely gaze returning. "There's food in my pack and all this talk has left me hungry."

"I might have something, if I didn't eat it already. No one told me that high magic would be such hungry work..."

Raul untied a pouch from his belt and rummaged through its contents, but this one turned out to be full of sketches for charms and war machines. Opening another, he knocked his elbow against his wounded side and the jolt of pain made him jerk his arm away. Nuts and dried berries scattered across the grass.

He almost flung the pouch on the ground. It was so frustrating, so exhausting, working around his limits every day, using twice as much energy on even the smallest tasks, constantly having to pay attention to each little detail yet still managing to mess it up, to step the wrong way and have his leg give out from under him or to knock against a chair and end up consumed with pain. Some days he wanted to just sit down and weep, but he couldn't because they were all counting on him.

When this was over, then he could truly rest.

If this was ever over.

There was a rustle of movement. Prisca crouched in front of him, gathering up the spilled food with hands that trembled just as much as his.

"I expect I'm missing some," she said, "and I daresay the squirrels will be grateful later, if gratitude is within their capabilities."

"Thank you." Raul swallowed the tears threatening to burst from him. Carefully, he pulled the mouth of the pouch open and held it for her to fill.

Another rustle of movement, this time behind him.

"Your Highness," one of his guards said, and there was an edge to her voice.

Trying not to strain his wounds, he turned to look around. Prisca's guard had returned. She wasn't carrying a pack, but she was accompanied by another dozen warriors, all wearing the livery of Queen Junia, all carrying clubs.

"What is this?" Raul asked, looking from the new arrivals to Prisca, who had risen to stand over him, her expression apologetic.

"I'm sorry, Raul," Prisca said, "but events have reached a critical juncture, and we cannot risk the kingdom on a child's vision of government."

Ferns rustled and twigs snapped as the warriors moved out around the clearing, circling them. Raul's two guards stepped closer to him, drawing their axes, watching the others.

"At my insistence, Her Majesty agreed that we would give you one last chance to see sense. But I must reluctantly accept that Queen Junia is right. You simply don't have the maturity our nation needs right now. Perhaps, in time, you will. Or perhaps, in this regard, I failed in raising you. Regardless, I need you to understand that this is not about you or me, it is about the greater good. Once the nation has been securely restored, you will be released to some small, safe life, perhaps in another country where the recollection of your endeavours cannot disturb the status quo.

"For now, I recommend that you don't resist. As both your minister and your mother, I wouldn't want to see you hurt."

Raul felt as if the bottom of the world had opened up and he was plummeting down a pit with no end. Nothing he said or did seemed equal to the moment.

His guards backed toward him, weapons raised, while the warriors with clubs closed in. There was no way he could escape, but he had to let the others know. He couldn't let Prisca's pride and Junia's ambition undo the things they'd fought for.

"Give me a moment," he said, wrapping his hands around his staff. He forced himself upright, legs trembling even more than usual. His body felt like a lead weight dragging him down.

It would have been easier if he could see the triumph in Prisca's eyes, but there was something closer to resignation.

"You made your choices," she said.

"And now I'm making one more."

Fast as he could, he whipped the staff up and swung it with all his strength. The blow knocked one warrior off his feet and sent another staggering back. Unable to keep his balance,

Raul flung himself into Prisca and the two of them fell, pain blazing through him as he hit the ground.

"Run!" he screamed.

One of his guards moved to protect him, but the other understood. Swinging her axe as a deterrent, she charged through the gap Raul had made, running for all she was worth. Three of Prisca's warriors sprinted after her, into the trees and toward the meadow.

There were thuds as his other guard went down under a flurry of clubs, while hands hauled Raul roughly to his feet.

"Come," Prisca hissed, heading for the deeper forest. "We need to get out of here."

Chapter Twenty-Five
Land and People

Yasmi wasn't sure how she had ended up in charge of the casualties. Valens had been organising their surviving forces, Ferra coordinating scouts to watch the Dunholmi, Drusil checking supplies. Everyone was playing their part, but the dead and wounded had been left out of the script. So here she was, checking on the progress of the physicians and overseeing the digging of graves, with help from anyone who would listen when she gave a command. That turned out to be more people than she expected.

She'd chosen one side of the meadow as a graveyard, at the edge of the trees. Each body got a grave of its own, whether anyone knew their name or not. Estian, Dunholmi, mercenary, they were all as deserving of a respectful resting place.

There was Raul's influence again, insisting that she care about everyone. She smiled and shook her head.

Princess Nydia was approaching with some of her corsairs, dressed in their black armour over yellow, wearing helmets and weapons as if marching to war. Even battered from the battle, Nydia managed to look stunning, a bruise on her cheek coordinating with her uniform. Yasmi straightened the bronze charm around her neck and tugged the sleeves of her tunic up, revealing the silver bracelet that Raul had given her.

The Saditchi stopped a few strides from three yellow-clad bodies and the holes waiting for them. So pale in life, Yasmi might have thought they were only playing the roles of corpses.

"Your Highness." Yasmi bowed her head. "I'm sorry for your loss."

"Thank you." Nydia knelt by one of the bodies, a young woman, and pushed a few strands of white hair back behind her ear.

"We have two priests of Yorl and one of Avgar, if you would like them to attend."

"We sail with our own gods, and our own chaplain."

At a gesture from Nydia, a young woman stepped forward, bareheaded and with a stole hanging across her breastplate, a gold whale embroidered on blue. The others took off their helmets.

"For each of us, one final tide will come," the chaplain said, "and the wave of our lives will break. For Yisprani, Malam, and Yay, that wave came in courage and honour. Though they will not find their find berth in the brine, but here in the dry dirt, still their—"

"Help!" a voice cried out. "Help for the Warborn!"

Yasmi whirled around, reaching for her masks. A warrior came running out of the woods, dressed in the red and black of the Imperial Legion. Her face was flushed, an axe swinging in her hand. Behind her, someone else moved in the forest, then turned and hurried away.

"What is it?" Yasmi ran across the loose dirt of freshly filled graves.

"Minister Prisca," the legionary said, panting for breath between her words. "She's taken... taken Prince Raul."

"Taken him where?"

"Don't know. She had... armed men... caught us by surprise... Julio was..."

The exposed skin on Yasmi's arms prickled as dread wrapped its cold hands around her chest, followed a heartbeat later by the hot flush of rage. After everything they'd been through, everything they'd forgiven her, Prisca had betrayed Raul again? Seized him by force? Her fingers clenched the muscles of an arm twice as thick as her own, dragging the woman's head down to hers.

"Where?"

"Back in the woods, I can show you."

"We'll come." Nydia was there, turning to whistle to her corsairs. "Harito, run to General Valens, tell him my prince is taken. The rest of you, with me."

As they followed the legionary into the woods, Yasmi reached for her masks. She wished that she still had the wolf, to follow Prisca's trail and hunt her down. Or the ogre, so she could rip the treacherous minister apart. But more than anything else, she wished that this wasn't happening, that Raul was safely back behind the walls of Barrowblack, that his mother hadn't found a way to prove herself worse than ever.

For a little while, it had seemed that Raul might get back what he wanted, not just his family but his trust in the world, and Yasmi hated Prisca for ruining that sweetness as much as for anything else. Why couldn't she let her son be who he was?

"This must be Junia's doing," Nydia said as they ran. "Not wanting to give up her family's throne."

Yasmi barked a bitter laugh. "Never underestimate the cruel depths of Prisca Servita."

In a clearing, another legionary lay crumpled on the ground, blood oozing from his scalp. As they ran over, he pushed himself up on one elbow and pointed into the woods.

"That way," he croaked.

The guilt she felt at leaving him didn't even give Yasmi pause. She'd never run so fast in human form as she did now, leaping over fallen branches and flinging aside the undergrowth, Nydia running beside her, the corsairs and legionary behind.

They reached a dip in the ground, a slope down to a stream with a bed of stones.

"Which way now?" Nydia asked, setting an arrow to her bowstring.

Again, Yasmi longed for the wolf, the power of a hunter's body, the scent of prey in the air. But she had other forms, others senses she could use. She took the deer mask from her belt and placed it on her face.

There was a pounding in her ears as she sank to four legs, her body bending in places and stretching in others, arms elongating. Some of the corsairs gasped, not used to seeing a shifter change. She ignored them and focused on the world around her, what the senses of prey revealed.

Playing the role of the deer had always been an edgy experience, as the shape of her body shaped her mind. While the wolf relished the rich scents of the world, the deer smelled harsh and dangerous things that left her gulping in panic. Every sound was an alarm bell. Muscles twitched at the least movement in the undergrowth.

She forced herself to stand still, to accept the stench of the humans around her while she noted other sounds and smells. There was little wind to carry anything here, under the shelter of the trees and a summer's day, but a lingering stink of sweat and the rattle of displaced stones downstream.

Water splashed beneath her hooves as she bounded into the stream and, fighting every instinct in her body, followed the sounds instead of fleeing them. She dashed downriver, momentum keeping her stable as pebbles flew from beneath her hooves. More splashing and clattering followed, but it grew distant as she ran, the sounds ahead clearer. Now she caught a scent she had missed in among the rest, one that made her heart swell and her muscles tighten, pushing her on for all she was worth. The scent of Raul.

Tall trees gave way to shorter, slender ones and dense undergrowth, then the stream flowed out of the woods and into a pool at the edge of fields. The ground here had been divided into strips planted with different crops: the thick stalks of broad beans, low leaves of turnips, rows of half-grown corn. A clear line was trampled through it all to a track at the far side where warriors in the heraldry of Estian noble houses were hauling something toward a mule.

Not something, someone. Raul, dressed in the green

diviner's robes of which he was so proud, feet trailing in the dirt. Another of the warriors was carrying his staff. Off to one side, Prisca gave orders and watched them all with her habitual disdain.

There were dozens of warriors, perhaps a hundred even, more than Yasmi had brought with her even if she waited for support.

She didn't.

Racing out of the woods, she brought a hoof up and swept the mask from her face. Her back twisted and her forelegs became arms, almost dropping her in the dirt, but she kept running, cast the mask aside, found another by touch and tore it from her belt.

Across the fields, Prisca looked up and her brow creased. She snapped a command and warriors lined the edge of the field, clubs in hand, while others kept hauling Raul toward the mule. Was he moving? Could he? Fear for him fuelled Yasmi's fury as she pressed the lion to her face and flung herself into a powerful, bounding pace. When she roared, it was a sound so deep and merciless that the fields rippled and shook.

"No blades," Prisca snapped as one of the warriors reached for a sword. "No killing our own."

An arrow hissed past Yasmi's head and hit the ground by Prisca's feet. Nydia's people weren't far behind and they seemed ready to spill blood, but whatever advantage that gave them would be nothing compared with how many people Prisca had brought.

It didn't matter. All that mattered was Raul, who turned his head at the sound of her coming, eyes wide, pleading with his captors.

Yasmi leapt, hit one of the warriors with her full weight, ribs cracking as she slammed him into the ground. Another swung a club, but she caught his arm between her teeth, twisted, crunched, tasted blood, then flung him aside. The third raised a shield and Yasmi hooked her claws over the top, wrenched it down, ripped it from her arm. The warrior yelled and dropped her club, clutching a hand to her dislocated shoulder.

Others circled around Yasmi, trying to close her in. Too late, she realised her mistake. Flinging herself into the heart of them, she'd let herself be surrounded, and the Saditchi couldn't shoot at these troops without risking her. Not that Nydia was holding them back. She and her corsairs came loping across the fields, round black shields on their arms, hooked spears and hatchets in their hands, their battle cry a wild gale of laughter.

The Saditchi hit one end of Prisca's force, clubs and hatchets and shields clashing, both sides roaring oaths. Through the chaos, Yasmi could still see Raul, his captors preparing to sling him over the mule. She snapped and slashed and roared, tried to force a way through, but more of them stood in her way and some had given up on not spilling blood, drawing swords and axes.

"Stop this nonsense!" Prisca shouted over the fighting. "Yasmi, you cannot win. Nydia, what I'm doing serves you. Would your brother rather see you marry a councillor or a king?"

"Hold!" Nydia raised her hatchet, backing off from the fighting. Her corsairs followed suit, backing away from the

Estians. Only Yasmi was left up close with her foes, and they backed off, caging her with a ring of weapons. "You want to talk, Minister Servita? Stop taking my prince from me."

Yasmi growled in frustration. Betrayed again. Was no one else loyal to Raul? She snapped at one of the warriors, but an outstretched spear stopped her from getting close.

Prisca's gaze flicked from Nydia to Raul, then she nodded curtly. His bearers lowered him to the ground.

"Well?" Nydia said. "Explain yourself, and make it good, Minister. My brother isn't easily impressed, and I take after him."

"Your brother. Exactly." Prisca's slender smile curved up beneath hollow, sunken eyes. There was so little flesh left on her face, she seemed almost a skull, but her mouth worked all too well. "King Yazadi enjoys being a monarch on a throne, doesn't he? Upheld by his connections to others? The same as Dunholm. The same as Estis should be. One nation, one leader, queen or king, and you know who you're dealing with."

"Are you going to tell me that the ocean is wet?" Nydia asked, and she was smiling too. How could they be like this when Raul was lying there, fingers scraping at the dirt, one hand pressed against his injured belly?

"I'm telling you that this is how you buy stability and security, a reliable ally in the north. Queen Junia will consolidate our victory and ensure a solid heir on the throne, whoever that might be. Then you get the marriage alliance you wanted, our nations bound in blood, and between us we can crush Dunholm."

Nydia's head swayed from side to side and the feathers on her helmet swayed with it. She looked around, her gaze running across Raul, across the Estians, across her corsairs, across the fields, then briefly over Yasmi, those blue eyes striking her with an intensity of expectation, some meaning that she didn't see.

Prisca found it first.

"Oh." The minister sounded disappointed as she looked toward the woods. "Of course. You're delaying. I presume you've left people behind to direct the reinforcements. If we talk long enough, even Valens will have time to organise, and I can't allow that."

"It was worth a try." Nydia swung a foot around, taking up a fighting stance. "Shall we return to our dance?"

"Wait." Raul had pushed himself to his knees. His face was drawn, almost as pale as the Saditchi. One hand was pressed against his belly, the other lying in his lap, fingers covered in dirt. On the ground in front of him, he'd drawn a row of stick people.

"What is this nonsense?" Prisca snapped, frowning at what he'd done.

"You know what I did at Barrowblack," Raul said. "Don't make me use it against you."

"At Barrowblack you had a coven, days of preparation, the perfect place to draw power from its meaning. What are you going to do here?" She waved at the fields. "Make us hungry for turnips?"

Raul was trembling so badly it made Yasmi sick with fear, but he held his mother's gaze in spite all of it.

"Places don't make themselves special," he said. "People do that to them. This place is special to me. Estian farmland like where I grew up, where I first took a stand against Dunholmi injustice. A place where, in this moment, the people I'm closest to have both betrayed and saved me. You think I won't remember this place as long as I live?"

"You can't just make a thin place in the world."

"It's not about thinness. It's about the thickness of meaning." Raul took a ragged, pained breath. "I'm asking you once more, don't do this. We can talk, find ways to keep working together, in spite of everything you've done." He looked at her with an expression Yasmi hadn't seen in a long time, an innocent, wide-eyed pleading that broke her heart. "Ma, please."

The world seemed frozen. Not a gust of wind. Not a bird flying by. Not a single breath from a hundred warriors primed to fight. All Yasmi saw was Raul and his mother staring at each other, Prisca's face as still as stone except for the frantic blinking of her eyes. Just for that moment, Yasmi believed in redemption, because if anyone could draw mercy from this woman, it was Raul.

But Prisca Servita hadn't bent to twenty years of Dunholmi rule, and she wouldn't bend to her son's pleas.

"Put him on the mule. We're going."

The warriors stood uncertainly for a moment, and in that moment Raul spoke again.

"The land of Estis," he said, pressing his hand to the dirt, "is connected to the people of Estis." He ran his fingers across the stick figures he'd drawn, then gestured at the flesh-and-blood people around him. "Is connected to the figurehead of rising Estis." He pressed his hand to his chest, smearing dirt across robes the green of the moon on their banners. "Is filled with the pain of Estis—homes burned down, loved ones lost, communities torn apart." The fingers of his other hand pressed against his belly, tips pointing in. "All of our pains."

He shoved hard with those fingers, pressing them through his robes and his bandages, pushing against the wounds beneath, and Yasmi almost screamed as blood soaked through the green.

Then she did scream as a burst of pain ran through her. The others screamed too, Prisca and her warriors, dropping their weapons and sinking to the ground, some of them writhing, others sobbing, none left on their feet. Yasmi's heart hammered and she clenched her teeth, holding back the anguished howl that filled her chest. She could barely see straight through her agony, but she could see the twitching bodies all around.

And stepping through them, the Saditchi, clad in the yellow and black of their distant land, detached from Estis and its pain. Nydia rushed to Raul, hauled him up in her arms and flung him over her shoulder, blood seeping red down her sleeve. She shouted and others ran to Yasmi, hauled her lion body onto their shoulders, set off across the fields at a jog while their comrades drew bows to cover their backs.

Jolting around on the corsairs' shoulders, Yasmi looked back across the fields. She saw Estian warriors peeling themselves off the ground; saw Prisca pull herself up, leaning on one of them; saw distance open up while pain kept throbbing through her. She saw the Saditchi chaplain stoop to pick something out of the corn, then hurry after the rest.

Then they were entering the soothing shadows at the edge of the woodland. Other voices and footsteps came down the stream, the clink of armour and weapons, Valens's distinctive growl. She was lowered onto the earth and lay there, letting the pain pass, seeking the strength to shift into human form.

A Saditchi corsair crouched next to her. It was the chaplain, her stole hanging across her armour, though one side had got twisted around, hiding the embroidered whale. One of her hands was thrust through her belt, the forearm above it broken in the fight, not bloody but bent in a way no forearm should. Her other hand reached out and she placed Yasmi's deer mask between her forepaws, returning the precious treasure Yasmi had discarded in the rush to rescue Raul.

"You were there for our fallen," the chaplain said. "That means we're here for you."

Chapter Twenty-Six
By Royal Command

Alder galloped across the cobbles, his chosen guard beside him, spears pointing at the pitiful band of rebels at the far side of the square. These weren't proper warriors like the North Marchers had brought back from exile, not even the dishevelled and amateurish fighters the early rebels had flung at him. They were people of Pavuno, untrained and barely armed, scruffy ingrates who didn't appreciate what Dunholm had done for their city, how he had brought order and prosperity, saved them from the corrupt sorcerers who once ruled this place. They had dared to rise up while he was away fighting the real rebellion, and they deserved everything that was coming to them.

His war cry was a guttural scream as he thrust the spear forward, past the pitchfork some fool was fighting with, felt the thud of its impact and the resistance of flesh for just a moment before it gave way, the spear skewering the man in a spray of blood. Fellstride's hooves hammered another of them into the dirt, bones crunching, body falling. The rest didn't even try to make a stand. Wide-eyed with panic, they turned and ran, screaming, dropping weapons, knocking into each other in their haste. The weight of a body dragged the spear from his hand, but he drew his sabre as he kept galloping on, hacking left and right. Blood sprayed, hot and satisfying. Screams rose and were abruptly cut short.

He reached the end of the square and turned to look back. Some of his warriors were still chasing down the scattered rebels. Others were dismounting to finish off the survivors. Downhill, smoke streamed in thick dark clouds above the rooftops, from where those cursed merchant families had tried to make a stand in a pair of warehouses. They must have felt so smug, but the barricades that held him out had trapped them in as the flames started to rise.

From the moment he arrived, he had despised this city, but he had thought that he could make something worthwhile out of it. Perhaps the best he could make was ashes. It would be a shame, as he'd put so much effort into rebuilding, but some steeds refused to be broken in.

More riders trotted out of a side street, Captain Brook and several of her company. She dragged a man along, grey-haired and dressed in robes, a patch over his left eye. Some of her other riders brought prisoners as well, all stumbling to keep up with the horses, their wrists bound at the end of ropes.

"My lord." Brook bowed her head. "We believe these are the ringleaders. We found them in the Temple of Yorl, scheming over a map of the city. They had this too."

She held up a cage with a magpie inside, a knotted string wrapped around its leg.

"A messenger bird?" Alder asked. "Were you hoping to summon the rebel horde?"

The man with the eye patch stood with his head high and his wrinkled face steady, staring intently at Alder.

"I am Holy Cirillo, High Priest of Yorl," he intoned. "The blessed father watches over us in his wisdom and he calls upon you to end this bloodshed. Our people will not surrender again, and you have nothing to gain by ruling over a city of ashes and bones."

"On the contrary, Holy Cirillo." Alder drew a cloth from his belt and tried to wipe the blood from his sword, but the cloth was already soaked through and it only spread the stains. "I will gain fear. I will gain respect. I will gain the understanding that actions have consequences." He felt the heat rising through him, heard the crackle of flames in his own voice. "I will drag your rebel friends across the country to fight me here on my own terms."

He dropped the cloth and caught another that Brook tossed to him. This time, his blade came away clean and he sheathed it before descending from the saddle. Fellstride snorted and tugged at his reins, trying to pull away, but Alder held him in place. In the distance, there was a crash as a burning building collapsed.

"Young man, this is a desperate, foolish thing you are doing," Cirillo warned, holding Alder's gaze. "The bitterness this stirs will poison our people against you for generations. There can be no peace, no collaboration with the likes of you."

"On the contrary, many of your merchant houses still provide me with fighting companies. Someone will always see sense."

To his surprise, Cirillo took a step closer, right up in Alder's face.

"Learn from the past so that you will not lose the future. Like Yorl among the ogres, we must—"

"Do you think I care about stories from a dead man?"

"Yorl is no man, but a god."

"I meant you." Alder drew the silver dagger from his belt, its edge gleaming with menace. "You understand that I'm going to have you killed, right? And not in a nice, clean way. Something terrible and memorable, something that gives your followers nightmares so horrific their great-great-grandchildren wake up sweating and terrified in the night."

Cirillo swallowed and turned his face away.

"What happened to you, that you can treat the world like this?" he asked.

Over the priest's shoulder, Alder saw a figure watching them. Not his grandmother anymore, but a being of pure flames, the essence of her spirit and her strength. Raw ambition unleashed.

"I found a higher power." Alder summoned flames to dance along the dagger's edge. It was a relief to let them out, their fire suppressed within him for too long. "Or perhaps it found me. You know how that feels, don't you, priest? This power gives me what no one else has: the strength to do what is needed and the will to recognise what that is, not to be held back by the softness of the world."

"You're an abomination."

"I'm a saviour, as you'll all soon see." Alder jerked his head. "Take this one away. String him up above the docks and slice him open so the passing boats can see his guts slowly sliding out."

Cirillo closed his eye, shoulders shaking, hands clasped tight in front of him. Then he raised his head to stand as proud as when he'd first arrived.

"Yorl's blind eye watch over me in my final hour, Selthin strengthen me for what I must endure, and Avgar guide you all to the suffering you deserve."

Then he was led away over the litter of bodies, past more people approaching across the square.

"What about the bird?" Brook asked, holding up the cage.

"Kill it. Word will reach them in the end, but I want time to regroup. Once that's done, Prince Raul will come rushing after us, his people shaken with alarm, his forces in chaos. I want him here in the city we've held for a generation and which we will prepare for him. I want him to falter in every advance and attack for fear of hurting his precious people.

"We're going to turn his weakness against him, and we're going to unleash all our strength."

Flames flared around his dagger and swirled down his hand. Fellstride whinnied and tugged at the reins again. Brook opened the cage, took the magpie in her fist, and squeezed until it went limp.

Alder's chosen warriors parted to make way for the group coming up the square. Some of them were locals who had stayed loyal to Dunholm through the war, warriors drawn from Pavuno's merchant households like the Tisco boy. At their head was a woman Alder knew well, decked out in furs and gold chains, one who had stayed loyal without facing the fight.

"My lord." Gallia Tisco bowed to him. "I trust my son has served you well."

Alder shrugged. "He has served. That is more than I can say for many around here."

The Tisco boy was terrible at hiding his disappointment. Alder hoped that Gallia had a better heir to run the business once she was gone.

"I'm pleased to see you return, my lord," she continued. "As always, I stand ready to provide whatever supplies your army needs. Some of the trade routes have been disrupted, but we will adapt."

"You're not siding with these rebels?"

"I side with whoever brings prosperity to Pavuno and the North March, something Dunholm has long done."

"Good, because I'm going to need those supplies. Food, fodder, arrows, whatever weapons and armour you can find. Fresh horses."

"And this will be paid for from the royal purse? I heard tell that King Lorrin was with you."

"He will be here soon." The fire grew brighter around Alder's hand and Gallia Tisco stared at it with wide eyes. "All will be well."

"Of course, my lord."

Fellstride yanked at the reins, snorting and slamming his hooves against the cobbles, straining to draw away.

"What is the matter with you?" Alder snapped, flames flaring.

Fellstride reared up, almost dragging Alder off his feet. Hooves flailed wildly through the air.

"Blasted beast!" Alder let go of the reins and drew his sword, but before he could swing it Fellstride galloped away, scattering warriors as he went. Other horses bucked and reared, while some threw their riders and followed him, a panicked herd dashing down the dirt streets.

The sword shook in Alder's fist and flames leapt across its blade. He took a long, rasping breath, tasted blood and smoke, took another, calmed himself. He had to stay in control. He couldn't make the mistakes his father had.

In the back of his mind, part of him was screaming that he'd already made those mistakes. But he'd done what was needed to beat the rebels, to control the North March, to do what the crown demanded. Once he beat Raul Warborn and got the king back, he would prove to all of Dunholm that the House of Alder was worthy, that they deserved their place of power within the kingdom. All this waste and ruin would be put behind him. He just had to take the decisive action needed to reach that point.

He had to burn.

He had to make them bleed.

He grinned. Yes, that was what was needed. More reminders of why no one should cross him. Not the peasant people of the North March. Not his own courtiers like that snivelling wretch Tur. Not even a horse, though it was the best he had ever known.

"We'll draw them to the flat ground outside the city," he said, "force them to fight in the open, trample them under the hooves of our cavalry. All their little tricks won't save them then."

Gallia Tisco looked across the city, at the smoke rising from the dockside warehouses, the bodies littering the ground, the warriors with their bloody blades, and finally back to Alder. Gold chains dangled around her neck as she bowed.

"Whatever you say, my lord."

The wagon creaked as it hit a rut in the road, the lurch of its movement almost knocking Yasmi over. She clung to the bundle of costume she was sitting on while Tenebrial held on to his papers and his quill pens, even as ink dripped down his tunic. After years during which they were barely allowed to bring the tools of writing into Estis at all, the playwright was relishing the opportunity to gather papers and parchments around him, to set down different drafts of his plays instead of working out the best lines in his head and then teaching them to the cast.

"Could the hero be a farmhand instead of a blacksmith?" she asked. "It gets us around that awkwardness in the first act and explains why he does so well with the animals in act three."

"No, no, no." Tenebrial shook his head. "Have you seen how many plays begin with an innocent farmhand dreaming of a higher destiny? Audiences will yawn us out of town."

"An innkeeper's child, then." Yasmi tried not to look up the marching column to another wagon, its canvas roof sheltering wounded passengers from the sun. She wished Raul had let them leave him somewhere to rest in peace, though she understood why he wouldn't. He wasn't going to miss out on the climax of the story, however battered he was.

"Really?" Tenebrial raised an eyebrow. "I thought you wanted to get away from the established stories and clichés."

"I want us to tell a story about what war's really like. Not the battles and the dramatic speeches, not the strength and courage or the moments of self-sacrifice. A story about the things we saw when we went out into the country, the loss and suffering, the people struggling to get by."

Tenebrial's thin fingers twitched around his quill.

"I can bear to do without battles." He shuddered. "Especially after the bodies we buried at Barrowblack. But dramatic speeches are my stock in trade and the foundation of the actor's very art. Would you leave a smith without a hammer, a seamstress without a needle, a warrior without a sword?"

"Fine, we can keep the dramatic speeches." It was the concession she'd been ready to give in return for things she wanted. "Speaking of which, you should write down what you just said. It's got the makings of a solid monologue."

She peered through the dust that rose in the army's wake, across the open land of rural Estis. That morning, they'd passed through another village ruined by Alder during his retreat, but he'd clearly rushed this stretch because the fields were barely touched, only one small patch of oats blackened and trampled. At a lake a short way from the road, reed cutters were squeezed out by a team of warriors filling barrels to supply the army. At this time of year, many of the smaller streams would have dried up, and marching was thirsty work.

"Permission to come aboard?"

Yasmi looked down to see Nydia walking along beside the wagon. The Saditchi princess had left her armour elsewhere, along with most of her weapons, only a hatchet hanging from the belt around her yellow tunic.

"If you can get up here," Yasmi replied.

"I've been climbing rigging since I was the size of a cat." Nydia scrambled up the side of the wagon, using bundles of props and the ropes that held them in place. "This mess of a vessel is nothing." She flung herself up the last few feet and landed next to Yasmi, then stretched out across the heap of costume, hands pillowing her head, eyes closed as she soaked in the sunshine. "I might have to start sleeping up here. It's the most comfortable I've been in months."

"Careful." Tenebrial pulled papers from under her boots. "You might smudge something."

The sun shone down and the army kept marching, boots stamping against the road, wheels creaking under the wagons. They passed an orchard, most of its trees intact, and a burned-out shell of a windmill. Whatever had brought Nydia to them, she wasn't in a rush, but Yasmi's agitation grew sitting next to her. She tapped her fingers against her masks and tried not to pull a face.

"Tenebrial, could you please check on my father?" she said. "He hasn't been sleeping well since Barrowblack. I don't want him dozing off at the reins and steering us into a ditch. Our lives are tragedies at the moment, and it would be uncouth to shift into farce."

"The horses will follow the rest," Tenebrial said without looking up from his writing.

"Tenebrial," she said more sharply. "Who do you think will take over this company when my father retires?"

Tenebrial snorted. "Efron will never retire, the theatre's in his blood."

"My dear little man," Nydia interjected without opening her eyes, "your mistress is politely signalling you to depart. If you prefer, I can tell you to fuck off instead."

In spite of herself, Yasmi stifled a laugh. This wasn't how princesses were meant to speak, and Nydia's smile said she knew it.

"No, no." Tenebrial hurriedly gathered up his papers and pens. "I'll go do the... with the horses and the..."

"Good chap. Off you go."

With far less dignity and agility than the princess, Tenebrial scrambled down the side of the wagon and out of view.

The wheels kept creaking. The army kept marching. Yasmi opened her mouth and tasted dust as she tried to muster her words.

"Thank you," she said at last, "for helping me save Raul."

"You fought more than me, and he did a chunk of saving himself."

"Still, I..."

Yasmi wet her lips and looked around her again. She could jump off the wagon and run away, leave Nydia to enjoy her well-earned rest. But the longer she held on to what needed saying, the more tension clenched her body, squeezing the breath from her chest. According to her father, she'd started grinding her teeth at night, and it was a bad sign if he could hear that over his snoring.

"When the time comes, I'll leave before the wedding," Yasmi said. "Better if I'm not around, his old girlfriend watching from the back row."

Better not to see it too. That wasn't something she could bear.

"Really?" Nydia half opened her eyes.

"You've fought so hard for him, brought all these troops from your country, pretty much saved us from disaster. I know Prisca made the deal and she's..."

"Out there somewhere sulking?" Another comment that didn't sound very regal but almost made Yasmi smile.

"We have to think about the future. About the friends we'll need to deter another invasion, to keep people safe from the horrors of war. An alliance with Saditch is an important part of that."

Cloth rustled as Nydia pushed herself up on her elbows, looking at Yasmi with eyes blue as the sky.

"You do know that I was sent to marry a prince, don't you?"

"Half the army still calls him prince, and more of them every day. Someone will make it official when this is done."

"Every monarchy's got to start from somewhere."

"And marrying a Saditchi princess will make his more secure."

Yasmi gazed down at her hands, thought of what it had been like to hold Raul's, to wrap herself around him when they'd first kissed in the woods. That felt so long ago now, and she was too weary for words to describe, as if a year of fighting had caught up with her all at once.

"Did you know that this isn't the first time my brother's offered me up for marriage?" Nydia asked.

"No." Yasmi looked over, curious in spite of herself.

"I never know how far the gossip spreads. The first fiancé was a lord Yazadi needed on side while he was securing the throne. I was too young to marry, which is a mercy because that man was ugly as sin and vicious with it. I spilled a few secrets about him that might or might not have been true, politics shifted, and suddenly he wasn't what the crown needed.

"The next one was an Esvadellian princess. Better-looking than him, and I did consider going through with it, but I generally prefer men. Less competition to be the prettiest one in the room. I persuaded her that she should look for alliances elsewhere on the Golden Ocean.

"Then there's Raul Warborn. Kind, friendly, an impressive warrior, smarter than average when he's not being too innocent, and believe me, I can solve that part. Quite the looker too, has all his own teeth. And of course, he comes with a kingdom, even if it's a little storm-tossed. Hard to argue with an offer like that, when I've seen the alternatives."

Yasmi swallowed, clasped her hands tighter, breath stuck in her throat.

"Perhaps I should go help with the horses," she mumbled.

Nydia sat up and rolled her head from side to side until something clicked in her neck.

"That's better. Now, where was I?" Her voice softened. "Look, if he wasn't half-broken at the moment, there would be nothing I'd like more than to take your little princeling home to the palace and ride his mainmast raw. But marrying is a whole other business, and as my past voyages show, I'm not settling for less than what suits me.

"That boy is so determined to look after others, he'll destroy himself at every turn. Leaping into danger. Burning his brain out with divination. Sticking fingers into his own wounds. He'll run a kingdom the same way, and his whole life with it, one sacrifice after another.

"That sounds noble, but really it's exhausting. Anyone who loves him is going to spend their life worrying, and he'll be sacrificing their heart as much as he sacrifices himself. I'm not saying I couldn't fall in love with that boy if I gave it a chance, but I'd spend the rest of my life having my heart broken, and I'd rather go back out to sea."

Yasmi blinked as she tried to make sense of it all.

"Are you telling me that you're not going to marry him?" she asked. "Even if it's offered? Even if he's a prince?"

Nydia leaned forward and, to Yasmi's immense surprise, took her hand.

"I'm telling you to take care of your own heart," she said gently but firmly. "No one else will."

The princess let go and Yasmi, stunned, let her hand flop back into her lap. Nydia swung her legs over the edge of the wagon and started climbing down.

"Wait!" Yasmi had been so caught up in her own concerns, she'd forgotten something far more important. "What about the alliance? If you're not marrying Raul, are you going to leave us?"

Nydia cocked her head. "Why would I do that? The Dunholmi are the biggest threat we face. Far better to fight them here than do it back home. Not every alliance has to have a marriage."

She dropped to the ground and strode off up the column, waving goodbye.

Caught in an exhausting mix of anxiety and relief, Yasmi flopped onto the crumpled costumes. She wanted to laugh, to howl, to batter her hands against the ground like a child having a tantrum.

Then she grinned, the sort of hysterical joy that filled her whole body. All this time, she'd been trying to focus on what mattered while worrying that this beautiful older woman might take Raul from her. Now that threat was lifted, washed away in a torrent of fine words.

Such fine words.

She went scrambling back across the top of the wagon.

"Tenebrial!" she called out, and his head popped up at the front. "Get your papers and pens. I've worked out who our hero is, and I've got *such* a speech for her."

Chapter Twenty-Seven
Hungry for More

Raul pressed his lips together, holding back a gasp of pain, trying not to let Yasmi know how much it hurt as she wrapped him in fresh bandages.

"I know there's not much light in here," she said, "but even if I couldn't see you flinch, I could feel it."

She tied the bandage off and carefully tucked its loose ends away. Outside the tent, the rest of the rebels were going about the evening business of an army camp: eating, drinking, training, hauling supplies, and digging pits. There was something comforting in the familiarity of those routines, the same old people shouting the same old curses.

"I'm sorry," Raul said.

"Don't be sorry for flinching, be sorry for doing this to yourself, just when you were getting better."

"I had to. The magic needed it."

"And I need you." The brush of her lips against his shoulder sent an excited shiver through him. "No more throwing yourself away."

He knew she wouldn't like his answer to that, so instead he focused on other things.

"Do you have my shirt?"

"In a moment." She shuffled back, and there was just enough washed-out light to see her smile by.

"What are you doing?"

"Enjoying the view. It'll be better when you're rid of the bandages, but still…" She tossed the shirt to him. "I didn't want to rush this part."

He was getting better at dressing without straining his wounds or pressing against them too hard. The movements were awkward, especially in a tent, but they gave him a sense of control over his own life, a sense that had been missing when he let Yasmi or a physician dress him.

"Did you hear me, about not throwing yourself away?" she asked as he pulled his boots on.

"I was listening."

"And?"

"And the council will be waiting for us."

Yasmi sighed. "We're not done talking."

Raul picked up his staff, pushed the tent flap open, and stepped out.

"That's fine with me," he said. "I'd be happy talking with you for the rest of my life."

Yasmi screwed up her face as she emerged and clutched her bronze charm, the one he'd made to carry her safely home.

"Have I told you how perfectly infuriating you are?" she asked.

"I like the perfect part."

"And I liked it when you didn't know how to answer back." She took his hand. "I've clearly taught you too well."

As they walked through the camp, almost everyone they passed wore a round pewter charm, and every one of them offered a greeting. Some raised fists or shouted out Raul's name. Folk from the Withered Hills slapped their chests in salute. Red-clad imperial legionaries raised their fists. Strange to think that when he'd first come down the country to Pavuno, no one had known who he was. This was much more like living in the family inn in the Vales, where everybody knew his name. Except that there, he'd known their names too, and here he couldn't possibly know everyone. He didn't even know all of their faces. How many of these people had been with him since before Barrowblack, before Hound's Gap, before the Withering? He ought to know how much they had committed, how much they had sacrificed, but it was beyond him. All he could do was grab hold of the biggest moments and try to control them.

At least one familiar face was emerging from the crowd: Efron Dellest, his moustache quivering as he puffed his way through the camp.

"My queen of the boards!" he exclaimed, clasping Yasmi's hands. "Might I beg a few moments of your time before you're swept up in the base business of government?"

"Of course, Father." Yasmi smiled apologetically to Raul. "See you there?"

"I'll save you a seat."

As Efron leaned toward his daughter with a look of deep

intensity, Raul walked on, his staff tapping against the ground. Even in summer, the nights could get very cold, especially when there were clear skies like these, so fires were lit all around the camp. He headed for the one next to Quintae's trebuchet, a distinctive landmark wherever they went.

Unlike the camp's other fires, this one was guarded, a ring of legionaries warding off anyone who approached. Raul didn't like that, but he didn't even try to argue about security anymore. Prisca had changed that conversation.

Thinking about her, his hand tightened around the staff. He had thought that his mother couldn't hurt him any further, but he'd been sorely mistaken. The worst of it was that she would never see how wrong she'd been. The world worked one way in the mind of Prisca Servita, and everything had to bend in that direction. He'd come close to ending up that way himself, wanting the world to be simple, choices black and white, everything existing in a single state. But Prisca herself had made that impossible. She was his ma, so he loved her. She had betrayed him, so he hated her. She was an old woman, her mind broken for a noble cause, so he pitied her and admired her.

What would he do if she walked back into camp and demanded her seat at the fire?

Right now, those seats were taken by people he would much rather see. Valens, Drusil, Silvano, Ferra, a few other captains who had fought with them for the past year or who had taken the place of those lost along the way. They sat on folding stools around the fire, eating roasted meat and vegetables from bread platters.

"Here," Valens said as Raul took a seat next to him. "Eat."

Raul eagerly dived in, gobbling down chunks of carrot, parsnip, and swede. No fancy preparation out here on the march, food simply cooked even by the standards of their old inn, but even though he rode in a wagon half the time, he felt ferociously hungry. Recovery was a famine of its own.

"Here." Drusil passed him a charm like the ones he'd seen walking through camp. It was a simple pewter disk stamped with the outline of a swift, hanging on a piece of rough twine. "They're banking the fires now for tonight's forging. We should have the last few hundred made by dawn."

Raul set his food aside and held the charm up to catch the firelight, now that the sky was too dim to illuminate the workmanship. It was crude by Drusil's standards but good by anyone else's. Not as neat or polished as the one she'd given him to take into the Withered Hills, but a mist-thin twin of that other charm. While mist might be nothing when it was one person thick, an army's worth of mist was solid enough to blot out the sun. He hoped the power of charms could work the same way.

"For speed and for luck." He slipped it around his neck, the twine tickling his skin. "It's brilliant. Thank you."

Drusil handed them out to the rest of the council, and small conversations emerged as they tied them around their necks, wrists, belts, or wherever seemed best. Just as Raul started eating again, Yasmi settled in the seat next to him.

"How's your father?" he asked quietly.

"Dramatic, as always," she whispered back. "Apparently he's decided that once the war is over, he's going to take over an inn in some small town, put in a stage, and encourage local performers. He wants to take art to the masses."

"That sounds lovely."

"What it sounds like is his version of your old family inn, looking for a way he and Valens can settle down."

"Which sounds even more lovely." Raul glanced at his da, who was too busy comparing charms to overhear what they were saying. "What about the Company Dellest?"

"That depends on how the others react, of course, but if I want it..." She pushed her hair back behind her ear and looked at him with an uncertain smile. "I have stories I want to tell, and I'll have more before this is over. I'd be young for a director, but I think I can do it."

"Of course you can." He squeezed her hand. "You'll be amazing, just like always."

Valens back in an inn and Yasmi leading a touring company, that felt like a future beyond all the marching and pain. Even thinking about it for a moment, Raul could see the edges of awkward conversations, choices he didn't want to face, people he would miss. But right now, he had even bigger issues.

He clapped his hands together and everyone turned to look at him, the firelight shining in their eyes.

"It's going to be a short night, and we all need our sleep," he said. "So let's get to business. What's the latest on Count Alder's army?"

"We frayed half his forces away at Barrowblack," Ferra said. "And I've got folk out chasing stragglers, in case they're fixing to find him again. But we've not seen his main force in days."

"Which way were they going?"

"Into the heartland."

"Pavuno," Valens said. "Got to be."

"Unless he's running back to Dunholm," Silvano said.

"Not Count Alder." Raul thought of the hate burning in the count's eyes the last time they'd fought. "He won't give up until we're dead or he is. Maybe not even then." He clasped his hand around his knee, trying to stop it from jiggling. "How are our numbers?"

The fire flickered. His captains looked at each other awkwardly, then jerked around at a sharp crack.

Valens opened his fist and the snapped pieces of a wooden spoon fell into the dirt.

"I don't know where Prisca Servita's gone," Valens said, staring into the flames. "But if she comes back here, I'll rip her head off and shove that mind full of smart words back down her throat."

"Da..." Raul said, reaching for him.

"No." Valens shook off his son's hand. "This time was too far. She's done."

Around the fire, others muttered their agreement and angry suggestions for what should happen to Prisca. Hearing that wasn't as hard as thinking about what she'd done, but it still wasn't easy.

"It's all right," Raul said. "I doubt she'd be coming back, but where does that leave us?"

"Junia's gone too," Silvano said. "Her treasury paid for the mercenaries, so they've melted away."

"And the other exiles?"

"I can speak to that." Earl Tordesse stepped into the

firelight. He looked dusty and dishevelled, the skin dark and dropping beneath his eyes, but he held himself with dignity.

Valens rose, fist clenched, and for a moment Raul thought he might leap across the fire to strike the earl.

"Where the fuck have you been?" Valens growled. "And who else is with you?"

"Not Queen Junia, and not Minister Servita." Tordesse stood his ground beneath the ferocity of Valens's glare. "The minister asked me to tell you that she has chosen what she believes to be right—tradition and the authority of the crown. She doesn't expect you to agree, but she hopes that you will understand."

"You mean she chose power over family." Valens's chest shook with every breath.

"Some might say that." Tordesse turned his attention to Raul. "I don't know how to address you now, but I assume you're still in charge."

"We all are, equally," Raul replied.

"If you insist." Tordesse gestured to a seat. "May I?"

Raul looked around the fire, trying to judge people's responses, but while none of them were happy, they all still looked to him.

"Best we take what help we can," Ferra said, and the bat on her shoulder made a clicking sound. "Let him speak his piece."

Slowly, Valens lowered himself into his seat, and when no one else objected, Tordesse sat.

"My news isn't what you're going to want," he said. "Her Majesty no longer trusts your judgement as servants of the Estian crown."

Drusil snorted. "Like I'm here to serve her."

Tordesse rubbed a hand across his face. Raul felt sorry for him, caught between a long-standing loyalty and the reality of the world he lived in. More importantly, he needed to move this conversation on before it became an argument between people who could be allies.

"The people around this fire have done their best to accommodate the earls," Raul said. "We've listened to their concerns and treated them as equals, though aside from yourself none of them showed the rest of this council the same respect. But while you've been a huge help, we fought for a year without you, and we'll do it again if we must."

"That's just as well," Tordesse said, "because most of them aren't coming back. The only Estis they'll fight for is the one they remember. They've gone with Junia, and they've taken their warriors with them."

"Most?" Raul asked.

"Some of them value their homeland more than they value their titles."

"And you?"

"I said that I would fight for you until we won, and then I would serve Queen Junia. We haven't won yet."

"Word is word." Ferra slapped her chest.

"Indeed." Tordesse looked at Valens. "General, I have a small force waiting two miles from here. With your permission, I'd like to bring them into this camp and under your command."

Valens's fingers twitched. He tilted his head, eyes narrowed and studying Tordesse, then nodded slowly. "Bring them."

"Thank you."

Tordesse rose, bowed to the council, and headed back out

into the night. Around the circle, everyone seemed to let out a single held breath. Ferra chuckled and tossed the burned end of a roasted carrot into the fire.

"Nowt so strange as town folk, so."

Silvano cleared his throat.

"There's something else we've been discussing." He looked around and other captains nodded eagerly. "When this is over, we'll need a new way of keeping the nation secure. We can't trust the nobility to raise our armies—they'll use them to bring us back into line. But those of us who raised companies for the war, the guilds and towns and so on, we plan to keep training and to raise funds for arms and armour.

"We'll need someone to take charge of it all, so some of that money will go to paying them. Someone who can travel the country training troops, building barracks, planning how we'll fight off the next invasion. Someone we can trust to lead us when the time comes, serving the people instead of the crown." All of them turned to look at Valens. "We're agreed, it should be you."

Raul grinned with pride. Of course they wanted his da to do this. He was the best choice there could be and everyone knew it. He would enjoy the challenge too; Raul had seen the satisfaction he took in his work as a general, in talking with those who followed him, in caring for them in his gruff warrior's way. But then Yasmi squeezed his hand, and when he saw the worry in her eyes he remembered Efron's dreams of a small-town inn, a very different vision of happiness.

"I'm honoured." Valens rubbed his stump across his scalp. "I…"

There was a commotion from outside the circle of firelight. A legionary appeared at Valens's shoulder.

"General, there's a rider galloping into camp. He's wearing the colours of the collaborator companies and he says he needs to talk with our prince." The legionary looked at Raul. "No disrespect, I wasn't sure if we even still had one."

Valens looked at Raul, one eyebrow raised.

"Bring him to the council," Raul said. "Make sure he's not armed."

He tore a chunk from the edge of his bread platter and thrust it into his mouth. The hunger was there still, clawing at his insides. He would end up even hungrier after they distributed all the swift charms, when he and his coven tried their next work. A charm like that had let him move faster in the wilderness, and if he got this right, if he tapped into the nature of the road as well as what that symbol meant, he was sure he could speed up the whole army, cut Alder off wherever he was going. But something like that would draw on his reserves even more than recovering from the wound. He only had a few experiences to judge it by—the charm in the snow, Barrowblack, the magic he'd used to escape Prisca—but they always left him the same way in the aftermath: exhausted, bewildered, hungry, struggling to assemble his thoughts.

Yasmi squeezed his hand again, and he smiled at her around a mouthful of bread. There was something in her expression, almost sadness in her smile.

Two legionaries marched into the firelight, holding a young man by the arms. His armour and surcoat were in the Dunholmi style but embroidered with the seal of an Estian merchant family. He was sweat-stained, the dust of the road plastered to a face that looked familiar, though Raul wasn't sure where from.

"Which of you is the prince?" the man asked, looking around the fire.

"Not how this works," Valens growled. "Tell us all why a traitor's in our camp."

The young man tried to stand proud, but the hands around his arms got in his way, as did the dirt and sweat.

"My name is Senius Tisco," he said. "I'm sent by my mother, Gallia, head of Tisco Trading. She says to tell you that Count Alder is in Pavuno, and that he is burning the city down."

Chapter Twenty-Eight
Fortune's Thread

The noise of the army was overwhelming, a cacophony closing in on Raul from every direction, like a raging river that had caught him in its current. He stumbled through the chaos, clutching his staff, shoulders pulled in tight, but however much he tried to shrink away all the people still came to him, some saluting or shouting his name, some asking for orders, some whose words and intentions he couldn't make out. He did his best to smile and nod, to direct those who needed it to other commanders, but he still saw the way they looked at him, the worry in their eyes. Worry for him or worry for themselves, when...when...

He reached a copse at the edge of camp and sagged to the ground, his back against a tree. Even with his eyes half-closed, he could make out the banners flying, the people hurrying back and forth, the frantic activity of it all. So many of them, but so few compared with what they had been before. Battered by the Dunholmi and deserted by people who called this country their own. Could they still stand against...

They had to try, and they had to do it now. Every evening brought messenger bats from Ferra's scouts near Pavuno, and every message was worse than the last. Neighbourhoods burned. Innocents killed. Terror in the streets. He drew a string from his belt and ran it through his hand, knowing that its knots were a message, one that had sent a hush through the group when Ferra read it out. Holy Cirillo of Yorl, the most powerful and respected priest in Estis, one of the earliest agents of their cause, was dead. Prisca had known him since before the conquest, and this news should hit her hard, but Raul was starting to wonder if his mother felt anything at all beyond her ambition.

No, that was bitterness talking. Bitterness and exhaustion. His feet were sore, his legs ached, he didn't have the energy to sit up straight, and his mind kept drifting away from him, thoughts fading like... like...

"Raul?"

He blinked, looked up. When had dusk arrived?

"Raul, look at me."

Yasmi. Her hands on his knees, her face so close, framed by that hair, so soft, so golden. He caught its ends between his fingers, smiling.

"I love you," he murmured.

Why was she still frowning? She liked it when he said that he loved her.

Had he said the wrong words? He'd done that earlier, mixed up "sword" and "shears." The warriors he'd been talking to as he passed had laughed about it, thinking that he was labelling Count Alder a sheep, but Raul had known better. He was using his mind like Prisca had used hers, but pushing so much harder, so much sooner. Was this how it had been for her, feeling thoughts starting to fade, fighting to hold them in place?

"Here."

Yasmi had a slice of bread and honey, practically holding it to his lips. When he took it he couldn't taste the sweetness, but his body responded as if it was there, a rush of sunlight through his limbs. He gobbled it down like a small child, would have licked his fingers if she hadn't given him a second slice. He held his head up, smiled, shook some of the fog away.

"How are you feeling?" she asked.

"A bit tired." He wanted to tell someone the truth, but he didn't want to worry any of them, her least of all.

"I'm not surprised. You've been striding in circles around the army all day while the army marches twice as fast as it should. Three days now, Raul. Don't you want to take a rest?"

"Resting now."

"A proper rest. A day lying in a wagon while we walk at normal speed."

"Can't." He smiled weakly. "It's all right, we're nearly there."

"Then let your coven do it tomorrow."

He shook his head. "No time to teach them. I found the swift's speed in the Withered Hills, that's why I can do this."

"Have you even tried teaching them?"

He looked down. There was another slice of that sticky bread in her hand. He reached out, and after a moment, she gave it to him.

Saying that he hadn't taught his coven the magic sounded wrong. He wasn't holding back because he didn't want them to know; few things gave him more pleasure than sharing what he'd learned. But he didn't want them to bear the weight. He didn't want anyone else to feel like he did now.

One more day of marching, two at most, and they'd be at Pavuno. Then he would work whatever charms were needed to beat Alder, and then...

His hand was empty. He licked his fingers. They didn't taste of much, but still...

"Raul?"

He blinked, looked up. Yasmi was there.

"I should go read the signs," he mumbled. "Need to... to... to know what we might find tomorrow."

"Raul, we're putting on our new play tonight."

"Play?"

"A short version, but I think it works. I think people will want to see it."

Raul rubbed his eyes. He enjoyed the plays, but he was so weary.

"Will people watch?" he asked.

"You mean because they're tired and demoralised, because a madman's burning their country down and they're worried he'll do that to them next?"

"Something like that."

"That's why they need to see this." She squeezed his hand. "And you do too."

For a moment, he almost argued. They were in the middle of a war, marching past burned homes and trampled fields every day, their people tired and injured, dispirited at the desertion of allies they'd been counting on. They could spend the time sleeping or sharpening their weapons. Was a play really worth that precious hour?

But then he remembered Yasmi on the stage, transforming from a tree into a woman and kneeling over Efron dressed as a king. He remembered the folk from the Withered Hills playing with puppets around their campfire, sharing stories of their lives. He remembered marching songs and jokes passed from mouth to ear through the camp, the flicker of a smile at the darkest time.

Maybe those things mattered because they allowed people to keep going, or maybe people kept going because those things mattered. In a day or two, they would reach Pavuno, and they would have to fight for their lives. He'd almost been killed once in battle already, and that was when he'd been stronger. If these were the last few evenings he had left, then there was nothing he wanted more than to watch Yasmi perform.

Weakly, he squeezed her hand and smiled.

"I'll be there."

Proper darkness was falling at last, the sort of darkness the stage craved. Darkness in which firelight would blur the makeup on their faces into real human features, would add depth to landscapes painted onto canvas, would exaggerate the movements of the players. The darkness that Yasmi had been waiting for.

"I do believe this to be our largest audience ever," Efron

said, peering out around the wagon. "An entire army come to see what wonders we can perform."

Yasmi swallowed. Normally, she would have loved to hear a thing like that, but normally she wasn't the one who'd come up with the words, or at least this many of them.

"Half an army at most." Tenebrial paced back and forth, rubbing the back of his neck. "Some are on watch, some scouting, some sleeping."

"Merely thousands then, not tens of thousands." Efron's eyes were wide with excitement. "We must give a performance worthy of the moment."

"That takes time and rehearsal. We should not have rushed into this."

"We had to," Yasmi said. "Listen to them."

After a lifetime of performances, the three were experts in the sounds of an audience. They could hear the difference between wariness, boredom, excited anticipation, and drunken belligerence. They knew how to adapt to those moods, to shape the relationship between audience and performers. But as they cocked their heads and took in the sounds past the theatre wagons, it was the first time they'd ever heard an audience full of doubt and fear.

"They need us," Yasmi said.

"And I need to watch the show," Tenebrial said. "To see where our weaknesses lie, so we can do better next time. Best of luck, both of you."

He tapped his foot against the ground three times, then headed out to join the audience.

Flies were buzzing in Yasmi's stomach.

"I wish he hadn't said that," she said. "About our weaknesses. I know they'll be there, but it's not what I want to think about."

"My dear." Her father took her hands. "You have nothing to fear. In all my years upon the stage, this is the finest work I have ever had the pleasure of performing."

She couldn't help smiling. "You say that every time."

"And Tenebrial worries about our cock-ups every time, but it always works out in the end."

"Do you not remember that town where they pelted us with cabbages?"

"Those people don't count, far too ignorant."

"Or the village where—"

"My sweet girl." Efron squeezed her hands. "I love you as dearly as I loved your mother, so please do not take the least measure of offence when I tell you that it is time to shut up and step up. My imminent retirement from the touring stage will be a shocking blow to good audiences everywhere, but no salve could soothe that wound more perfectly than you and the story you have created.

"Now if you'll excuse me." He stepped back, curled up the points of his moustache, and went to stand at the stage left steps. "I must be ready when our esteemed director gives my cue."

Yasmi felt as if she was ready to fly apart, a dozen conflicting emotions tugging her this way and that. Fear for Raul and for their future, nervousness in case the play went wrong, excitement that it might go right, pride in her company for getting it ready with only a few days' rehearsal in the backs of wagons rumbling along rough and jolting roads. Love and amusement as she watched her father preen.

Being adored by the crowd had always been her greatest thrill, but tonight they would see what was inside her heart, not the performance she donned with her masks. Tonight, she lay exposed. What would they make of her?

She straightened her shifter greys and lined the masks up carefully on her belt. Then she tapped her toe against the ground three times before stepping past her father, through a gap in the canvas backdrop, and onto the stage.

Thousands of firelit faces stared. For a moment, the noise of the crowd grew louder as they shouted at each other to be quiet. Then something almost like silence fell as she reached the middle of the stage.

The gentlest of summer winds brushed her face and hands, making hairs stand on end. She licked dry lips and took a breath that felt like it could lift her off the stage.

"Gentles all," she began, "though not so gentle those hands which make rough work of war's wrath. Not so gentle those hearts whose scars have hardened in the glare of grief. Not so gentle the words screamed on the battlefield or when memory rises like a ghoul in the night.

"Tonight, the Company Dellest presents a play not of the past but of our own times, a story saved from the shadows of all we have seen and done, a truth trapped in the amber of imagining. Tonight, we share with you *Fortune's Thread*."

As she spoke, her hands found a mask on her belt, the humble yet expressive features of a cat. As she bowed, she brought it to her face.

When she'd first shifted in front of an audience, back on the fixed stage at Pavuno, it had been a moment that shattered taboo and helped trigger a riot, but over the past two years she had shifted numerous times in front of members of the rebellion, changing shape as battle demanded. She had thought that the novelty of it must have worn off. But as she curled over and her whiskers sprang out, as her paws hit the stage and she was struck by the hidden richness of the night, a roar of applause rolled across her.

Perhaps she still had the power to move them.

For the next hour, she lost herself in the play. She and Tenebrial had kept it short by necessity, and though she hoped to expand it to full length later, the story had everything at its core. A community ravaged by war and a family struggling with the stresses it brought. The terrible choices survival forced upon them. Pain and grief, but also the hope that came through them. No monarchs or generals. No battles.

She wished that Biallo could have been there to play his part, though then they might not have named the second brother after him. He had always enjoyed a good tragedy and now his name would be preserved in one. She hoped that he would have approved.

As the end approached, a family found themselves lost in the wild, threatened by a lion that lived near their cave. Efron, playing the father, gave his favourite speech of the evening, in which he promised to draw the lion away, giving his life so that the others could escape. But for Yasmi, watching from the wings with the lion mask clutched in her hands, the older son's response was the speech that truly mattered.

"You think that you're so special, Father, throwing your life away," Claudio declared, strutting across the stage. For once, to Yasmi's relief, he'd remembered all of his lines. "But just like the lords who brought this war to our land, you're making it all about yourself, you're looking for the easy path."

"How dare you?" Efron grabbed Claudio's doublet, roaring the words from the top of his lungs, projecting across a silent audience thousands strong. "Everything I do here, I do for you. I give my life for you. I give my death for you."

"I don't want your death!" Claudio flung him off and Efron sank to his knees. "You talk and talk about sacrifice as if it were the hardest thing in the world. Sacrifice an oxen to appease the gods. Sacrifice yourself to keep the lion from our door. Always these moments of grandeur and grief, sharp and final and decisive, moments when you can cry out, 'I did this, look what a great man I am!'

"But there is something harder than sacrifice, and that is compromise. Instead of cutting off a part of yourself and casting it aside, accepting something from others into yourself. Truly making your life about theirs, instead of making theirs all about you."

"Compromise is weakness! If we try to compromise with the lion, it will devour us."

"Compromise is the strength to change while remaining yourself, and it lets us work together, the weak threads of our separate skills twisting into a rope so strong that it cannot be broken. It will let us drive that lion back, together. More than that..." Claudio knelt and took Efron's hands. "It will let us live together when this is done."

Efron had always had a gift for projecting his voice while sounding weak and broken. He brought all of that to bear as he turned his face to the crowd, one hand clutched to his chest.

"I do not wish this risk for you, or the pain that will be its price."

The second son, the character she'd named Biallo, knelt at his other side, arm wrapped around his shoulders. "That is our choice, Father, and we make it for your sake just as you make it for ours."

"Pain lessens in its sharing," Claudio said, "while strength grows. Let us twine our threads together and haul fortune in on that rope."

Yasmi winced. She liked that image, but the phrasing needed work. Still, the audience seemed happy, cheering and clapping as the actors bowed their heads for the scene's end. There was a swish of cloth as the next backdrop fell into place and the players lined up for the penultimate scene. She held her mask, but before donning it she peered at the crowd, hoping to pick out a face in the darkness. Was he there? Had he heard? Would he listen?

Too many faces and too little time to find him in the dark, if he was even awake. All she could do was follow the script through to its end.

———————•———————

Standing with Raul near the back of the crowd, dishing out tankards of beer until the barrel was empty, Valens almost felt like he was back at the inn, enjoying those special few days each year when the players were in town. Except the beer here was better, not having been made by him, and this crowd never would have fitted into their yard.

He watched the play from beginning to end, but he watched the audience too. The spirit of an army could be a powerful thing, but it could be a fragile one when things went wrong, and they hadn't all been going right. He wanted to believe in Efron and his players, in what they had planned, but he'd fought too many wars to believe in the power of wanting.

Through the first two-thirds of the play, his shoulders tightened until they ached, and that ache spread up his neck toward his head. He'd never seen an army so hushed, watching characters on the stage who could have been their friends and families. Innocents caught up in war. A village destroyed. Loss. Grief. These didn't seem like things to raise a warrior's spirits, but none of them walked away, and the faces he could see showed a hardness that might not be so bad. Then came the last act, some grand speeches and the business with the lion. The clapping and cheering as the family worked together to survive, and then to raise a barn at the end, that was some of the loudest cheering he'd ever heard. Even he leapt to his feet when he saw the green moon in its black ring on the side of the barn.

He got it now. The family was Estis. The lion was Dunholm. The barn was...some barns? It didn't matter exactly, it felt right, and he thought Efron would be proud of him for understanding. He was so swept up in the excitement of that ending, for a moment he forgot what else he was worried about. But he could never forget his son for long.

"They're really good, aren't they?" He leaned toward Raul, checking that the lad was awake. He was so still, but at least his eyes were open.

On the stage, the Company Dellest took a collective bow, Efron and Yasmi in the middle of the line.

"They're great." Raul rubbed his face. "And I'm exhausted. I should sleep."

"Don't you want to see Yasmi before you go to bed?"

"Everyone will want to see Yasmi. Just tell her... Tell her I'll be working with the coven on the road tomorrow."

"Shouldn't I tell your coven that?" Valens asked.

Raul yawned so wide it looked like his jaw was about to drop off.

"Them too," he managed.

Valens scratched his head. He felt like there was something else from the play they ought to talk about, something from those speeches near the end, something that tugged at the worries he felt whenever he looked at Raul. But it was late and he didn't know how to start that conversation. Maybe he should ask Efron or Yasmi, see if they could give him the right words.

"Good night, then," he said instead, raising his voice to be heard above the cheering, which was somehow growing louder over time.

"Good night, Da."

Chapter Twenty-Nine
The Heroes I Know

Back home at the Dunholmi court, they would have called it a racing day. Clear skies, bright sunshine, and a gentle breeze. Perfect for sitting out on the plains, watching courtiers push their finest horses to the limits as they sought to prove their riding skills and the quality of their stables. A fine day for living, but for the North March rebels appearing on the far side of the fields outside Pavuno, it would be a day for dying. Count Alder would see to that.

He patted his horse's neck. She was a fine steed, but not his best. He hoped that Fellstride was out there somewhere still, running free. That left hope that he could be recaptured and retrained, restoring Alder's stable to its full glory. Right now, though, that didn't matter. It wouldn't take the finest warhorses in Dunholm to crush these foot-slogging peasants.

"What do you make of their numbers?" he asked, watching the enemy spread out across the meadows, forming up for the fight.

Between the two armies, skirmishers loosed desultory shots back and forth, keeping each other out of reach. There was an argument for attacking now, before the rebels could assemble their fighting line, but then the rebels could pull back into the woods and hedgerows of less open ground, obstructing cavalry charges. Better to let them advance into the open. Each side knew what the other was doing here, but neither had a better option than letting it play out, a dance as old as war.

At least, that was how it looked.

"Far fewer of them than before, my lord," Captain Brook said. "Are they trying to catch us in a pincer movement?"

"Where would their other column come from?" Alder shook his head. "No, I think the rumours are true. Our enemies are divided."

"More fool them. They could have had us outnumbered, and now numbers are on our side."

Alder touched his stomach, where the rebels' would-be prince had run him through once before. He'd had his revenge for that blow, but there was an important reminder in it. These people weren't to be underestimated.

"Do we still have patrols in the streets?" he asked.

"Yes, my lord, but I have riders ready to fetch them before the battle begins."

"Leave them there. We have enough troops here, and I don't want to leave our soft belly exposed."

"Yes, my lord."

He looked along the line. In the centre were his cavalry, Dunholmi nobles leading armoured knights trained and equipped by their households, the greatest warriors ready to smash a hole in the enemy's centre, to break their strength and their will. To either side were the infantry levies who would follow up and finish them off. Their left flank was anchored against the river, while on the right, where the ground rose sharply toward the foothills and the mountains beyond, were the troops of local loyalists.

"Who's commanding the collaborators today?" Alder asked.

"Gallia Tisco. No one's seen her take the field in over twenty years, but apparently she insisted. Something about her family's honour."

"That useless son of hers, is he there?"

"I haven't seen him in days, my lord. He always looked like a strong current would wash him away, maybe he's lost his taste for war."

"Maybe." Alder narrowed his eyes against the sunlight gleaming off armour and spear tips. "I want you up there, Brook." He pointed toward the locals. "Take ten of my best."

"You think something's amiss?"

"Call it a morale boost, reminding our local friends that we're here for them." He smiled a half smile. "Whatever they decide to do."

"That's it, General," Silvano said. "Everybody's in line."

Valens looked up at the sun, then down at the dirt on his boots. There was enough of the day left to fight, he just wished they weren't doing it after a morning's march. He also wished they weren't outnumbered, but at least they had plans for that. Flimsy plans, but better than nothing. And if he was going to wish, he shouldn't just wish for warriors; he should wish it all away—invasion, defeat, twenty years in the wilderness, good comrades lost. But as Fabia used to point out, wishes were like piss: you needed to let them out once in a while, but they didn't do any good.

He crouched, fumbled in the dirt, found four small stones. Cupping them in his hands, he walked to the side of the road and made them into a tiny cairn.

"Laughing Loftus, I offer you this gift in joy, that joy may return to me when next we meet." Maybe praying was no better than wishing, but it was no worse either.

He rose and headed for the front of the army, Silvano marching beside him. In the centre of the line, other commanders were waiting, Ferra, Nydia, Tordesse, and Drusil among them. Normally, the blacksmith stayed back, managing logistics and artillery. Today she was dressed in overlapping steel plates and carrying a two-handed hammer with a vicious pick on its back.

"New?" Valens asked.

"D'you think I'd sit this out?" She tapped the mountain charm hammered into the armour over her heart. "Got to put some faith in my own handiwork."

Valens stepped forward into the meadow so he could look up and down the massed ranks of the rebellion. This was his handiwork, forging an army like none he'd fought with before. Foreigners and refugees, cripples and labourers, people who'd taken up arms out of conviction, not because they didn't know what else to do. If Raul was the best thing he'd ever done with his life, this was the second. If today was his day, he could die proud.

Given the numbers against them, this moment might be as good as his life got.

"Listen up!" he bellowed, and they all turned to look.

Those out on the flanks shouldn't have been able to hear him, but Drusil had made him a charm for the occasion, a chain with images of mouths and carriers pigeons stamped onto its links. Maybe it was working. Maybe he was just louder than he thought on a still day like this. That was the thing with charms; you were never sure what worked and what didn't.

Tenebrial had written him a speech, short but powerful, a simple thing for simple warriors. He'd practised it as they marched along until the words were hammered into his tongue. But now the time came, he found some of his own.

"I've been fighting near my whole life," he shouted. "I'm fucking good at it." They laughed at that and he grinned, swelling with pride. "But if I live through today, it won't be because of how good I am—it'll be because of you lot. Look at who's standing next to you. You'll save them, and they'll save you, and that's how we win.

"In the old stories, a hero comes to save the day, but one person alone can't save us. We all have to be heroes. We all get to be heroes. Be the heroes I know you are."

He almost raised his fist, then thought better of it and raised his stump, the remnant of another bitter fight, of loss and recovery.

"A new moon rises!" he bellowed.

"A new moon rises!" the whole army roared.

———•———

As the boat rowed quietly up the river, Raul wished that he could have worked the oars, but his belly screamed with pain if he lifted anything heavier than a book, so he had to leave that to the rest of his coven. Instead, he dipped his hand in the river, then watched the way the water dripped from his fingers, the shapes it made on the wooden seat.

"Divining the future?" Yasmi asked quietly. She was dressed in her shifter greys, hair tied back, no scarf covering the masks on her belt, her only jewellery the bronze charm around her neck.

"I'm not sure divination is really about the future," Raul said. "It's more about what exists now, what we might find if we carry on along our path."

"That sounds like the future to me."

He shook his head. "There will only be one future, but from where we are now there are countless possibilities."

He tapped a rower on the shoulder, then gestured with his hand, pointing to where the fast-flowing Rack joined the slower, steadier river that carried Pavuno's trade. In a whisper, the rower passed the message on to the others and the prow of their craft turned. The coven members strained at their oars as they rowed against the ever-fiercer current, into the mouth of the Rack.

A short way up, amid the stumps of trees cut down during

the invasion, a bald man in threadbare scholar's robes stood on the bank. As the boat ploughed into the mud and the coven stowed their oars, he came down to meet them.

"Pomponius." Raul held out his hand. "It's been too long."

Instead of shaking, the man bowed. "Your Highness, an honour to assist you on such an auspicious day."

"I'm not sure I count as a Highness anymore. How is the accountancy business?"

"Ah, ah, ah!" Pomponius wagged a finger. "I'm not sure I would call myself an accountant either. The more appropriate term is 'scribe.'"

"You're out in the open now?"

Pomponius shrugged. The sweat on his brow spoke to more than the heat of the day. "Either we emerge victorious and I am free to openly pursue my endeavours, or we face an abject end. If I must die, I shall do it as who I am."

The others were out of the boat and all followed Raul's lead in raising their hoods, each embroidered with a crossed-out eye. A charm only provided so much concealment in an occupied city, but it was the second best protection they could get. The best was someone who knew the city as it was, the safe ways to go and the patterns of patrols.

"Come." Pomponius gestured urgently up the bank. "We don't have long. The armies have met."

———— • ————

The Dunholmi cavalry hit the shield wall with a crash like mountains colliding. Spears splintered, flinging shards of wood through the air. Steel punched through armour and bodies. Blood sprayed. Bones shattered. Warriors stepped over the fallen, holding the line as it bent inward beneath the staggering impact of the assault.

Standing on a stool behind the line, his shield over his shoulder and hand resting on the pommel of his sword, Valens stared over the heads of the intervening companies, holding his breath. If they didn't withstand this moment, then the rebellion was doomed already. If they did, it at least meant there was a chance, time for other people to play their parts.

"Hold!" he roared, spittle flying from his lips, as if anyone could hear him over the clangs and thuds and screams. "Don't let the horse-fuckers through!"

The centre swayed, the Dunholmi pushed, riders hacking left and right. Blue pennants fluttered over their heads while the green moon flew above the Estian line, the lightness of cloth signalling the power of whole nations colliding, the terrible, glorious weight of life and death.

There in the centre stood the National Legion, as the Imperial Legion had been renamed the previous night. There was pride in sharing a name that had stood for centuries, but Estis was done with empires. The red line of legionaries and the green of their banners seemed to waver, on the verge of giving way. But then it pushed back, started to straighten, finding its strength, and Valens's teeth bared in his most savage smile. Heavy cavalry were brutal in the charge, ruiners of bodies and demolishers of fighting lines. But in the slow grind where armies were locked together, in the push and press of a packed fight, so close you could feel a warrior's breath on your cheek as she tried to stab out your eyes, at that point nothing beat a solid shield wall and nobody stood their ground like the warriors of Estis.

"Lestavo, take your people's fighting beasts to the right, see if you can push back on the riverbank," he shouted. "Osten, I want your reserves in with Tordesse. Go!"

There was a fresh wave of shouting and clashing weapons as the Dunholmi infantry hit. Now they were engaged across the meadow, nearly all the forces of Estis committed, while the Dunholmi were still marching a column along the flank, close to the hills. A column of Estians who'd marched out of Pavuno, collaborators who'd thrived in the shadow of the invaders. Where did their loyalties lie now? Better to ask where their profit was, with the merchant families at their head. Whichever way they went, it was a bad day for someone.

Valens's fingers tightened around his sword. At this distance, it was hard for him to make out the banners they flew, but he could see blue shapes above the massed warriors.

Then that blue fell and the merchant houses of Pavuno advanced.

———————•———————

Paws flexing and monkey tail raised, Yasmi bounced from rooftop to rooftop, running ahead of Raul and his companions, watching for the Dunholmi troops who still patrolled the streets.

For the most part, Pavuno was silent, its residents sheltering behind closed doors and shuttered windows, waiting for the storm of war to pass. A few scurried furtively across street junctions, but most remained out of sight. Only the occupying patrols marched confidently between the warehouses and workshops, homes and taverns, between the buildings still standing and those recently burned down, smouldering holes in the cityscape around which the stench of ashes swirled. Those blackened gaps and the bodies swinging from nooses were a grim reminder of what was at stake. Her stomach felt like lead, but she still bounded lightly from one building to the next, stretching out to leap across those terrible absences, pausing to chitter a warning when she saw the opposition approach.

Pomponius led them along a winding route down narrow back streets, avoiding the places where the patrols were most likely to be. The coven weren't the most athletic members of the Estian rebellion and Raul limped along with his staff and his wounds, but they went as fast as they could, moving in silence except for the swish of robes and the patter of footsteps.

At the next junction, she hissed down to them, hoping not to be heard in the next street. Pomponius held up a hand and they stopped in a house's shadow.

The patrol she'd seen turned, walked straight toward them. Seeing the hooded figures, an officer raised his hand. Sabres swished from scabbards. Five against twelve, but those five were armoured warriors, the twelve scholars carrying clubs and knives. Raul stepped forward with his staff. Yasmi reached for her face, ready to shift into a deadlier form.

A door creaked. A woman emerged, a mallet in her hand and a determined look on her face. Three teenagers followed her, all carrying kitchen knives.

From another house came two men, one holding a shovel, the other a pair of hefty hooks like the dockers used to haul cargo.

Another door. Another. Another. People stepping into the streets, half of them shaking with fear but none of them backing down.

The Dunholmi looked at their chances, then ran. No one tried to stop them. Yasmi lowered her hand and breathed.

Pomponius laughed.

"Come." He gestured up the hill. "Before word spreads."

Death and destruction filled the air around Alder, the stink of blood and sweat, the screams and cries and groans. He clutched reins tight as he watched his forces advance, their numbers pushing the rebels back. The North Marchers and their Saditchi allies were holding, but not for much longer. Soon, the line would collapse, and with the day secure he could seize his moment, could join in the fray. He longed to feel the heat of blood and flames, the thrilling shudder up his arm as his blade parted flesh, to see his enemies trampled before him.

Through a great act of will, he held himself back. Things could still change, and he didn't trust anyone else to lead for him.

"My lord!" A rider galloped down the line, helmet missing and blood streaming from her scalp. Captain Brook, red staining her sword and half her horse's flank. "Treachery!"

Alder bared his teeth as the fire of fury swelled. His horse bucked and he yanked at the reins, holding her in place.

Brook pulled up in front of Alder and his reserves. Her arm hung limp, blood soaking the sleeve, and she slumped halfway out of her saddle.

"You were right," she said. "Tisco. The merchants. They've turned coats. They're attacking our own flank."

Here it was, the reason he'd held back and the moment to let restraint go. He'd given these people a chance to show that they were better than their misbegotten country and they'd thrown that opportunity in his face, but he would make them regret it. Flames burst from his empty hand and then subsided, leaving his fingers smeared with soot. He wiped one of them across his forehead, marking his face with a dark V, a sign of the ruin he brought. Then he drew his sabre and flames leapt along the blade. His horse reared again and this time he let her, holding the sword aloft as he called to his reserves.

"Warriors of Dunholm, let's make the traitors pay!"

Fire flew as he galloped to the attack.

Behind him, Brook slid from her saddle, bleeding out into the dirt.

———————•———————

There were a dozen guards at the palace gates and more on the walls above, bows in hand. They stood their ground as Raul approached, backed by his coven and a growing band of the most courageous townspeople, Yasmi walking at his side with a mask in her hand.

Originally, he'd hope to get around the outside and sneak into the palace through a back way. But time was short, people were dying in the meadows outside the city, and if he had the numbers for a faster approach, then he had to try it.

"My name is Raul Warborn," he announced. "You might have heard of me."

He didn't like leaning on his own story anymore. It had been a crutch at the start of the rebellion, something sturdy and obvious to rally people around, and the rebellion wasn't about him anymore. But perhaps some of that old myth remained, maybe even enough to save them a struggle here.

"Heard the count cut you up," one of the guards replied, levelling his spear.

"Heard you're a cripple." Another of them spat in the dirt, though her darting eyes said there was a false front to her bravado. "Not so much of a warrior now."

"Yet here I am, while Count Alder is outside the city, fighting for his life." Raul gestured to the people around him. The guards were better armed. His best hope was that numbers intimidated them. "If you let us have our nation's palace back, we won't hurt you."

One of the guards snorted. Another laughed. They pointed their weapons at Raul.

"Or you could drop that staff and we won't knock you about too much before we lock you up."

Raul sighed. He'd tried, and he couldn't waste more time talking. He only hoped that they could get through.

"I'm sorry," he said.

Yasmi raised her mask and a lion roared. Shocked by the beast before them, the guards were too slow raising their weapons. She tore two of them down before they even fought back, and by then the mob was on the rest. Arrows flew from the walls, the screams that followed them ripping at Raul's heart, but he couldn't falter. He followed Yasmi and his coven followed him, through the middle of the fight.

The gates were barred from the inside. Yasmi switched masks, loomed over them all as a massive bear, then slammed her body against the middle of the gates. They held against the first hit, the second, the third, though there was creaking and cracking that time. On the fourth blow, wood splintered and the gates burst open.

"Hold off the guards," Raul called to the mob as he rushed through the gates and across the courtyard beyond.

He needn't have worried. A crowd of ordinary Estians, driven by desperation and the pain of the past year, came streaming in behind him, rushing up the walls to where the archers stood, wrestling with warriors who charged at them.

Two guards ran out of the keep as the coven approached. Still a bear, Yasmi thudded across the dirt of the yard, knocked aside their attacks, grabbed their heads and slammed them together. Raul strode past the limp bodies and followed the bear through grand hallways, under arches of stone that had stood for centuries, into the room from which Estis had been ruled for centuries, the greatest symbol there could be for where power lay in the land. The makings of his greatest charm.

The last time Raul had ascended the steps to the throne room, he'd had his allies with him, on their way to seize the palace and free Estis. He remembered the bodies littering the stairs, the crushing weight of failure and the savage cut of truths slicing away the life he had believed in. The day he learned it was all a lie.

But he didn't need to be special to fight for what was right. He didn't need prophecies or destiny. He didn't need powers beyond what he could learn from hard work and share with the people around him.

The throne room was dark and empty except for the throne itself, sitting on a dais at the far end, a goblet made from a skull on a table next to it. Yasmi grabbed shutters with her great paws and ripped them off their hinges, letting in the brightness of the day. With it came the distant sounds of battle, but also the scent of flowers on the mountainside and of bakeries down in the city, the song of birds and the rush of the River Rack, the warmth of the summer sun. Some part of life went on, a life that was worth fighting for.

The coven pulled back their hoods, exposing themselves to the palace and to the land. With the tip of his staff, Raul scratched a drawing of flames into the dark stones of the floor. Ivus lit a candle and placed it in the centre of that symbol, real fire amid its image. The others took out bags of ashes and drew long, straight lines across it all, the cold aftermath of fire marking out a cage to contain the heat. Then they all stood in a circle, hands held toward each other but not touching, a sign of connection instead of its reality, charms instead of closeness, drawing out abstractions and power.

Part of Raul wanted to pray that this would work, like he'd seen others pray. But if this worked, it wouldn't be because of a god.

"We are Estis," they chanted together. "Land, people, will. We are one and we are many, shattered and united."

As he spoke, Raul let himself feel the truth of the words, the nature of the land beneath his feet, solid, enduring. He felt something else as well, something brighter and sharper that had crept in. Something destructive.

"A new moon rises," they chanted. "An old land heals itself."

When he had first envisioned this moment, he had thought to call that terrible power into him. He knew that it could occupy a body, so why not draw it into his? It might burn through him, but wasn't that a price worth paying?

Except that there were other ways.

"At the birth of this country, the king of Estis went to Jarrag for his power," Raul said. "At the rebirth of this country, the people of Estis call Jarrag to us."

"We call you," the others intoned, and Raul could feel their minds alongside his, all connecting to the land.

In the middle of the ash cage, the candle flared.

Count Alder's sabre was more than steel. It was an arc of flame that sliced through weapons, through armour, through bodies, that tore the traitors into charred ruins and watered the meadow with their blood. It was glorious, furious destruction, shattering the merchants of Pavuno, scattering their turncoat troops. Cowards fled in terror before him, and he hacked down those foolish enough to stand.

He was power and fury.

He was strength.

He was the one who would bend this cursed nation to his will and save Dunholm from ignominy.

Then the flames of the sword faltered. Alder willed them back but they flickered, died. He stared aghast at the bare blade of his sword.

Closing his eyes, he reached for the power that had carried him home from the Withered Hills and to victory since. He felt it flow away. Turning to face the current, he looked across the battlefield to the city and the palace looming over it all. Someone was ripping the power of Jarrag from him.

He grasped at it with all of his strength, clung on tight. This power was him and he would not let it go.

Unable to resist, he turned his horse's head from the fight and galloped across the meadow, toward Pavuno.

Chapter Thirty
Never Done

Fire roared across the throne room, scorching Raul's robes as it blazed past him, forming a column above the charms on the floor. It was so bright it hurt to look at, but he forced himself to face it.

"How dare you!" the voice of the fire crackled and spat. "I will blister your skin, melt your flesh, leave charcoal for bones."

The candle in the centre of the ash cage evaporated in the heat, leaving a greasy smear and a smell of animal fat. Raul focused on those things instead of on the terrible power facing him. It was easier to swallow his fear and stand his ground that way.

"You won't," he said. "We have you trapped."

"You cannot hold me. I am Jarrag. I am destruction. I am fire and blood. I am pain and terror. I will peer into your heart and bind it with your own hopes and fears."

In the back of Raul's mind, other voices called to him,

familiar echoes of his own twisted by something darker. One said that he should surrender, that he couldn't win. Another urged him to embrace this opportunity, to strike a deal with Jarrag, to become stronger for himself and for his nation. A third spoke of the chance to release his enemy and face him in fair battle, like a hero should. Whichever voice he turned his attention to grew louder, and every one of them touched something that felt true.

The faces of the coven shifted, some determined, some scared. Some backed away, while others stepped closer.

"Those voices aren't you." Across the circle, Cloia was already saying it, her fingers twisting through the curls of her hair. "They come from outside."

"It's Jarrag," Raul said. "Listen to each other, not to it."

Jarrag kept talking, sometimes pleading, sometimes screeching, sometimes addressing one of them, sometimes all. Its flames shifted toward one of them and then another, singeing their brows and drenching them in sweat.

The coven stood their ground, held the fire in place.

"Are you done?" Raul asked at last, in a pause between the shrieks.

"I am never done," Jarrag hissed. "I am desolation, the god of the wild."

"Maybe you are, maybe you aren't." Raul shrugged. "What I know is the price we would pay to have a power like you, and we're not willing to pay it."

"So you'll banish me?" Jarrag laughed, the fire forming a vast mouth with teeth of flame and a throat of smoke. "I told you, I am destruction, I am fury, I am strength bared. Those things are a part of every one of you, and you can never be rid of them."

"Sadly, I think you're right. We all have a little darkness in here." Raul tapped his chest. "But we don't have to bring it together, to let it dictate our fate. We can accept who we are without using it to hurt others." He held his arms wide and the others did the same. "I accept you, Jarrag."

———————•———————

Alder galloped through the streets of Pavuno, through the city that was meant to be his to the palace on the top of the hill, toward the fire blazing from its windows. He didn't know if anyone had followed him. He didn't care.

He felt hollow inside, his sabre cold in his hand. Jarrag was gone, and the creature's power with it. No flames rising inside him or before him. No vision of his grandmother urging him on. The heady heat that had driven him for the past year left only ash in his soul.

Without it, he could see more clearly, could look back across his mistakes. That power had taken his will from him, driven him along the most destructive path at every turn. It had torn him away from caution, from calculation, from compromise. It was a storm that had swept him here.

Free now, he could make his own choices. If he wanted, he could withdraw his troops and ride home.

But he was a noble of Dunholm, born to the fight.

He was the heir of a great house, destined for power.

He was Count Brennett Alder, and he had to show the

world that he was a man of greatness, one of those chosen few who would shape the world.

Hooves clattered across cobbles as he approached the palace gates. Seeing peasants with knives and sticks outside, he grinned. There might not be flames along his blade, but it was good Dunholmi steel, painted with the blood of his foes. If that wasn't enough to put the fear of all the gods into them, then nothing would.

He raised his sabre and galloped toward the power that was his to claim.

Raul trembled as he opened himself up to Jarrag. What if he had misunderstood all of this? What if he was letting this monster destroy him, or worse yet, take him over? What if he became the one tearing the land apart?

The power flowed through him, as it did through the others around the circle. It was like fire flowing through his chest, like anger raging in his heart, like every dark and terrible thing he had ever thought. He wanted to close it out, to tear it down, to reject everything the magic represented. He wanted to take this fire and thrust it into his mother's face, to scream at her that this was what she'd brought him to, destroyed by the magic she'd raised him with.

And then, like flames shifting in the wind, his feelings changed. He realised that the power was running out through him. He was losing. He should have known that he wasn't good enough for this. He wasn't unique. He wasn't special.

He was a country boy dressed up in a costume, playing at being a hero or a prince or a diviner. Trying to be something he wasn't.

He sank to his knees. Around the room, the other diviners were doing the same. They reached out for one another, finding the shared strength to endure. But Raul didn't know if he could bear it. Not the pain, but the hateful, angry thoughts. The part of him that wanted to grab hold of Quintae, to stop his twitching and snap at him to shut up. The part that wanted to punch Queen Junia, to watch blood stream across that wrinkled, self-satisfied face. The part that wanted to scream at his da, to vent all the hurt and disappointment at knowing their life together was a lie.

The part of him that wanted to kill every last Dunholmi warrior, then march into their country and let the people there know how it felt.

Those thoughts were part of him, the part of him that was somehow also Jarrag. He had to accept them along with the pain of the flames, to let it drain through him. That inferno in the centre of the room was diminishing, screaming as its strength flowed away, but there was still so much left of it, and he didn't know how long he could cling on.

"You can do this." Yasmi stood beside him, and her voice was the one good thing among the horror of his thoughts. She took the charm from around her neck and hung it around his, pressing it to his chest with the flat of her hand. "You're my home."

He clung to those words, to that feeling, to knowing there was a part of him that Yasmi could love, and that let him hold the blaze of hate and destruction from his mind even as it flowed through him and away.

With a thud, Ivus fell to the ground. Another of the coven lay groaning. Raul looked around the circle, caught the gazes of those who remained. He smiled and nodded, tried to show that he believed in them. It was so little, and yet it was so much.

Footsteps echoed from the stones of the hall outside. Count Alder appeared in the doorway, a sabre in his hand. He stared at them, the dwindling firelight playing across his face, his expression haughty beneath the blood and ashes.

"I knew I shouldn't underestimate you." He looked from Raul to the flames, then tipped his head as if listening to a voice the rest of them couldn't hear. "No, that bargain is over. I've had as much from you as I need. Now it's time to fix things for myself."

He prowled into the room, blood dripping from his blade. The blood of innocent Estians, spilled in this man's lust for power. Raul had never hated anyone more, hated so hard that he wanted to leap up, grab his staff, and batter Alder to a pulp. He had to remind himself that the force of that hate came from Jarrag's power still draining through him, that however worthy Alder was of hate, Raul didn't want it to be a part of him.

"You can walk away," Raul said. "Take your people and leave us in peace."

He wanted to say more, to summon all the eloquence he'd learned from Yasmi and her troupe, but the fire was a pain scorching through him, stealing his focus. He could barely do more than grit his teeth and hang on.

"Walk away, when I'm about to finish you off?" Alder sneered. "Why would I give up this close to victory?"

"Because you're not close to victory." Yasmi gestured out of the window, across the balcony and the city to the fields beyond. "Come and see for yourself. Your army is losing. Estis is going to be free."

Alder walked over to the window and looked out. Sunshine gleamed off a gold bracelet on his wrist and a silver ring on his finger, both warped where heat had melted them, and off the handle of a silver dagger on his belt, its pommel marked with a charm for sharpness. He gave a mocking half smile.

"It's not over yet."

His sabre swung. Yasmi flung herself from him, hit the ground, rolled, sprang back to her feet with a performer's grace. Snatching the bear mask from her belt, she slapped it onto her face and shifted, growing until her head was near the ceiling, looming over the count.

"Really, that's your answer?" Alder asked. "Wild animals?"

In the circle, Jarrag's voice was growing weak, not the roar of flames now but the faint crackle of fading embers. Almost done, Raul and the coven just had to endure a little longer.

Alder advanced on Yasmi, sabre raised. He lunged and she dodged the blow, brought her claws around, missed him as he sidestepped. The blade lashed out again, hit Yasmi's arm. She bellowed in pain. Raul flinched, forced himself not to run to her rescue; he had to finish this first.

Blood oozed through Yasmi's fur and dripped to the floor. Alder, grinning, swung at her again. The bear was too large to dodge the blow, but she pivoted, caught the blade between her body and her arm. More blood flowed but she held on, roaring out her pain as she kept the sabre trapped, then slammed her other paw down. Alder let go of the sabre and staggered back, his arm limp.

With a sound like a dying gasp, the last of the flames died. Raul staggered to his feet and grabbed his staff. Yasmi kicked the sabre away, then raised her hand to her face and became a woman again.

"Please." Raul hobbled over to face Alder by the window. The Dunholmi count was pressing his broken arm to his chest, his other hand resting on his belt. "You don't have to go down fighting. Can't we end this now?"

It would have been good to hold out his hand, to offer a sign of peace, but he didn't trust Alder that much. Instead he clung to his staff, ready to fight if he had to.

"Never."

Alder's good hand slashed out, his silver knife glittering as it sliced through Raul's staff. Alder hurled himself at Raul, dagger drawing back to stab again.

With a screech, a monkey leapt onto the count's head, tugging at his hair, scratching at his eyes. He tried to stab his attacker with the knife but the monkey kept moving, dodging attacks, throwing the count off balance. He staggered out onto the balcony, face bloody, eyes squeezed shut, slashing and stabbing at empty air where the monkey had been moments before.

Alder hit the rail, lost his balance, and the two of them tumbled over.

There was a thud from the courtyard below.

"Yasmi!" Raul screamed and ran to the railing.

A small furry face looked up at him, its owner clinging to the balcony with long fingers and tail. Sobbing with relief, he leaned over and held out his hand.

Below them, Count Alder lay broken by the land he had governed, while in the distance the last of the Dunholmi retreated, broken, from the battlefield.

Chapter Thirty-One
Voice of Estis

The border ran along a broad river separating the farmland of two towns, places that had more kin and customs in common with each other than with the nations that divided them. Just like the inn where Raul had grown up, those towns didn't often see people from the big cities, never mind ministers, generals, and royalty, so their inhabitants came down to the river with the visitors who had camped in their fields the previous night. While those visitors walked across plank bridges to the platform Quintae had rigged in the middle of the river, the locals sheltered under trees that were turning to orange and brown.

Raul breathed deeply. He loved the smell of the first fallen leaves, their crunch beneath his feet, though he probably shouldn't go kicking through piles of them today. Of course, he loved the smells of spring as well, and those of summer and winter. There was a lot to love in the world.

"Harvest festival seems an auspicious time for this," Yasmi said as they approached the bank, along with the other Estian dignitaries. " 'The sweet kiss of fruit and the bulging bounty of golden grain promise us their prosperity,' as Nole says in *Time's Tide*."

"It does seem a good omen, doesn't it?" Raul replied.

"Have you..." She gestured toward a flock of geese honking as they flew south for the winter.

Raul shook his head. "After months of negotiation, no signs are going to change this."

The walkway to the raft creaked as he headed across it, his staff tapping against the boards. The Saditchi were already in place, their boat moored off the raft's south side, and Nydia flashed him a smile. The man standing next to her had many of the same features, as well as a golden crown shaped like crashing waves. At last, here was King Yazadi, the brother he'd heard so much about.

Most of the Dunholmi stood at their side of the raft, but two were at the table in the middle, where Pomponius was counting coins from one chest to another. Satisfied, he waved a hand.

Valens stomped his way across the raft, bringing a manacled King Lorrin with him. At the table, Pomponius ostentatiously drew a key from his belt and unshackled the Dunholmi monarch, while Valens hauled the ransom chest up under his arm and carried it away.

One part done, now for the rest. Pomponius laid out four identical and elegantly written manuscripts, one at each side of the table, then quill pens and jars of ink to go with them. Meanwhile, Dunholmi nobles gathered around their king, hastily providing him with fresh robes, chains, and a crown, decking him out in appropriate ostentation while carrying out a tense and hurried conversation. When he returned to the table, several of them stood stiffly behind him.

"Under the circumstances..." Lorrin pointed at the chains in the middle of the table. "...I shan't stand on ceremony."

He took a seat. To his left, King Yazadi did the same.

A small knot of folk from the Withered Hills stood opposite the Saditchi. After a moment of hissing and muttering, Ferra was thrust forward to take the third seat.

At their side of the raft, the representatives of Estis stood in clusters, looking at each other with varying levels of friendship or suspicion. Raul had tried to gather them the previous night, but some people wouldn't sit down with others, the exiles had stalled at every turn, and he'd given up on it all in favour of sleep. He could stay active for longer now, but busy days left his side aching and his whole body weary.

Junia was the first to speak. "As the last remaining representative of—"

"Don't even try it," Valens growled.

The former queen glared at him, but then Prisca tapped her on the arm and gave a small shake of her head. For all her many faults, the minister understood this settlement, and she understood the other parties well enough to see what could tear it apart. Raul was sure that she was working on schemes to restore the old monarchy, but for now she was part of the mortar holding the new order together. The alternative for the exiles had been exclusion from all of this, and none of them wanted to leave the fruits of peace to the people who had won it.

It was still hard to be around Prisca, after everything she'd done. The first time, he'd had to fight the urge to scream in her face, and they hadn't let Valens near her for weeks out of fear for what he might do. But in the end, they all had to make concessions to the future.

"It should be you, my prince," Drusil said. While the nobles had come dressed in finery, she was wearing her most scorched and stained working leathers. Like the dockers' gloves and cargo hooks hanging from Silvano's belt, those leathers sent a message about what Estis had become.

"No more princes," Raul said. "That lie served its purpose; now it's time to move forward honestly."

Drusil opened her mouth, on the verge of saying more. But he'd already turned down the offer of the crown and a fresh royal line, even though the council offering it had represented all the Estians who stood by him through the war, as well as the merchants and guilds of Pavuno and several large cities. Even if he'd still thought that having a monarch was a good idea, trying to raise one like that would have led to fresh violence. Like Prisca, he understood the script they were playing out. Perhaps because of her and how well she'd raised him, feeding him all those lessons from history, those examples of how nations thrived or fell.

Most of the old nobles didn't deserve to be here, but that wasn't all that mattered. Bringing them into government removed an outside threat, and besides, weren't they as Estian as anyone?

He untied a pouch from his belt. Stones rattled when he shook it.

"One of them is painted green," he said. "Whoever draws it will be the voice of Estis today. Agreed?"

They nodded. What else were they going to do? One by one, they reached in, keeping their stones clasped tight until all were done. Only Earl Tordesse refused when the bag was offered. Even Raul took one of the stones, clutching it in his palm while he let others take their turns. Of course, it would be better for someone else to do this, but if everyone on the council was equal, then that should include him.

Keeping his fingers curled close so the others wouldn't see, he looked at his stone. Dull grey. He lowered his head, surprised by his own disappointment.

"Well?" He looked around.

Prisca held out her hand, a green stone on a pale palm. Her smile was as restrained as ever, but he could see the triumph in her eyes.

"Congratulations, Minister Servita," Raul said. "You're about to sign our nation up to a lasting peace."

"Peace never lasts," Junia snapped.

"Perhaps." Raul shrugged. "But won't you feel safer now, knowing that Saditch and the Withered Hills are sworn to defend us if Dunholm attacks? Just like we're sworn to defend Dunholm or Saditch or the Withered Hills if one attacks another."

"Terribly clever, but are you fool enough to think people will be held to this?"

"It's a nice story, and those have a lot of power, whether you wrap them up in plays, prophecies, or treaties." He looked at Prisca. "Unless you don't want to do this?"

She looked up as another flock of geese flew past, studying their formation. Then she looked back at Raul and he forced himself to meet her eyes. This would have been easier if all he'd felt was pain and hate, but love's roots ran deep, enduring even when they shouldn't.

In spite of everything, in some corner of his mind she would always be his ma.

"I am a minister of the nation of Estis," Prisca said. "And it seems I have a duty to fulfil."

She stood tall, as proud as he had ever seen her, and walked over to take the final seat at the table. After scanning the manuscript for a moment, she lifted it between trembling fingers.

"Shall we begin? I believe that a verbal affirmation was agreed, to ensure that we share our understanding of this undertaking. So, beginning with the first clause..."

Raul turned and, his staff clacking against the planks, started walking back to the bank.

Silvano grabbed his sleeve. "Don't you want to stay and see it through?"

"Thank you, but no." Raul shook his head. "I'm done with this."

And with her.

The boards creaked as others followed him, Valens's footsteps thudding down the bridge, Yasmi with a lighter step. They took up places either side of him as he walked up the road, and Yasmi slipped her arm through his.

It was a pleasant day, warm enough not to need cloaks, just a few clouds blowing across the sky. More grain grew here than up in the Winding Vales, but the sight of farmers at work still reminded Raul of his old home, and he smiled to think that it would now be free of Dunholmi patrols. How much did the people he'd left behind know about what had happened? How much difference would it make to them? Maybe he could go back and find out; he knew some travelling players who would pass that way in the spring.

"Efron's found a place for the tavern," Valens said. "Town called Abetti."

"I know it," Yasmi said. "Does the place need much work?"

"He wants me to build a stage before I fix the roof." Valens laughed and shook his head. "Says the show's more important than keeping our heads dry."

"You're not going to be a general, then?" Raul asked. "Prepare the armies of Estis against invasion?"

"It's tempting, but I'll enjoy peace more. Think I've earned it."

"I'll make sure that you're in the company's touring schedule," Yasmi said.

"Like Efron would let you miss us."

Yasmi looked back and Raul looked with her. On the slow-flowing river, an era was coming to an end, and Prisca Servita's name would forever be bound to it.

"Do you think she'll be happy?" Yasmi asked.

"I fucking hope not," Valens growled, his hand clenching into a fist. Then a deep breath swelled his chest, and when he let it go his face was no longer scrunched in fury. "Efron says I should let my anger go, that it'll be good for me." He flexed his fingers. "And you made me swear not to throttle her."

Through a gap in the gathered dignitaries, Raul saw the slender figure of his mother dip her quill pen in an ink pot.

"I'm not sure she can ever be happy," he said. "But she did get what she wanted."

Chapter Thirty-Two
The Fortune Teller

Inina's favourite day of the whole year was when the travelling players came into town. They were pale, enchanting people from a place that her father said was called Estis, and who he said only came this far south once a year, in the depths of winter, because where they came from, the cold was so harsh it turned water to stone. That sounded like nonsense to Inina, but so did some of the things in the plays, which proved that nonsense could be wonderful.

She rushed into the town square, where the boards were being laid between the wagons. The company's director, a woman with hair like golden flames and a row of masks hanging from her belt, stood on top of one of the wagons, calling to the crowd as they gathered.

"Gentlemen, ladies, and all other folk, you do us a great honour with this welcome, the warmest we could ever hope for. It is a delight to be back in Valdeblanc.

"Please, allow us one brief night of rest, a moment of calm

amid time's surging tide in which to recover from the road. Then, tomorrow, we will perform for you all."

The director winked directly at Inina, who cheered as loudly as any of the adults, though she was barely up to their elbows. Then the woman peered around, as if watching for guards who might carry her away. A conspiratorial hush fell and Inina's chest swelled with excitement.

"Would you care for a preview?"

More cheering. This next part was always good, and Inina would have stayed if she hadn't seen the director's husband walking away from the wagons. He leaned on a staff with a lump of flint bound into its head, smiling and greeting people as if he'd known them all his life. Outside an inn at the side of the square, he eased himself onto a bench and stretched his leg out while rubbing his side.

Her stomach fluttering, Inina walked up to him.

"Excuse me," she said, her voice coming out as a high squeak.

The man smiled at her and she blushed.

"Have I shrunk, or are you twice as tall as you were last winter?" he asked.

"I've grown this much." Inina gestured with her hand. "And I've been practising my letters, like you said."

"Are you enjoying it?"

"I am. Did you know that there's a tree in the middle of the ocean that all the fishes grow from?"

"I didn't, but I'd love to see that one day." He patted the bench next to him. "Join me?"

Eagerly, Inina took her place on the bench, just as the

innkeeper emerged with a tray of cups. She handed one to the man, then took the rest toward the players and their audience. The man on the bench looked up at the parrots fluttering past, at the clouds drifting across the sky. He dipped his fingers in his drink and flicked droplets into the dust, then peered at them.

"Are you reading the signs?" Inina asked eagerly. It always amazed her, the shapes that he could see in the world, the way he used them to guide people when he came to town. Thanks to him, they'd found the turtles in the south cove last winter, and Lolala had finally taken up with Toft, one of the happiest couples in town.

"I am," he said. "Just enough to be helpful without hurting me."

"It can hurt you?" Inina asked, eyes wide. Was that why he had to walk with a staff?

"Not if you're careful, though it took me a long time to work out what careful meant."

"You must be very special, to read the signs."

"All of us are special." He smiled the smile that made Inina want to run away and become an actor. "Especially inquisitive young people with sharp minds."

Across the square, the preview had come to its end, and the director had taken her place on the stage again.

"Tell your friends!" she proclaimed. "Tell your neighbours! Tell your enemies, if they have coin to pay and hands to clap! Be here tomorrow tonight, for the grand premiere of the latest offering from the Company Dellest. Gasp and laugh and cry as you behold *The New Moon's Tale*."

She bowed and the crowd cheered. Inina tugged at the man's sleeve, then looked down at the pattern of dark droplets in the dust.

"What does it mean?" she asked, eager for some hint of her future.

He looked at the droplets, then back at her. "You tell me."

ACKNOWLEDGMENTS

Thanks to the team at Orbit, in particular Stephanie Lippitt Clark, for helping me see this story through. And huge thanks once again to Milena for encouraging and inspiring me.

MEET THE AUTHOR

Richard Wilson

ANDREW KNIGHTON's goal growing up was to go on fantastical adventures in impossible worlds. When that didn't work out, he started imagining the adventures instead, and a writer was born. He's now the author of the Forged for Destiny trilogy and the Executioner series, as well as assorted short stories, comics, novellas, and murder mystery games. He lives in Yorkshire with an academic and a cat, growing vegetables and striving for a brighter future, while still hoping that a magical portal will open between the broad beans. You can find more of him at andrewknighton.com.

Find out more about Andrew Knighton and other Orbit authors by registering for the free monthly newsletter at orbitbooks.net.

RAISING READERS
Books Build Bright Futures

Thank you for reading this book and for being a reader of books in general. We are so grateful to share being part of a community of readers with you, and we hope you will join us in passing our love of books on to the next generation of readers.

Did you know that reading for enjoyment is the single biggest predictor of a child's future happiness and success?

More than family circumstances, parents' educational background, or income, reading impacts a child's future academic performance, emotional well-being, communication skills, economic security, ambition, and happiness.

Studies show that kids reading for enjoyment in the US is in rapid decline:
- In 2012, 53% of 9-year-olds read almost every day. Just 10 years later, in 2022, the number had fallen to 39%.
- In 2012, 27% of 13-year-olds read for fun daily. By 2023, that number was just 14%.

Together, we can commit to **Raising Readers** and change this trend. How?

- Read to children in your life daily.
- Model reading as a fun activity.
- Reduce screen time.
- Start a family, school, or community book club.
- Visit bookstores and libraries regularly.
- Listen to audiobooks.
- Read the book before you see the movie.
- Encourage your child to read aloud to a pet or stuffed animal.
- Give books as gifts.
- Donate books to families and communities in need.

Books build bright futures, and **Raising Readers** is our shared responsibility.

For more information, visit **JoinRaisingReaders.com**

Sources: National Endowment for the Arts, National Assessment of Educational Progress, WorldBookDay.com, Nielsen BookData's 2023 "Understanding the Children's Book Consumer"

Follow us:

 /orbitbooksUS

 /orbitbooks

 /orbitbooks

Join our mailing list to receive alerts on our latest releases and deals.

orbitbooks.net

Enter our monthly giveaway for the chance to win some epic prizes.

orbitloot.com